A Romance of the Equator

A Romance of the Equator

BEST FANTASY STORIES

BRIAN ALDISS

LONDON
VICTOR GOLLANCZ LTD
1989

First published in Great Britain 1989
by Victor Gollancz Ltd
14 Henrietta Street, London WC2E 8QJ

British Library Cataloguing in Publication Data
Aldiss, Brian W.
    A romance of the equator.
    I. Title   II. Best Fantasy Stories
    823'.914[F]   PR6051.L3

ISBN 0-575-04211-7

Photoset in Great Britain by
Rowland Phototypesetting Ltd, Bury St Edmunds, Suffolk
and printed by St Edmundsbury Press Ltd,
Bury St Edmunds, Suffolk

Contents

Introduction

INTERVIEWER: How would you define *fantastic* then?

BORGES: I wonder if you *can* define it. I think it's rather an intention in a writer. Really, nobody knows whether the world is realistic or fantastic, that is to say, whether the world is a natural process or whether it is a kind of dream, a dream that we may or may not share with others.

Thus Jorge Luis Borges, in an interview in *The Paris Review* in 1967. If Borges cannot define fantasy, I am exempted from attempting the task.

Since Borges was interviewed, our view of nature has changed. Between 1967 and today, Jim Lovelock's theory of Gaia, which seeks to prove that our planet is suitable for life because the living organisms on it maintain that suitability, has claimed many adherents. Looked at from this fresh vantage point, the world becomes less of a natural process and more of a dream in which all living things unknowingly conspire. Much depends on what you mean by those two magic words, *the world*.

As the world is changing, so too is the word fantasy. It once meant an illusory appearance, or some supposition resting on no verifiable grounds. Only in this century has the word taken on other meanings, the psychoanalyst's-couch connotation of a day-dream arising from the unconscious or, later still, the sense of a label for a kind of literary genre rather looked down upon. Thus, Queenie Leavis in her *Fiction and the Reading Public* speaks of "A habit of fantasying which will lead to maladjustment in actual life."

Fantasy is a quicksandy word, very different from the firm, straight path trodden by the likes of Queenie Leavis. Yet that

"actual life" of which she speaks, so plausible on first appearance –
how deceptive when approached, as Borges perceived. "Actual
life" may be a fantasy too. It's many centuries since Chuang Tzu
woke from a dream that he was a butterfly to ponder whether he
was a man who had dreamed he was a butterfly or a butterfly who
now dreamed he was a man.

The question still teases us because of the duality of our nature.
Teases or pleases. I prefer having a dual nature. Robots have single
natures. Humans need binocular vision to see each other with.

Much that was once considered fantastic, like the Gaian theory,
sets like concrete and becomes reality. And the opposite is true.
Much that was once considered reality, like the idea that the planet
Mercury turned one face always to the sun and one always away,
has become fantasy. Science is often the switch which transforms
one thing into its opposite. If you turn on the light quickly enough,
you can see what the darkness looks like.

Some of the stories in this volume were conceived as science
fiction. They turn out to have been fantasy. Such a story as "Old
Hundredth" – written to celebrate the hundredth number of a
science fiction magazine and reprinted dozens of times – has always
been accepted as science fiction. As Borges says, it is the intention
in the writer that counts.

Some of the stories were conceived as fantasy and turn out to be
science fiction. "Creatures of Apogee", for instance, brief bulletin
from the nether regions as it is, gave birth to one of the two cardinal
ideas in my *Helliconia* novels. Switch on the darkness quickly
enough, you can see light standing naked.

Such illumination as these stories give is based on the notion – it
is practically the only theory of writing I have – that all kinds of
fiction are devised to reveal truth, or a truth, but that truth can best
be conveyed when hidden in an ambush of fibs. This is the method
of fairy tales. For what is the truth when we get to it? Perhaps what
the cynic said is right, that what is inexpressible would hardly be
worth expressing if it were expressed. I believe that one interest a
reader has in reading is in determining for himself what is truth,
what mere fabrication. In this respect, SF is perhaps more challenging than fantasy, since SF sometimes lays claim – mistakenly
to my mind, but then Magritte calls himself a realistic painter – to
being realistic writing.

That having been said, I try in my fiction to keep the nutty element within bounds. Dragons, vampires, elves, singing swords, etc., do not enter here. For all my aspirations towards madness, an old rationalist taint remains.

Not surprisingly, I prefer some stories to others. "The Blue Background", "Old Hundredth", "The Small Stones of Tu Fu", "The Moment of Eclipse", still hold their original interest for me – perhaps not solely because they concern art in one form or other.

"The Source" was written when I was getting excited about Jungian psychology and published by Michael Moorcock just before his magazine, *New Worlds*, went into its nova phase. It contains a frightening and alluring question with which I have sought to deal on a larger scale: how does modern mankind come to terms with nature and with his/her own nature?

"The Village Swindler" carries a Sell By date. It was published in a long vanished magazine called *International* in 1968, when heart transplants were news. Yet the point it makes is less to do with new medical techniques than with the imbalance dividing rich and poor, which has no Sell By date.

"Bill Carter Takes Over" has (I hope) a lovable idiocy. Perhaps it embodies a paradox: God cannot be omnipotent because he is unable to make good and happy a species which, in his omnipotence, he has endowed with a measure of free will.

"Day of the Doomed King" was written while I was travelling in Yugoslavian Macedonia, and reflects a love of that beautiful country as well as curiosity about an ancient line of monarchs, the Nemanijas, whose portraits one still comes across on the walls of churches set in the heart of Serbia, looking out sightlessly at their communist congregations.

"A Romance of the Equator" is also staged in sunshine – properly, since it is about love, the love that cannot make up its mind.

"North Scarning" is a ghost story, the only one I have ever written, based on a ghost with which I was familiar for many years. We tried to treat it kindly, but ghosts resist humanitarian impulses and its evil nature was slowly revealed.

It would be tedious to go turning over stories in this way. Readers should make their own discoveries. What we find by accident is often more valuable than what we are led to, which is bad luck on those who try to educate us.

One principle of fantasy is to have the magical event happen far away. Not only does distance lend enchantment; it makes facts harder to check on. These stories move from Barnstaple, a damp town in which I once lived, and Prague, to New York, Greece, India, Cythera, the Goat Star, Malacia, Helliconia, and beyond. Of course the journeys are only imaginary, but imagination is more valuable than we can imagine.

This volume is a companion to a collection of science fiction stories. Its contents are chosen from about three hundred short stories published over the years. I am not enthusiastic about categorising, while recognising its necessity. In fact I am planning to issue a third volume entitled *Best Nondescript Stories*.

Boars Hill
Oxford
January 1989

Old Hundredth

The road climbed dustily down between trees as symmetrical as umbrellas. Its length was punctuated at one point by a musi-column standing on the sandy verge. From a distance, the column was only a faint stain in the air. As sentient creatures neared it, their psyches activated it, it drew on their vitalities, and then it could be heard as well as seen. Their presence made it flower into pleasant noise, instrumental or chant.

All this region was called Ghinomon, for nobody lived here any more, not even the old hermit Impure. It was given over to grass and the weight of time. Only a few wild goats activated the musicolumn nowadays, or a scampering vole wrung a brief chord from it in passing.

When old Dandi Lashadusa came riding down that dusty road on her baluchitherium, the column began to intone. It was just an indigo trace on the air, hardly visible, for it represented only a bonded pattern of music locked into the fabric of that particular area of space. It was also a transubstantio-spatial shrine, the eternal part of a being that had dematerialised itself into music.

The baluchitherium whinnied, lowered its head, and sneezed on to the gritty road.

"Gently, Lass," Dandi told her mare, savouring the growth of the chords that increased in volume as she approached. Her long nose twitched with pleasure as if she could feel the melody along her olfactory nerves.

Obediently, the baluchitherium slowed, turning aside to crop fern, although it kept an eye on the indigo stain. It liked things to have being or not to have being; these half-and-half objects disturbed it, though they could not impair its immense appetite.

Dandi climbed down her ladder on to the ground, glad to feel the ancient dust under her feet. She smoothed her hair and stretched as she listened to the music.

She spoke aloud to her mentor, half the world away, but he was not listening. His mind closed to her thoughts, he muttered an obscure exposition that darkened what it sought to clarify.

". . . useless to deny that it is well-nigh impossible to improve anything, however faulty, that has so much tradition behind it. And the origins of your bit of metricism are indeed embedded in such a fearful antiquity that we must needs –"

"Tush, Mentor, come out of your black box and forget your hatred of my 'metricism' a moment," Dandi Lashadusa said, cutting her thought into his. "Listen to the bit of 'metricism' I've found here, look at where I have come to, let your argument rest."

She turned her eyes about, scanning the tawny rocks near at hand, the brown line of the road, the distant black and white magnificence of ancient Oldorajo's town, doing this all for him, tiresome old fellow. Her mentor was blind, never left his cell in Peterbroe to go farther than the sandy courtyard, hadn't physically left that green cathedral pile for over a century. Womanlike, she thought he needed change. Soul, how he rambled on! Even now, he was managing to ignore her and refute her.

". . . for consider, Lashadusa woman, nobody can be found to father it. Nobody wrought or thought it, phrases of it merely *came* together. Even the old nations of men could not own it. None of them knew who composed it. An element here from a Spanish pavan, an influence there of a French psalm tune, a flavour here of early English carol, a savour there of later German chorals. Nor are the faults of your bit of metricism confined to bastardy . . ."

"Stay in your black box then, if you won't see or listen," Dandi said. She could not get into his mind; it was the mentor's privilege to lodge in her mind, and in the minds of those few other wards he had, scattered round Earth. Only the mentors had the power of being in another's mind – which made them rather tiring on occasions like this, when they would not get out of it. For over seventy years, Dandi's mentor had been persuading her to die into a dirge of his choosing (and composing). Let her die, yes, let her transubstantio-spatialise herself a thousand times! His quarrel was not with her decision but her taste, which he considered execrable.

Leaving the baluchitherium to crop, Dandi walked away from

the musicolumn towards a hillock. Still fed by her steed's psyche, the column continued to play. Its music was of a simplicity, with a dominant-tonic recurrent bass part suggesting pessimism. To Dandi, a savante in musicolumnology, it yielded other data. She could tell to within a few years when its founder had died and also what kind of a creature, generally speaking, he had been.

Climbing the hillock, Dandi looked about. To the south where the road led were low hills, lilac in the poor light. There lay her home. At last she was returning, after wanderings covering half a century and most of the globe.

Apart from the blind beauty of Oldorajo's town lying to the west, there was only one landmark she recognised. That was the Involute. It seemed to hang iridal above the ground a few leagues on; just to look on it made her feel she must at once get nearer.

Before summoning the baluchitherium, Dandi listened once more to the sounds of the musicolumn, making sure she had them fixed in her head. The pity was her old fool wise man would not share it. She could still feel his sulks floating like sediment through his mind.

"Are you listening now, Mentor?"

"Eh? An interesting point is that back in 1556 by the old pre-Involutary calendar your same little tune may be discovered lurking in Knox's Anglo-Genevan Psalter, where it espoused the cause of the third psalm –"

"You dreary old fish! Wake yourself! How can you criticise my intended way of dying when you have such a fustian way of living?"

This time he heard her words. So close did he seem that his peevish pinching at the bridge of his snuffy old nose tickled hers too.

"What are you doing *now*, Dandi?" he inquired.

"If you had been listening, you'd know. Here's where I am, on the last Ghinomon plain before Crotheria and home." She swept the landscape again and he took it in, drank it almost greedily. Many mentors went blind early in life, shut in their monastic underwater dens; their most effective visions were conducted through the eyes of their wards.

His view of what she saw enriched hers. He knew the history, the myth behind this forsaken land. He could stock the tired old landscape with pageantry, delighting her and surprising her. Back and forward he went, flicking her pictures; the Youdicans, the Lombards, the Ex-Europa Emissary, the Grites, the Risorgimento, the Involuters – and catchwords, costumes, customs, courtesans, pelted briefly through Dandi Lashadusa's mind. Ah, she thought admiringly, who could truly live without these priestly, beastly, erudite, erratic mentors?

"Erratic?" he inquired, snatching at her lick of thought. "A thousand years I live, for all that time to absent myself from the world, to eat mashed fish here with my brothers, learning history, studying rapport, sleeping with my bones on stones – a humble being, a being in a million, a mentor in a myriad, and your standards of judgement are so mundane you find no stronger label for me than erratic? Fie, Lashadusa, bother me no more for fifty years!"

The words nattered and squeaked in her head as if she spoke herself. She felt his old chops work phantom-like in hers, and half in anger half in laughter called aloud, "I'll be dead by then!"

He snicked back hot and holy to reply, "And another thing about your footloose swan song – in Marot and Beza's Genevan Psalter of 1551, Old Time, it was musical midwife to the one hundred and thirty-fourth psalm. Like you, it never seemed to settle!" Then he was gone.

"Pooh!" Dandi said. She whistled Lass.

Obediently the great rhino-like creature, eighteen feet high at the shoulder, ambled over. The musicolumn died as the mare left it, faded, sank to a whisper, silenced; only the purple stain remained, noiseless, in the lonely air. Lass reached Dandi. Lowering its great Oligocene head, it nuzzled its mistress's hand. She climbed the ladder on to that ridged plateau of back.

They made contentedly towards the Involute, lulled by the simple and intricate feeling of being alive.

Night was settling in now, steady as snow. Hidden behind banks of mist, the sun prepared to set. But Venus was high, a gallant half-crescent four times as big as the Moon had been before the Moon, spiralling farther and farther from Earth, had shaken off its parent's clutch to go dance round the sun, a second Mercury. Even by that time Venus had been moved by gravito-traction into

Earth's orbit, so that the two sister worlds circled each other as they circled the sun.

The stamp of that great event still lay everywhere, its tokens not only in the crescent in the sky. For Venus put a strange spell on the hearts of man, and a more penetrating displacement in his genes. Even when its atmosphere was transformed into a muffled breath-ability, it remained an alien world; against logic, its opportunities, its possibilities, were its own. It shaped men, just as Earth had shaped them. On Venus, men bred themselves anew.

And they bred the so-called Impures. They bred new plants, new fruits, new creatures – original ones, and duplications of creatures not seen on Earth for aeons past. From one line of these familiar strangers Dandi's baluchitherium was descended. So, for that matter, was Dandi.

The huge creature came now to the Involute, or as near as it cared to get. Again it began to crop at thistles, thrusting its nose through dewy spiders' webs and ground mist.

"Like you, I'm a vegetarian," Dandi said, climbing down to the ground. A grove of low fruit trees grew nearby; she reached up into the branches, gathered and ate, before turning to inspect the Involute. Already her spine tingled at the nearness of it; awe, loathing and love made a part-pleasant sensation near her heart.

The Involute was not beautiful. True, its colours changed with the changing light, yet the colours were fish-cold, for they be-longed to another universe. Though they reacted to dusk and dawn, Earth had no stronger power over them. They pricked the eyes. Perhaps too they were painful because they were the last signs of materialist man. Even Lass moved uneasily before that ill-defined lattice, the upper limits of which were lost in thickening gloom.

"Don't fear," Dandi said. "There's an explanation for this, old girl." She added sadly, "There's an explanation for everything, if we can find it."

She could feel all the personalities in the Involute. It was a frozen screen of personality. All over the old planet the structures stood, to shed their awe on those who were left behind. They were the essence of man. They were man – all that remained of him.

When the first flint, the first shell, was shaped into a weapon, that action shaped man. As he moulded and complicated his tools, so they moulded and complicated him. He became the first scientific animal. And at last, via information theory and great computers, he gained knowledge of all his parts. He formed the Laws of Integration, which reveal all beings as part of a pattern and show them their part in the pattern. There is only the pattern, the pattern is all the universe, creator and created. For the first time, it became possible to duplicate that pattern artificially; the transubstantio-spatialisers were built.

All mankind left their strange hobbies on Earth and Venus and projected themselves into the pattern. Their entire personalities were merged with the texture of space itself. Through science, they reached immortality.

It was a one-way passage.

They did not return. Each Involute carried thousands or even millions of people. There they were, not dead, not living. How they exulted or wept in their transubstantiation, nobody left could say. Only this could be said: man had gone, and a great emptiness was fallen over the Earth.

"Your thoughts are heavy, Dandi Lashadusa. Get you home." Her mentor was back in her mind. She caught the feeling of his moving round and round in his coral-formed cell.

"I must think of man," she said.

"Your thoughts mean nothing, do nothing."

"Man created us; I want to consider him in peace."

"He only shaped a stream of life that was always entirely out of his control. Forget him. Get on to your mare and ride home."

"Mentor –"

"Get home, woman. Moping does not become you. I want to hear no more of your swan song, for I've given you my final word on that. Use a theme of your own, not of man's. I've said it a million times and I say it again."

"I wasn't going to mention my music. I was only going to tell you that . . ."

"What then?" His thought was querulous. She felt his powerful tail tremble, disturbing the quiet water of his cell.

"I don't know . . ."

"Get home then."

"I'm lonely."

He shot her a picture from another of his wards before leaving her. Dandi had seen this ward before in similar dreamlike glimpses. It was a huge mole creature, still boring underground as it had been for the last twenty years. Occasionally it crawled through vast caves; once it swam in a subterranean lake; most of the while it just bored through rock. Its motivations were obscure to Dandi, although her mentor referred to it as "a geologer". Doubtless if the mole was vouchsafed occasional glimpses of Dandi and her musicolumnology, it would find her as baffling. At least the mentor's point was made: loneliness was psychological, not statistical.

Why, a million personalities glittered almost before her eyes!

She mounted the great baluchitherium mare and headed for home. Time and old monuments made glum company.

Twilight now, with just one streak of antique gold left in the sky, Venus sweetly bright, and stars peppering the purple. A fine night for being alive in, particularly with one's last bedtime close at hand.

And yes, for all her mentor said, she was going to turn into that old little piece derived from one of the tunes in the 1540 *Souter Liedekens*, that splendid source of Netherlands folk music. For a moment, Dandi Lashadusa chuckled almost as eruditely as her mentor. The sixteenth-century Old Time, with the virtual death of plainsong and virtual birth of the violin, was most interesting to her. Ah, the richness of facts, the texture of man's brief history! Pure joy! Then she remembered herself.

After all, she was only a megatherium, a sloth as big as an elephant, whose kind had been extinct for millions of years until man reconstituted a few of them in the Venusian experiments. Her modifications in the way of fingers and enlarged brain gave her no real qualifications to think up to man's level.

Early next morning, they arrived at the ramparts of the town Crotheria where Dandi lived. The ubiquitous goats thronged about them, some no bigger than hedgehogs, some almost as big as hippos – what madness in his last days provoked man to so many variations on one undistinguished caprine theme? – as Lass and her mistress moved up the last slope and under the archway.

It was good to be back, to push among the trails fringed with bracken, among the palms, oaks, and treeferns. Almost all the town was deeply green and private from the sun, curtained by swathes of Spanish moss. Here and there were houses – caves, pits, crude piles of boulders or even genuine man-type buildings, grand in ruin. Dandi climbed down, walking ahead of her mount, her long hair curling in pleasure. The air was cool with the coo of doves or the occasional bleat of a merino.

As she explored familiar ways, though, disappointment overcame her. Her friends were all away, even the dreamy bison whose wallow lay at the corner of the street in which Dandi lived. Only pure animals were here, rooting happily and mindlessly in the lanes, beggars who owned the Earth. The Impures – descendants of the Venusian experimental stock – were all absent from Crotheria.

That was understandable. For obvious reasons, man had increased the abilities of herbivores rather than carnivores. After the Involution, with man gone, these Impures had taken to his towns as they took to his ways, as far as this was possible to their natures. Both Dandi and Lass, and many of the others, consumed massive amounts of vegetable matter every day. Gradually a wider and wider circle of desolation grew about each town (the greenery in the town itself was sacrosanct), forcing a semi-nomadic life on its vegetarian inhabitants.

This thinning in its turn led to a decline in the birth rate. The travellers grew fewer, the towns greener and emptier; in time they had become little oases of forest studding the grassless plains.

"Rest here, Lass," Dandi said at last, pausing by a bank of brightly flowering cycads. "I'm going into my house."

A giant beech grew before the stone façade of her home, so close that it was hard to determine whether it did not help support the ancient building. A crumbling balcony jutted from the first floor. Reaching up, Dandi seized the balustrade and hauled herself on to the balcony.

This was her normal way of entering her home, for the ground floor was taken over by goats and hogs, just as the second floor had been appropriated by doves and parakeets. Trampling over the greenery self-sown on the balcony, she moved into the front room. Dandi smiled. Here were her old things, the broken furniture on which she liked to sleep, the vision screens on which nothing could be seen, the heavy manuscript books in which, guided by her know-all mentor, she wrote down the outpourings of the musicolumns she had visited all over the world.

She ambled through to the next room.

She paused, her peace of mind suddenly shattered by danger.

A brown bear stood there. One of its heavy hands was clenched over the hilt of a knife.

"I am no vulgar thief," it said, curling its thick black lips over the syllables. "I am an archaeologer. If this is your place, you must grant me permission to remove the man things. Obviously you have no idea of the worth of some of the equipment here. We bears require it. We must have it."

It came towards her, panting doggy fashion with its jaws open. From under bristling eyebrows gleamed the lust to kill.

Dandi was frightened. Peaceful by nature, she feared the bears above all creatures for their fierceness and their ability to organise. The bears were few: they were the only creatures to show signs of wishing to emulate man's old aggressiveness.

She knew what the bears did. They hurled themselves through the Involutes to increase their power; by penetrating those patterns, they nourished their psychic drive, so the mentor said. It was forbidden. They were transgressors. They were killers.

"Mentor!" she screamed.

The bear hesitated. As far as he was concerned, the hulking creature before him was merely an obstacle in the way of progress, something to be thrust aside without hate. Killing would be pleasant but irrelevant; more important items remained to be done. Much of the equipment housed here could be used in the rebuilding of the world, the world of which bears had such high haphazard dreams. Holding the knife threateningly, he moved forward.

The mentor was in Dandi's head, answering her cry, seeing through her eyes, though he had no sight of his own. He scanned the bear and took over her mind instantly, knifing himself into place like a guillotine.

No longer was he a blind old dolphin lurking in one cell of a cathedral pile of coral under tropical seas, a theologer, an inculcator of wisdom into feebler-minded beings. He was a killer more savage than the bear, keen to kill anything that might covet the vacant throne once held by men. The mere thought of men could send this mentor into sharklike fury at times.

Caught up in his fury, Dandi found herself advancing. For all the bear's strength, she could vanquish it. In the open, where she could have brought her heavy tail into action, it would have been an easy matter. Here, her weighty forearms must come into play. She felt them lift to her mentor's command as he planned for her to clout the bear to death.

The bear stepped back, awed by an opponent twice its size, suddenly unsure.

She advanced.

"No! Stop!" Dandi cried.

Instead of fighting the bear, she fought her mentor, hating his hate. Her mind twisted, her dim mind full of that steely fishy one, as she blocked his resolution.

"I'm for peace!" she cried.

"Then kill the bear!"

"I'm for peace, not killing!"

She rocked back and forth. When she staggered into a wall, it shook; dust spread in the old room. The mentor's fury was terrible to feel.

"Get out quickly!" Dandi called to the bear.

Hesitating, it stared at her. Then it turned and made for the window. For a moment it hung with its shaggy shabby hindquarters in the room. Momentarily she saw it for what it was, an old animal in an old world, without direction. It jumped. It was gone. Goats blared confusion on its retreat.

"Bitch!" screamed the mentor. Insane with frustration, he hurled Dandi against the doorway with all the force of his mind.

Wood cracked and splintered. The lintel came crashing down. Brick and stone shifted, grumbled, fell. Powdered filth billowed up. With a great roar, one wall collapsed. Dandi struggled to get free. Her house was tumbling about her. It had never been intended to carry so much weight, so many centuries.

She reached the balcony and jumped clumsily to safety, just as the building avalanched in on itself, sending a great cloud of plaster and powdered mortar into the overhanging trees.

For a horribly long while the world was full of dust, goat bleats, and panic-stricken parakeets.

Heavily astride her baluchitherium once more, Dandi Lashadusa headed back to the empty region called Ghinomon. She fought her bitterness, trying to urge herself towards resignation.

All she had was destroyed – not that she set store by possessions: that was a man trait. Much more terrible was the knowledge that her mentor had left her for ever; she had transgressed too badly to be forgiven this time.

Suddenly she was lonely for his pernickety voice in her head, for the wisdom he fed her, for the scraps of dead knowledge he tossed her – yes, even for the love he gave her. She had never seen him, never could: yet no two beings could have been more intimate.

She missed too those other wards of his she would glimpse no more; the mole creature tunnelling in Earth's depths, the seal family that barked with laughter on a desolate coast, a senile gorilla that endlessly collected and classified spiders, an aurochs – seen only once, but then unforgettably – that lived with smaller creatures in an Arctic city it had helped build in the ice.

She was excommunicated.

Well, it was time for her to change, to disintegrate, to transubstantiate into a pattern not of flesh but music. That discipline at least the mentor had taught and could not take away.

"This will do, Lass," she said.

Her gigantic mount stopped obediently. Lovingly she patted its neck. It was young; it would be free.

Following the dusty trail, she went ahead, alone. Somewhere far off one bird called. Coming to a mound of boulders, Dandi squatted among gorse, the points of which could not prick through her thick old coat.

Already her selected music poured through her head, already it seemed to loosen the chemical bonds of her being.

Why should she not choose an old human tune? She was an antiquarian. Things that were gone solaced her for things that were to come.

In her dim way, she had always stood out against her mentor's absolute hatred of men. The thing to hate was hatred. Men in their finer moments had risen above hate. Her death psalm was an instance of that – a multiple instance, for it had been fingered and changed over the ages, as the mentor himself insisted, by men of a variety of races, all with their minds directed to worship rather than hate.

Locking herself into thought disciplines, Dandi began to dissolve. Man had needed machines to help him to do it, to fit into the Involutes. She was a lesser animal: she could unbutton herself into the humbler shape of a musicolumn. It was just a matter of *rearranging* – and without pain she formed into a pattern that was not a shaggy megatherium body . . . but an indigo column, hardly visible . . .

Lass for a long while cropped thistle and cacti. Then she ambled forward to seek the hairy creature she fondly – and a little condescingly – regarded as her equal. But of the sloth there was no sign.

Almost the only landmark was a faint violet-blue dye in the air. As the baluchitherium mare approached, a sweet old music grew in volume from the dye. It was a music almost as old as the landscape itself and certainly as much travelled, a tune once known to men as "The Old Hundredth". And there were voices singing: "All creatures that on Earth do dwell . . ."

(1960)

Day of the Doomed King

Through his heavy lids, the church hardly appeared to grow nearer until they were upon it. The summer and the wound at his chest made him dizzy. As he stumbled from his horse, the great daisies in the long grass made it seem to him that he was walking across a starry sky, and his perspectives would not come right.

A priest with a rich mantle thrown over his black frock came hurrying to them. He heard Jovann say to the priest, "It is King Vukasan, and he is sore wounded. Make ready a couch for him to rest on."

He muttered into his horse's flank, "We must get to Sveti Andrej and warn them to arm themselves against the Turk," and then the daisies and the sky and dappled shade rippled like a banner, and he had a near view of his silver stirrup before blackness closed upon him.

When he roused again, things were better for him. He lay on a bunk in a cool cell, and his head was clearer. Propping himself on one elbow, he said, "Now I am able to go on to my kinsmen at Sveti Andrej."

Jovann and the old black priest were at his side, smiling with anxiety. "My lord king," said the priest, "you have taken grievous harm, and must stay with us until you have strength for the rest of the journey."

His mouth was stiff, but he said, "Priest, yesterday we fought a battle all daylight long against the scimitared Muslim, until the River Babuna flowed with their blood and ours. Courage does not trifle with numbers, that I know, but we had only one blade to every six of theirs, and so in the end every one of my soldiers fell. My cousins at Andrej must be told to make ready to fight, and there is only my general, Jovann, and me to tell them. Bind me up and let me go on."

Then Jovann and the priest conferred together, first with Jovann's moustache at the priest's furry ear, and then with the priest's beard at Jovann's ear. Then Jovann came to his king and knelt by the bed, taking his hand and saying, "My lord, though we did not slay the vile Muslim, at least we stayed him; he also has his wounds to bind. So the urgency is only in you, and not in the situation. It is the heat of noonday now. Rest, take some soup and rest, and we will go on later. I must have care of you and not forget that you are of the house of Josević and your wound bleeds authority."

So he learnt to be persuaded, and they brought him a thin soup and a trout culled from the nearby lake, and a pot of wine, and then they left him to rest.

He could eat no more than a mouthful of the fish. Though he was not conscious of his wound, he was sick inside with worry, wounded to think that the consuming Turk ate his lands away and was never defeated. His people were brave and terrible in battle; why then did God not allow them to triumph? It was as if a vast tide of time flowed continually against them.

Listlessly, he stared through the open window by his bed. This room in the priests' quarters closely overlooked the lake, so that the waters seemed to flow even to the sill. All that punctuated the expanse of his view was a reed bed near at hand; the further shore was an uncertain line of blue, there merely to emphasise the water. He stared at it a long time until, growing tired of its excessive vacancy, he turned his gaze instead to the view within the room.

Although the cell itself was simple, it contained a number of objects, cloaks and instruments and even a field hoe. These had been hastily concealed, at least to some extent, from the royal view by a screen, interposed between the foot of the bed and the miscellany. Slowly his stare fixed itself on this screen.

It was carved of wood, elaborately, in a manner he recognised as that of the masters of Debar, for some of their work graced his own stronghold. Intertwined among leaves and vines were large birds swallowing fruit, and boys lying piping, and hogs rolling in flowers, and turrets, and lizards that curled like Turkish scimitars. These little religious foundations, scattered like jewels throughout his kingdom, hid many such treasures, but at this time of emergency he took no delight in them.

For a long while, he lay between lake and screen, thinking he must move and speed on to his kinsmen. Many times he dreamed he had already climbed from his bed before Jovann arrived at the door, staring anxiously at his face and asking, "Are you strong enough, my lord, to take the road again?"

"Fetch me my sword," he said.

So they set forth again, and this time, the path leading upland, they went by a more complicated way. The horses were fresh from their rest but nervous, and started violently at the jays that flashed across their track. Their nervousness conveyed itself to him, and he sweated inside his shirt until its heavy embroidery knocked cold against his ribs. He started against his will to speak of what was in his mind, of things that he knew a king had better keep hidden from even the most faithful of his generals.

"I fear an evil enchantment upon me," he said through his teeth. "When the wolves howled as my child-wife died of the fever at Bitola, I thought they cried my name, and now I know they did. There is a mark on me, and the mark is disaster."

"Then it is on me as well, and all who love you," said Jovann. "You are our common wealth, and as surely as the pig-fearing Muslim shall slay you, he shall slay all Serbia."

Then he regretted he had spoken, for it was not in Jovann's position to answer in such a way, but still the words shuddered from his lips. "As our fine clothes cannot hide our nakedness from God, so the trees that make my kingdom fair cannot hide his curse from me. For you know what the legends say, that we south Slavs rode from the East in great numbers when barbaric enemies drove us from the lands of our ancestors. Though our people have for many centuries broken the earth here, and lie under it numerously, yet it is still not our homeland; and I am afeared, Jovann, afeared lest this land fall all to the dark-visaged Muslim and the distant pashas."

"Your royal brethren will take arms with us against them, and turn them back so roughly that they never again dare cross the Vardar," said Jovann stoutly. But under the thick trees his face seemed to have a green shade that was not of nature; and even as he spoke, he reined his horse and stared anxiously ahead.

On the path where they must ascend, a magpie crouched with a lizard in its gullet. With wings outspread, it beat at the dust and the horses rattled their reins with dislike of the sight. Jovann sucked in a sharp hissing breath, and slid from the saddle, drawing his sword as he moved forward. The black bird flopped dead at his feet, the lizard still protruding from its beak. He made to strike it, but the king cried to him to stay.

"I never knew a magpie to choke to death before, nor to take a lizard," he said. "Better not to touch them. We will ride about them."

So they pricked their horses through the mantle of trees, forcing them along the mountain, and rode with some difficulty until they achieved the plain once more. Here grew the red poppies in their multitudes, millions and millions of them, the hue of dried blood in the distance, of fresh blood underfoot. In the king's head, there was only this colour, as he tried to understand the meaning of the lizard and the magpie.

With a heavy hand, he pointed across the plain. "Jakupica Planina lies there, with snow still on its ridge. When we have forded the Topolka, we can camp by the foot of the hills. By tomorrow night, we will rest ourselves by the stoves of Sveti Andrej and lay our story in sympathetic hands. But first I shall call at a small monastery I know of, Sveti Pantelimon by name, where lives a strange and wise seer who shall explain what ails me and my kingdom."

So they slowly drew near to the river in the afternoon heat, and came on a shepherd sitting by a flock of sheep, some white and many black, with half-grown lambs among them. The shepherd was a youth who greeted the king without an excess of respect.

"My humble home lies there," he said, when Jovann spoke sharply to him, and he stretched a finger towards a distant hut perched on a rock. "And there waits your enemy, the grinning musilman!" And the finger raised to crags over which a falcon circled. The king and his general looked there, and made out smoke ascending.

"It is impossible they should be here so soon, my lord. Plainly the boy lies," Jovann said in a small voice.

"There is, alas, more than one force of the enemy on my fertile lands," he said and, turning to the boy, asked, "If you know the stinking Muslim is there, why do you not fight? Why do you not join my arms? Have you nothing, even your life, that is precious to you, that you must defend?"

But the boy was not perturbed, answering straightly, "King Vukasan, because you are a king and therefore rich, the laughing musilman wants all from you, and will take all. But I have nothing, being poor, that he could want. Think you these are my sheep? Then my master would laugh to know. Think you my life is my own? Then you have a different creed from mine. No, your enemies in the hills will pass me by and leave me as I am."

Jovann drew his sword, and the boy retreated a step, but the king said, "Leave him, for only baseness comes from the base, and he is right to hold that even the thieving Muslim can wish nothing from him. Meanwhile, we have one more reason to press on swiftly towards Sveti Andrej."

But when they had crossed the broad and shallow stream of the Topolka, they came on wide shingle beds, on which the hooves of the horses could obtain small purchase. The heat rose up from these shingle beds, dazzling their eyes, and nothing grew save an occasional poppy and frail yellow flowers with five wide-spread petals to each blossom. And the shingle crunched and seemed to wish to draw them back to the river. So they were tired when they gained the bank, and the weight of the sun grew heavy on their shoulders. When they reached the first foothill, Jovann, taking as little regard for majesty as the shepherd boy had done, flung himself off his horse and declared he could go no further. They climbed down beneath a tree where a slight breeze stirred, so that the shadows of its branches crawled like vines on the stony ground. They pulled ripening figs from the tree and ate, and the horses cropped at scanty grass. Heavy blood was in their foreheads; they fell asleep as they sprawled.

He stirred, and the foliage above his head was patterned with fruit like the wooden screen from Debar, and there were greedy birds there, screaming and devouring the fruit. The sun was low over the hills, and he sat up guiltily, crying, "Jovann, Jovann, we must go on! Why are we waiting here, my general?"

His companion sat up, rubbing his head and saying grumpily, "As I will die for you, my lord, when the time comes, so when the time comes must I sleep."

But they got to their feet then, and the king forced them to go on, though Jovann would have eaten the cold fish, wrapped in leaves, that he had brought with him for their evening fare. Looking back over the plain of poppies, they heard the clank of a sheep bell as the sheep were ushered towards protection for the night, and they saw the fires of the Turk burning on the forehead of the mountain. These sights and sounds were soon hidden from them as they rounded the shoulders of the new hills and as night brought down its gentle wing upon them.

Wrapped safe in shadow, the king let his mind wander from the ride, until he imagined he had no wound and his child-wife Simonida was alive again; then said he gently to her, "My daughter, you see how the boundaries of our kingdom widen, and how the soldiers and merchants grow as rich as was my grandfather, great Orušan himself. The Bulgars now pay us tribute as far as Bess-Arabia, and the Byzantines are so poor and weak that their cities fall to us every month."

And he imagined that she smiled and answered, "My sweet lord Vukasan, it is good as you say, but let us establish a state that will make the name Serbia sweet even to those it conquers. Let there be not only executions, but laws; not only swords and armies but books and universities, and peace where we can instil peace."

Then did the king smile and stroke her hair, saying, "You know that way shall be my way, even as it would be your way or the way of my father and grandfather. We will bring wise men to speak to the people from distant Hilander, on the Mount called Athos, and there shall be artists and masons summoned from Thessaloniki, who work less rudely than our native craftsmen. And we shall start new arts and works with men from Ragusa and Venezia, and even beyond, from the courts of Europe, and the Pope in Rome shall heed us . . ."

"You dream too largely, my sweet lord. It is not good so to do." She had often said it.

"Dreams cannot be too large. Do you know what I dream, my daughter? I dream that one day I may ride into Constantinople and have myself crowned king of Byzantium – Emperor! – while you shall wear no dress but jewels."

"Then how your subjects will stare at me!" she said with a laugh, but the sound came faint and unnatural, more like the clink of a horse's bridle, and he could not see her for shade, so that Jovann said at his elbow, "Steady, my lord, as you go, for the way is rocky here."

And he answered heavily and confusedly, saying, "You are not the companion she was, though I grant you are bolder. What a change has come these last few years! Perhaps you were right in holding I dreamed too largely, for now my dreams are no more and you are gone from me, sweet child of my bed, and all I hear of is the rattle of swords, and for the designing of your jewellery I have exchanged battle plans against the fuming Muslim. Ho, then, and hup, or we'll die before we get to the gates of Constantin's town!"

The horse plunged under his sharp-digging stirrup, and he returned to his senses, more tired from the mental journey than the actual one.

"Did I speak to myself then, Jovann?"

"It is my lord's privilege," said the general.

"Did I speak aloud, tell me?"

"My lord, no, on my oath." But he knew the man lied to hide his sovereign's weakness, and bit his lip to keep silence until he had the pleasure of feeling the blood run in the hairs of his beard.

They followed a vague track, not speaking. At last they heard the noise of a bullock-cart creaking and bumping along, and emerged on the dusty road that would take them to Sveti Andrej. Now that the trees stood further apart, and their eyes were adjusted to the night journey, they could see the shape of the bullock-cart ahead. He was well awake now, and motioned to Jovann to follow. They rode up to the cart and hailed the driver.

Deciding they now had no cause to go further, the two bullocks dragging the cart stopped and cropped grass in the middle of the road. With an oath, Jovann jumped to the ground, his sword again ready in his hand. The driver of the cart sprawled face up to the stars with his throat cut. Rags lay under his outspread arm which they examined after a little, and found them to be a peasant woman's clothes.

"This they dare do, so near to home, to kill one of my peasants for the sake of his wife, so near to home, so near to home!"

In a storm of anger and weakness, he felt the tears scald from his eyes, and sat on the bank to weep. Jovann joined him, and put an arm about his shoulders, until he stopped for shame. At that, Jovann thrust a jug into his hands.

"The man's rakija, lord. We might as well profit from it, since he no longer can. Drink it, for we have not many hours' travel left, and then we will eat the fish and pluck some of the cherries that are growing above our heads."

He was secretly angry that Jovann could speak of these trivial matters when the urgency of the situation was so great. But a sort of fear gripped him; he was unnerved by the way the bullock-cart had arrived so punctually to deliver its message of death, and he needed to feel the bite of the rakija as it plunged down his throat. They drank in turns, quaffing out of the jug.

After a while, the bullocks took the cart off down the road again, creaking and bumping every inch of the way. The two men began to laugh. The king sang a fragment of song:

"How happy are they who dwell in Prilep
Where the birds nest under every eave
And the green tree grows."

Although he recalled that the Turk now stood at the gates of Prilep, he sang the verse again into the leafy night. He told Jovann stories of the old days to raise his spirits, of how his grandfather Orušan had in his youth leaped across the fissure in the rock on Pelister and would not marry till he found a girl of hot enough breath to do likewise, no, not though five bare-legged maidens lost their life trying; and of how he himself had swum underground a *vrst* in a cold and unknown river in the same region; and of his father's day-long fight, alone in the hills, with Alisto, the Shiptar prince. And then he thought of his little wife dying in Bitola, and was solemn, and reproached himself. They got to their feet and climbed once more stiffly into their saddles, though Jovann took a great bunch of cherries from the tree as they went, pulling half a branch along with him.

So they rode on through the night, and shivered in their jackets. When dawn leapt over the hills again, they were near to the holy place that the king had mentioned, called Sveti Pantelimon.

He halted his steed by a side track and said, "The way is steep here. I will leave the horses here with you and be back in under an hour, after I have consulted the holy man about the future."

But Jovann protested. "My lord, we are but two hours' travel now from the house of your kinsmen at Sveti Andrej. Let us first carry our ill news to them and set their warlike intentions astir, and then we can return here to your holy man tomorrow, after we have rested."

But he was set in his course, and said so. "Then," said the faithful Jovann with a sigh, "I will follow after you on foot, leading the horses, that where we may ride we can. Heaven guide you, sweet lord, that you know best."

"There is no room for doubt of that," he said sharply, though in his own head there was room enough.

Now they climbed amid sharp spurs of rock, on which the first lizards already crawled to sun themselves. Tortoises ambled from their path, and the progress they made was no faster than that of the tortoise, for the track led back and forth about the hillside. The noise grew of a fast mountain stream by which they could guide themselves. When they found it, they saw how it ran deep between two cliffs, and how the path to Sveti Pantelimon followed beside it, as man's paths must ever be slave to those of nature.

Here, after a brief discussion, the horses were hobbled and left, and the king and Jovann went forward together, the one behind the other because the path was so narrow. The water rushed by their feet, making unpleasant music. The rocks above overhung dangerously, so that the trees growing slantwise from one side were often trapped in the vines growing from the other. In one place, a great boulder had fallen and wedged itself between the two sides above their heads, making a bridge for any who were foolhardy enough to pass that way. At another point, where blue flowers clung to the damp rock, they had to bend double, for the path had been painfully chipped through the rock itself.

It was thus, bent double like cripples at Bitola fair, that they reached the monastery of Sveti Pantelimon. Roses grew by it, otherwise it was a grim place, a tiny church built into the rock on a widening ledge of the rock, with a dwelling hut attached. The modest brick cupola of the church was almost scraped by fingers of rock stabbing from the cliff-face.

The intruders were seen. Only four brothers lived here; three of them hurried out to meet their royal guest, whom they recognised. But it was the fourth the king desired to see and, after taking slatko, the traditional dish of Serbian hospitality, he asked to see this priest.

Jovann rose. "My lord king, I fear for your safety even here, since we know not that even now the foul-stomached Muslim may be riding along this very canyon. I am a soldier. I will guard outside, and give you warning if they come – in a place like this, we might hold off an army."

"Guard well, my general," said the king, and was prompted to give Jovann his hand.

The holy man he wished to see sat in the bare adjoining room. With his wrinkled visage, he represented antiquity rather than old age; but his most notable feature was his left eye which, unlike its brown neighbour, was entirely and featurelessly white. To the king, it appeared that this priest, by name Miloš, often saw best with his white eye.

When their courtesies were concluded, the king said, "I am here to ask you only one question, and I need from you only one answer."

"Often, my lord king Vukasan, there is more than one answer to a question. Question and answer are not simple and complete opposites, as are black and white."

"Do not tease me, for I am weary, and the freedom of my kingdom is at stake."

"You know I will do what I can."

"I believe you are among the wisest men in my lands, and that is why I come to you now. Here is the question. Only a few years ago, in the reign of my father and grandfather, whom we all recall and bless, this our kingdom was expanding, and with it the life of our peoples. Life and knowledge and art and worship were gaining strength every day. Now we see all that we hoped for threatened with ruin, as the red-tipped Muslim bites into our lands. So I ask you what will the future be, and how can we influence it for good?"

"That sounds, my lord king, like two questions, both large; but I will reply to you straightly." Miloš opened the palm of his hand and stared at it with his white eye. "There are as many futures as there are paths in your kingdom, my lord; but just as some paths, if followed to their end, will take you to the west and others if followed to their end will take you to the east, so there are futures which represent the two extremes of what may be – the best and the worst, we might say. I can, if you will, show you the best and the worst."

"Tell me what you can."

The priest Miloš rose and stared out of his small window, which afforded a view to the gloomy rock beyond. With his back to the king, he said, "First, I will tell you what I see of the good future.

"I see you only a year from now. You lead a great army to a beleaguered city set under an isolated mountain, as it might be Prilep. There you smite the sacrilegious Turk, and scatter the entrails of his soldiery far over the blossoming plain, so that he does not come again to our Serbian lands. For this great victory, many petty princes turn to your side and swear allegiance to you. The Byzants, being corrupt, offer you their crown. You accept, and rule their domain even as your father hoped you might."

He turned to look at the king, but the king sat there at the bare table with his head bowed, as if indifferent to the tidings the priest bore. The latter, nodding, turned back to contemplate the rock and continued in an even tone as previously.

"You rule wisely, if without fire, and make a sensible dynastic marriage, securing the succession of the house of Josević. The arts and religion flourish as never before in the new kingdom. Many homes of piety and learning and law are established. Now the Slavs come into their inheritance, and go forth to spread their culture to other nations. Long after you are dead, my king, people speak your name with love, even as we speak of your grandfather, Orušan. But the greatness of the nation you founded is beyond your imagining. It spreads right across Europe and the lands of the Russian. Our gentleness and our culture go with it. There are lands across the sea as yet undiscovered; but the day will dawn when our emissaries will sail there. And the great inventions of the world yet to come will spring from the seed of our Serbian knowledge, and the mind of all mankind be tempered by our civility. It will be a contemplative world, as we are contemplative, and the love in it will be nourished by that contemplation, until it becomes stronger than wickedness."

He ceased, and the king spoke, though his eyes were fixed on the bare floor. "It is a grand vision you have, priest. And . . . the other, the ill future?"

Miloš stared out with his white eye at the rock and said, "In the ill future, I see you leading no grand army. I see a series of small battles, with the shrieking Turk winning almost all of them by superior numbers and science. I see you, my lord king, fall face forward, down into the Serbian dust, never to rise again. And I see eventually Serbia herself falling, and the other nations that are our neighbours and rivals, all falling to the braying enemy, until he stands hammering at the gates even of Vienna in the European north. So, my lord, I see nigh on six centuries in which our culture is trampled underfoot by the conqueror."

Silence came into the chilly room, until the king said heavily, "And the other lands you spoke of, and overseas, how fare they in this ill future?"

"Perhaps you can imagine, my lord. For those six centuries, lost is the name of Serbia, and the places we know and love are regarded simply as the domain of the ginger-whiskered Turk. Europe grows into a fierce and strifeful nest of warring nations – art they have, but little contemplation, power but little gentleness. They never know what they lack, naturally. And when Serbia finally manages to free itself from its hated bondage, the centuries have changed it until your name is lost, and the very title King no longer reverenced. And though she may grow to be a modest power in the world, the time when she might have touched the hearts of all men with her essence is long faded, even as are last year's poppies."

After he had heard Miloš out, the king rose to his feet, though his body trembled. "You give me two futures, priest and, even as you said, they differ as does a speckled trout from a bird. Now answer my question and say which of them is to be the real future, and how I can realise the good vision of which you spoke first."

The priest turned to face him. "It is not in my power to tell you which future will happen. No man can do that. All I can do is give you an omen, hoping that you will then take power into your own hands. Seers see, rulers rule."

"Give me then an omen!"

"Think for yourself where the futures divide in the prospects I laid before you."

He groaned and said, "Ah, I know full well where they divide. We do not bring enough men against the devilish Muslim at one time. We are as you say a contemplative people, and the floods must lap our doorstep before we take in the rug at the portal."

"Suppose it were not a question of being warlike but of being . . . well, too contemplative, my lord."

"Then Jovann and I must rouse the whole nation to fight. This I will do, priest, this is what I was hastening to Sveti Andrej to do."

"But you called here. Was not that a delay?"

"Priest, I came bleeding from the battle at the River Babuna with all haste."

"All?"

He put a weary hand to his forehead and stared at the bare wall. He recalled the long hours of delay at the monastery, the sleep under the trees, the feast of fish and cherries and rakija, and then the diversion here, and he blamed himself deeply for this ineradicable tardiness in his nature, so characteristic of his people also. But there were some more warlike than he, and on them, he saw, the new burden of militarism must rest.

"Jovann," he said. "My bold General Jovann stands outside even now, defending us. He will lend metal to the Serbian arm even if I by my nature cannot."

Miloš looked at him with the white eye and said, "Then there is your omen. Come now to the window, my lord king."

By leaning a little way out of the window, it was possible to see the path by the stream below. Jovann lay with his back to a rock, a pink rose between his teeth. All thought of the Turk had plainly left him, for he sat drawing a heart in the dust, and his sword lay some distance from him beneath a bush.

"As we are contemplative, I fear it will not be a contemplative future," Miloš said, taking the arm of the king to prevent him swooning.

When the dizziness wore off, King Vukasan shook off the hand that held his. He saw, looking wearily up, that it was Jovann who squatted by his bed. He lay breathing heavily, conscious of the terrible weight on his chest, trying to measure where his spirit had been. He saw the wooden screen at the bottom of his couch, he

regarded the still lake outside his window, and he forced a few
words through his swollen lips.

"We should have been in Sveti Andrej today."

"My lord, do not fret yourself, there is plenty of time in the
world."

And that, my dear unhastening Jovann, is only the truth,
thought he, unable to turn the thought into words; but the fate of
the coming centuries has to be decided now, and you should have
left me here to die and dream of death, and hurried on with the
news that my kinsmen must unite and arm . . . But he could only
look up into the trusting and gentle face of his general and speak no
word of all he feared.

Then his focus slipped, and rested momentarily on the carved
screen. He saw that among the wilderness of flowers and leaves a
bird strained at a lizard, and a bullock-cart traced a path along a
vine, and there were little cupolas appearing amid the buds, and
shepherd boys and fat sheep, and even a wooden river. Then his
head rolled to one side, and he saw instead the vast vacancy of the
lake, with the rushes stirring, and the sky reflected in the lake,
until it seemed to his labouring mind that all heaven stood just
outside the window. He closed his eyes and went to it.

And Jovann moved on tiptoe out to the waiting priests and said,
"A mass must be sung, and the villagers must come at once with
flowers and mourn their king as he would have it. And all
arrangements must be made properly for the burial of this, our
great and loved King. I will stay and arrange it for a day or so before
taking the news on to Sveti Andrej. There is plenty of time, and the
king would not wish us to spoil things by haste."

And one of the priests walked along with him along the narrow
way, to summon mourners from the nearest village in the
beleaguered hills.

(1965)

The Source

Only two of the detachment of Seekers left the human settlement and set off across the desert in the direction they had been advised to take. They were the leader of the whole expedition, Kervis XI, and his year-wife, Ysis, who sat beside him in the front of the crawler.

In the sand about them lay memorials of old time. Occasionally they passed a cultivated patch of ground, where men and women stood silent in ragged grandeur to watch them go by, framed perhaps in the entrance of a glassless block of flats or an old railway station.

Kervis said, "I don't understand it. I only hope this place Ani-mykey will offer a clue to where we can find mankind's greatest achievement, as the settlement promised it would."

Ysis regarded the sessions in the settlement as great nonsense. She said quietly, "You have made a mistake, Kervis, haven't you?"

He did not reply. His flow of thought had become confused over the last months as they spiralled through the unending light years towards Earth, and the confusion had increased since they landed. He had been a hard and crystal-clear man. As he grew woollier, Ysis became more indifferent to him and the crew of the Seeker ship more restless. Unhappy though he was, he welcomed the confusion in a curious way.

"This is Earth, *the* Earth," he said.

"It's primitive, more primitive than I could have imagined."

"That's right," he said eagerly. "It is, isn't it?"

"You can see it is," she said contemptuously. "It's a disgusting planet. You can't tell me this is what we are looking for."

"I don't find it disgusting," he said quietly.

"Stop being so simple, Kervis. From Andromeda to here, we have travelled through stupendous civilisations far more glorious than anything in our own remote galaxy. So wonderful is it, it seems as if science can have no end and man's achievements no limit. Yet we never found what we were searching for –"

"We were looking in the wrong place."

"No, no, it was there on Playder, on Doruchak, Millibine, on any one of a million planets encrusted with the tall towers of man's faith. But you did not stay to look. So you are a – well, I won't say you are a failure, because I believe a man to be a failure only when he pronounces himself one, but you have failed in your main Life Objective; to lead us instinctively to the peak of man's greatness."

He said gently, "Ysis, you speak above yourself. Do not forget I was trained on Ravensour itself for a hundred years to be a Seeker, and the instilled instinct of which you speak is still with me and my Life Objective is still untarnished. Accordingly, I have led the Seekers to Earth, which may have been the cradle of mankind, and you must hold your tongue."

"The cradle of mankind! Who needs to go back to the cradle?"

Kervis made no answer. He was tired, divided against himself. He acknowledged much of what Ysis said; yet there seemed nothing to do but press on with his investigation.

They had arrived at the settlement to experience only crushing disappointment. All the cities of Earth stood in ruins or sprawled into dust; only in the settlements was there a fair degree of order. But it was immediately obvious to them that political and governmental organisations, without which great civilisations cannot survive, were entirely lacking. The buildings were low and modest, hugging the ground with broad eaves; within, men and women could be seen going naked, though outside they wore casual clothing.

Kervis was immensely disturbed to find what he had been taught to regard as only semi-aware behaviour. The people were singing and making music with punctured wooden pipes; they danced together in the evenings in intricate patterns, round stinking wood fires. Even worse, they let their children run free and play with various species of animal which were allowed to foul where they would and go into the dwellings. Throughout the rest of this galaxy, all this was unheard of. It seemed indeed that Earth was an unlikely place on which to go looking for man's greatest achievement.

Yet it must be said that the people in the settlement had some virtue. They listened quietly enough while the Seekers told them of the wonders of the universe, of the treatments that could make them purely rational creatures, or extend their lifespans for thousands of years, or transfer their intelligences to other minds. And they seemed willing enough to divulge their alarming habits to the recorders of the party. Among these alarming habits was religion.

It was when Ysis and the Senior Seekers found how much attention Kervis paid to the pathetic details of the local religion that they first officially voiced their impatience to him. Bandareich came before him and said ceremonially, "O Kervis XI, it was not to occupy our great minds with these trifles that we travelled these last two and a half thousand subjective years. The Machines report to us that on the last occasion when we were expunging our minds of dross, you did not undergo Ablution; we believe that consequently your brain grows tired. We therefore ask you to undergo Ablution or not to stand at the next Election."

Bandareich's words had made it plain how seriously his leadership had slipped. Yet Kervis had not undergone Ablution. The truth was, it had been a psychic shock to him to visit the source of his race, and thus of his being. He had continued to listen to the vague rumours of the settlement's religion. He had become so interested that he had embarked on this expedition to find their place of pilgrimage, Ani-mykey. The declaration of his intentions had caused a serious split in the ranks of Senior Seekers, most of whom were for leaving Earth immediately. Under the guidance of Bandareich, they waited now in the settlement, letting Kervis go off with his year-wife in one vehicle across unknown land.

The desert outside the crawler was giving place to semi-scrubland. He saw a small armoured creature scuttle away into thorn, but could not get a clear glimpse of it because the light was poor. In fact the light was extremely bad. Although the sun was shining, its rays seemed to be absorbed by the layers of cloud that piled up evenly from the horizon. The clouds were black and looked as if they would belch forth torrential rain at any moment.

As Kervis stared up at them, he saw Ysis's face from the corner of his eye. She had withered and aged into an old crone.

The truck swerved under his shock. He swung round to see what had happened. Her face was as normal: pale, unlined, lofty of brow, thin of lip, dark of hair. She stared at him curiously.

"Kervis, are you ill?"

"I thought – I'm sorry, the light's so bad."

"Switch the searchlight on. Are you tired? Do you wish me to drive? Put it on automatic."

Muttering to himself, he switched on the searchlight. As he turned to do it, the crone was back there at the corner of his eye. This time, slowly and fearfully, he turned his head, the illusion vanished; Ysis was as usual, and looking at him in challenging and unfriendly fashion.

He shook his head and tried to concentrate on the road. From the half-seen seat next to his, the withered mummy mocked him.

Now trees were closing in on the road. In the distance, they reared against the smudgy sky where hills were. At any moment, the downpour would start, for though the sun still shone, the clouds made a sickly yellow light that seemed to baffle visibility.

The mummy said, "A suitable setting for your final hour, Kervis."

He watched it dissolve into the calm features of Ysis as he turned and asked, "What did you say?"

"I said that the sun will be set before our return. What are you so nervous about?"

"Nothing. It's curious country, don't you think?"

"It's vile country," she said contemptuously.

His hands shook on the wheel. The track was good through the forest, but it wound in baffling fashion. The trees seemed like smudges on the glass before his eyes and he lost speed. What have I got next to me? he wondered. Has some change come over Ysis, once so loving; or is this some new thing which has taken Ysis's place; or is my mind collapsing because I have refused the Ablutions? And what do I do? How my mother, the Matriarch, would grieve to see me like this!

The mummy told him: "Incest won't help you."

Gritting his teeth, he swung round on it and demanded as it turned into Ysis, "What did you say then?"

"I said that it was as still as hell here."

"Oh, you did, did you? And where did you find the concept of hell?"

"You forget I had to attend those boring talks with the religious man in the settlement with you."

Had he nearly trapped her/it there? Hell: the primitive belief in a sub-world devoted to suffering; and some idea the Earthmen had that you had to go into hell to rise a full man. Well, perhaps this forest was hell; it was dark enough to be far underground.

"What's the matter with you, Kervis? It *is* still, isn't it? Why do you challenge every remark I make?"

Anxious, for some obscure reason, not to agree with her, he gestured at the landscape outside. "It's full of animals," he said.

As he spoke, he saw to his horror it was true. The sable trees were as blurred as a bad water-colour under the distortion of light. Among them, so that the trees themselves seemed to be alive, moved huge ungainly forms, more primitive than he could imagine. Try as he might, he could not get a clear glimpse of one. It seemed to him there were several varieties. He yanked the search-light about, sending its yellow tooth biting into the foliage. The foliage heaved and glittered and kept its secrets; only an odd armoured scale or a vanishing hoof or eye could be caught.

"See those creatures?" he asked, turned to Ysis.

"They're only rodents," she said indifferently.

Struck by an idea, he turned away so that the aged crone was back beside him and said, "Would you mind repeating what you just said?"

"I said, 'You know them, don't you?'" the crone told him.

He nodded his head slowly, some of the fright leaving him. He found the crone's answer more reassuring than Ysis's evasive remark; the crone at least faced him with the truth, awful though it was.

Kervis screwed up his eyes and pressed his forehead, wondering why he had just thought that; for he didn't know the animals in the forest – did he? He looked again. They were still there, bigger perhaps now, for he fancied that now and again one stood on its hind legs and looked at him over the forest. He nearly drove over the tail of one, but it fortunately flicked out of the way just in time. At least he could not see anyone he knew walking in the forest,

which was lucky. He had a suspicion that there might be – but that
was silly, for he didn't know any Twins. At least. *Perhaps if he went
back . . .*

"Why have we stopped?" Ysis asked, as his rolling eye sought
her.

"It's so hot in here," he said. "Do you mind if I take my clothes
off?"

Impatiently, she reached over and adjusted the airconditioning,
switching the fan on at the same time. "Are you ill? Shall I take
over the driving?"

"I must keep control."

"You're losing your grip. Let me into your seat. You can rest.
You're no longer responsible."

"No, no, it's important – I must steer us out of this –" And as he
was talking, her fine flesh was withering and turning brown and
her eyes sinking back into her skull and little blotches were rising
through her flesh and her mouth altering shape, the lips turning a
flecked purple, opened to reveal dusty old gums guarded by an odd
broken bastion of tooth. And the old crone rocked with laughter
and said –

As Ysis: "You're in too much of a state to drive. Let go!"

As Mummy: "You're too young and innocent to drive – let's
go!"

She was right, though he feared her. He dived past her, opening
the door as he went, and jumped down to the ground, rolling
lightly over and picking himself up off his hands and knees. All
round him was the barbarous and moist dark. Though it was
strange to him, he thought he recognised something, perhaps a
haunting smell.

He walked swiftly along the track, which was so narrow that it
could only be traversed on foot. As he went, he realised that he had
been mistaken about the forest, that in fact what he had taken for
conifers were gigantic ferns, their fronds rolling and uncurling as if
under the pressure of accelerated growth. It was difficult to catch
sight of the gorillas, although he could hear them clearly, but he
was not afraid of them. His personal worry was that he should not
miss sight of the mountain – the Jungfrau, was it? – that would
guide him on his way.

But the thought was parent to the deed, or perhaps vice versa, for the forest of ferns was thinning, and beyond was the white-capped spire of the mountain, his landmark, shining clear in the murk. Ani-mykey must be very close.

It seemed that he had been a long while in the forest. As he stood looking ahead, a string of primitive men emerged from among the giant fronds, carrying amorphous objects; the mist prevented him seeing clearly. Ysis was among them, wearing a dress she had worn at the beginning of their association. He was glad to see that she was not entirely unfriendly to the Earth people, and held out his arms to welcome her.

"I thought you were lost."

"I thought you were!"

He attempted to kiss her lips, but she turned in his arms and pointed ahead. "Is that where you are hoping to get?" she asked.

The ground sloped away steeply before them. In the depression, the spires of a stone building could be seen.

"That looks like Ani-mykey," he said. He took her hand and led her forward – she had lost her own volition.

They climbed down a steep hillside. At the bottom, there flowed a narrow but swift stream, with Ani-mykey standing on the further bank.

"Now we shall have to undress," Kervis said.

As they stood there, absolutely naked and hairless, he recalled how the primitive men had been covered with hair over their bodies. Ysis wanted to take her camera across, but he persuaded her to unstrap it from her wrist and leave it on the bank. Similarly, he unstrapped the chronometer that fed him an injection against sleep every nine hours, and left it on the bank beside the micro-camera. They plunged into the stream.

Fortunately, it was not deep, for neither could swim. He took her hand and led her across, the water splashing under his armpits. It was dauntingly cold; they flopped up the far bank in the mud like two sea creatures climbing from the sea.

"You'd have thought the pilgrims would have built a bridge here for their own convenience," Ysis said.

"The river may be part of the plan."

"What plan?"

"Finding whatever they seek in their religion."

"It's all nonsense to me, and I'm cold." As she spoke, she looked up at the building. The spires grew from the ground all round it, ancient and veined with moss. The great walls themselves, punctuated by windows of diamond shape, set high, were stone; and the stone was covered with obscure patterns. Kervis moved nearer to observe the pattern; any small area of it seemed to be intelligible, formed as it was from letters and leaves and the entwined bodies of man and animal; but the structure was so immense that the meaning of the overall pattern – if indeed there was a meaning – was impenetrable.

He began to stride along the walls, which proved to hold bays and towers and recesses, looking for an entrance. Ysis moved reluctantly behind him.

"Come on!" he exclaimed, generally dissatisfied with her. "Faster!"

"If you're looking for a door," she said, "you've just passed one."

He went back, amazed he could have missed it.

The entrance was set in a square tower, narrow and with a low threshold. The door was of wood, its carvings continuing the riot of carving on the stonework to either side.

Kervis exclaimed in disappointment. "This can't be the main door!"

"Why do you need the main door? Any door will do if you just want to get in. You do think a lot of yourself if you must have the main door!"

"You're mistaken. This is the main door."

"But you just said it wasn't! The whole thing's a trick, isn't it? You just want to prove that you're right."

"That's not so. I wish to better the whole human race. That's why we're here, aren't we?"

"I don't know why we're here. And I'm not coming in there with you."

"It's important that you should come in."

"I'm not coming. Sorry."

"Suit yourself. It doesn't matter to me."

"Oh? Then why did you say it was important?"

He looked at her searchingly; perhaps she had aged. "Did you ever think something might be important to *you*, Ysis?" He bowed his head, and made his way into Ani-mykey.

Inside, in the semi-dark, he tripped over a litter of stuff on the floor, and fell among it, squelching as he rolled over. His hands were sticky and slimy, and he saw the modest hall was littered with dead flowers and fruit, presumably offerings brought here by people from the settlements. As he climbed to his feet, he glimpsed robes hanging on one side, and gratefully took one to cover his nakedness. Moving carefully, he walked down the corridor ahead.

The corridor was perfectly plain and austere, only the thick gloom rendering it mysterious. It turned corners and divided more than once before he realised that he was well on the way to getting lost, and that it would be advisable to go back to the beginning if he could and start again. Then he saw something staring at him from the next corner, and dread blotted out thought.

From under lowered horns, eyes could be seen, eyes too full of evil to be other than intelligent, though the form seemed to be that of a beast. It appeared to be waiting. He seemed to discern that its eyes were four. In his ears was a roaring noise like organ music. He could only clutch his gown to him and shiver in it.

He stood there for a long time, and the thing waited patiently for him. Finally it occurred to him that it might be a statue or a model—at least not alive. Very slowly, he approached it. Very slowly, it dissolved into something else.

When he got to it at the corner, he saw that he was looking at nothing at all resembling the terrifying beast he had imagined. From here on, the corridor was elaborately decorated by carving that often stood away from the wall altogether. The horns were the end of an elephant's tusk, the eyes acorns clustered on a little bush bowing under the elephant's tread. Yet he still felt his fear as he walked along the new stretch of corridor, ducking and pushing through a forest of carving. The air was laden with ancient fears.

Whereas the carving on the stonework outside had been extremely formalised, approaching abstraction, here it was executed in the severely naturalistic vein. Fierce animals of prey raked the sides of ruminants whose wounds spurted beads of wooden blood; venomous thorn and gossamer creeper intertwined caught wooden pearls of dew between them; shy forest sprites, arrested in mid-motion, held their heads high with an inquiring eye that seemed to blink; scavenger birds leaned forward with ruffled grainy feathers.

In this unyielding forest which knew only simulated life, it was almost impossible to discover the next turn of the corridor, so prolific was the contorted wood. Kervis wished devoutly that he had brought an axe with him, or one of the weapons from the vehicle, but he was empty-handed. The noise still sounded in his ears. He thought it might be music; it was as loud and intimate as the sound of his bloodstream.

He passed the representation of a primitive being carrying a woman over its shoulder. The being was shown as almost noseless and without forehead; so bestial was its wooden glance that he shrank by it. The girl, tumbled carelessly over the brute's shoulder, had her eyes closed in a faint. Uneasily past them, he came up against a dead end. A jungle of unliving leaves and creepers united to bar his way. He stood there a moment, looking and probing, and then was forced to return past the brute.

The girl's eyes were open.

As his own mouth hinged open in terror, so did hers, and she let out a piercing scream. Unthinking, taken over by a superior and mindless force, Kervis lashed out with all the force of his body and caught the brute between the eyes with his fist. It blinked and dropped the woman, slowly raising its great oaken arms towards him. Ignoring the pains shooting up his arms, Kervis hit it again.

In a shower of splinters, it fell slowly forward. He ducked out of its grasp. One great paw rasped his shoulder and it hit the floor face down. Where it had stood, a new corridor lay open. Panting, sobbing with fright and hurt, Kervis jumped over the great riven body and ran down the new avenue.

Here the maze was wider and the walls free of all but the most elusive pattern. He leant against the wall, gasping the thick air into his lungs. He lifted his injured wrist and saw the dark hair growing on the backs of his fingers. Beyond surprise, he recalled only that before he had been naked; now there was a light thatch of hair up his arms. Looking at his legs, he saw they too were not hairless as formerly. Opening the gown, his whole body was revealed, patched here and there with wiry hair in the manner of the people's bodies in the settlement.

The visibility had much improved for him to be able to glimpse such detail. Looking up, he saw that the source of illumination must indeed be bright, and was moving towards him.

By now, he took it for granted that he was in a maze. The light seemed to be several passages away; only intuition told him it was approaching. Some of his former alarm returned, but in the main he felt only an apprehension that he might be somehow unprepared for whatever was coming next. He hurried forward down the corridor, clutching his robe about him.

At the next turn, the corridor divided. Instinctively, he took the left turn, ran through a shadowy arch, found himself in a circular chamber, to which four arches permitted entrance. Exhilaration filled him; he knew he stood at the heart of the place.

The light was coming nearer. From the arch opposite him, a woman appeared, bearing in her hand a lamp that glowed with a living white luminance. She stopped before him and looked at him. Overcome, he went down on his knees.

Afterwards, he was unable to recall what she looked like; he retained only the general idea that her beauty was of a severe and yet exotic kind, and that there was a sort of seriousness about her which seemed as if it might easily melt, either into laughter or erotic welcome. Nor was their conversation any more easy to recall; it always slipped away, though he knew it was the most momentous conversation in which he had participated.

He thought that at first she spoke about strange wild animals being wrenched from their natural habitat and being put to strange work under a yoke. He thought that he in some manner disclaimed all connection with this, and that she then produced a yoke which he did not recognise as such. Either she told him, or he gathered without being told, that a yoke might still be a yoke even when it was not recognisable. She seemed to talk of recognition, and say that millions of years might render things like yokes difficult to recognise without changing their essential natures. Someone – it was as if a third party were speaking for him at times – claimed something about essential natures; that man's essential nature was not known. But the woman knew it; that was her function. He saw she knew it, and that she was unlike Ysis. He thought he said that he recognised her essential nature. It was enough, whatever was said, to release a great wave of loving trust between them. He thought she or he said that he had come here seeking something, and that it had been found. What happened, what was "said" was on a plane below the vocal one; but he understood, even when afterwards he was not sure if he did, and he had the task of interpreting the experience into words.

When she was gone, he walked dazedly through the nearest arch and out into the open air. He saw that it had rained heavily; the air was fresh, everything gleamed. Ysis was coming towards him. He staggered forward in a faint.

That yoke had been very complex, an intricately manufactured thing, as elaborate in its own way as a city, and that he could not understand. He roused in puzzlement, to find that Ysis had driven him back to the settlement. She was sitting by him, looking doubtful.

"I thought you would die."

"I'm all right."

"Bandareich is holding a meeting. I must ask you, Kervis – did you see the *thing* in the maze?"

"What thing?"

"I followed you in after a moment. I had to. But there was a hairy – a man, all hairy, with burning eyes, clad in steel. I ran away."

After a while he said, "I didn't see him." It seemed useless to pursue that subject; she was not like him. He said, heavily, "What is the meeting for?"

"They want to replace you. They say you are finished. They asked me if we found anything, and I had to say no."

"I'll speak to them." He rose. He felt curiously well. Ysis was dressed in one of her more elaborate and artificial costumes; he still had on his mud-spattered gown.

"You can't go in that," she said. "You know you'll lose your chance of winning if you appear like that. You look like an Earthman."

He took her face between his hands. "Do you love me, Ysis?"

"Darling, you know our year is nearly up, do try and be rational."

"Ha!" He pulled the gown round him and strode out into the open.

Bandareich and five of the Senior Seekers were approaching, their faces telling him much that he had guessed.

They raised hands to him in the traditional greeting, and Bandareich said, "Kervis XI, we come to you after a meeting convened according to the articles of Seeking, tabled –"

"Thank you, Bandareich, I'm satisfied it was all legal. I take it I've offended?"

"You know how you have offended, not only by refusing to undergo Ablution, but by leaving the vehicle of which you had command and by –"

"I have offended in more ways than you can know, Seniors, so spare me an incomplete list. If you wish to replace me, I am entirely willing to be replaced."

Ysis had come up beside him. She said, "Defend yourself! Your record was blameless until we reached Earth."

"Quiet, woman!" Bandareich exclaimed. But one of his companions, Wolvorta IV, said, "She has reason on her side. Kervis, have you anything to say in your defence? Did you find on your excursion any artifact or object that might be ranked among man's greatest achievements?"

"Nothing you would recognise as such," Kervis said.

The group of Seekers conferred among themselves. A group of Earthmen had come up and stood at a distance in easy attitudes, watching with an amount of leisurely interest.

Bandareich broke from the group and said, "Kervis XI, regretfully we must ask for your resignation as leader. You will be returned to home galaxy as soon as possible."

He looked down at his feet in the dusty ground. The blow was none the less heavy for being expected, even wanted; no Kervis before him had suffered such disgrace – but the disgrace was imposed by them and no real part of him.

Looking across at his erstwhile companions, he said, "I offer you my resignation."

"Accepted," they said in unison. Bandareich snapped his fingers. "Then we will leave Earth immediately; this idle mission has wasted enough time." As he spoke, he thumbed the button set in his metal lapel, and a ghostly cage descended from the sky and materialised before them. A door swung open. They began to move towards it. More cages were descending for men and vehicles, to carry them up to the great celestial city orbiting above the planet.

"Come along, Kervis," Bandareich called. "We can't leave you behind."

Ysis wept, clung to him in unexpected pain, finally ran to the cage as its door was closing. They made one last gesture to him; he shook his head. He stood alone, the Earthmen coming slowly up to him. The cage door closed; they were impatient to be off, seeking again man's greatest achievement. The cage vanished.

He stared upwards into the clear sky, wetting his lips, wondering what would become of them all. He sighed. "You idiots, you won't see that you have your hands on it as surely as I do! The greatest human achievement is to fulfil one's destiny."

He turned to the ragged Earthmen, nearer now, playing their simple pipes.

(1965)

The Village Swindler

The great diesel train hauled out of Naipur Road, heading grandly south. Jane Pentecouth caught a last glimpse of it over bobbing heads as she followed the stretcher into the station waiting-room.

She pushed her way through the excited crowd, managing to get to her father's side and rejoin the formidable Dr Chandhari, who had taken charge of the operation.

"My car will come in only a few moments, Miss Pentecouth," he said, waving away the people who were leaning over the stretcher and curiously touching the sick man. "It will whisk us to my home immediately, not a mile distant. It was extremely fortunate that I happened to be travelling on the very same express with you."

"But my father would have been –"

"Do not thank me, dear lady, do not thank me! The pleasure is mine, and your father is saved. I shall do my level best for him."

She had not been about to thank this beaming and terrifying Hindu. She trembled on the verge of hysterical protest. It was many years since she had felt so helpless. Her father's frightening attack on the train had been bad enough. Then all those terrible people had flocked round, all offering advice. Then Dr Chandhari had appeared, taken command, and made the conductor stop the train at Naipur Road, this small station apparently situated in the middle of nowhere, claiming that his home was nearby. Irresistibly, Jane had been carried along on the steamy tide of solicitude and eloquence.

But she did believe that her father's life had been saved by Dr Chandhari. Robert Pentecouth was breathing almost normally. She hardly recognised him as she took his hand; he was in a coma. But at least he was still alive, and, in the express, as he bellowed and fought with the coronary attack, she had imagined him about to die.

The crowd surged into the waiting-room, all fighting to give a hand with the stretcher. It was oppressively hot in the small room; the fan on the ceiling merely caused the heat to circulate. As more and more men surged into the room, Jane stood up and said loudly, "Will you all please get out, except for Dr Chandhari and his secretary!"

The doctor was very pleased by this, seeing that it implied her acceptance of him. He set his secretary to clearing the room, or at least to arguing with the crowd that still flocked in. Bending a yet more perfect smile upon her, he said, "My young intelligent daughter Amma is fortunately at home at this very present moment, dear Miss Pentecouth, so you will have some pleasant company just while your father is recovering his health with us."

She smiled back, thinking to herself that the very next day, when her father had rested, they would return to Calcutta and proper medical care. On that she was determined.

She was impressed by the Chandhari household despite herself.

It was an ugly modernistic building, all cracked concrete outside – bought off a film star who had committed suicide, Amma cheerfully told her. All rooms, including the garage under the house, were air-conditioned. There was a heart-shaped swimming pool at the back, although it was empty of water and the sides were cracked. High white walls guarded the property. From her bedroom, Jane looked over the top of the wall at a dusty road sheltered by palm trees and the picturesque squalor of a dozen hovels, where small children stood naked in doorways and dogs rooted and snarled in piles of rubbish.

"There is such contrast between rich and poor here," Jane said, surveying the scene. It was the morning after her arrival here.

"What a very European remark!" said Amma. "The poor people expect that the doctor should live to a proper standard, or he has no reputation."

Amma was only twenty, perhaps half Jane's age. An attractive girl, with delicate gestures that made Jane feel clumsy. As she herself explained, she was modern and enlightened, and did not intend to marry until she was older.

"What do you do all day, Amma?" Jane asked.

"I am in the government, of course, but now I am taking a holiday. It is rather boring here, but still I don't mind it for a change. Next week, I will go away from here. What do you do all day, Jane?"

"My father is one of the directors of the new EGNP Trust. I just look after him. He is making a brief tour of India, Pakistan, and Ceylon, to see how the Trust will be administered. I'm afraid the heat and travel have over-taxed him. His breathing has been bad for several days."

"He is old. They should have sent a younger man." Seeing the look on Jane's face, she said, "Please do not take offence! I am meaning only that it is unfair to send a man of his age to our hot climate. What is this trust you are speaking of?"

"The European Gross National Product Trust. Eleven leading European nations contribute one percent of their gross national product to assist development in this part of the world."

"I see. More help for the poor overpopulated Indians, is that so?" The two women looked at each other. Finally, Amma said, "I will take you out with me this afternoon, and you shall see the sort of people to whom this money of yours will be going, if they live sufficiently long enough."

"I shall be taking my father back to Calcutta this afternoon."

"You know my father will not allow that, and he is the doctor. Your father will die if you are foolish enough to move him. You must remain and enjoy our very simple hospitality and try not to be too bored."

"Thank you, I am not bored!" Her life was such that she had had ample training in not being bored. More even than not being in command of the situation, she hated failing to understand the attitude of these people. With what grace she could muster, she told the younger woman, "If Dr Chandhari advises that my father should not be moved, then I will be pleased to accompany you this afternoon."

After the light midday meal, Jane was ready for the outing at two o'clock. But Amma and the car were not ready until almost five o'clock, when the sun was moving towards the west.

Robert Pentecouth lay breathing heavily, large in a small white bed. He was recognisable again, looked younger. Jane did not love him; but she would do anything to preserve his life. That was her considered verdict as she looked down on him. He had gulped down a lot of life in his time.

Something in the room smelt unpleasant. Perhaps it was her father. By his bedside squatted an old woman in a dull red-and-maroon sari, wrinkled of face, with a jewel like a dried scab screwed in one nostril. She spoke no English. Jane was uneasy with her, not certain whether she was not Chandhari's wife. You heard funny things about Indian wives.

The ceiling was a maze of cracks. It would be the first thing he would see when he opened his eyes. She touched his head and left the room.

Amma drove. A big new car that took the rutted tracks uneasily. There was little to Naipur Road. The ornate and crumbling houses of the main street turned slightly uphill, became mere shacks. The sunlight buzzed. Over the brow of the slope, the village lost heart entirely and died by a huge banyan tree, beneath which an old man sat on a bicycle.

Beyond, cauterised land, a coastal plain lying rumpled, scarred by man's long and weary occupation.

"Only ten miles," Amma said. "It gets more pretty later. It's not so far from the ocean, you know. We are going to see an old nurse of mine who is sick."

"Is there plague in these parts?"

"Orissa has escaped so far. A few cases occur down in Cuttack. And of course in Calcutta. Calcutta is the home town of the plague. But we are quite safe – my nurse is dying only of a malnutritional disease."

Jane said nothing.

They had to drive slowly as the track deteriorated. Everything had slowed. People by the tattered roadside stood silently, silently were encompassed by the car's cloud of dust. A battered truck slowly approached, slowly passed. Under the annealing sun, even time had a wound.

Among low hills, little more than undulations of the ground, they crossed a bridge over a dying river and Amma stopped the car in the shade of some deodars. As the women climbed out, a beggar sitting at the base of a tree called out to them for baksheesh, but Amma ignored him. Gesturing courteously to Jane, she said, "Let us walk under the trees to where the old nurse's family lives. It perhaps would be better if you did not enter the house with me, but I shall not be long. You can look round the village. There is a pleasant temple to see."

Only a few yards farther on, nodding and smiling, she turned aside and, ducking her head, entered a small house with mud walls.

It was a long blank village, ruled by the sun. Jane felt her isolation as soon as Amma disappeared.

A group of small children with big eyes were following Jane. They whispered to each other but did not approach too closely. A peasant farmer, passing with a thin-ribbed cow, called out to the children. Jane walked slowly, fanning the flies from her face.

She knew this was one of the more favoured regions of India. For all that, the poverty – the stone-age poverty – afflicted her. She was glad her father was not with her, in case he felt as she did, that this land could soak up EGNP money as easily, as tracelessly, as it did the monsoon.

Walking under the trees, she saw a band of monkeys sitting or pacing by some more distant huts, and moved nearer to look at them. The huts stood alone, surrounded by attempts at agriculture. A dog nosed by the rubbish heaps, keeping an eye on the monkeys.

Stones were set beneath the big tree where the monkeys paced. Some were painted or stained, and branches of the tree had been painted white. Offerings of flowers lay in a tiny shrine attached to the main trunk; a garland withered on a low branch above a monkey's head. The monkey, Jane saw, suckled a baby at its narrow dugs.

A man stepped from behind the tree and approached Jane.

He made a sign of greeting and said, "Lady, you want buy somet'ing?"

She looked at him. Something unpleasant was happening to one of his eyes, and flies surrounded it. But he was a well-built man, thin, of course, but not as old as she had at first thought. His head was shaven; he wore only a white dhoti. He appeared to have nothing to sell.

"No, thank you," she said.

He came closer.

"Lady, you are English lady? You buy small souvenir, some one very nice thing of value for to take with you back to England! Look, I show – you are please to wait here one minute."

He turned and ducked into the most dilapidated of the huts. She looked about, wondering whether to stay. In a moment, the man emerged again into the sun, carrying a vase. The children gathered and stared silently; only the monkeys were restless.

"This is very lovely Indian vase, lady, bought in Jamshedpur, very fine hand manufacture. Perceive beautiful artistry work, lady!"

She hesitated before taking the poor brass vase in her hands. He turned and called sharply into the hut, and then redoubled his sales talk. He had been a worker in a shoe factory in Jamshedpur, he told her, but the factory had burned down and he could find no other work. He had brought his wife and children here, to live with his brother.

"I'm afraid I'm not interested in buying the vase," she said.

"Lady, please, you give only ten rupees! Ten rupees only!" He broke off.

His wife had emerged from the hut, to stand without motion by his side. In her arms, she carried a child.

The child looked solemnly at Jane from its giant dark eyes. It was naked except for a piece of rag, over which a great belly sagged. Its body, and especially the face and skull, were covered in pustules, from some of which a liquid seeped. Its head had been smeared with ash. The baby did not move or cry; what its age was, Jane could not estimate.

Its father had fallen silent for a moment. Now he said, "My child is having to die, lady, look see! You give me ten rupees."

Now she shrank from the proffered vase. Inside the hut, there were other children stirring in the shadows. The sick child looked outwards with an expression of great wisdom and beauty – or so Jane interpreted it – as if it understood and forgave all things. Its very silence frightened her, and the stillness of the mother. She backed away, feeling chilled.

"No, no, I don't want the vase! I must go –"

Muttering her excuses, she turned away and hurried, almost

ran, back towards the car. She could hear the man calling to her.

She climbed into the car. The man came and stood outside, not touching the car, apologetic, explaining, offering the vase for only eight rupees, talking, talking. Seven-and-a-half rupees. Jane hid her face.

When Amma emerged, the man backed away, said something meekly; Amma replied sharply. He turned, clutching the vase, and the children watched. She climbed into the driving seat and started the car.

"He tried to sell me something. A vase. It was the only thing he had to sell, I suppose," Jane said. "He wasn't rude." She felt the silent gears of their relationship change; she could no longer pretend to superiority, since she had been virtually rescued. After a moment, she asked, "What was the matter with his child? Did he tell you?"

"He is a man of the scheduled classes. His child is dying of the smallpox. There is always smallpox in the villages."

"I imagined it was the plague . . ."

"I told you, we do not have the plague in Orissa yet."

The drive home was a silent one, voiceless in the corroded land. The people moving slowly home had long shadows now. When they arrived at the gates of the Chandhari house, a porter was ready to open the gate, and a distracted servant stood there; she ran fluttering beside the car, calling to Amma.

Amma turned and said, "Jane, I am sorry to tell you that your father has had another heart attack just now."

The attack was already over. Robert Pentecouth lay unconscious on the bed, breathing raspingly. Doctor Chandhari stood looking down at him and sipping an iced lime juice. He nodded tenderly at Jane as she moved to the bedside.

"I have of course administered an anti-coagulant, but your father is very ill, Miss Pentecouth," he said. "There is severe cardiac infarction, together with weakness in the mitral valve, which is situated at the entrance of the left ventricle. This has caused congestion of the lungs, which means the trouble of breathlessness, very much accentuated by the hot atmosphere of the Indian sub-continent. I have done my level best for him."

"I must get him home, doctor."

Chandhari shook his head. "The air journey will be severely taxing on him. I tell you frankly I do not imagine for a single moment that he will survive it."

"What should I do, doctor? I'm so frightened."

"Your father's heart is badly scarred and damaged, dear lady. He needs a new heart, or he will give up the ghost."

Jane sat down on the chair by the bedside and said, "We are in your hands."

He was delighted to hear it. "There are no safer hands, dear Miss Pentecouth." He gazed at them with some awe as he said, "Let me outline a little plan of campaign for you. Tomorrow we put your father on the express to Calcutta. I can phone to Naipur Road station to have it stop. Do not be alarmed! I will accompany you on the express. At the Radakhrishna General Hospital in Howrah in Calcutta is that excellent man, K. V. Menon, who comes from Trivandrum, as does my own family – a very civilised and clever man of the Nair caste. K. V. Menon. His name is widely renowned and he will perform the operation."

"Operation, doctor?"

"Certainly, certainly! He will give a new heart. K. V. Menon has performed many, many successful heart-transplants. The operation is as commonplace in Calcutta as in California. Do not worry! And I will personally stand by you all the while. Perhaps Amma shall come too because I see you are firm friends already. Good, good, don't worry!"

In his excitement, he took her by the arm and made her rise to her feet. She stood there, solid but undecided, staring at him.

"Come!" he said. "Let us go and telephone all the arrangements! We will make some commotion around these parts, eh? Your father is OK here with the old nurse-woman to watch. In a few days, he will wake up with a new heart and be well again."

Jane sent a cable explaining the situation to the Indian head-quarters of EGNP in Delhi (the city which ancient colonialist promptings had perhaps encouraged the authorities to choose). Then she stood back while the commotion spread.

It spread first to the household. More people were living in the Chandhari house than Jane had imagined. She met the doctor's wife, an elegant sari-clad woman who spoke good English and who apparently lived in her own set of rooms, together with her servants. The latter came and went, enlivened by the excitement. Messengers were dispatched to the bazaar for various little extra requirements.

The commotion rapidly spread further afield. People came to inquire the health of the white sahib, to learn the worst for themselves. The representative of the local newspaper called. Another doctor arrived, and was taken by Dr Chandhari, a little proudly, to inspect the patient.

If anything, the commotion grew after darkness fell.

Jane went to sit by her father. He was still unconscious. Once, he spoke coherently, evidently imagining himself back in England; although she answered him, he gave no sign that he heard. Amma came in to say goodnight on her way to bed.

"We shall be leaving early in the morning," Jane said. "My father and I have brought you only trouble. Please don't come to Calcutta with us. It isn't necessary."

"Of course not. I will come only to Naipur Road station. I'm glad if we could help at all. And with a new heart, your father will be really hale and hearty again. Menon is a great expert in heart-transplantation."

"Yes. I have heard his name, I think. You never told me, Amma – how did you find your old nurse this afternoon?"

"You did not ask me. Unhappily, she died during last night."

"Oh! I'm so sorry!"

"Yes, it is hard for her family. Already they are much in debt to the moneylender."

She left the room; shortly after, Jane also retired. But she could not sleep. After an hour or two of fitful sleep, she got dressed again and went downstairs, obsessed with a mental picture of the glass of fresh lime-juice she had seen the doctor drinking. She could hear unseen people moving about in rooms she had never entered. In the garden, too, flickering tongues of light moved. A heart-transplant was still a strange event in Naipur Road, as it had once been in Europe and America; perhaps it would have even more superstition attached to it here than it had there.

When a servant appeared, she made her request. After long delay, he brought the glass on a tray, gripping it so that it would not slip, and lured her out on to the verandah with it. She sat in a wicker chair and sipped it. A face appeared in the garden, a hand reached in supplication up to her.

"Please! Miss Lady!"

Startled, she recognised the man with the dying child to whom she had spoken the previous afternoon.

The next morning, Jane was roused by one of the doctor's servants. Dazed after too little sleep, she dressed and went down to drink tea. She could find nothing to say; her brain had not woken yet. Amma and her father talked continuously in English to each other.

The big family car was waiting outside. Pentecouth was gently loaded in, and the luggage piled round him. It was still little more than dawn; as Jane, Amma, and Chandhari climbed in and the car rolled forward, wraithlike figures were moving already. A cheerful little fire burned here and there inside a house. A tractor rumbled towards the fields. People stood at the sides of the road, numb, to let the car pass. The air was chilly; but, in the eastern sky, the banners of the day's warmth were already violently flying.

They were almost at the railway station when Jane turned to Amma. "That man with the child dying of smallpox walked all the way to the house to speak to me. He said he came as soon as he heard of my father's illness."

"The servants had no business to let him through the gate. That is how diseases spread," Amma said.

"He had something else to sell me last night. Not a vase. He wanted to sell his heart!"

Amma laughed. "The vase would be a better bargain, Jane!"

"How can you laugh? He was so desperate to help his wife and family. He wanted fifty rupees. He would take the money back to his wife and then he would come with us to the Calcutta hospital to have his heart cut out!"

Putting her hand politely to her mouth, Amma laughed again.

"Why is it funny?" Jane asked desperately. "He meant what he said. Everything was so black for him that his life was worth only fifty rupees!"

"But his life is not worth so much, by far!" Amma said. "He is just a village swindler. And the money would not cure the child, in any case. The type of smallpox going about here is generally fatal, isn't it, Pappa?"

Dr Chandhari, who sat with a hand on his patient's forehead, said, "This man's idea is of course not scientific. He is one of the scheduled classes – an Untouchable, as we used to say. He has never eaten very much all during his life and so he will have only a little weak heart. It would never be a good heart in your father's body, to circulate all his blood properly." With a proud gesture, he thumped Robert Pentecouth's chest. "This is the body of the well-nourished man. In Calcutta, we shall find him a proper big heart that will do the work effectively."

They arrived at the railway station. The sun was above the horizon and climbing rapidly. Rays of gold poured through the branches of the trees by the station on to the faces of people arriving to watch the great event, the stopping of the great Madras-Calcutta express, and the loading aboard of a white man going for a heart-transplant.

Furtively, Jane looked about the crowd, searching to see if her man happened to be there. But, of course, he would be back in his village by now, with his wife and the children.

Intercepting the look, Amma said, "Jane, you did not give that man baksheesh, did you?"

Jane dropped her gaze, not wishing to betray herself.

"He would have robbed you," Amma insisted. "His heart would be valueless. These people are never free from hookworms, you know – in the heart and the stomach. You should have bought the vase if you wanted a souvenir of Naipur Road – not a heart, for goodness sake!"

The train was coming. The crowd stirred. Jane took Amma's hand. "Say no more. I will always have memories of Naipur Road."

She busied herself about her father's stretcher as the great sleek train growled into the station.

(1968)

The Worm that Flies

When the snow began to fall, the traveller was too absorbed in his reveries to notice. He walked slowly, his stiff and elaborate garments, fold over fold, ornament over ornament, standing out from his body like a wizard's tent.

The road along which he walked had been falling into a great valley, and was increasingly hemmed in by walls of mountain. On several occasions, it had seemed that a way out of these huge accumulations of earth matter could not be found, that the geological puzzle was insoluble, the chthonian arrangement of discord irresolvable: and then vale and drumlin created between them a new direction, a surprise, an escape, and the way took fresh heart and plunged recklessly still deeper into the encompassing upheaval.

The traveller, whose name to his wife was Tapmar and to the rest of the world Argustal, followed this natural harmony in complete paraesthesia, so close was he in spirit to the atmosphere ruling here. So strong was this bond, that the freak snowfall merely heightened his rapport.

Though the hour was only midday, the sky became the intense blue-grey of dusk. The Forces were nesting in the sun again, obscuring its light. Consequently, Argustal was scarcely able to detect when the layered and fractured bulwark of rock on his left side, the top of which stood unseen perhaps a mile above his head, became patched by artificial means, and he entered the domain of the human company of Or.

As the way made another turn, he saw a wayfarer before him, heading in his direction. It was a great pine, immobile until warmth entered the world again and sap stirred enough in its wooden sinews for it to progress slowly forward once more. He brushed by its green skirts, apologetic but not speaking.

This encounter was sufficient to raise his consciousness above its trance level. His extended mind, which had reached out to embrace the splendid terrestrial discord hereabouts, now shrank to concentrate again on the particularities of his situation, and he realised he had arrived at Or.

The way bisected itself, unable to chose between two equally unpromising ravines, and Argustal saw a group of humans standing statuesque in the left-hand fork. He went towards them, and stood there silent until they should recognise his presence. Behind him, the wet snow crept into his footprints.

These humans were well advanced into the New Form, even as Argustal had been warned they would be. There were five of them standing here, their great brachial extensions bearing some tender brownish foliage, and one of them attenuated to a height of almost twenty feet. The snow lodged in their branches and in their hair.

Argustal waited for a long span of time, until he judged the afternoon to be well advanced, before growing impatient. Putting his hands to his mouth, he shouted fiercely at them. "Ho then, tree-men of Or, wake you from your arboreal sleep and converse with me. My name is Argustal to the world, and I travel to my home in far Talembil, where the seas run pink with the spring plankton. I need from you a component for my parapatterner, so rustle yourselves and speak, I beg!"

Now the snow had gone, and a scorching rain driven away its traces. The sun shone again, but its disfigured eye never looked down into the bottom of this ravine. One of the humans shook a branch, scattering water drops all round, and made preparations for speech.

This was a small human, no more than ten feet high, and the old primate form which it had begun to abandon perhaps a couple of million years ago was still in evidence. Among the gnarls and whorls of its naked flesh, its mouth was discernible; this it opened and said, "We speak to you, Argustal-to-the-world. You are the first ape-human to fare this way in a great time. Thus you are welcome, although you interrupt our search for new ideas."

"Have you found any new ideas?" Argustal asked, with his customary boldness. "I heard there were none on all Yzazys."

"Indeed. But it is better for our senior to tell you of it, if he so judges good."

It was by no means clear to Argustal whether he wished to hear what the new idea was, for the tree-men were known for their deviations into incomprehensibility. But there was a minor furore among the five, as if private winds stirred in their branches, and he settled himself on a boulder, preparing to wait. His own quest was so important that all impediments to its fulfilment seemed negligible.

Hunger overtook him before the senior spoke. He hunted about and caught slow-galloping grubs under logs, and snatched a brace of tiny fish from the stream, and a handful of nuts from a bush that grew by the stream.

Night fell before the senior spoke. As he raspingly cleared his gnarled throat, one faded star lit in the sky. That was Hrt, the flaming stone. It and Yzazys' sun burnt alone on the very brink of the cataract of fire that was the universe. All the rest of the night sky in this hemisphere was filled with the unlimited terror of vacancy, a towering nothingness that continued without end or beginning.

Hrt had no worlds attending it. It was the last thing in the universe. And by the way its light flickered, the denizens of Yzazys knew that it was infested already by the Forces, which had swarmed outwards from their eyries in the heart of the dying galaxy.

The eye of Hrt winked many times in the empty skull of space before the senior of the tree-men of Or wound himself up to address Argustal. Tall and knotty, his vocal cords were clamped within his gnarled body, and he spoke by curving his branches until his finest twigs, set against his mouth, could be blown through, to give a slender and whispering version of language. The gesture made him seem curiously like a maiden who spoke with her finger cautiously to her lips.

"Indeed we have a new idea, O Argustal-to-the-world, though it may be beyond your grasping or our expressing. We have perceived that there is a dimension called time, and from this we have drawn a deduction.

"We will explain dimensional time simply to you like this. We know that all things have lived so long on Earth that their origins are forgotten. What we can remember carries from that lost-in-the-mist thing up to this present moment; it is the time we inhabit, and we are used to think of it as all the time there is. But we men of Or have reasoned that this is not so."

"There must be other past times in the lost distance of time," said Argustal, "but they are nothing to us because we cannot touch them as we can our own pasts."

As if this remark had never been, the silvery whisper continued, "As one mountain looks small when viewed from another, so the things in our past that we remember look small from the present. But suppose we moved back to that past to look at this present! We could not see it – yet we know it exists. And from this we reason that there is still more time in the future, although we cannot see it."

For a long while, the night was allowed to exist in silence, and then Argustal said, "Well, I don't see that as being very wonderful reasoning. We know that, if the Forces permit, the sun will shine again tomorrow, don't we?"

The small tree-man who had first spoken, said, "But 'tomorrow' is expressional time. *We* have discovered that tomorrow exists in dimensional time also. It is real already, as real as yesterday."

"Holy spirits!" thought Argustal to himself. "Why did I get myself involved in philosophy?" Aloud he said, "Tell me of the deduction you have drawn from this."

Again the silence, until the senior drew together his branches and whispered from a bower of twiggy fingers, "We have proved that tomorrow is no surprise. It is as unaltered as today or yesterday, merely another yard of the path of time. But we comprehend that things change, don't we? You comprehend that, don't you?"

"Of course. You yourselves are changing, are you not?"

"It is as you say, although we no longer recall what we were before, for that thing is become too small back in time. So: if time is all of the same quality, then it has no change, and thus cannot force change. So: there is another unknown element in the world that forces change!"

Thus in their fragmentary whispers they reintroduced sin into the world.

Because of the darkness, a need for sleep was induced in

Argustal. With the senior tree-man's permission, he climbed up
into his branches and remained fast asleep until dawn returned to
the fragment of sky above the mountains and filtered down to their
retreat. Argustal swung to the ground, removed his outer garments, and performed his customary exercises. Then he spoke to
the five beings again, telling them of his parapatterner, and asking
for certain stones.

Although it was doubtful whether they understood what he was
about, they gave him permission, and he moved round about the
area, searching for a necessary stone, his senses blowing into nooks
and crannies for it like a breeze.

The ravine was blocked at its far end by a rock fall, but the
stream managed to pour through the interstices of the detritus into
a yet lower defile. Climbing painfully, Argustal scrambled over the
mass of broken rock to find himself in a cold and moist passage, a
mere cavity between two great thighs of mountain. Here the light
was dim, and the sky could hardly be seen, so far did the rocks
overhang on the many shelves of strata overhead. But Argustal
scarcely looked up. He followed the stream where it flowed into the
rock itself, to vanish forever from human view.

He had been so long at his business, trained himself over so
many millennia, that the stones almost spoke to him, and he
became more certain than ever that he would find a stone to fit in
with his grand design.

It was there. It lay just above the water, the upper part of it
polished. When he had prized it out from the surrounding pebbles
and gravel, he lifted it and could see that underneath it was slightly
jagged, as if a smooth gum grew black teeth. He was surprised, but
as he squatted to examine it, he began to see that what was
necessary to the design of his parapatterner was precisely some
such roughness. At once, the next step of the design revealed itself,
and he saw for the first time the whole thing as it would be in its
entirety. The vision disturbed and excited him.

He sat where he was, his blunt fingers round the rough-smooth
stone, and for some reason he began to think about his wife
Pamitar. Warm feelings of love ran through him, so that he smiled
to himself and twitched his brows.

By the time he stood up and climbed out of the defile, he knew
much about the new stone. His nose-for-stones sniffed it back to

times when it was a much larger affair, when it occupied a grand position on a mountain, when it was engulfed in the bowels of the mountain, when it had been cast up and shattered down, when it had been a component of a bed of rock, when that rock had been ooze, when it had been a gentle rain of volcanic sediment, showering through an unbreathable atmosphere and filtering down through warm seas in an early and unknown place.

With tender respect, he tucked the stone away in a large pocket and scrambled back along the way he had come. He made no farewell to the five of Or. They stood mute together, branch-limbs interlocked, dreaming of the dark sin of change.

Now he made haste for home, travelling first through the borderlands of Old Crotheria and then through the region of Tamia, where there was only mud. Legends had it that Tamia had once known fertility, and that speckled fish had swam in streams between forests; but now mud conquered everything, and the few villages were of baked mud, while the roads were dried mud, the sky was the colour of mud, and the few mud-coloured humans who chose for their own mud-stained reasons to live here had scarcely any antlers growing from their shoulders and seemed about to deliquesce into mud. There wasn't a decent stone anywhere about the place. Argustal met a tree called David-by-the-moat-that-dries that was moving into his own home region. Depressed by the everlasting brownness of Tamia, he begged a ride from it, and climbed into its branches. It was old and gnarled, its branches and roots equally hunched, and it spoke in grating syllables of its few ambitions.

As he listened, taking pains to recall each syllable while he waited long for the next, Argustal saw that David spoke by much the same means as the people of Or had done, stuffing whistling twigs to an orifice in its trunk; but whereas it seemed that the tree-men were losing the use of their vocal cords, it seemed that the man-tree was developing some from the stringy integuments of its fibres, so that it became a nice problem as to which was inspired by which, which copied which, or whether – for both sides seemed so self-absorbed that this also was a possibility – they had come on a mirror-image of perversity independently.

"Motion is the prime beauty," said David-by-the-moat-that-dries, and took many degrees of the sun across the muddy sky to say it. "Motion is in me. There is no motion in the ground. In the ground there is not motion. All that the ground contains is without motion. The ground lies in quiet and to lie in the ground is not to be. Beauty is not in the ground. Beyond the ground is the air. Air and ground make all there is and I would be of the ground and air. I was of the ground and of the air but I will be of the air alone. If there is ground, there is another ground. The leaves fly in the air and my longing goes with them but they are only part of me because I am of wood. O, Argustal, you know not the pains of wood!"

Argustal did not indeed, for long before this gnarled speech was spent, the moon had risen and the silent muddy night had fallen with Hrt flickering overhead, and he was curled asleep in David's distorted branches, the stone in his deep pockets.

Twice more he slept, twice more watched their painful progress along the unswept tracks, twice more joined converse with the melancholy tree – and when he woke again, all the heavens were stacked with fleecy cloud that showed blue between, and low hills lay ahead. He jumped down. Grass grew here. Pebbles littered the track. He howled and shouted with pleasure. The mud had gone.

Crying his thanks he set off across the heath.

". . . growth . . ." said David-by-the-moat-that-dries.

The heath collapsed and gave way to sand, fringed by sharp grass that scythed at Argustal's skirts as he went by. He ploughed across the sand. This was his own country, and he rejoiced, taking his bearing from the occasional cairn that pointed a finger of shade across the sand. Once, one of the Forces flew over, so that for a moment of terror the world was plunged in night, thunder growled, and a paltry hundred drops of rain spattered down; then it was already on the far confines of the sun's domain, plunging away – no matter where!

Few animals, fewer birds, still survived. In the sweet deserts of Outer Talembil, they were especially rare. Yet Argustal passed a bird sitting on a cairn, its hooded eye bleared with a million years of danger. It clattered one wing at sight of him, in tribute to old reflexes, but he respected the hunger in his belly too much to try to dine on sinews and feathers, and the bird appeared to recognise the fact.

He was nearing home. The memory of Pamitar was sharp before

him, so that he could follow it like a scent. He passed another of his kind, an old ape wearing a red mask hanging almost to the ground; they barely gave each other a nod of recognition. Soon on the idle skyline he saw the blocks that marked Gornilo, the first town of Talembil.

The ulcerated sun travelled across the sky. Stoically, Argustal travelled across the intervening dunes, and arrived in the shadow of the whiteblocks of Gornilo.

No one could recollect now – recollection was one of the lost things that many felt privileged to lose – what factors had determined certain features of Gornilo's architecture. This was an ape-human town, and perhaps in order to construct a memorial to yet more distant and dreadful things, the first inhabitants of the town had made slaves of themselves and of the other creatures that now were no more, and erected these great cubes that now showed signs of weathering, as if they tired at last of swinging their shadows every day about their bases. The ape-humans who lived here were the same ape-humans who had always lived here; they sat as untiringly under their mighty memorial blocks as they had always done – calling now to Argustal as he passed as languidly as one flicks stones across the surface of a lake – but they could recollect no longer if or how they had shifted the blocks across the desert; it might be that that forgetfulness formed an integral part of being as permanent as the granite of the blocks.

Beyond the blocks stood the town. Some of the trees here were visitors, bent on becoming as David-by-the-moat-that-dries was, but most grew in the old way, content with ground and indifferent to motion. They knotted their branches this way and slatted their twigs that way, and humped their trunks the other way, and thus schemed up ingenious and ever-changing homes for the tree-going inhabitants of Gornilo.

At last Argustal came to his home, on the far side of the town.

The name of his home was Cormok. He pawed and patted and licked it first before running lightly up its trunk to the living-room.

Pamitar was not there.

He was not surprised at this, hardly even disappointed, so serene was his mood. He walked slowly about the room, sometimes swinging up to the ceiling in order to view it better, licking and sniffing as he went, chasing the after-images of his wife's presence. Finally, he laughed and fell into the middle of the floor.

"Settle down, boy!" he said.

Sitting where he had dropped, he unloaded his pockets, taking out the five stones he had acquired in his travels and laying them aside from his other possessions. Still sitting, he disrobed, enjoying doing it inefficiently. Then he climbed into the sand bath.

While Argustal lay there, a great howling wind sprang up, and in a moment the room was plunged into sickly greyness. A prayer went up outside, a prayer flung by the people at the unheeding Forces not to destroy the sun. His lower lip moved in a gesture at once of content and contempt; he had forgotten the prayers of Talembil. This was a religious city. Many of the Unclassified congregated here from the waste miles, people or animals whose minds had dragged them aslant from what they were into rococo forms that more exactly defined their inherent qualities, until they resembled forgotten or extinct forms, or forms that had no being till now, and acknowledged no common cause with any other living thing – except in this desire to preserve the festering sunlight from further ruin.

Under the fragrant grains of the bath, submerged all but for head and a knee and hand, Argustal opened wide his perceptions to all that might come: and finally thought only what he had often thought while lying there – for the armouries of cerebration had long since been emptied of all new ammunition, whatever the tree-men of Or might claim – that in such baths, under such an unpredictable wind, the major life forms of Earth, men and trees, had probably first come at their impetus to change. But change itself . . . had there been a much older thing blowing about the world that everyone had forgotten?

For some reason, that question aroused discomfort in him. He felt dimly that there was another side of life than content and happiness; all beings felt content and happiness; but were those qualities a unity, or were they not perhaps one side only of a – of a shield?

He growled. Start thinking gibberish like that and you ended up human with antlers on your shoulders!

Brushing off the sand, he climbed from the bath, moving more swiftly than he had done in countless time, sliding out of his home, down to the ground without bothering to put on his clothes.

He knew where to find Pamitar. She would be beyond the town, guarding the parapatterner from the tattered angry beggars of Talembil.

The cold wind blew, with an occasional slushy thing in it that made a being blink and wonder about going on. As he strode through the green and swishing heart of Gornilo, treading among the howlers who knelt casually everywhere in rude prayer, Argustal looked up at the sun. It was visible by fragments, torn through tree and cloud. Its face was blotched and pimpled, sometimes obscured altogether for an instant at a time, then blazing forth again. It sparked like a blazing blind eye. A wind seemed to blow from it that blistered the skin and chilled the blood.

So Argustal came to his own patch of land, clear of the green town, out in the stirring desert, and his wife Pamitar, to the rest of the world called Miram. She squatted with her back to the wind, the sharply flying grains of sand cutting about her hairy ankles. A few paces away, one of the beggars pranced among Argustal's stones.

Pamitar stood up slowly, removing the head shawl from her head.

"Tapmar!" she said.

Into his arms he wrapped her, burying his face in her shoulder. They chirped and clucked at each other, so engrossed that they made no note of when the breeze died and the desert lost its motion and the sun's light improved.

When she felt him tense, she held him more loosely. At a hidden signal, he jumped away from her, jumping almost over her shoulder, springing ragingly forth, bowling over the lurking beggar into the sand.

The creature sprawled, two-sided and misshapen, extra arms growing from arms, head like a wolf, back legs bowed like a gorilla, clothed in a hundred textures, yet not unlovely. It laughed as it rolled and called in a high clucking voice, "Three men sprawling under a lilac tree and none to hear the first one say, 'Ere the crops crawl, blows fall', and the second abed at night with mooncalves, answer me what's the name of the third, feller?"

"Be off with you, you mad old crow!"

And as the old crow ran away, it called out its answer, laughing, "Why Tapmar, for he talks to nowhere!" confusing the words as it tumbled over the dunes and made its escape.

Argustal and Pamitar turned back to each other, vying with the strong sunlight to search out each other's faces, for both had forgotten when they were last together, so long was time, so dim was memory. But there were memories, and as he searched they came back. The flatness of her nose, the softness of her nostrils, the roundness of her eyes and their brownness, the curve of the rim of her lips: all these, because they were dear, became remembered, thus taking on more than beauty.

They talked gently to each other, all the while looking. And slowly something of that other thing he suspected on the dark side of the shield entered him – for her beloved countenance was not as it had been. Round her eyes, particularly under them, were shadows, and faint lines creased from the sides of her mouth. In her stance too, did not the lines flow more downward than heretofore?

The discomfort growing too great, he was forced to speak to Pamitar of these things, but there was no proper way to express them, and she seemed not to understand, unless she understood and did not know it, for her manner grew agitated, so that he soon forewent questioning, and turned to the parapatterner to hide his unease.

It stretched over a mile of sand, and rose several feet into the air. From each of his long expeditions, he brought back no more than five stones, yet there were assembled here many hundreds of thousands of stones, perhaps millions, all painstakingly arranged, so that no being could take in the arrangement from any one position, not even Argustal. Many were supported in the air at various heights by stakes or poles, more lay on the ground, where Pamitar always kept the dust and the wild men from encroaching them, and of these on the ground, some stood isolated, while others lay in profusion, but all in a pattern that was ever apparent only to Argustal – and he feared that it would take him until the next sunset to have that pattern clear in his head again. Yet already it started to come clearer, and he recalled with wonder the devious and fugual course he had taken, walking down to the ravine of the tree-men of Or, and knew that he still contained the skill to place the new stones he had brought within the general pattern with reference to that natural harmony – completing the parapatterner.

And the lines on his wife's face: would they too have a place within the pattern?

Was there sense in what the crow beggar had cried, that he talked to nowhere? And . . . and . . . the terrible and, would nowhere answer him?

Bowed, he took his wife's arm, and scurried back with her to their home, high in the leafless tree.

"My Tapmar," she said that evening as they ate a dish of fruit, "it is good that you come back to Gornilo, for the town sedges up with dreams like an old riverbed, and I am afraid."

At this he was secretly alarmed, for the figure of speech she used seemed to him an apt one for the newly-observed lines on her face, so that he asked her what the dreams were in a voice more timid than he meant to use.

Looking at him strangely, she said, "The dreams are as thick as fur, so thick that they congeal my throat to tell you of them. Last night, I dreamed I walked in a landscape that seemed to be clad in fur all round the distant horizons, fur that branched and sprouted and had sombre tones of russet and dun and black and a lustrous black-blue. I tried to resolve this strange material into the more familiar shapes of hedges and old distorted trees, but it stayed as it was, and I became . . . well, I had the word in my dream that I became a *child*."

Argustal looked aslant over the crowded vegetation of the town and said, "These dreams may not be of Gornilo but of you only, Pamitar. What is *child*?"

"There's no such thing in reality, to my knowledge, but in the dream the child that was I was small and fresh and in its actions at once nimble and clumsy. It was alien from me, its notions and ideas never mine – and yet it was all familiar to me, I was it, Tapmar, I was that child. And now that I wake, I become sure that I once was such a thing as a *child*."

He tapped his fingers on his knees, shaking his head and blinking in a sudden anger. "This is your bad secret, Pamitar! I knew you had one the moment I saw you! I read it in your face which has changed in an evil way! You know you were never anything but Pamitar in all the millions of years of your life, and that *child* must be an evil phantom that possesses you. Perhaps you will now be turned into *child*!"

She cried out and hurled a green fruit into which she had bitten. Deftly, he caught it before it struck him.

They made a provisional peace before settling for sleep. That night, Argustal dreamed that he also was small and vulnerable and hardly able to manage the language; his intentions were like an arrow and his direction clear.

Waking, he sweated and trembled, for he knew that as he had been *child* in his dream, so he had been *child* once in life. And this went deeper than sickness. When his pained looks directed themselves outside, he saw the night was like shot silk, with a dappled effect of light and shadow in the dark blue dome of the sky, which signified that the Forces were making merry with the sun while it journeyed through the Earth; and Argustal thoughts of his journeys across the Earth, and of his visit to Or, when the tree-men had whispered of an unknown element that forces change.

"They prepared me for this dream!" he muttered. He knew now that change had worked in his very foundations; once, he had been this thin tiny alien thing called *child*, and his wife too, and possibly others. He thought of that little apparition again, with its spindly legs and piping voice; the horror of it chilled his heart; he broke into prolonged groans that all Pamitar's comforting took a long part of the dark to silence.

He left her sad and pale. He carried with him the stones he had gathered on his journey, the odd-shaped one from the ravine at Or and the ones he had acquired before that. Holding them tightly to him, Argustal made his way through the town to his spatial arrangement. For so long, it had been his chief preoccupation; today, the long project would come to completion; yet because he could not even say why it had so preoccupied him, his feelings inside lay flat and wretched. Something had got to him and killed content.

Inside the prospects of the parapatterner, the old beggarly man lay, resting his shaggy head on a blue stone. Argustal was too low in spirit to chase him away.

"As your frame of stones will frame words, the words will come forth stones," cried the creature.

"I'll break your bones, old crow!" growled Argustal, but inwardly he wondered at this vile crow's saying and at what he had said the previous day about Argustal's talking to nowhere, for Argustal had discussed the purpose of his structure with nobody, not even Pamitar. Indeed, he had not recognised the purpose of the structure himself until two journeys back – or had it been three or four? The pattern had started simply as a pattern (hadn't it?) and only much later had the obsession become a purpose.

To place the new stones correctly took time. Wherever Argustal walked in his great framework, the old crow followed, sometimes on two legs, sometimes on four. Other personages from the town collected to stare, but none dared step inside the perimeter of the structure, so that they remained far off, like little stalks growing on the margins of Argustal's mind.

Some stones had to touch, others had to be just apart. He walked and stooped and walked, responding to the great pattern that he now knew contained a universal law. The task wrapped him round in an aesthetic daze similar to the one he had experienced travelling the labyrinthine way down to Or, but with greater intensity.

The spell was broken only when the old crow spoke from a few paces away in a voice level and unlike his usual sing-song. And the old crow said, "I remember you planting the very first of these stones here when you were a child."

Argustal straightened.

Cold took him, though the bilious sun shone bright. He could not find his voice. As he searched for it, his gaze went across to the eyes of the beggarman, festering in his black forehead.

"You know I was once such a phantom – a child?" he asked.

"We are all phantoms. We were all childs. As there is gravy in our bodies, our hours were once few."

"Old crow . . . you describe a different world – not ours!"

"Very true, very true. Yet that other world once was ours."

"Oh, not! Not!"

"Speak to your machine about it! Its tongue is of rock and cannot lie like mine."

He picked up a stone and flung it. "That will I do! Now get away from me!"

The stone hit the old man in his ribs. He groaned painfully and danced backwards, tripped, lay full length in the sand, hopeless and shapeless.

Argustal was upon him at once.

"Old crow, forgive me! It was fear at my thoughts made me attack you – and there is a certain sort of horror in your presence!"

"And in your stone-flinging!" muttered the old man, struggling to rise.

"You know of childs! In all the millions of years that I have worked at my design, you have never spoken of this. Why not?"

"Time for all things . . . and that time now draws to a close, even on Yzazys."

They stared into each other's eyes as the old beggar slowly rose, arms and cloak spread in a way that suggested he would either fling himself on Argustal or turn in flight. Argustal did not move. Crouching with his knuckles in the sand, he said, ". . . Even on Yzazys? Why do you say so?"

"You are of Yzazys! We humans are not – if I call myself human. Thousands of thousands of years before you were child, I came from the heart stars with many others. There is no life there now! The rot spreads from the centre! The sparks fly from sun to sun! Even to Yzazys, the hour is come. Up the galactic chimneys the footprints drum." Suddenly he fell to the ground, was up again, and made off in haste, limbs whirling in a way that took from him all resemblance to humankind. He pushed through the line of watchers and was gone.

For a while, Argustal squatted where he was, groping through matters that dissolved as they took shape, only to grow large when he dismissed them. The storm blew through him and distorted him, like the trouble on the face of the sun. When he decided there was nothing for it but to complete the parapatterner, still he trembled with the new knowledge: without being able to understand why, he knew the new knowledge would destroy the old world.

All now was in position, save for the odd-shaped stone from Or, which he carried firm on one shoulder, tucked between ear and hand. For the first time, he realised what a gigantic structure he had wrought. It was a businesslike stroke of insight, no sentiment involved. Argustal was now no more than a bead rolling through the vast interstices around him.

Each stone held its own temporal record as well as its special position; each represented different stresses, different epochs, different temperatures, materials, chemicals, moulds, intensities. Every stone together represented an anagram of Earth, its whole composition and continuity. The last stone was merely a focal point for the whole dynamic, and as Argustal slowly walked between the vibrant arcades, that dynamic rose to pitch.

He heard it grow. He paused. He shuffled now this way, now that. As he did so, he recognised that there was no one focal position but a myriad, depending on position and direction of the key stone.

Very softly, he said, ". . . That my fears might be verified . . ."

And all about him – but softly – came a voice in stone, stuttering before it grew clearer, as if it had long known of words but never practised them.

"Thou . . ." Silence, then a flood of sentence.

"Thou thou art, O thou art worm thou art sick, rose invisible rose. In the howling storm thou art in the storm. Worm thou art found out O rose thou art sick and and found out flies in the night thy bed thy thy crimson life destroy. O – O rose, thou art sick! The invisible worm, the invisible worm that flies in the night, in the howling storm, has found out – has found out thy bed of crimson joy . . . and his dark dark secret love, his dark secret love does thy life destroy."

Argustal was already running from that place.

In Pamitar's arms he could find no comfort now. Though he huddled there, up in the encaging branches, the worm that flies worked in him. Finally, he rolled away from her and said "Whoever heard so terrible a voice? I cannot speak again with the universe."

"You do not know it was the universe." She tried to tease him. "Why should the universe speak to little Tapmar?"

"The old crow said I spoke to nowhere. Nowhere is the universe – where the sun hides at night – where our memories hide, where our thoughts evaporate. I cannot talk with it. I must hunt out the old crow and talk to him."

"Talk no more, ask no more questions! All you discover brings you misery! Look – you will no longer regard me, your poor wife! You turn your eyes away!"

"If I stare at nothing for all succeeding aeons, yet I must find out what torments us!"

In the centre of Gornilo, where many of the Unclassified lived, bare wood twisted up from the ground like fossilised sack, creating caves and shelters and strange limbs on which and in which old pilgrims, otherwise without a home, might perch. Here at nightfall Argustal sought out the beggar.

The old fellow was stretched painfully beside a broken pot, clasping a woven garment across his body. He turned in his small cell, trying for escape, but Argustal had him by the throat and held him still.

"I want your knowledge, old crow!"

"Get it from the religious men – they know more than I!"

It made Argustal pause, but he slackened his grip on the other by only the smallest margin.

"Because I have you, you must speak to me. I know that knowledge is pain, but so is ignorance once one has sensed its presence. Tell me more about childs and what they did! Tell me of what you call the heart stars!"

As if in a fever, the old crow rolled about under Argustal's grip. He brought himself to say, "What I know is so little, so little, like a blade of grass in a field. And like blades of grass are the distant bygone times. Through all those times come the bundles of bodies now on this Earth. Then as now, no new bodies. But once . . . even before those bygone times . . . you cannot understand . . ."

"I understand well enough."

"You are scientist! Before bygone times was another time, and then . . . then was childs and different things that are not any longer, many animals and birds and smaller things with frail wings unable to carry them over long time . . ."

"What happened? Why was there change, old crow?"

"Men . . . scientists . . . make understanding of the gravy of bodies and turn every person and thing and tree to eternal life. We now continue from that time, a long long time – so long we forgotten what was then done."

The smell of him was like an old pie. Argustal asked him, "And why now are no childs?"

"Childs are just small adults. We are adults, having become from child. But in that great former time, before scientists were on Earth, adults produced childs. Animals and trees likewise. But with eternal life, this cannot be – those child-making parts of the body have less life than stone."

"Don't talk of stone! So we live forever . . . You old ragbag, you remember – ah, you remember me as child?"

But the old ragbag was working himself into a kind of fit, pummelling the ground, slobbering at the mouth.

"Seven shades of lilac, even worse, I remember myself a child, running like an arrow, air, everywhere fresh rosy air. So I am mad, for I remember!" He began to scream and cry, and the outcasts round about took up the wail in chorus. "We remember, we remember!" – whether they did or not.

Clapping his hand over the beggar's mouth, Argustal said, "But you were not child on Yzazys – tell me about that!"

Shaking, the other replied, "Earlier I tell you – all humans come from hearts stars. Yzazys here is perched on universe's end! Once were as many worlds as days in eternity, now all burned away as smoke up the chimney. Only this last place was safe."

"What happened? Why?"

"Nothing happened! Life is life is life – only except that change crept in." And what was this but an echo of the words of the tree-men of Or who, deep in their sinful glade, had muttered of some unknown element that forced change? Argustal crouched with bowed head while the beggarman juddered beside him, and outside the holy idiots took up his last words in a chant: "Change crept in! Change crept in! Daylight smoked and change crept in! Change crept in!"

Their dreadful howling worked like spears in Argustal's flank. He had pictures afterwards of his panic run through the town, of wall and trunk and ditch and road, but it was all as insubstantial at the time as the pictures afterwards. When he finally fell to the ground panting, he was unaware of where he lay, and everything was nothing to him until the religious howling had died into silence.

Then he saw he lay in the middle of his great structure, his cheek against the Or stone where he had dropped it. And as his attention came to it, the great structure round him answered without his having to speak.

He was at a new focal point. The voice that sounded was new, as cool as the previous one had been choked. It blew over him in a cool wind.

"There is no amaranth on this side of the grave, O Argustal, no name with whatsoever emphasis of passionate love repeated that is not mute at last. Experiment X gave life for eternity to every living thing on Earth, but even eternity is punctuated by release and suffers period. The old life had its childhood and its end, the new had no such logic. It found its own after many millennia, and took its cue from individual minds. What a man was, he became; what a tree, it became."

Argustal lifted his tired head from its pillow of stone. Again the voice changed pitch and trend, as if in response to his minute gesture.

"The present is a note in music. That note can no longer be sustained. You find what questions you have found, O Argustal, because the chord, in dropping to a lower key, rouses you from the longer dream of crimson joy that was immortality. What you are finding, others also find, and you can none of you be any longer insensible to change. Even immortality must have an end. Life has passed like a long fire through the galaxy. Now it fast burns out even here, the last refuge of man!"

He stood up then, and hurled the Or stone. It flew, fell, rolled . . . and before it stopped he had awoken a great chorus of universal voice.

The whole Earth roused, and a wind blew from the west. As he started again to move, he saw the religious men of the town were on the march, and the great sun-nesting Forces on their midnight wing, and the stars wheeling, and every majestic object alert as it had never been.

But Argustal walked slowly on his flat simian feet, plodding back to Pamitar. No longer would he be impatient in her arms. There, time would be all too brief.

He knew now the worm that flew and nestled in her cheek, in his cheek, in all things, even in the tree-men of Or, even in the great impersonal Forces that despoiled the sun, even in the sacred bowels of the universe to which he had lent a temporary tongue. He knew now that back had come that Majesty that previously gave to Life its reason, the Majesty that had been away from the world for so long and yet so brief a respite, the Majesty called DEATH.

(1968)

The Moment of Eclipse

Beautiful women with corrupt natures – they have always been my life's target. There must be bleakness as well as loveliness in their gaze: only then can I expect the mingled moment.

The mingled moment – it holds both terror and beauty. Those two qualities, I am aware, lie for most people poles apart. For me, they are, or can become, one! When they do, they coincide, ah . . . then joy takes me! And in Christiania I saw many such instants promised.

But the one special instant of which I have to tell, when pain and rapture intertwined like two hermaphrodites, overwhelmed me not when I was embracing any lascivious darling but when – after long pursuit! – I paused on the very threshhold of the room where she awaited me: paused and saw . . . that spectre . . .

You might say that a worm had entered into me. You might say that there I spoke metaphorically, and that the worm perverting my sight and taste had crept into my viscera in childhood, had infected all my adult life. So it may be. But who escapes the maggot? Who is not infected? Who dares call himself healthy? Who knows happiness except by assuaging his illness or submitting to his fever?

This woman's name was Christiania. That she was to provoke in me years of pain and pursuit was not her wish. Her wish, indeed, was at all times the very opposite.

We met for the first time at a dull party being held at the Danish Embassy in one of the minor East European capitals. My face was known to her and, at her request, a mutual friend brought her over to meet me.

She was introduced as a poet – her second volume of poetry was just published in Vienna. My taste for poetry exhibiting attitudes of romantic agony was what attracted her to me in the first place; of course she was familiar with my work.

Although we began by addressing each other in German, I soon discovered what I had suspected from something in her looks and mannerisms, that Christiania was also Danish. We started to talk of our native land.

Should I attempt to describe what she looked like? Christiania was a tall woman with a slightly full figure; her face was perhaps a little too flat for great beauty, giving her, from certain angles, a look of stupidity denied by her conversation. At that time, she had more gleaming dark hair than the fashion of the season approved. It was her aura that attracted me, a sort of desolation in her smile which is, I fancy, a Scandinavian inheritance. The Norwegian painter Edvard Munch painted a naked Madonna once, haunted, suffering, erotic, pallid, generous of flesh, with death about her mouth; in Christiania, that madonna opened her eyes and breathed!

We found ourselves talking eagerly of a certain *camera obscura* that still exists in the Aalborghus, in Jutland. We discovered that we had both been taken there as children, had both been fascinated to see a panorama of the town of Aalborg laid out flat on a table through the medium of a small hole in the roof. She told me that that optical toy had inspired her to write her first poem; I told her that it had directed my interest to cameras, and thus to filming.

But we were scarcely allowed time to talk before we were separated by her husband. Which is not to say that with look and gesture we had not already inadvertently signalled to each other, delicately but unmistakably.

Inquiring about her after the party, I was told that she was an infanticide currently undergoing a course of mental treatment which combined elements of Eastern and Western thought. Later, much of this information proved to be false; but, at the time, it served to heighten the desires that our brief meeting had woken in me.

Something fatally intuitive inside me knew that at her hands, though I might find suffering, I would touch the two-faced ecstasy I sought.

At this period, I was in a position to pursue Christiania further;

my latest film, *Magnitudes*, was completed, although I had still some editing to do before it was shown at a certain film festival.

It chanced also that I was then free of my second wife, that *svelte*-mannered Parsi lady, ill-omened star alike of my first film and my life, whose vast promised array of talents was too quickly revealed as little more than a glib tongue and an over-sufficient knowledge of tropical medicine. In that very month, our case had been settled and Sushila had retreated to Bombay, leaving me to my natural pursuits.

So I planned to cultivate my erotic garden again: and Christiania should be the first to flower in those well-tended beds.

Specialised longings crystallise the perceptions along the axes concerned: I had needed only a moment in Christiania's presence to understand that she would not scruple to be unfaithful to her husband under certain circumstances, and that I myself might provide such a circumstance; for those veiled grey eyes told me that she also had an almost intuitive grasp of her own and men's desires, and that involvement with me was far from being beyond her contemplation.

So it was without hesitation that I wrote to her and described how, for my next film, I intended to pursue the train of thought begun in *Magnitudes* and hoped to produce a drama of a rather revolutionary kind to be based on a sonnet of the English poet Thomas Hardy entitled "At a Lunar Eclipse". I added that I hoped her poetic abilities might be of assistance in assembling a script, and asked if she would honour me with a meeting.

There were other currents in my life just then. In particular, I was in negotiation through my agents with the Prime Minister of a West African republic who wished to entice me out to make a film of his country. Although I nourished an inclination to visit this strange part of the world where, it always seemed to me, there lurked in the very atmosphere a menace compounded of grandeur and sordidness which might be much to my taste, I was attempting to evade the Prime Minister's offer, generous though it was, because I suspected that he needed a conservative documentary director rather than an innovator, and was more concerned with the clamour of my reputation than its nature. However, he would not be shaken off, and I was avoiding a cultural attaché of his as eagerly as I was trying to ensnare – or be ensnared by – Christiania.

In eluding this gigantic and genial black man, I was thrown into the company of an acquaintance of mine at the university, a professor of Byzantine Art, whom I had known for many years. It was in his study, in the low, quiet university buildings with windows gazing from the walls like deep-set eyes, that I was introduced to a young scholar called Petar. He stood at one of the deep windows in the study, looking intently into the cobbled street, an untidy young man in unorthodox clothes.

I asked him what he watched. He indicated an old newspaper-seller moving slowly along the gutter outside, dragging and being dragged by a dog on a lead.

"We are surrounded by history, monsieur! This building was erected by the Habsburgs; and that old man whom you see in the gutter believes himself to be a Habsburg."

"Perhaps the belief makes the gutter easier to walk."

"I'd say harder!" For the first time he looked at me. In those pale eyes I saw an aged thing, although at the start I had been impressed by his extreme youth. "My mother believes – well, that doesn't matter. In this gloomy city, we are all surrounded by the shadows of the past. There are shutters at all our windows."

I had heard such rhetoric from students before. You find later they are reading Schiller for the first time.

My host and I fell into a discussion concerning the Hardy sonnet; in the middle of it, the youth had to take his leave of us; to visit his tutor, he said.

"A frail spirit, that, and a tormented one," commented my host. "Whether he will survive his course here without losing his mental stability, who can say. Personally, I shall be thankful when his mother, that odious woman, leaves the city; her effect on him is merely malevolent."

"Malevolent in what respect?"

"It is whispered that when Petar was thirteen years old – of course, I don't say there's any truth in the vile rumour – when he was slightly injured in a road accident, his mother lay beside him – nothing unnatural in that – but the tale goes that unnatural things followed between them. Probably all nonsense, but certainly he ran away from home. His poor father, who is a public figure – these nasty tales always centre round public figures –"

Feeling my pulse rate beginning to mount, I enquired the family name, which I believe I had not been given till then. Yes! The pallid youth who felt himself surrounded by the shadows of the past was her son, Christiania's son! Naturally, this evil legend made her only the more attractive in my eyes.

At that time I said nothing, and we continued the discussion of the English sonnet which I was increasingly inspired to film. I had read it several years before in a Hungarian translation and it had immediately impressed me.

To synopsise a poem is absurd; but the content of this sonnet was to me as profound as its grave and dignified style. Briefly, the poet watches the curved shadow of Earth steal over the moon's surface; he sees that mild profile and is at a loss to link it with the continents full of trouble which he knows the shadow represents; he wonders how the whole vast scene of human affairs can come to throw so small a shade; and he asks himself if this is not the true gauge, by any outside standard of measurement, of all man's hopes and desires? So truly did this correspond with my own lifelong self-questionings, so nobly was it cast, that the sonnet had come to represent one of the most precious things I knew; for this reason I wished to destroy it and reassemble it into a series of visual images that would convey precisely the same shade of beauty and terror allied as did the poem.

My host, however, claimed that the sequence of visual images I had sketched to him as being capable of conveying this mysterious sense fell too easily into the category of science-fiction, and that what I required was a more conservative approach – conservative and yet more penetrating, something more inward than outward; perhaps a more classical form for my romantic despair. His assertions angered me. They angered me, and this I realised even at the time, because there was the force of truth in what he said; the trappings should not be a distraction from but an illumination of the meaning. So we talked for a long time, mainly of the philo-sophical problems involved in representing one set of objects by another – which is the task of all art, the displacement without which we have no placement. When I left the university, it was wearily. I felt a sense of despair at the sight of dark falling and another day completed with my life incomplete.

Half-way down the hill, where a shrine to the virgin stands within the street wall, Petar's old news-vendor loitered, his shabby dog at his feet. I bought a paper from him, experiencing a tremor at the thought of how his image, glimpsed from the deep-set eye of the university, had been intertwined in my cogitations with the image of that perverted madonna whose greeds, so hesitatingly whispered behind her long back, reached out even to colour the imaginings of dry pedants like my friend in his learned cell!

And, as if random sequences of events were narrative in the mind of some super-being, as if we were no more than parasites in the head of a power to which Thomas Hardy himself might have yielded credulity, when I reached my hotel, the vendor's newspaper folded unopened under my arm, it was to find, in the rack of the ill-lit foyer, luminous, forbidding, crying aloud, silent, a letter from Christiania awaiting me. I knew it was from her! We had our connection!

Dropping my newspaper into a nearby waste bin, I walked upstairs carrying the letter. My feet sank into the thick fur of the carpet, slowing my ascent, my heart beat unmuffled. Was not this – so I demanded of myself afterwards! – one of those supreme moments of life, of pain and solace inseparable? For whatever was in the letter, it was such that, when revealed, like a fast-acting poison inserted into the bloodstream, would convulse me into a new mode of feeling and behaving.

I knew I would have to have Christiania, knew it even by the violence of my perturbation, greater than I had expected; and knew also that I was prey as well as predator. Wasn't that the meaning of life, the ultimate displacement? Isn't – as in the English sonnet – the great also the infinitely small, and the small also the infinitely great?

Well, once in my room, I locked the door, laid the envelope on a table and set myself down before it. I slit the envelope with a paper knife and withdrew her – her! – letter.

What she said was brief. She was much interested in my offer and the potential she read in it. Unfortunately, she was leaving Europe at the end of the week, the day after the morrow, since her husband was taking up an official post in Africa on behalf of his government. She regretted that our acquaintance would not deepen.

I folded the letter and put it down. Only then did I appreciate the writhe in the serpent's tail. Snatching up the letter again, I re-read it. She and her husband – yes! – were taking up residence in the capital city of that same republic with whose Prime Minister I had been long in negotiation. Only that morning had I written to his cultural attaché to announce finally that the making of such a film as he proposed was beyond my abilities and interests!

That night, I slept little. In the morning, when friends called upon me, I had my man tell them I was indisposed; and indisposed I was; indisposed to act, yet indisposed to let slip this opportunity. It was perversity, of course, to think of following this woman, this perverted madonna, to another continent; there were other women with whom the darker understandings would flow if I merely lifted the somewhat antique phone by my bedside. And it was perhaps perversity that allowed me to keep myself in indecision for so long.

But by afternoon I had decided. From a lunar distance, Europe and Africa were within the single glance of an eye; my fate was equally a small thing; I would follow her by the means so easily awaiting me.

Accordingly, I composed a letter to the genial black attaché, saying that I regretted my decision of yesterday, explaining how it had been instrumental in moving my mind in entirely the opposite direction, and announcing that I now wished to make the proposed film. I said I would be willing to leave for his native country with camera team and secretaries as soon as possible. I requested him to favour me with an early appointment. And I had this letter delivered by hand there and then.

There followed a delay which I weathered as best I could. The next two days I spent shut in the offices I had hired in a quiet part of the city, editing *Magnitudes*. It would be a satisfactory enough film, but already I saw it merely – as is the way with creative artists – as pointing towards the next work. Images of Africa already began to steal upon my brain.

At the end of the second day, I broke my solitude and sought out a friend. I confided to him my anger that the attaché had not condescended to give me a reply when I was so keen to get away. He laughed.

"But your famous attaché has returned home in disgrace! He was found robbing the funds. A lot of them are like that, I'm afraid! Not used to authority! It was all over the evening papers a couple of days ago – quite a scandal! You'll have to write to your prime minister."

Now I saw that this was no ordinary affair. There were lines of magnetism directed towards the central attraction, just as Remy de Gourmont claims that the markings on the fur of certain luxurious female cats run inescapably towards their sexual quarters. Clearly, I must launch myself into this forceful pattern. This I did by writing hastily – hastily excusing myself from my friend's presence – to the distant statesman in the distant African city, towards which, on that very evening, my maligned lady was making her way.

Of the awful delays that followed, I shall not speak. The disgrace of the cultural attaché (and it was not he alone who had been disgraced) had had its repercussions in the far capital, and my name, becoming involved, was not sweetened thereby. Finally, however, I received the letter I awaited, inviting me to make the film in my own terms, and offering me full facilities. It was a letter that would have made a less perverse man extremely happy!

To make my arrangements to leave Europe, to brief my secretary, and settle certain business matters took me a week. In that time, the distinguished film festival was held, and *Magnitudes* enjoyed from the critics just such a reception as I had anticipated; that is to say, the fawners fawned and the sneerers sneered, and both parties read into it many qualities that were not there, ignoring those that were – one even saw it as a retelling of the myth of the wanderings of Adam and Eve after their expulsion from Eden! Truly, the eyes of critics, those prideful optics, see only what they wish to see!

All irritations were finally at an end. With an entourage of five, I climbed aboard a jet liner scheduled for Lagos.

It seemed then that the climactic moment of which I was in search could not be far distant, either in time or space. But the unforeseen interposed.

When I arrived at my destination, it was to discover the African capital in an unsettled state, with demonstrations and riots every day and curfews every night. My party was virtually confined to its hotel, and the politicians were far too involved to bother about a mere film-maker!

In such a city, none of the pursuits of man are capable of adequate fulfilment: except one. I well recall being in Trieste when that city was in a similar state of turmoil. I was then undergoing a painful and exquisite love affair with a woman almost twice my age – but my age then was half what it now is! – and the disruptions and dislocations of public life, the mysterious stoppages and equally mysterious pandemoniums that blew in like the bora, gave a delectable contrapuntal quality to the rhythms of private life, and to those unnerving caesura which are inescapable in matters involving a beautiful married woman. So I made discreet inquiries through my own country's embassy for the whereabouts of Christiania.

The republic was in process of breaking in half, into Christian South and Muslim North. Christiania's husband had been posted to the North and his wife had accompanied him. Because of the unrest, and the demolition of a strategic bridge, there was no chance of my following them for some while.

It may appear as anticlimax if I admit that I now forgot about Christiania; the whole reason for my being in that place and on that continent. Nevertheless, I did forget her; our desires, particularly the desires of creative artists, are peripatetic: they submerge themselves sometimes unexpectedly and we never know where they may appear again. My imp of the perverse descended. For me the demolished bridge was never rebuilt.

Once the army decided to support the government (which it did as soon as two of its colonels were shot), the riots were quelled. Although the temper of the people was still fractious, some sort of order was restored. I was then escorted about the locality. And the full beauty and horror of the city – and of its desolated hinterland – were rapidly conveyed to me.

I had imagined nothing from West Africa. Nobody had told me of it. And this was precisely what attracted me now, as a director. I saw that here was fresh territory from which a raid on the inarticulate might well be made. The images of beauty-in-despair for which I thirsted were present, if in a foreign idiom. My task was one of translation, of displacement.

So immersed was I in my work, that all the affairs of my own country, and of Europe, and of the western world where my films were acclaimed or jeered, and of the whole globe but this little troubled patch (where, in truth, the preoccupations of all the rest were echoed) were entirely set aside. My sonnet was here; here, I would be able to provide more than a dead gloss on Hardy's sonnet. The relativity of importance was here brought to new parameters!

As the political situation began to improve, so I began to work further afield, as if the relationship between the two events was direct. A reliable Ibo hunter was placed at my disposal.

Although man was my subject and I imagined myself not to be interested in wildlife, the bush strangely moved me. I would rise at dawn, ignoring the torment of early-stirring flies, and watch the tremendous light flood back into the world, exulting to feel myself simultaneously the most and least important of creatures. And I would observe – and later film – how the inundating light launched not only flies but whole villages into action.

There was a vibrance in those dawns and those days! I still go cold to think of it.

Suppose – how shall we say it? – suppose that while I was in Africa making *Some Eclipses*, one side of me was so fully engaged (a side never before exercised in open air and sunlight) that another aspect of myself slumbered? Having never met with any theory of character which satisfied me, I cannot couch the matter in any fashionable jargon. So let me say brutally: the black girls who laid their beauty open to me stored, in their dark skins and unusual shapes and amazing tastes, enough of the unknown to hold the need for deeper torments at bay. In those transitory alliances, I exorcised also the sari-clad ghost of my second wife.

I became temporarily almost a different person, an explorer of the pysche in a region where before me others of my kind had merely shot animals; and I was able to make a film that was free from my usual flights of perversity.

I know that I created a masterpiece. By the time *Some Eclipses* was a finished masterpiece, and I was back in Copenhagen arranging details of premières, the regime that had given me so much assistance had collapsed; the prime minister had fled to Great Britain; and Muslim North had cut itself off from Christian South. And I was involved with another woman again, and back in my European self, a little older, a little more tired.

Not until two more years had spent themselves did I again cross the trail of my perverted madonna, Christiania. By then, the lines of the magnet seemed to have disappeared altogether: and, in truth, I was never to lie with her as I so deeply schemed to do: but magnetism goes underground and surfaces in strange places; the invisible suddenly becomes flesh before our eyes; and terror can chill us with more power than beauty knows.

My fortunes had now much improved – a fact not unconnected with the decline of my artistic powers. Conscious that I had for a while said what I needed to say, I was now filming coloured narratives, employing some of my old tricks in simpler form, and, in consequence, was regarded by a wide public as a daring master of effrontery. I lived my part, and was spending the summer sailing in my yacht, *The Fantastic Venus*, in the Mediterranean.

Drinking in a small French restaurant on a quayside, my party was diverted by the behaviour of a couple at the next table, a youth quarrelling with a woman, fairly obviously his paramour, and very much his senior. Nothing about this youth revived memories in me; but suddenly he grew tired of baiting his companion and marched over to me, introducing himself as Petar and reminding me of our one brief meeting, more than three years ago. He was drunk, and not charming. I saw he secretly disliked me.

We were more diverted when Petar's companion came over and introduced herself. She was an international film personality, a star, one might say, whose performances of recent years had been confined more to the bed than the screen. But she was piquant company, and provided a flow of scandal almost unseemly enough to be indistinguishable from wit.

She set her drunken boy firmly in the background. From him, I was able to elicit that his mother was staying nearby, at a noted hotel. In that corrupt town, it was easy to follow one's inclinations. I slipped away from the group, called a taxi, and was soon in the presence of an unchanged Christiania, breathing the air that she breathed. Heavy lids shielded my madonna's eyes. She looked at me with a fateful gaze that seemed to have shone on me through many years. She was an echo undoubtedly of something buried, something to resurrect and view as closely as possible.

"If you chased me to Africa, it seems somewhat banal to catch up with me in Cannes," she said.

"It is Cannes that is banal, not the event. The town is here for our convenience, but we have had to wait on the event."

She frowned down at the carpet, and then said, "I am not sure what event you have in mind. I have no events in mind. I am simply here with a friend for a few days before we drive on to somewhere quieter. I find living without events suits me particularly well."

"Does your husband –"

"I have no husband. I was divorced some while ago – over two years ago. It was scandalous enough: I am surprised you did not hear."

"No, I didn't know. I must still have been in Africa. Africa is practically soundproof."

"Your devotion to that continent is very touching. I saw your film about it. I have seen it more than once, I may confess. It is an interesting piece of work – of art, perhaps one should say only –"

"What are your reservations?"

She said, "For me it was incomplete."

"I also am incomplete. I need you for completion, Christiania – you who have formed a spectral part of me for so long!" I spoke then, burningly, and not at all as obliquely as I had intended.

She was before me, and again the whole pattern of life seemed to direct me towards her mysteries. But she was there with a friend, she protested. Well, he had just had to leave Cannes on a piece of vital business (I gathered he was a minister in a certain government, a man of importance), but he would be back on the morning plane.

So we came gradually round – now my hands were clasping hers – to the idea that she might be entertained to dinner on *The Fantastic Venus*; and I was careful to mention that next to my cabin was an empty cabin, easily prepared for any female guest who might care to spend the night aboard before returning home well before any morning planes circled above the bay.

And so on, and so on.

There can be few men – women either – who have not experienced that particular mood of controlled ecstasy awakened by the promise of sexual fulfilment, before which obstacles are nothing and the logical objections to which we normally fall victim less than nothing. Our movements at such times are scarcely our own; we are, as we say, possessed: that we may later possess.

A curious feature of this possessed state is that afterwards we recall little of what happened in it. I recollect only driving fast through the crowded town and noticing that a small art theatre was showing *Some Eclipses*. That fragile affair of light and shadow had lasted longer, held more vitality, than the republic about which it centred! I remember thinking how I would like to humble the arrogant young Petar by making him view it – "one in the eye for him", I thought, amused by the English phrase, envious of what else his eyes might have beheld.

Before my obsessional state, all impediments dissolved. My party was easily persuaded to savour the pleasures of an evening ashore; the crew, of course, was happy enough to escape. I sat at last alone in the centre of the yacht, my expectations spreading through it, listening appreciatively to every quiet movement. Music from other vessels in the harbour reached me, seeming to confirm my impregnable isolation.

I was watching as the sun melted across the sea, its vision hazed by cloud before it finally blinked out and the arts of evening commenced. That sun was flinging, like a negative of itself, our shadow far out into space: an eternal blackness trailing after the globe, never vanquished, a blackness parasitic, claiming half of man's nature!

Even while these and other impressions of a not unpleasant kind filtered through my mind, sudden trembling overcame me. Curious unease seized my senses, an indescribable *frisson*. Clutching the arms of my chair, I had to fight to retain consciousness. The macabre sensation that undermined my being was – this phrase occurred to me at the time – that *I was being silently inhabited*, just as I at that moment silently inhabited the empty ship.

What a moment for ghosts! When my assignation was for the flesh!

Slightly recovering from the first wave of fear, I sat up. Distant music screeched across the slaty water to me. As I passed a hand over my bleared vision, I saw that my palm bore imprinted on it the pattern of the rattan chair arm. This reinforced my sense of being at once the host to a spectral presence and myself insubstantial, a creature of infinite and dislocated space rather than flesh.

That terrible and cursed malaise, so at variance with my mood preceding it! And even as I struggled to free myself from it, my predatorial quarry stepped aboard. The whole yacht subtly yielded to her step, and I heard her call my name.

With great effort, I shook off my eerie mood and moved to greet her. Although my hand was chill as I clutched her warm one, Christiania's imperious power beamed out at me. The heavy lids of Munch's voluptuous madonna opened to me and I saw in that glance that this impressive and notorious woman was also unfolded to my will.

"There is something Venetian about this meeting," she said, smiling. "I should have come in a domino!"

The trivial pleasantry attached itself to my extended sensibilities with great force. I imagined that it could be interpreted as meaning that she acted out a role; and all my hopes and fears leaped out to conjure just what sort of a role, whether of ultimate triumph or humiliation, I was destined to play in her fantasy!

We talked fervently, even gaily, as we went below and sat in the dim-lit bar in the stern to toast each other in a shallow drink. That she was anxious I could see, and aware that she had taken a fateful step in so compromising herself: but this anxiety seemed part of a deeper delight. By her leaning towards me, I could interpret where her inclinations lay; and so, by an easy gradation, I escorted her to the cabin next to mine.

But now, again, came that awful sense of being occupied by an alien force! This time there was pain in it and, as I switched on the wall-lights, a blinding spasm in my right eye, almost as though I had gazed on some forbidden scene.

I clutched at the wall. Christiania was making some sort of absurd condition upon fulfilment of which her favours would be bestowed; perhaps it was some nonsense about her son, Petar; at the same time, she was gesturing for me to come to her. I made some excuse – I was now certain that I was about to disintegrate! – I stammered a word about preparing myself in the next cabin – begged her to make herself comfortable for a moment, staggered away, shaking like an autumn leaf.

In my cabin – rather, in the bathroom, jetty lights reflected from the surface of the harbour waters projected a confused imprint of a porthole on the top of the door. Wishing for no other illumination, I crossed to the mirror to stare at myself and greet my haggard face with questioning.

What ailed me? What sudden illness, what haunting, had taken me – overtaken me – at such a joyful moment?

My face stared back at me. And then: *my sight was eclipsed from within* . . .

Nothing can convey the terror of that experience! Something that moved, that moved across my vision as steadily and as irretrievably as the curved shadow in Hardy's sonnet. And, as I managed still to stare at my gold-haloed face in the mirror, I *saw* the shadow move in my eye, traverse my eyeball, glide slowly – so eternally slowly! – across the iris from north to south.

Exquisite physical and psychological pain were mine. Worse, I was pierced through by the dread of death – by what I imagined a new death: and I saw vividly, with an equally pain-laden inner eye, all my vivid pleasures, carnal and spiritual alike, and all my gifts, brought tumbling into that ultimate chill shadow of the grave.

There at that mirror, as if all my life I had been rooted there, I suffered alone and in terror, spasms coursing through my frame, so far from my normal senses that I could not hear even my own screams. And the terrible thing moved over my eyeball and conquered me!

For some while, I lay on the floor in a sort of swoon, unable either to faint or to move.

When at last I managed to rise, I found I had dragged myself into my cabin. Night was about me. Only phantoms of light, reflections of light, chased themselves across the ceiling and disappeared. Faintly, feebly, I switched on the electric light and once more examined the trespassed area of my sight. The terrible thing was transitory. There was only soreness where it had been, but no pain.

Equally, Christiania had left – fled, I learned later, at my first screams, imagining in guilty dread perhaps that her husband had hired an assassin to watch over her spoiled virtue!

So I too had to leave! The yacht I could not tolerate for a day more! But nothing was tolerable to me, not even my own body; for the sense of being inhabited was still in me. I felt myself a man outside society. Driven by an absolute desperation of soul, I went to a priest of that religion I had left many years ago; he could only offer me platitudes about bowing to God's will. I went to a man in Vienna whose profession was to cure sick minds; he could talk only of guilt-states.

Nothing was tolerable to me in all the places I knew. In a spasm of restlessness, I chartered a plane and flew to that African country where I had once been happy. Though the republic had broken up, existing now only in my film, the land still remained unaltered.

My old Ibo hunter was still living; I sought him out, offered him good pay, and we disappeared into the bush as we had previously done.

The thing that possessed me went too. Now we were becoming familiar, it and I. I had an occasional glimpse of it, though never again so terrifyingly as when it eclipsed my right eye. It was peripatetic, going for long submerged excursions through my body, suddenly to emerge just under the skin, dark, shadowy, in my arm, or breast or leg, or once – and there again were terror and pain interlocked – in my penis.

I developed also strange tumours, which swelled up very rapidly to the size of a hen's egg, only to disappear in a couple of days. Sometimes these loathsome swellings brought fever, always pain. I was wasted, useless – and used.

These horrible manifestations I tried my best to keep hidden from everyone. But, in a bout of fever, I revealed the swellings to my faithful hunter. He took me – I scarcely knowing where I went – to an American doctor who practised in a village nearby.

"No doubt about it!" said the doctor, after an almost cursory examination. "You have a loiasis infestation. It's a parasitic worm with a long incubation period – three or more years. But you weren't in Africa that long were you?"

I explained that I had visited these parts before.

"It's an open-and-shut case, then! That's when you picked up the infection."

I could only stare at him. He belonged in a universe far from mine, where every fact has one and only one explanation.

"The loiasis vector is a blood-sucking fly," he said. "There are billions of them in this locality. They hit maximum activity at dawn and late afternoon. The larval loiasis enters the bloodstream when the fly bites you. Then there is a three–four year incubation period before the adult stage emerges. It's what you might call a tricky little system!"

"So I'm tenanted by a worm, you say!"

"You're acting as unwilling host to a now adult parasitic worm of peripatetic habit and a known preference for subcutaneous tissue. It's the cause of these tumours. They're a sort of allergic reaction."

"So I don't have what you might call a psychosomatic disorder?"

He laughed. "The worm is real right enough. What's more, it can live in your system up to fifteen years."

"Fifteen years! I'm to be haunted by this dreadful succubus for fifteen years!"

"Not a bit of it! We'll treat you with a drug called diethyl-carbamazine and you'll soon be OK again."

That marvellous optimism – "soon be OK again!" – well, it was justified in his sense, although his marvellous drug had some unpleasant side effects. Of that I would never complain; all of life has unpleasant side effects. It may be – and this is a supposition I examine in the film I am at present making – that consciousness itself is just a side effect, a trick of the light, as it were, as we humans, in our ceaseless burrowings, accidentally surface now and again into a position and a moment where our presence can influence a wider network of sensations.

In my dark subterranean wanderings, I never again met the fatal Christiania (to whom my growing aversion was not strong enough to attract me further!); but her son, Petar, sports in the wealthier patches of Mediterranean sunshine still, surfacing to public consciousness now and again in magazine gossip columns.

(1969)

So Far from Prague

The chauffeur stopped the car and walked smartly round to open the door for Slansky. Slansky climbed out into the ruinous street. A crowd of children gathered to watch him as he walked up the hotel steps. Its double doors were closed; abstractedly, he took in the elaborate fret of the woodwork. As he pushed, one of the doors creaked open. As he walked into the dark hall, his driver came up behind him, deposited his suitcase, and saluted, one hand to his turban, the other cupped before him.

Hardly thinking, Slansky gave him a rupee note. The man disappeared, the door closed, Slansky was left standing in the sweet dusk of the hall. I must get back home.

His despair and anger were such that he stood alone for a minute completely lost to his surroundings, mentally back in Prague. Then the sweat trickling down his collar reminded him of his physical presence.

In the gloom of the hall, flies buzzed. From a hidden radio somewhere came the hum of a *veena*. The smells too were Indian: the prickle of woodsmoke, a faulty drain somewhere, a musky perfume, the aroma of spiced food.

"Anyone here?" he asked in English.

It's a curious sort of hotel. Was there even a sign over the door? I didn't look. But Bihari Das gave me the address – he would know it was all right. No matter. Nothing here's important.

Now that he was alone, away from Sadal Bihari Das and his multitudinous friends, Slansky was reluctant to feel anything but anger and despair. It was curious how those emotions could be eclipsed by a much slighter irritation. True, he had broken rudely away from Sadal's party, given in his honour, but surely Sadal would not have played a mean trick on him by sending him to some impossible place? Would he have to get a taxi back to Delhi?

There was a cubbyhole for reception. A dim light burned there, but all looked absolutely dead. Closed doors all round. The very air unmoving.

And growing in my wife, the world of the future – a little curled up thing with little nails and gills, hair already forming, rudimentary dreams in its head, going to live in a happier world, didn't we hope, oh Gordana, my dearest precious darling!

A glass-bead curtain hung to one side of the reception desk. Slansky pushed through it into a dim side-hall that had three doors opening from it. The smell of food lay more heavily here. Horizontal sunlight lay here at disconcerting angles, as if reflected from tarnished mirrors. Stepping forward, Slansky pushed open the nearest door and walked in.

He found himself in a living-room full of furniture, encumbered by sofas, chairs, small tables, potted plants, bureaux, bookcases, and a massive upright piano. Large photographs – faded and brown-stained, showing posed scenes or family groups, it appeared – hung in heavy frames from the walls. Detail did not present itself to Slansky, since the only illumination came from windows at the far end of the tangled room and an open door looking out across a veranda onto bright gardens beyond; the horizontal evening light insinuated itself into the room, reflecting off table-tops and the front of the piano, creating shadows that stood like solid obstacles in Slansky's way.

This much, he took in at a glance, and the fact that a second door, open in the right-hand wall, revealed a bedroom beyond, in which he glimpsed a bed veiled in mosquito netting. Then a movement caught his eye, and he saw, outlines made indistinct by the confusion of light and shadow, a man standing against the post of the door leading to the veranda. He gazed across the length of the room at Slansky.

The man was young and appeared to be wearing a uniform. He was well-built and fair; his face looked square and honest. Evidently he was a European. The expression on his face was friendly and the movement by which he revealed himself was evidently intended to be one of welcome.

Overcome by a form of embarrassment which sometimes

attacked him, Slansky withdrew himself from the room before the stranger could complete his gesture. He had intruded, and was angry with himself. This evidently was a private room.

Fearing that the stranger might follow him, he walked quickly through the side-hall into a rear passage, and thus into an inner courtyard.

This was where the music came from. An Indian family was lunching here, sitting on stone flags in the shade of a further wall. They saw Slansky as soon as he stepped into the sunlight.

A grey-haired lady in a sari stood up and came to him, shooing back a pair of small boys who dared to follow her. She greeted Slansky courteously and asked if he were Slansky Sahib.

"Antonin Slansky, madam. You were expecting me?"

"Yes, sahib, we are expecting you. My son has had to go to the bazaar or he would welcome you more properly. Nevertheless, may I allow to show you your rooms?"

As he followed her back into the building, with the two boys struggling to take his luggage, he asked her if this was a hotel.

"This is the hotel for friends of Sadal Bihari Das only, sahib. He own this hotel and keeps it closed except for his personal guests. In his Delhi flat is not many room for comfort."

"I see. And are there many guests here now beside me?"

"In the hot season is not many guests, sir. Later they come."

She showed him into an upstairs room. It was a lounge; a bedroom and a modern bathroom led off it. Smiling and bowing, she left him, ushering the boys along with her, and at once he was left with his anger and despair, isolated in another foreign room.

My dear Czech land, your peace and beauty – what are the Russians doing to you at this hour! Their heavy armour grinding down the hopes we had this spring. My comrades – I can't stay here, I must go and join them and die, let the blood of my fingers rust the tank tracks! That our socialist allies, our brother Slavs should so betray us, and after Bratislava and Cierna – Honour is dead! I can't stay! I must fly back to Prague! To hell with the damned film project!

A radio stood on a side table, decorously covered by a linen drape decorated with beads. He swept the cover aside and switched on the set. Music came, to his impatience a wailing and barbarous noise. He looked at his watch. Six minutes to the hour.

He passed the six minutes impatiently, striding up and down the room or gazing from his balcony at the pattern below of courtyard, tiles, and garden, with fields beyond fringed with palms. At the hour, a radio announcer began to read the news in Hindi. At five past, he read the news in English.

"Units of the Russian army are now moving into Czechoslovakia unopposed. Polish, East German, Hungarian, and Bulgarian units are also involved. Firing has been reported from Prague and other large cities such as Brno and Bratislava; in the capital itself, twenty people are reported killed, but in the main the occupation is proceeding without opposition –"

Gordana, I beg you still to be enjoying your holiday down on the Dalmatian coast and not back in Prague, don't be back in Prague, don't be back in Prague, please don't be back in Prague, stay out of Prague, stay out of our beloved country! Stay down in Yugoslavia! Now that you're pregnant, you shouldn't drive so fast. Because I know you secretly hope it will be a girl, I also hope it will be a girl.

Opening his suitcase, he stared down at its contents, seeing only the creases in the crushed clothes, trying to decipher them.

"There is still no news of the whereabouts of Mr Dubcek, key figure in the liberalisation programme implemented in the spring . . ."

It is only two months since we talked together, Alexander Dubcek! You wanted me to continue to experiment in the cinema. Now where are you? I really wouldn't put it past them to shoot you. And Svoboda. They'll want a puppet government. Could they really have shot him? Is it all true? My madness, an Indian madness? Am I dreaming? It's true enough – and the Warsaw Pact . . . Communism is betrayed. It's worse than a dream!

He paced about the room, walked into the bedroom, strode onto the balcony, looked aimlessly about. Below was the veranda. On it stood the stocky fair-haired man from the suite below. He turned and went in as Slansky glimpsed him. "Friend of Bihari Das". English perhaps. American? Will the Americans do anything? Oh, Gordana, and we have plans we haven't even planned yet. Next month you are twenty-nine and the liberalisation was proceeding. It's been so good to be alive.

The sun had almost finished its tyrannous day's business with the Ganges plain. In nearby trees, thousands of birds gathered, screaming, struggling, and excreting. People walked in the shadowed streets. He could not stay where he was, could not stay.

Pacing downstairs, he passed an old man now sitting at the reception desk and strode out into the rear courtyard. The music was playing, laden with discord. He ignored the people and the children, marching through the rear archway into the garden he had noted from his balcony.

The garden was small; imprisoned within its walls lay the heat of the day. It had a well, the swivelling arm of which, perched awkwardly on two legs, dipped down into the well like a wooden beak. There was a rear gate set in the white wall, closed and barred with a cross-beam. A battered charpoy stood by the door under a crude shelter. A lantern burned, hanging from one of the poles supporting the shelter's thatched roof. On the bed sat an old man, reading to a child. The child was almost naked; it sprawled elegantly against the side of the bed, listening abstractedly as the old man read, his ancient face pressed close to the page.

It's a real deep betrayal, destroying everything! Not the anaesthesia of a mere political betrayal, like the Anglo-French betrayal of 1938. No, this is a personal betrayal, almost brother against brother. It's only a few days since they signed the Bratislava agreement, the dogs! It's us they assassinate, each one of us, not just the liberalisation, us, us, us. In Eastern Europe, the personal life is done to death, the way the capitalist countries do it to death with financial manipulation. I'll have to go back to find Gordana. Oh my darling, stay safe!

As Slansky stood in the gathering gloom, the old man became aware of his presence. He ceased his reading and looked up. His broad old face was deformed by age, the cheeks puckered almost like blisters over the cheekbones, the white beard fibrous and clinging like cat-scratches far down the throat. Gravely marking his place in the book, he set it down and raised his hands, fingertips together, in salute. The boy copied the gesture.

"Hello. I had no intention of interrupting."

A stick of agarbatti, held firm in a crack of the bed, smouldered into the greying air. The old man said something interrogatively.

"I don't speak any Indian languages," Slansky said sharply. Even exchanging a salute implied more involvement than he could manage just now.

Behind his thick glasses, the old man's eyes floated, large, apparently detached. Then he said something to the small boy and resumed his reading, holding the book high to catch the feeble light of his lantern.

Slansky resumed his pacing, slapping occasionally at a mosquito.

Bihari Das should have called the celebration off when he heard the news from Prague. He was always insensitive in some ways. Garrulous people are always insensitive. I must speak to him before I leave. Everything's in ruins. The Dark Ages. Fascism. Machine-people crushing individuals down until machines take over the job. Gordana. Talking in the yard to old General Rambousek, filling the yard with her pleasantness. The cobbles, her neat ankles, legs, the vine on the wall. Coming to the studios, working on those first documentaries together. Helping to improvise equipment. Her idea for the cartoon. Haven't we suffered enough . . . The economy being deliberately run down, and now where is she? What would that old Indian man say if he knew? Poor old fellow . . . But being dull and stupid – maybe he isn't – he would never know our anguish.

There was no peace for him in the garden.

With one last slap at the mosquitoes, he walked back into the hotel and approached the desk clerk.

"Do you speak English? I wish to talk to Mr Bihari Das on the phone. Will you please ring him at his Delhi flat for me?"

"Certainly, sir. I will get him immediately, although there is possibly an hour's delay on the Delhi line."

"Will you try at once? I will wait here."

He turned impatiently in the narrow hall. Bihari Das entered at the front door. He ran and embraced his friend.

"Antonin, my dear man, you see I escaped away from the awful party! Let them fiddle while Rome burns, what do I care for it if my guest of honour cannot be there?"

"I was just trying to phone you, Sadal!"

"Yes, yes, well, that will no longer be necessary! Here I am! I shall be in hot water, you mark my words, for leaving those people, but it positively does not matter to me. Let's go upstairs to your room, if we may, eh, and have a chat?" He signalled to the desk clerk to attend them.

In the room upstairs, darkness was plunging down. Looking from the balcony, Slansky could see the little glow-worm light at the far corner of the garden, where the old man read to the child. From the street came people's voices and music. Lightning flickered round the serrated edges of the horizon.

As he took a drink from Bihari Das, he said, "To concentrate on film-making is beyond me. I'll have to get the first flight back to Prague tomorrow."

Bihari Das was still in his twenties, small, dapper, full of energy, with a great crop of blue-black hair. His light blue suit and silk shirt were immaculate. He shone Slansky a smile that had ravished many a screen in the days before he took to directing instead of starring.

"I know what you are thinking, my dear man. You think I have been terribly insensitive to your predicament. Well, it is not so, though I admit I don't understand this private row between two allied Communist states. I hate politics, hate it absolutely, with the true loathing of an artist. I have phoned the airport and made a reservation for you already on the Air India flight at 10.05 hours tomorrow back to Prague. Does that make you feel better towards me?"

"I always thought well of you, Sadal. That is most thoughtful of you. Again I owe you my gratitude."

"Say no more. Thank my secretary – it was he who executed all the painful details. He will produce the tickets tomorrow. And now – now your mind is more at ease, let us talk cinema and forget all the boredom and horror of politics. Once the Russians have helped your government stamp out all the subversive elements in the country, conditions will be back to normal and we can resume planning our joint film about the petrification of time."

Reluctantly, Slansky said, "It's not like that, Sadal! The subversive elements in our country are all imposed there by the Soviet Union. We have had years of rule by Moscow stooges, running down the economy, limiting our freedom of speech. They are being weeded out by Dubcek and Svoboda, and the nation is behind them. We must be our own bosses. Now the Soviet Union is trying to reimpose her rule, and we must resist in every way possible, short of taking up arms. Passive resistance – Mahatma Gandhi would have approved, for sure."

"Gandhi's a long time ago! Let's discuss our film, Antonin, my dear man, since our time is so cut short." He sat on a sofa and lounged back, cocking his legs up till his ankles rested on the sofa-arm. Looking dreamily at the ceiling, he said, "Czechoslovakia after all gets economic aid and military protection from Russia all the while. She is not a strictly neutral country, like India. How can you complain?"

"Complain! When that so-called military protection means tanks sitting in the central square of every town, when the hoodlums in the Kremlin kidnap our Dubcek like Chicago hoodlums. Can you not understand what a blow has fallen, even this far from Prague?"

Bihari Das waved a hand. "So far from Prague, we perhaps understand better. This is just a European power-brawl, isn't it, not to be rated in importance with the concerns of art."

"Sadal – I beg you! Don't try to anger me! Even if it were just a power-brawl, it concerns *people*, it concerns *truth*, it concerns *art*. The Soviet rulers don't care for people, they don't know what truth is, they hate and fear art. They will stamp out art and truth in our country if they get the chance!"

He pressed his fingertips to his forehead. Don't tell me art and truth can never be stamped out! They have been! We have seen them stamped out twice in my country in my lifetime, by Hitler and by Stalin, and now that fearful spectre rises again. It taints all our lives. It is never dormant. It lurks here too, Bihari Das, lurks in your decadent attitude – you're never so far from Prague that you can escape the forces of evil and night. Gordana, let everything else die but you and the future you carry in your sweet belly – let truth and the rest die! They're all meaningless without their dear embodiment in you, wherever you now are, wherever you are at this very minute. Oh, I should have made you come with me and laughed at your fear of air travel, my dearest – your first presence when we were working together on that iron-ore documentary, only five years ago. That terrible hotel in Brno. "You must try to understand that I'm going back to fight for things you take here for granted."

Bihari Das waved a hand in disdain.

"Nonsense, my dear man, we chucked the British out, you know – oh, sure, it was almost before I was pupped! But we are no better since they have been gone and, frankly, my sympathy is rather with the British. We gave them a lot of trouble, you know. They are very simple and orderly people, much like the Russians."

"The Soviets are imperialists, just as the British were. They have just committed a naked act of imperialist aggression against my country. Who has made you believe otherwise?"

Bihari Das sat up. "Come on, dear man, don't give me propaganda after you are speaking so highly of art. I sympathise with you as a husband, but your country has surely got what it asked for as a troublesome satellite, and the Russians will merely restore order. Order is important, even if a few people get hurt. You must forgive me if I see the Russian point of view. Now, let's get off this boring subject and speak of what lies more closely to our hearts, for heaven's sake!"

Once, there were private places. They've gone – even here, they've gone, so far from Prague! Art has got to wear a sword. I can't talk to him. Someone has fed him lying propaganda. I can't . . . "Sadal, I can't – I don't feel well enough to talk. I'm upset."

He sat on a chair opposite Bihari Das and the two men stared at one another.

At last, Bihari Das broke into his disarming smile. "You should have some exercise before dinner, Antonin. You know what? At the back of this building and its garden lies my *bagh* – well, it's quite a scientific little farm really, forty acres where we grow the latest wheat varieties and hybrid millets. I have installed a tubewell and a tractor. I hoped to drive you round it."

"Your latest craze, Sadal?"

"More than a craze! Gentlemen farmers are springing everywhere. We help the government and get rich ourselves. It's a very big development everywhere. Nowadays, it's as easy to become a millionaire in agriculture as it once was in film-making."

"So you're going to make a second fortune!"

The winning smile again. "I am forced to, my dear man, to pay off the tax I owe on the first. Come, we will go down, and I'll give you a fresh sniff of air, since you aren't up to talking."

She came back from the seaside directly she heard that the Russian tanks were rolling in, while her Yugoslav friends, preparing to defend their own frontiers, talked of "the most monstrous event in history". She drove overnight, ignoring tiredness, and reached Prague early in the morning. She stopped in Wenceslas Square, in order to go to my office.

Already there were people in the square, mainly youngsters, surrounding the Russian tanks. Already each Russian tank had its neat little stinking pile of rubbish and excrement at the back. The Russian troops had to keep to their posts. Their nerves were on edge. Swastikas had been chalked on their vehicles. Close-up.

One tank crew could stand the tension no more. Its commander gave the order to fire. Students scattered wildly as the guns opened up. A figure in the background, uninvolved. Startled, taken by surprise. Zoom in as she falls. Blood running from some hidden place.

Oh no, my darling, no, no, not you, not my Gordana!

Beyond the torment of the stairs, the ordinary mysterious evening, still hardly advanced since last time he was here. But dark now, and everywhere the sounds of happiness of people – happiness perhaps a little hard to believe in face of that hysterical note in the *veena* music. We had it ourselves, it was ours, and above all the hope of more, if we pushed for it.

Lightning still burnished the night's darkness. Smell of fires, the family cooking in the courtyard, several vague figures squatting, talking, smoking. In the garden, the rear wooden gate propped open and a lightbulb burning among the frangipani branches, haloed with dancing insects.

"You see, we have done away with the old historic plough even in India, Antonin," Bihari Das said. "I am not only a very avant-garde director but a progressive in other ways!"

As he spoke, laughing relaxedly and gesticulating with an open hand, a tractor came through the gates from fields beyond and stopped beneath the shelter inside. The driver jumped down and saluted Bihari Das.

The ugly old man, evidently the watchman, still sat on his bed. As the tractor arrived, he rose slowly and shuffled over to close the gate, while the boy to whom he had been reading sped round the yard making driving noises. Bihari Das called to the old man to wait; as he and Slansky walked through into the farm, the old man bowed low to them.

Bihari Das was voluble and expert on the workings of his farm.

He summoned a foreman who walked with them, a keen young man, scarcely more than a student, who had to keep silent while Bihari Das rattled off facts and figures. They showed Slansky a small vineyard with especial pride.

"The profits on grapes amount to fifteen thousand rupees per acre," said the foreman proudly.

"That's not all profit by any means," said Bihari Das quickly.

Why should I care how much money you make? What's going to happen to us if the Russians do stay? The old bleak censorship again, truth stifled, unable to know if your colleague is your friend or your enemy. That old creaking system of corruption that was the only possible system for obtaining necessary equipment. And you, darling, with our future growing lips inside you – we had hoped to see Communism freed from its old Stalinist straitjacket of paranoia . . .

They walked back at last, silent, through into the garden. Before closing the gate for them, the old watchman picked up his little friend, pressing his shining cheek so lovingly to his blistered lips in a goodnight kiss that his spectacles were pushed against his eyes. When the boy was set down again, he ran along the path, calling to his mother, "Mother, Mother, now I'm ready for bed at long last."

And the tractor was a Russian model, a Belarus, made in Minsk, such as I have seen many a time slowly ploughing the clayey fields of Bohemia or the alluvial lands of Moravia, not as good as our Czech tractors, either . . .

"Antonin, you know what a busy man I am – a partygoer this afternoon, a farmer this evening, and tomorrow again an artist, when I fly to Agra for a day's shooting, on which I once hoped you would join me. So we must say farewell now. My secretary will get the air tickets to you first thing. I am of course terribly sorry for all the upsets in your country, and I hope you will be able to come back here again when matters have sorted themselves out."

"I hope so, Sadal, and next time I shall bring Gordana with me. Then I hope I shall make a more receptive guest. Thank you for your hospitality, and tell me one thing before you leave –"

"Yes, yes, of course."

"Who is the other guest in the suite below mine?"

The famous smile slowly emerged again, expressing itself in crinkling eyes and perfect teeth. You said he was the most handsome man in the world when I introduced you in Prague, but I believe his smile would not capture you quite so much today, my love!

"He won't interfere with you, Antonin. He turns in early after dinner and will be away before the dawn."

"Another of your guests who wasn't at your party!"

"That's because he was not invited exactly, you see, my dear man, since he is more of a business acquaintance. A mere travelling salesman, let's say, doing a lucrative business among gentlemen farmers in the Delhi region."

"He's a Russian, isn't he?"

The smile went out and came on again.

"He's just a businessman, I am telling you. He is tired, like you, and does not speak English, only Hindi, so you could not converse. You should take a leaf out of his book and turn in early, get a good night's kip. After all, you have to be moving pretty smartly in the morning."

"So he is Russian."

"Just a Moscow businessman."

They shook hands at the door of the private hotel. Waving, smiling, Bihari Das walked down the steps to his car, where a chauffeur patiently waited. Slansky closed the hotel door and stood in the hall a minute, trembling. The man sitting in the reception desk watched him politely and openly.

"Good evening," said Slansky, and started to walk upstairs, up the drab marble steps, watching his feet tread on the carpet.

He moved swiftly over to the balcony and looked down. The Russian's veranda was not far below. He lowered himself over, hung for a second, then dropped. From inside his cluttered room, the Russian asked, "Who's there?" An ancient standard lamp threw light and shadow over his face. He sat in his shirt sleeves writing at a table. I pulled my gun out and walked into the room. "So you're the guy who's been stuffing Bihari Das with lying propaganda!"

At the top of the stairs, he paused. From the street came a mixture of noises; people noises, not traffic noises. In the hotel itself, silence. He went into his room and locked the door. Stood with the light off, still trembling. The enemy. Fellow Communist. When the shot rang out, he fell against the table and then slipped

down, while his order books – so many pumps, so many tractors –
No!

Slansky switched on the lamp and poured himself a glass of fresh
lime juice and a strong tot of gin from the drinks cabinet. There
were books on a shelf running right along one wall. Bihari Das's
personal books – cast-outs probably, but at least they made it seem
more like home.

Dostoevsky, Kafka, Koestler, dated theories of aesthetics,
Reik's *The Unknown Murderer*. He was sleeping heavily and
drunkenly. As I crept up to his bedside, I could see a grey pulse
beating in his throat. Hurling myself on him, I sank my clawed
fingers into his neck. "This for Bohemia and truth!" I cried.

The poor old untouchable kissing the kid goodnight. What love
in the gesture, the whole of everything there, his old deformed
hands supporting the boy. "Tata", the boy called him. "Grandfather". Maybe just an honorary position. That harmless old man,
all his life opening and shutting gates. Does Bihari Das even know
his name?

And if I killed Ivan down below, would it open Bihari's eyes?
Famous Czech director on murder charge. As I opened his door, a
creaking board gave me away. He fired from his bed, through the
mosquito net, through the open bedroom doorway. I fell in
agony –

There's no principle involved. I just can't kill him. He's a
private person.

Suppose I captured him, held him hostage here in exchange for
the safety of Alexander Dubcek? He isn't important enough. He
counts for no more than the old watchman. We fell onto the floor
together, grappling. I reached out for a heavy wooden ornament
standing on the table. Even as she ran across the square, the tank
crew opened fire again.

"No!"

I'll go down, properly dressed, and speak to him in Russian.
Argue with him. Just convince one of them. That is what a civilised
man should do. Behave here as if I were in Prague facing the
enemy. Always correct.

He drank the gin quickly and then sipped at the cold lime.

He would hear no more. "You Czechs by your revisionism have
betrayed the Warsaw Pact," he said. "On the contrary," he said

coldly, "it is you Russians who have betrayed it, as well as betraying many unspoken pacts of friendship. We knew you were old-fashioned and inclined to be heavy. We didn't know you were liars and swindlers and killers –" "I don't wish to be offensive, sir, or spoil your visit to India, in any way, but some friends of yours who were visiting Prague as uninvited guests raped and killed my wife."

Setting the glass down, he went to the door. As he went to the door, it was opened from the other side. The young Russian stood there. "I came to apologise for the actions of my government," he said. As he was opening the door – the Russian stood there with two armed men behind him. "You are Czech?" he asked coldly. A figure stood on the landing. "Come with me."

It was the old lady. "We will be serving dinner in ten minutes, sir. Will you like to come down for it or eat in your room?"

They confronted each other across the table. No, it would have to be a cool dialectical argument. "How do you justify an armed act of aggression against a friendly fellow-country that has at no time offended against socialist morality or made overtures to imperialist powers?"

"Will any other guests be eating downstairs, madam?"

"Only the other guest, Mr Dabrynin, the Russian gentleman."

No melodramatics. It was simple. Gordana, take care of yourself; I will come for you.

"Then I will eat downstairs with Mr Dabrynin. Perhaps you will be kind enough to inform him that I shall be present."

"No, Mr Dabrynin, there was no threat from any West German federal intelligence agents – no infiltration in any way from the anti-Communist powers. We would have welcomed them then as little as we now welcome the Soviet Occupation."

He went back into his room, closing the door firmly behind him. The man's only some minor engineer. No threat to anyone. All the more reason to talk to him.

Gordana, I swear I would kill him if I thought anything had happened to you.

Death is not my weapon. Being an artist, I must fight with life. I must remain true to my vision. There is a commitment greater than any one situation.

My head's clear of those foul images.

Read something, anything, before the dinner gong goes!

He scanned the bookshelf, put on his reading glasses, looked again, picked out almost at random a collection of the writings of the painter Giorgio de Chirico, opened it almost at random, began to read.

"Yet our minds are haunted by visions; they are anchored to everlasting foundations. In public squares shadows lengthen their mathematical enigmas. Over the walls rise nonsensical towers, decked with little multicoloured flags; infinitude is everywhere, and everywhere is mystery. One thing remains immutable, as if its roots were frozen in the entrails of eternity: our will as creative artists . . .

"Inside a ruined temple the broken statue of a god spoke a mysterious language. For me, this vision is always accompanied by a feeling of cold, as if I had been touched by a winter wind from a distant unknown country."

(1969)

The Day We Embarked
for Cythera

The ruined hillside above the lake was an idyllic place for conversation and fête. We could see the town but not the palace, and the river beyond the town, and flowers grew in the warm bank on which we sat. The pines were shattered, the dells incredible, the scents of acacia all that mid-June could demand. I had forgotten my guitar, and my stout friend Portinari insisted on wearing his scarlet conversing-jacket.

So he was conversing on grandiose scarlet themes, and I was teasing him. "Mankind lives between animal and intellectual worlds by reason of its cerebral inheritance. I am mathematician and scholar. I am also dog and ape."

"Do you live in the rival worlds alternately or both in the same moment?"

He gestured, looking down the hillside to where young men fought with yellow poles. "I am not speaking of rival worlds. They are complementary, one to another, mathematician, scholar, dog, ape, all in one capacious brain."

"You surprise me." I took care to look unsurprised as I spoke. "The mathematician must find the antics of the dog tedious, and does not the ape revolt against the scholar?"

"They all fight it out in bed," said Clyton, cuttingly. We thought he had left our conversation to our own devices, for he squatted at our feet under one of the shattered tombstones, presenting the fantastic patterns of his satin-covered back to us as he examined the ancient graves.

"They fight it out in science," offered Portinari: less a correction than a codicil.

"They truce it out in art," I said: less a codicil than a coda.

"How about this fossil of art?" Clyton asked. He rose, smiling at us under his Punchinello mask, and held out the fragment of tomb he had been scrutinising.

It bore a human figure crudely outlined in stone, blurred further by lichen, one patch of which had, with mycotic irony, provided the figure with a fuzz of yellowing pubic hair. In one hand the figure clutched an umbrella; the other hand, offered palm outwards, was enlarged grotesquely.

"Is he supplicating?" I asked.

"Or welcoming?" Portinari asked.

"If so, welcoming what?"

"Death?"

"He's testing for rain. Hence the umbrella," Clyton said. We laughed.

Through the low hills, screams rang.

Nothing here attracted life, for the drought of some centuries' standing had long since withered all green things. The calm was the calm of paralysis, which even the screams could not break. Through the hills, making for the edge of a distant horizon, ran the double track of a railway line. Along this line, a giant steam locomotive fled, screaming. Behind it, pursuing, came the carnivores.

There were six carnivores, their headlights blazing. They were now almost abreast of their quarry. Their klaxons echoed as they called to each other. It could be only a short while before they pulled their victim down.

The locomotive was untiring. For all its superb strength, it could not outdistance the carnivores. Nor was there any help for it here; the nearest station was still many hundreds of miles away.

Now the leading carnivore was level with its cab. In desperation, the locomotive suddenly flung itself sideways, off the confining rails, and charged into the dried riverbed that lay on one side. The carnivores halted for a moment, then swung to the side also and again roared in pursuit. Now the advantage was more than ever with them, for the locomotive's wheels sank into the ground.

In a few minutes, it was all over. The great beasts dragged down their prey. The locomotive keeled heavily on its side, thrashing out vainly with its pistons. Undeterred, the carnivores hurled themselves on to its black and vibrating body.

Through the hills, screams rang.

Though the king had decreed a holiday, we still had our wards strapped to our wrists. I punched for Universal Knowledge and asked about rainfall in the area four centuries previously. No figures. Climate reckoned equable.

"Machines are so confoundedly imprecise," I complained.

"But we live by imprecision, Bryan! That's how Portinari's mathematician and puppy dog manage to co-exist in his well-endowed head. We made the machines, so they bear our impress of imprecision."

"They're binary. What's imprecise about either-or, on-off?"

"Surely either-or is the major imprecision! Mathematician-dog. Scholar-ape. Rain-fine. Life-death. It's not the imprecision in the things but in the hiatus between them, the dash between the either and the or. In that hiatus is our heritage. Our heritage the machines have inherited."

While Clyton was saying this, Portinari was brushing away the pine-needles on the other side of the tomb (or perhaps I might make that stout friend of mine sound more mortal if I said on the *opposite* side of the tomb). A metal ring was revealed. Portinari pulled it, and dragged a picnic basket from the earth.

As we were exclaiming over the basket's contents, pretty Columbine arrived. She kissed us each in turn and offered to lay a picnic for us. From the top of the basket, she produced a snowy cloth, and spreading it out, commenced to arrange the viands upon it. Portinari, Clyton, and I stood about in picturesque attitudes and watched the four-man fliers flapping their way slowly across the blue sky above our heads.

Outside the wall of the town, a silver band played for the princess's birthday. Its notes came faintly up to us, preserved in the thin air. One could almost taste them, like the thin beaten sheets of silver in which duckling is cooked.

"It's so beautiful today – how fortunate we are that it will have an end. Permanent happiness lies only in the transitory."

"You're changing the subject, Bryan," Portinari said. "You were being taxed on imprecision."

I clutched my heart in horror. "If I am to be taxed for imprecision, then it is not the subject but the king who must be changed!"

Just a fraction late, Clyton replied, "Your tributary troubles make for streams of mirth."

Columbine laughed prettily and curtsied to indicate that our spread was ready.

The savannahs ended here, were superseded abruptly by a region of stone, a semi-desert place where few of the giant herbivores ever ventured. The same heavy sky lowered over all. Sometimes the rain fell for years at a time.

Compared with the slow herbivores, the carnivores were fleet. They ranged down their terrible black road, which cut through savannah and desert alike.

One lay by the edge of the roadside slowly devouring a two-legged thing, its engine purring. Fitful sun marked its flanks.

As we sat down to our picnic, removing our masks, one of the hill-dwarfs came springing up in his velvet and sat on the sward beside us, playing his electric dulcimer for Columbine to dance to. He had a face like a human foetus, hanging over the strings, but his voice was clear and true. He sang an old ditty of Caesura's:

> *"I listened to every phrase she uttered*
> *Knowing, knowing they'd be recorded only*
> *In my memory – and knowing, knowing my memory*
> *Would improve them all by and by . . ."*

To this strain, Columbine did a graceful dance, not without its own self-mocking quality. We watched as we ate iced melon and ginger, in which were embedded prawns, and silver carp and damson tart. Before the dance was over, boys in satins carrying banners and a tiny black girl with a tambor came scurrying out of the magnolia groves to listen to the music. With them on a chain they led a little green-and-orange dinosaur which waltzed about on its hind legs. We thought this party must be from the court.

A plump boy was with them. I remarked him first because he was dressed all in black; then I noticed the leathery flying creature on his shoulder. He could have been no more than twelve, yet was monstrously plump and evidently boasted abnormally large sexual appendages, for they were hung before him in a yellow bag. He gave us greeting, doffing his cap, and then stood with his back to the frolic, looking across the valley to the far woods and hills. He provided an agreeable foil to the merriment, which we watched as we ate.

Everyone pranced to the song of the hill-dwarf's dulcimer.

The carnivores ran along endless roads, indifferent to whether the land through which they passed was desert, savannah, or forest. They could always find food, so great was their speed.

The heavy skies overhead robbed the world of colour and time. The lumbering grass-eaters seemed almost motionless. Only the carnivores were bright and tireless, manufacturing their own time.

A group of them were converging on a certain crossroads in an area of heath. One of their number had made a kill. It was a big grey beast. Its radiator grill was bared in a snarl. It sprawled at its leisure on the roadside, devouring the body of a young female. Two others of her kind, freshly killed, lay nearby, to be dealt with at will.

This was long before internal parasites had labyrinthed their way into the mechanisms of eternity.

"Come now, Bryan," Portinari said as he opened up a second bottle of new wine. "Clyton here was quizzing you on imprecision. You twice evaded the point, and now pretend to be absorbed in the antics of these dancers!"

Clyton leaned back on one elbow, gesturing lordly in the air with a jellied chicken-bone. "What with the smell of the acacia blossom and the tang of this new vintage, I've forgotten the point myself, Portinari, so we'll let Bryan off for once. He's free to go!"

"To be let off is not necessarily to be free," I said. "Besides, I am capable of liberating myself from any argument."

"I believe truly you could slip out of a cage of words," said Clyton.

"Why not? Because all sentences contain contradictions, as we all contain contradictions, in the way that Portinari is mathematician and dog, ape and scholar."

"*All* sentences, Bryan?" Portinari asked, teasingly.

We smiled at each other, the way we did when preparing verbal traps for each other. The party of children from the court had gathered round to hear our talk, all except the plump boy dressed in black, who now leaned against an aspen trunk and regarded the blue distances of the landscape. With sweet gestures, the others lolled against one another to decide if we talked wisdom or nonsense.

Of course Columbine was not listening. More of the velvet-clad dwarfs had arrived. They were singing and dancing and making a great noise; only the first-comer of their tribe had laid down his dulcimer and was fondling and kissing the lovely bare shoulders of Columbine.

Still smiling, I passed my glass towards Portinari and he filled it to the brim. We were both of us relaxed but alert, coming to the test.

"How would you describe that action, Portinari?"

They all waited for his answer. Cautiously, smiling yet, he said, "I shall not be imprecise, dear Bryan. I poured you some newly-bottled wine, that was all!"

A toad hopped under one of the broken tombstones. I could hear its progress, so quiet had our circle become.

"'I poured you some newly-bottled wine'", I quoted. "You provide a perfect contradiction, my friend, as I predicted. At the beginning of your sentence, you pour the wine, yet by the end of the sentence it is newly-bottled. Your sequence contradicts utterly your meaning. Your time-sense is so awry that you negate what you did in one breath!"

Clyton burst out laughing – even Portinari had to laugh – the children squeaked and fluttered – the dinosaur plunged – and as Columbine clapped her pretty hands in mirth, the hill-dwarf flipped out of her corsage the two generous orbs of her breasts. Clutching them, she jumped up and ran laughing through the trees towards the lake, her pet fawn following her, the dwarf chasing her.

Over the lush grass rain swept in curtains of moisture. It seemed to hang in the air rather than descend, to soak everything between ground and sky. It was an enormous summer shower, silent and fugitive; it had lasted for tens of thousands of years.

Occasionally the sun broke through clouds, and then the moving moistures of the air burst into violent colour, only to fade to a drab brass tint as the clouds healed their wound.

The metal beasts that drove through this perpetual shower hooted and snarled on their way. Outwardly, they shone as if impervious, paint-

work and chromework as bright as knives; but, below their armour, the effects of the water, dashing up for ever from their spinning wheels, were lethal. Rust crept into every moving part, metal's cancer groping for the heart.

The cities where the beasts lived were surrounded by huge cemeteries. In the cemeteries, multitudinous carcases, no longer to be feared, lapsed into ginger dust, into poor graves.

As we were draining the wine and eating the sweetmeats, the dwarfs and boys danced on the sward. Some of the youths leapt on their goose-planes and pedalled up above our heads for aerial jousting-matches. All the while, the black-clad plump boy stood in lonely contemplation. Portinari, Clyton and I laughed and chatted, and flirted with some country wenches who passed by. I was pleased when Portinari explained my paradox of imprecision to them.

When the girls had gone, Clyton, rising, swept his cloak about him and suggested we should move back to the ferry.

"The sun inclines towards the west, my friends, and the hills grow brazen to meet its glare." He gestured grandly at the sun. "All its trajectory is dedicated, I am certain, towards proving Bryan's earlier aphorism, that the only permanent happiness lies in transitory things. It reminds us that this golden afternoon is merely of counterfeit gold, now wearing thin."

"It reminds me that I'm wearing fat," said Portinari, struggling up, belching, and smoothing his stomach.

I picked up Clyton's figured fragment from the tombstone and offered it to him.

"Yes, perhaps I'll keep this umbrella-bearing shade until I find someone to throw light on him."

"Is he supplicating you to?" I asked.

"Or welcoming you to?" Portinari.

"He's testing for rain," Clyton. We laughed again.

Almost hidden by a nauseous haze of its own manufacture, a pride of machines lay by the side of the road, feeding.

The road was like a natural feature. The great veldt, which stretched almost planet-wide, ended here at last. It appeared to terminate without reason. As inexplicably, the mountains began, rising from the dirt like

icebergs from a petrified sea. They were still new and unsteady. The
road ran along their base, a hem on the mighty skirt of plain.

It was a twenty-two lane highway, with provision for both mach-
negative and mach-positive traffic. The pride lay in one of the infre-
quent rest-places, gorging itself on the soft red-centred creatures that rode
in the machines. There were five machines in the pride, perpetually
backing and revving engines as they scrambled for better positions.

Juice spurted from their radiator grills, streamed over their cowling,
misted their windscreens. The tainted blue of their breath hung over
them. They were devouring their young.

"So we retreat from our retreat!" said Clyton, shouldering his
stone. The rabble still frolicked among the trees.

As we were moving off, it chanced I was just behind my friends.
On impulse, I plucked the sleeve of the plump boy in black and
asked him, "May a stranger inquire what has preoccupied your
thoughts all through this sumptuous afternoon?"

When he turned his face to me and removed his mask, I saw how
pale he was; the flesh of his body carried no echo on his face: it
resembled a skull.

He looked at me long before he said, slowly, "Perhaps truth is an
accident." And he cast his gaze to the ground.

His words caught me by surprise. I could find no rejoinder,
perhaps because his manner was grave enough to forbid repartee.

Only as I turned to leave did he add, "It may hap that you and
your friends talked truth all afternoon-long by accident. Perhaps indeed our time-sense is awry. Perhaps the wine is never
poured, or forever poured. Perhaps we are contradictions, each
one in himself. Perhaps . . . perhaps we are too imprecise to
survive . . ."

His voice was low, and the other party was still making its merry
noise – the dwarfs would continue to dance and frolic long after
sunset. Only as I hurried away through the saplings after Portinari
and Clyton did his words actually register on me: "Perhaps we are
too imprecise to survive . . ."

A melancholy thing to say on a gay day!

And there was the ferry, floating on the dark lake, screened by
tall cypresses and so rather gloomy. But already lanterns twinkled
along the shore, and I caught the sound of music and singing and

laughter aboard. Back at the tavern, our sweethearts would be waiting for us, and our new play would open at midnight. I had my role by heart, I knew every word, I longed to walk out of the wings into the glittering lights, cynosure of all eyes . . .

"Come on, my friend!" cried Portinari heartily, turning back from the throng and catching my arm. "Look, my cousins are aboard – we shall have a merry trip homewards! Will you survive?"

Survive?

Survive?

Survive

(1970)

Castle Scene with Penitents

The days in which I was recovering from a fever under my sister's care seemed like a long afternoon in childhood, when eternity begins punctually after the midday meal, to linger on long beyond twilight in an odour of flowers and warm rooms. Their comfort and idleness were almost more enslaving than the fever.

The chamber assigned me as a nest was high in the Mantegan castle, overlooking the ragged roofs of an inner court. Despite its height, honeysuckle had climbed up to the window and beyond, to the eaves, clinging wirily to the pitted stonework. During my time in bed, the sound of bees filled the room, together with the pale scent of blossoms.

My sister Katerina sat by my bed for hours. She allowed nobody but her personal servant to attend me. Mostly, she looked after me herself. Katerina was my one surviving sister. I would rouse and open an eye and there she would be, patiently sitting; I would drift off into a realm of feverish dreams, imagining her gone, and then open my eyes again, to the luxury of finding her still there. As I recovered, she took to sitting by the window, stroking her lovely amber-coloured cat, Poseidon, or working at her embroidery.

She still remained during my convalescence, tranquil by the sunlight, while I lolled in the shade of the room, weak from the effects of my illness, and we turned old times into spasmodic conversation.

"I'm truly grateful for your care, Katie. Now the summer is here, let's see more of one another than we have managed recently."

"I'm glad of the wish – and yet forces operate in life to separate people, whatever they wish."

"We'll take care that those forces avoid us. We'll remain lighthearted and rise above them."

Silence, save for the industrious bees, and then Katerina said, gesturing outside, "These elegant birds with forked tails are flying about our towers again. They arrive every year from somewhere – some say from the bottoms of ponds. They never alight on the ground. I believe they have no feet or legs, according to Aristotle."

"They're called cavorts, and are supposed to come from a continent of southern ice which no man has ever seen."

She made no answer, instead producing a small white comb with which she commenced to comb out the lustrous amber coat of Poseidon, till his purr was as loud as the noise of the bees.

"It's hard to imagine a land that no living person has ever seen."

"Is it? I believe *we* live in such a land. Close at our hand, everything is mysterious, undiscovered."

She laughed. "I'm sure that's a line from one of your plays!"

"Whenever I say anything profound, or even sensible, everyone tells me I stole it from some wretched comedy or other. Don't you recall how clever I was as a child?"

"I recall how you used to do living statues for us, and we had to guess whom you were supposed to represent. And you nearly drowned in the lagoon when you were doing Triton! I ruined my new dress, helping to rescue you."

"It was worth it for the sake of art. You were always the best at guessing, Katie!"

As she collected a combful of fur, she would pull it away and flick it out of the window. Combful after combful poured out of Poseidon's coat and drifted out into the warm air beyond.

"Could it be unlucky to see cavorts on a certain day, do you think?"

"I never heard so. Who told you that?"

"Perhaps it's an old wives' tale. They say that if you see a cavort on a certain day of the year, you will think about it ever after, and gradually the thought becomes so obsessive that you can think of nothing else."

"I've heard that theory expounded of other things, but surely not of a mere bird. It's ridiculous!"

"Possey, look at all this fur you are wasting, you silly cat!

People's thoughts are funny affairs – perhaps they could be attracted to one special thing, as a lodestone enchants metals."

I stretched and climbed off the bed, groaning and yawning pleasurably.

"Certainly I know people whose thoughts are obsessed by horses or precious stones or women or –"

"Women are different!"

"Different each from each other, sister, I agree –"

"And then there's poor father, whose thoughts are obsessed by his books . . ."

She released yet another handful of fur through the window. I went over to her, lolling against the side of the window and tickling the cat's head, saying idly, "I suppose we are all obsessed with something or other, even if we don't recognise the fact."

Katerina looked up at me. With a hint of reproach, she said, "You still generalise about life. You take it so lightly, don't you? You think everything's arranged for your amusement."

"I have no evidence to the contrary so far. You used to be carefree enough, Katie. Is Volpato unfaithful to you? Does he beat you? Why does he leave you here alone for so long?"

She did not remove her gaze from me for a while. Then she looked down at her slender hands and said, "I was fascinated by Volpato and the Mantegan family even as a carefree child. On my eighth birthday, an old soothsayer told me I would grow up to marry him. I did so, and I love him, so that's all there is to it."

"Predestination! Have you no will of your own, Katie?"

"Don't tease me! You are better, I see. You can leave the castle tomorrow, if you desire."

I kissed her hand and said, "Sweet sis, don't be cross with me! You are such a beautiful person and I have much liked being pampered by you. I shall marry a girl as much like you as possible – and I will leave the castle tomorrow in search of her!"

She laughed then, and all was well between us, and Poseidon purred more loudly than ever.

The window at which we all were was deep-set within its embrasure. Its ledge was fully wide enough for Katerina and her cat to sit there in comfort and gaze out at the world below. Or a man might stand there and, with no inconvenience to himself, discharge a musket from the coign of vantage. The woodwork round the window was lined like an aged peasant's brow with the ceaseless diurnal passage of sunlight; perhaps some such thought had crossed the mind of an old unknown poet who, with many a flourish, had engraved two tercets of indifferent verse on one of the small leaded panes of the window:

> What twain I watch through my unseeing eye:
> Inside, the small charades of men; outside,
> The tall parades of regulating sky!
>
> Thus I a barrier am between a tide
> Of man's ambitions and the heavens' meed –
> Of things that can't endure and things that bide.

Poseidon changed his position and lay stomach upward on my sister's lap, so that it was now combsfull of white fur which were released on the breezes to join the brown. The afternoon had created within the courtyard a bowl of warm air which spilled outward and upward, carrying the cat's fur with it; I was surprised to find that not a single strand had reached the ground. Instead, the brown and white tufts floated in a great circle, moving between the façades of the rooms on this side of the courtyard and the next, the stables and lofts with their little tower opposite us, and the tall and weather-blasted pines which stood on the fourth side, by the wall with the gatehouse. A whole layer of air, level with our window, and extending to each of the four limiting walls, was filled with Poseidon's fur. It floated like feathers on water, but in a perpetual stir. Katerina squeaked with amazement when I pointed it out; with her attention fixed on me, she had not noticed the pleasant phenomenon.

The cavorts were also busy. There were perhaps six pairs of them, and they swooped up from their positions in eaves and leads, tearing at the layer of fur, and whisking it down again to line their nests with. We stood watching, delighted by their activity. So intent were the little birds on their work that they often blundered almost near enough to our window to be caught. Majestically round and round floated the fur, and erratically up and down plunged the birds.

"When the baby birds are born, they'll be grateful to you,

Poseidon!" said Katerina. "They'll be brought up in proper luxury!"

"Perhaps they'll form a first generation of cat-loving birds!"

When at length we went downstairs, the fur was still circulating, the birds still pulling it to shreds, still bearing it back to their aerial nests.

"Let's play cards again tonight . . . Birds are so witless, they must always be busy – there's nothing to them but movement. I never find that time hangs heavy on my hands, Prian, do you?"

"Oh, I adore to be idle. It's then I'm best employed. But I wonder time doesn't hang heavy for you here, alone in the castello."

Placing a hand on my sleeve, smiling in a pleasant evasive way, Katerina said, "Why don't you employ yourself by visiting our wizard of the frescos, Nicholas Dalembert? There's a man with a mind obsessed by only one thing, his art. Like his wife, he's melancholy but interesting to talk to – when he feels disposed to talk."

"Dalembert's still here! It's many a moon since I last saw him, and then he was threatening to leave the castle on the morrow! The man is probably one of the geniuses of our age, if unrecognised."

As we descended to her suite of rooms, and her pretty black maid, Peggy, ran to open the doors for her, Katerina said, "Dalembert is always threatening to leave. I'd as soon believe him if he threatened to finish his frescos!"

"How can your husband afford to pay him?"

She laughed. "He can't! That's why Dalembert still lives here. He is so lazy! At least he has a free roof over his head. And he's safer here in isolation now there's plague again in Malacia."

"It always comes with the hot weather."

"Go and talk to him. You know the way. We'll meet this evening in the chapel."

It was always pleasant to stroll through the irregularities of the Mantegan family castle. Its perspectives were like none I knew in the world, with its impromptu landings, its unexpected chambers, its dead ends, its never-ending stairs, its descents from stone into wood, its fine marbles and rotting plasters, its noble statues and ignoble decay.

The Mantegan family had never been rich within memory of

living man; now they were positively bankrupt, and my brother-in-law, Volpato, was the last of the line. It was whispered of him that he had poisoned both his elder brother, Claudio, and his elder sister, Saprista, in order to gain control of what little family wealth remained: Claudio by spreading a biting acid on the saddle of his stallion, so that the deadly ichor moved from the anus upward to the heart; Saprista by smearing a toxic orpiment on a golden statue of the Virgin which she was wont to kiss during her private devotions, so that she died rotting from the lips inward. If all this was true or not, Volpato did not reveal. Evil stories clustered about him, but he acted kindly enough in his treatment of my sister, as well as having the goodness to be away for long periods, seeking his fortune among the megatherium-haunted savannahs of the New World.

Meanwhile, his castle on the banks of the Toi fell into decay, and his wife did not become a mother. But I was proud of it, and of my dear sister for marrying so well – the only one of us to marry into court circles.

The way to Dalembert's quarters lay through a long gallery in which Volpato displayed some of his treasures. Rats scuttled among them in the dim light. Among much that was rubbish were some fine blue-glazed dishes brought back from the lands of the Orinoco; ivories of mastodon carved during the last Neanderthal civilisation for the royal house of Itssobeshiquetzilaha; parchments rescued by a Mantegan ancestor from the great library at Alexandria (among them two inscribed by the library's founder, Ptolemy Soter) and portraits on silk of the seven Alexandrian Pleiades preserved from the same; a case full of Carthaginian ornament; jewels from the fairy smiths of Atlantis; an orb reputed to have belonged to Birsha, King of Gomorrah, with the crown of King Bera of Sodom; a figurine of a priest with a lantern from the court of Caerleon-on-Usk; the stirrups of the favourite stallion of the Persian Bahram, Governor of Media, that great hunter; tapestries from Zeta, Raška, and the courts of the early Nemanijas, together with robes cut for Milutin; a lyre, chalice, and other objects from the Mousterian Period; a pretty oaken screen carved with dim figures of children and animals which I particularly liked, said to have come from distant Lyonesse before it sank below the waves; together with other items of some interest. But all that was of real worth had been sold off long ago, and the custodian sacked, to keep the family in meat and wine.

Tempted by a whim for which I could not account, I paused on my way among the mouldy relics and flung open an iron-strapped chest at random. Books bound in vellum met my gaze, among them one more richly jacketed, in an embroidered case studded with beads of ruby and topaz.

Taking it over to the light, I opened it and found it had no title. It was a collection of poems in manuscript, probably compiled by their creator. At first glance, the poems looked impossibly dull, odes to Liberty and the Chase, apostrophes to the Pox and Prosody, and so on. Then, as I flicked the pages, a shorter poem in *terza rima* caught my eye.

The poem consisted of four verses – the first two of which were identical with those adorning my bedroom window! Its title had reference to the emblematic animal over the main archway of the castle: "The Stone Watchdog at the Gate Speaks." Whoever had transcribed part of the poem onto the window had been ingenious in accrediting its lines to the transparent glass. Amused by the coincidence, for coincidences were my daily dish, I read the final verses.

> No less, while things celestial proceed
> Unfettered, men and women all are slaves,
> Chaining themselves to what their hearts most need.

> Methinks that whatsoe'er the mind once craves,
> Will free it first and then it captive take
> By slow degrees, down into Free Will's graves.

Alas, Prosody had not replied when addressed! Yet the sentiment expressed might be true. I generally agreed with myself on the truth of the moralising in poems. Perhaps very little could be said that was a flat lie, provided it rhymed. Thoughtfully, I tore the page from its volume and tucked it in my doublet, tossing the book back into the chest, among the other antiquities.

Beyond the long gallery was the circular guard room, with its spiral stair up to the ramparts. Although the guard room had once been a building standing alone, it had long since come within the strangling embrace of the castle which, like some organic thing, had thrown out galleries and wings and additional courts, century by century, engulfing houses and other structures as it went. The old guard room retained something of its outdoor character despite being embedded inside the masonry of the castle; a pair of cavorts skimmed desperately round the shell, trapped after venturing in through carelessly boarded arrow slits on the inside-facing wall. On the floor lay a shred of Poseidon's fur which the birds had dropped in their panic.

The character of the building changed again beyond the guard room. Here were stables, now converted to the usages of the Mantegan family's resident artist, Nicholas Dalembert. Dalembert worked up in the loft, while his many children romped over the cobbles below.

I called to him. After a moment, his head appeared in the opening above, he waved, and began to climb down the ladder. He started to speak before he reached the bottom.

"So, Master Prian, it's almost a year – it's a long while since we've seen you at Mantegan. As God is my witness, this is an inhospitable place. I wonder what can have brought you here now. Not pleasure, I'll be bound."

I explained that I had been ill, that my sister was caring for me, and that I might be leaving on the morrow. "At first I thought it was the plague troubling me! There's much of it in Malacia, especially in the Stary Most district – brought from the East, the medicos say, on the backs of the Turkish armies. Whenever you fall into a fever these days, you fear the worst."

"You're safe from the plague here, that at least I'll say. The plague likes juices and succulence, and there's nothing of that in this place." He cast a gloomy eye down on his children, then busy flogging an old greyhound they had cornered; certainly they were not the plumpest of children.

Dalembert was a hefty fellow, as befits an artist who spends much time dissecting men, horses, and dinosaurs. The years had bowed his broad shoulders and trained a mass of grey hair about his shoulders. He had a huge cadaverous face with startling black eyes whose power was reinforced by the great black line of his eyebrows.

"I came to see how the frescos were progressing, Nicholas."

"They're as incomplete as they were last Giovedi Grassi Festival, when you and the players were performing here. Nothing can be done – I can't work anymore without pay and, although I don't want to complain to you about your own brother-in-law, Milord Volpato would be better employed setting his lands in order than involving me in his schemes for self-aggrandisement. I'm so hard up I've even had to sack the lad who was colouring in my skies for me."

As he was making this dismal speech, he was leading me through a side door and across a narrow court. His steps were heavy, his manner slow and deliberate. I wondered at him and his situation. I had no doubt that he was among the greatest painters in the land, and not just in Malacia; yet he had wasted a decade here – indeed, seemed to have settled here, forever dawdling on the Mantegan frescos, forever experimenting with a dozen other arts. Sometimes he quarrelled with Volpato and threatened to leave. All the while, he complained of Volpato's stinginess. Yet Volpato also seemed to have some justice on his side when he, in his turn, complained that he housed and supported an idle painter and got no reward for it.

We entered the banqueting hall, with its pendant vaulting and splendid lattice window, fantastic with carved transoms, overlooking the River Toi. Dalembert's unfinished frescos took their orientation from this window, and their lighting schemes. The theme was the Activities of Man and the Prescience of God. Only one or two pastoral scenes and the dinosaur hunt were complete; for the rest, one or two isolated figures or details of background stood out in a melancholy way behind the scaffolding.

As Dalembert plodded to and fro, expounding what he intended to do, I could see something of his vision, could see the entire hall as a sweet elegaic rhapsody of Youth, as he planned it to be. The cartoons scattered about showed that his wonderful fantasies, his glorious and ample figures, drawn together in grandiose colour orchestrations, opened new horizons of painting. In the marriage scene, sketched in and part painted, the wedding of an early Mantegan to Beatrice of Burgundy was commemorated. What delicacy and perception!

"The secret is the light," I said.

For light seemed to linger on the princess with a serene if sad intimacy, and on her banners and followers with no less lucidity.

The church with its galleries and the view beyond were carefully drawn in, proof of Dalembert's marvellous command of perspective.

The artist paused before a military scene, where soldiers were shooting birds and a peasant boy stood comically wearing a large helmet and holding a shield. In the background rose a small fantastic city, drawn and washed over.

Dalembert dismissed it all with a curt wave of one hand.

"That's all I've done here since we last met. The whole task is impossible without adequate funds. Adequate talent, too."

"It's beautiful, Nicholas. The city, with its ragged battlements, its towers, domes, and overhanging garde-robes – how well it's set amid its surroundings!"

"Well enough, perhaps, yet there's nothing there which my master, Albrecht, could not have done thirty years ago – fifty years ago."

"Surely perfection is more important than progression?"

He looked at me with his dark and burning eyes. "I didn't take you for a man who preferred a stagnant pond to running water. Ah, I can do nothing, nothing! Outside beyond these crumbling walls is that great burning world of triumphs and mobilities, while I'm here immobile. Only by art, only through painting, can one master it and its secrets! Seeing is not enough – we do not see until we have copied it, until we have faithfully transcribed everything . . . everything . . . especially the divine light of heaven, without which there is nothing."

"You would have here, if you could only continue with your work, something more than a transcription –"

"Don't flatter me. I hate it sincerely. I'll take money, God knows I'll take money, but not praise. Only God is worthy of praise. There is no merit anywhere but He gives it. See the locks of that soldier's hair, the bloom on the boy's cheek, the bricks of the walls of the fortifications, the plumage of the little bird as it flutters to the sward – do I have them exact? No, I do not! I have imitations! You don't imagine – you are not deceived into believing there is no wall there, are you?"

"But I expect the wall. Your accomplishment is that through perspective and colouring, you show us more than a wall."

"No, no, far less than a wall . . . A wall is a wall, and all my ambition can only make it less than a wall. You look for mobility and light – I give you dust and statuary! It's blasphemy – life offered death!"

I did not understand him, but I said nothing. He stood stock still, fixing his gaze in loathing on the fortified city he had depicted, and I was aware of the formidable solidity of him, as if he were constructed of condensed darkness inside his tattered cloak.

Finally he turned away and said, as if opening a new topic of conversation, "Only God is worthy of praise. He gives and takes all things."

"He has also given us the power to create."

"He gives all things, and so many we are unable to accept. We stand in a new age, Master Prian. This is a new age – I can feel it all about me, cooped up though I am in this dreadful place. Now at last – for the first time in a thousand years, men open their eyes and look about them. For the first time, they construct engines to supplement their muscles and consult libraries to supplement their meagre brains. And what do they find? Why, the vast, the God-given continuity of the world! For the first time, we may see into the past and into the future. We find we are surrounded by the classical ruins of yesterday and the embryos of the future! And how can these signs from the Almighty be interpreted save by *painting*? Painting gives and therefore demands universal knowledge . . ."

"And, surely, also the instincts are involved –"

"Whereas I know nothing – nothing! For years and years – all my life I've slaved to learn, to copy, to transcribe, and yet I have not the ability to do what a single beam of light can do – here, my friend, come with me, and I'll show you how favourably one moment of God's work compares with a year of mine!"

He seized my tunic and drew me from the hall, leaving the door to swing behind us. Again we retraced the court, which echoed to his grudging step. We returned to the stable that housed him. The little children sprawled and played. Dalembert brushed them aside. He climbed the ladder to his loft, pushing me before him. The children cried words of enticement to him to join their play; he shouted back to them to be silent.

The loft was his workshop. One end was boarded off. The rest was filled with his tables and materials, with his endless pots and brushes of all sizes, with piles of unruly paper, with instruments of every description, with geometrical models, and with a litter of objects which bespoke his intellectual occupations: an elk's foot, a buffalo horn, skulls of aurochs and hypsilophodon, piles of bones, a plaited hat of bark, a coconut, fir cones, shells, branches of coral, dead insects, and lumps of rock, as well as books on fortifications and other subjects.

He brushed through these inanimate children too. Flinging back a curtain at the rear of the workshop, he gestured me in, crying, "Here you can be in God's trouser pocket and survey the universe! See what light can paint at the hand of the one true Master!"

The curtain fell back into place. We were in a small, stuffy and enclosed dark room. A round table stood in the centre of it. On the table was a startling picture painted in vivid colours. I took one glance at it and knew that Dalembert had happened on some miraculous technique, combining all arts and all knowledge, which set him as far apart from all other artists as men are apart from the other animals with which they share the globe. Then something moved in the picture. A second glance told me this was nothing but a camera obscura! Looking up, I saw a little aperture through which the light entered. Directed by a lens, it shone in through a small tower set in the roof of the stable.

"Can our poor cobwebs of brains counterfeit a picture as vivid and perfect as this? Yet it is merely a passing beam of light! The lens in the roof has a better mastery of experience than I! Why should a man – what drives a man to compete against Nature itself? What a slave I am to my hopes!"

As he bewailed his lot, I stared at the scene laid out so curiously and captivatingly on the table. From the perspectives of the rooftops, we looked down on a stretch of track outside the castle, where the Toi ran beside a dusty climbing road. By the river, resting on grass and boulders, sat a group of people as dusty as the road, their mules tethered nearby. So enchanted was I to observe them, and to overlook such details as an elderly man who mopped his bald head with a kerchief and a widow woman in black who fanned her face with a hat, that it was a minute before I identified them as a group of pilgrims or penitents – evidently embarked on a long journey and making life hard for themselves.

"You see how they are diminished, my friend," said Dalembert.

"We see them as through God's eye. We believe them real, yet we are only looking at marks on a table, light impressions that leave no stain! Look, here comes my wife, toiling back up the hill – yet it is not my wife, only a tiny mark on the tabletop which I identify with my wife. What is its relation to her?"

"If you knew that, you would hold the secret of the universe, I daresay."

His great brows drew together.

"She has been copied by a master painter, who uses only light."

I watched as the small figure of his wife, in climbing up toward the castle gate, slowly traversed an inch or two of tabletop. I did not answer Dalembert, not having his religious convictions; but he never needed prompting to speak.

"We stand – our generation, I mean – on the verge of some tremendous discovery. All things may be possible . . . And yet, what man can say if we aren't ourselves little more than reflections of light."

"Or shadows, as Plato says in the seventh book of his *Republic* . . . As an actor, I've often thought it – I seem most substantial when I'm being a fictitious creature."

"Actors – they're nothing, they leave no trace."

"If that is so, then they are like Plato's shadows on the wall of his cave."

"Those that observed the shadows were captives, chained where they sat since childhood. That much at least is not allegory."

"Shall we go down to greet your wife?"

"She has nothing to say. She probably has nothing to eat either, poor jade!" As if to dismiss her, he stepped back and turned a handle, causing the lens or mirror attached to it to be moved. At once, the labouring woman and the penitents were swept away. Rooftops and gables appeared in our enchanted circle, and then an inner court.

The sharp diminution, the steep perspective, and the amazing brilliance of the scene gave the buildings so novel an air that at first I did not recognise where we were. Then I uttered a cry of surprise.

All at once the whole panorama was known and interpreted. Minute birds flittered here and there. These were the very cavorts I had watched with my sister. I could even see a haze of cat's fur, spread out like a web and stirred by the warm circulating breath of the courtyard. I looked for my bedroom window. Yes, there it was, and on the open sill Poseidon herself, glaring out at the creatures who were making so free with her abandoned coat! How bright and minute the colours were, like some living Schwabian miniature in enamel! The entire window with its parched woodwork was less than half the size of my little finger's nail, yet I saw every detail of it, and the cat, to perfection. What images of peace! I was watching them still when – with startling speed – the whole view was blotted out by a rapidly growing bird, which rose and rose, as if from the depths of the table, until it blotted everything out. A scrabbling sounded overhead, and a cavort fluttered down between Dalembert and me.

"Wretched creatures! How clumsy they are!" Dalembert said, lumbering about and striking at the bird – nearly clouting me in the process. "That isn't the first time one has tumbled in here. Get out of the way while I kill it!"

I descended the ladder while he hit out at the luckless bird, circling round and round in the darkness.

Below, the children were all crying in delight. Their mother had just entered by the street door. She greeted me wearily and sat down.

She was a heavy woman. Her face was withered now and had lost much of its former beauty. Her name among men was Charity; she was, in fact, a flying woman. Our laws in Malacia governing the flying people were very strict, but Charity, as child and young girl, had been one of those favoured few allowed to nest on top of the campanile, on account of her great beauty. I could recall her being pointed out to me as a boy, flying with some of her sisters – a lovely and remarkable sight; though the subject of lewd boyish jokes, for the flying people scorned clothes.

Now Charity kept her pinions folded. Since marrying her lover, Dalembert, for whom she had modelled, she never flew and had perhaps lost the art.

Seeing me, she rose and offered a hand in welcome. The children tugged at her robe so vigorously that she sat down again before pouring me a glass of wine. I accepted gladly – her husband had been too mean to offer me one.

"I hoped you would come to see us, Master Prian. Your good sister told me you were almost recovered from your fever."

"I would never come to Mantegan without visiting you and Nicholas. You know that. As ever, I have a great admiration for your husband's work."

"How do you find Dalembert?"

"As bursting with genius and ideas as ever!"

"*And* as religious, *and* as despairing?"

"A trifle melancholy, perhaps . . ."

"And as unable to paint a wall!"

Picking up a couple of the children, she went over to the water bin, dipped a ladle, and drank from it. The children then called out for a similar treat, and she gave to each in turn, the boys first and then the girls. Over their clamour, she said, "He is too ambitious, and you see the results. I've just been out washing for a wealthy family to earn enough to buy bread. How we shall manage when the winter comes, I don't know . . ."

"Genius seldom cares to earn its bread."

"He thinks he will be famous in two hundred years' time. What good will that do me or his poor children, I don't know! Come, I must find them something to eat . . . I shouldn't complain, Master Prian; it's just that I don't see matters in the same light as Dalembert, and the road up to the castle grows steeper week by week, I swear."

As I leaned against a wall, sipping the wine and watching how she managed to work while keeping the children entertained, I wondered if she still recalled the aerial views she had had of our city as a young girl – how enchanting it must have looked before she had to walk it! But I said nothing; it was best not to interfere.

It seemed as if the artist had forgotten me. I heard him pacing overhead. He would be working again at his figures.

Passing her the empty glass, I said to Charity, "I must go and rest now. Tell your husband that I hope to come and see him again before I leave the castle. And I'll ask my sister if she can get Volpato to pay him a little more money."

She shook her head and gestured dismissively with her hands in a gesture reminiscent of her husband's.

"Let well alone! Don't do that! You may not know it, but Volpato has threatened to throw us out, frescos or no frescos, if he is pestered ever again on the subject of money."

"As you wish, of course."

"It is not as I wish but as I must."

I went to the door. She pulled a long grey feather from her wing and stooped to give it to the smallest baby to play with. I was out of the door before she straightened up again.

The day was moving toward evening. The shadows were climbing the sides of the courtyard. As I crossed to my sister's quarters, I noticed that the cavorts had all gone. High above my head, the panes of my window were still catching the eye of the sun, but Poseidon had vanished. All was still. The fur had sunk down at last to the ground – a dusty twist of it rolled across the flags under my feet. Now only light filled the tranquil air.

I was well again: tomorrow I would probably quit the castle.

(1973)

The Game with the Big Heavy Ball

Perhaps this was the clue to the whole confused world in which I still managed to survive. That we love the things that frighten us. That wish and fear are close allied. That the proper study of mankind is menace.

The fear that placid morning, with the ocean so preternaturally still. I had woken with a start. Everything was strange. Another night had been survived. The sun shone again.

Poe's book of tales still lay on my pillow. The maroon leather binding caught my eye as I sat up. Those tales were among the things that frightened me. Some of the stories, such as "Premature Burial", "The Tell-Tale Heart", "The Game of the Lead Ball", and "The Pit and the Pendulum", were most terrifying, most loved, most read.

Often, in the days when Poe was still alive, I had read them to my sister, just for the pleasure of hearing her scream and whimper.

But now it was daylight and another move in the cosmic game was indicated.

I carried my sister very carefully, so as not to wake her. Dawn was breaking as I passed through the library door into the rear court-yard and round the north end of the house. The three massive pillars of wood which shored up the northern wall were still standing; but as I paused, resting one hand on the first beam to feel its cracked surface, I observed by the gouges in the earth at their base that the night's earthquake had shifted them.

Staring up the towering side of the house, I saw it remained intact. Even the ornate chimneys had not toppled. The windows looked down at me, blank, incurious, waiting.

"Ulysses should be back any day now," I said.

I walked slowly through the overgrown grass of the lawn – it was a field now, might as well acknowledge the fact – and into the shrubbery. The shrub I particularly liked was flowering; it flowered all winter, bearing its sprays of little white blossoms, from October till the next April or May, and the most savage winds, springing over the cliff top, could not shake off its little sprays of flower. This morning, there was no wind. It was a day of silence and of stillness after the uneasy night.

As I came out on to the cliff top and started down the twisting path to the beach, my sister stirred in my arms. I looked down at her face; she did not waken.

Half-way down the cliff, I paused and stared at the expanse of the beach. On a clear day, the coast could be seen doubling and redoubling itself into the distance in a series of bays and headlands. This morning, next to nothing of the coast showed; the sky and the sea closed together quite near at hand, pale as a fish's mouth. The main feature was the ruin of the old lifeboat house, its few battered timbers and massive barnacle-encrusted base looming black between shelving sand and water. Of the pirates there was no sign.

As usual, I went barefoot. I advanced over the sand, its dark peppery granules crunching under my feet; seawrack lay about in heaps like horse dung. Balancing precariously, I climbed one of the sloping buttresses and advanced along the base of the lifeboat house until I stood at the seaward end of its ramp.

I looked down into the clear dangerous water, into that dark lucid world of another element where pebbles lay like mouths and small fish flitted. Here the current was swift, unrelenting; a small person caught in it would be tumbled about as she was borne out to sea, would stand no chance of getting to dry land again. How often had I dreamed in terror that that might happen – not to me, but to her, whose outstretched hand always failed to reach my outstretched hand, whose eyes failed to close as waves broke over that last desperate glance passing between us!

Leaning over the water with her, sinking onto one knee, I looked out to sea and my eye was caught by a detail on the surface. At first I thought a bird floated there, yet the object was not a bird. Then I observed that all round it stretched something dark, a stain under the face of the water. Although I knew there was no rock here, certainly no rock so near to the surface – so near that the keel of our skiff in which we often sailed would surely have scraped it – I could only assume the dark patch to be rock, with one spike of it protruding above the water.

In the stillness, I stared at this apparition of rock where no rock had been, watching the swirl of water round it.

My sister's dark straight hair had fallen across her forehead. In her sleep her mouth had opened slightly, revealing the even white line of her teeth and something of her tongue. Her eyes were newly open, her pupils, brown and flecked with gold, regarded me with a remote look. The eyes were wide, deeply, neatly set in the flesh that rolled like pastry over her wide cheekbones. Slowly, she closed her mouth, as if about to form a syllable.

Taking my gaze away from hers, I lowered her so that her feet touched the little extinct volcano shells of barnacles and she could stand, which she did in an absent way, still retaining her left arm about my neck – loosely, and not as if fearing I might push her off our narrow platform.

"Is the town still on fire?" she asked.

All I seemed able to do was to stare down at the clear water by our feet, heaving up and down as if it breathed in sleep. Far up the beach, where the landscape's few colours faded into a universal drab white, a flock of gulls squabbled over something lying among the seawrack.

"Look out there, Bathsheba!" I said, pointing to the shadowy stain under the surface of the waves. "A whole shelf of rock has come up in the night and is invading our beach."

She did not look at first. Instead she brought up her right hand for inspection, staring at the little folded fingers and shining nails as if they were items fashioned of a new material.

"It was the earth-tremor, Bathsheba! It's thrown up a whole new continent. We'll be able to scramble over it at low tide."

She did look then, in a casual bored way, before turning back towards the land. "The earth must have been throwing up old bits of itself. Perhaps that's Atlantis. Are you coming to have breakfast?"

"I'll come in a little while." I felt sulky, just moderately sulky. I stooped down, trying to pry one of the barnacles from its hold until she had gone, running with her arms stretched wide, up the crinkling path towards the old house. Not attending properly to what I was doing, I cut a finger on a sharp ridge of shell. When I squeezed the cut, it bled slightly.

Lying flat on my stomach, I dipped the finger into the water below, watching a spiral of my blood emerge from my body like smoke and vanish into the lungs of the sea. A fancy entered my head that the scent of the blood might summon a monster swimming out of the depths; but nothing I did could alter the impersonal forces at work on the beach.

Similar feelings of powerlessness had once oppressed me greatly – when I was younger, say Bathsheba's age. I had wanted to make an effect, to leave a mark, to raise some sort of barrier that perhaps would have some duration against time or against the tides. So all one summer, rain or fine, I had laboured to fling up immense barricades in the sand, fortifying them with old timbers until they resembled the trenches that soldiers used to fight in during wars that grandfather talked about. To no avail. Always the sea returned up the beach, lapping its way up the sand in a foolish helpless manner, finally with its offhand power bowling over my timbers, washing away my cobbles, inundating my ramparts and in all ways fulfilling that horrible prophecy we used to sing about in the psalm: "Every valley shall be exalted and every hill shall be razed low."

Nowadays, I was much more powerful. Many years had passed.

I was hungry. I got to my feet, wrapped my finger in a handkerchief that I gripped in the palm of my hand as if it were a captured lizard, and headed towards breakfast.

Uncle Kenneth was one of the vaguely ill. His great bony structure, like an ancient castle overlooking some particularly damp stretch of the Rhine, was tenanted by numberless spectres: renal calculus, rattling its chains at dead of night; rheumatoid arthritis, flitting sheeted through the passageways; seborrhoea, an apparition like snow; hammer-toe, knocking away in the cellarage; dyspepsia with flatulence, doing its poltergeist best down the galleries; migraine, with its head tucked underneath its arm. These phantoms came and went; Uncle Kenneth crumbled but remained.

He sat at the breakfast table now, behind a barrage of packets, tins and bottles of health foods, powders, laxatives, pills and tonics. His lean jaw cracked over a spoonful of dry brown things.

"The darkest hour is just before the dawn," he said, looking up at me over his boxes.

I gave the countersign. "But westward look the land is bright. How are you this morning, Uncle?"

Grandfather, Mrs Gubernater and Bathsheba were already at the table. They kept their eyes down while Uncle Kenneth, flaunting a certain amount of medical knowledge, gave me a resumé of how his hours of agonising night had been spent. I helped myself to porridge.

When the catalogue of woes was over, I said, "There was a big earthquake in the night, Uncle. The whole house got heaved about, probably into a new dimension."

"That was me coughing, boy. You heard it in your sleep and thought it was an earthquake."

"I was awake all night with lumbago," Grandfather said, "and I didn't hear anything."

Uncle Kenneth pointed a spoon at Grandfather. "I don't reckon that's lumbago at all. I reckon it's Friedrich's Ataxia, or something like that."

"I ought to know what it is, I've got it." Grandfather pulled a horrible face across the table, as if to demonstrate what lumbago would look like if you could see it. "It's got so bad I can't even stand up if I close my eyes."

"Ah," said Uncle, closing his eyes. "That's a hint. And how long have you been staggering a bit as you walk? That's not lumbago – that's *tabes dorsalis*, more likely!"

"What?"

"*Tabes dorsalis* or *locomotor ataxia*. A form of GPI."

While they were arguing, I asked Mrs Gubernater if she would come out in the skiff with Bathsheba and me in the afternoon. Mrs Gubernater had been with the family for a long time but remained plump and rosy through it all. She was no longer young; the roses had become rather a bright red on her cheeks and nose. Three long grey hairs and a short black one sprouted from a mole on her left cheek.

"What have you been up to with Bathsheba this morning, Jeremy?"

"Nothing."

Mrs Gubernater rose, gathering her skirts with a characteristic gesture, and went to lean in one corner of the breakfast room against the Welsh dresser, piled with its precious china and engraved monumental glasses. I watched her, though it was not what I wished to do. Surely enough, she transposed a wrinkled finger between her eyes and mine and beckoned me with it.

I stood before her.

"I didn't do anything, Gooby. I just took her for a walk, that's all."

Speaking in a quiet voice so that the three at the table could not hear what she was saying above their passionately renewed discussion of Friedrich's Ataxia, she said, "You promised me that you would never renew your suicide pact."

"It wasn't anything like that," I said with false indignation.

Everything was very dark between us and our conversation was surrounded by white spaces. Her dress moved up and down where she mainly breathed.

Remorselessly, she repeated, "You promised that you would not turn into a sea creature and if you love me you must keep your promise. You must love me because I am the only human being here. You know that, don't you."

Fixing my eyes on that part of her which went up and down, I listened for the soft whirr of machinery. As ever, no conclusive findings, one way or another.

Hanging my head, I said, "I was just taking her for a walk, that's all."

"You must be strong, Jeremy," Mrs Gubernater said. "Remember, it's single combat. Now go and brush your teeth and do the other things and prepare to enjoy your day."

I had enjoyed the curve of the stairs since they had become curved. Dragging up them, scuffing my toes, I stared out of the tall, stained window and saw two men in some sort of ragged uniform running between the cedars on the lawn. They had broken from a slovenly escort and were making for the house. The escort had a quick argument among themselves, threw down their cigarettes, put their rifles to their shoulders, and fired. The two men ran on. One of the soldiers in the escort bent down and picked up his cigarette, drawing on it again. The others fired once or twice more. One of the escapers was hit. He staggered a few yards and fell against the trunk of a tree. His companion disappeared beyond the west wing of the house. I went on upstairs; they liked to keep me reminded.

In some incomprehensible way, Uncle Kenneth was pottering about the upper landing. Perhaps a new short-cut had developed in the house; there would be some "plausible explanation". Uncle carried a small enamel bowl, together with a short metal tube ending in a plastic bulb – some piece of medical equipment necessary to his health, I supposed.

He turned the old dog-fang-yellow smile on me, as ever with his air of having been caught doing something he should not have been, and said, "So there you are, Jeremy! I've got a riddle for you, my lad. I'm going to give you six things which were given as answers to a question, all right? And *you've* got to guess what the question was. All right? Six things that were given as answers to one question. What was the question?"

As he spoke, pointing the tube at me, he shuffled backwards along the passage, towards the bathroom door. From where I stood, I could see into the bathroom. A woman dressed all in black, wearing a black hat, was raising the blind. I had never seen her before and would never see her again. (I hated that kind of thing, as well they knew.)

"*Macbeth*. Jazz. God's creatures. Christ's life. Spring. Science."

He looked at me from behind the dog's fangs, clutching his chest and saying "Pardon" as it rumbled. I had long ago placed Uncle as one of the enemy; the whole aspect of caricature was too ridiculous. And yet were they not subtle enough even to flaunt being too ridiculous? Perhaps this poor broken reed was the only real person with me in the house. Either way, I could never trust him.

"Wyndham," I said, maliciously.

"That's unkind, and it's not a question, dear boy."

"Well, where is Wyndham, then?"

Dog's fangs, and his yellowing hand going back and clutching the bathroom doorknob. "The answer is, 'What begins with love and ends with murder?' Funny, isn't it?"

He disappeared into the room, and closed the door behind him.

I had to admit that I liked the idea of an answer being a question. It was part of the rules of single combat, and of life.

In my bedroom, I seized a pillow and sprawled on the floor by the windowseat. Idly, I took a book from the shelf under the windowseat, clutching it to me without opening it, almost certain of what I would read within its pages: they weren't that clever and, over the years, some of their tricks had become predictable. (When they all became predictable, would I have *won*? Was winning even possible?)

The book was entitled *The Boys' Book of Being*. I was supposed to have had it a long time, since, after the title on the title-page, a childish hand had scribbled in blue crayon the word *Sick*. The writing looked centuries old.

Opening the book at random, smiling in enjoyment of my cleverness, I read:

Axiom 241. *Always feel sympathy, particularly towards the weak.*

Jolly old Uncle Ken had only a short while to live, yet he never let his cheerfulness desert him. After a particularly trying night, he met his ungrateful young nephew, Billie, on the landing. Since his own son, Windy, had disappeared, Uncle Ken had treated Billie like a son. Yet his smiles brought no answering smile from Billie, which made the old man very sad.

Now he asked the young fellow a riddle he had devised during the long painracked hours of the night. Billie could not guess it.

All riddles are about communication. Once it was believed that only lucid things could and should be communicated, but this has since proved incorrect.

Billie said something which hurt his poor old uncle greatly. The old man retreated into a private room and wept bitter tears. He wished to win the young boy's love and trust. Little did either of them know that only another week's life was left to the boy. A terrible accident awaited in the near future.

I threw the book down, laughing. Tomorrow, a different piece of nonsense would have materialised in the book.

The door opened slowly. I tensed myself, ready for an unpleasant surprise, but it was only Bathsheba.

"I'm glad it's only you," she said. (By such means, the enemy sought to deceive me it was human.) "Let's go out while Gooby and Grandfather are busy downstairs and Uncle Gilroy is locked in the bathroom."

"You mean Uncle Ken?" I asked.

She looked all crafty at me and began to laugh in a panting way.

"Don't play that game with me," she said. "You know it scares me. Besides, there's no Uncle Ken. I'm not that silly."

Just for a moment, she must have seen something in my eyes that really frightened her. Then she bit her lower lip and pulled up her socks and came towards me in a determined fashion. Again I thought about hypnotising her and ordering her to fly – but whatever she was, she was the thing closest to me. Pointing imperiously, I made her stand in front of me.

"I'm going to ask you a riddle, Bathsheba."

"The answer's a question, isn't it?"

"No, it's not that riddle, and how did you know about that one, anyway?"

"Because – because I heard Uncle Gilroy ask it you on the landing."

"You sweet little girl, how you lie! Listen, this riddle is about me. There's a perfectly square featureless room – a cell, in fact. Just four corners and an even stone floor. A ping-pong ball is trapped in the room and cannot escape. It is continually pursued by a big heavy lead ball, many times its own size, which wishes to crush it. The ping-pong ball (that's me) has to keep on running, but it cannot climb the walls or fly through the air. How does it escape being crushed?"

Bathsheba sat down before me in a little heap, cradled her elbow, sucked her thumb.

"Does it get on top of the big heavy lead ball?"

"No, it can't."

"Uhhhh . . . does it find the big heavy lead ball is hollow and climb inside?"

"No, it can't do that either. Give up?"

"If the room got flooded with water, then it could float safely while the big heavy lead ball sank and was drowned."

"That's not the answer either. Give up?"

"Yes. How does it escape being crushed?"

I stuck my tongue out at her. "Tell you later. First, we're going out to discover what the soldiers are doing in the grounds. I'll say that about you – you always have something going on to interest me."

"First, tell me how the ping-pong ball escapes being crushed by the big heavy lead ball."

"You come along with me, Bathsheba, before you turn into a monster." I seized her wrist and led her from the room.

Outside my bedroom, the old house reverted to its secondary appearance, a cavernous, semi-ruinous structure presumably built by a well-meaning but cranky environmentalist. It was draughty and uncomfortable, but I had grown to like it: it appeared whenever I had scored a minor victory, as I had over Bathsheba, indicating that the enemy scarcely realised when it was showing pique.

Beyond the plate windows I saw that the old seaplane base had materialised. Disused hangars hung over the grey waters of the lake. Between the great squares of concrete, sorrel and grass grew rusty, and scrub flourished beyond them.

"Uh, oh, Environment Two!"

"It's nothing but reassuring. You people can only manage the two switches of surroundings. All your transformations are very limited. I sometimes feel as if I'm caught in a very technically limited life-size version of an electronic game. And since I know this is not technics but psychonics, I understand how limited your mind is despite its undoubted strength."

"Don't say 'your', Jeremy. 'Their' or 'its'. I'm on your side, just like Uncle and Grandfather and Mrs Gubernater. Really. Haven't you tested us enough to see that? I'm a ping-pong ball like you. If you can accept that, then the big heavy lead ball may not crush either of us."

"Whether or not you're part of the big heavy lead ball –" I had been going to add "is immaterial"; more deviously, I said, "– it must represent the projection of the psyche of an entire planetary biomass, human and animal and everything. And it has beamed itself right down on mankind on Earth. Where *I* have to fight it in single combat."

"Jeremy, you should hear how silly that sounds. Why would that happen?"

"I don't know why – or much care. But it's how things are, as even Gubernater admits in weak moments. Mankind has become stagnant for millions of years, in a kind of everlasting utopia, and this challenge by the big heavy lead ball has caught it unawares. So I have been thrown into the arena to fight."

She cringed away from me.

"You haven't told me that story for years. I thought you'd forgotten that crazy paranoid theory. I don't like that one. You know I'm a qualified mind-healer."

I smiled as nastily, twistedly, as I could, raising my hands like claws to either side of my ears. "Another slip in psychology. If you really thought me paranoid, it would be the last thing you would say to me!"

She slipped away, her arms stretched, dancing. I let her go. I was profoundly sorry for her. I loved her. Love thine enemy. Back in the Middle Ages of the Old Western Culture, legal proceedings had been taken against animals. Ideas of responsibility changed over the epochs. Human and animal nature also changed.

Outside, it was green all about the gaunt building. The very air was green. The carefully sited trees had grown with neglect, were pompous and heavy and thick like haystacks without foliage. I walked under them, looking for soldiers, stepping out on to the exposed ground of the seaplane ramps. From here, men and sea creatures had once soared under their own power to the very margins of space. Now all was deserted. Walking along the concrete by the water's edge, I heard my footsteps echo against the façade of the hangars.

One hangar was slightly open.

I walked in. A desk stood in the middle of emptiness with a cup of coffee steaming on it. I went over, sat down, sipped at the coffee.

There was a tapewriter on the desk. When I slipped a sheet of paper into it, it taped out the letter I dictated.

Dear Bathsheba,

The ping-pong ball simply kept to the walls. Then it could run round and round the whole room forever, and the big heavy lead ball could not crush it.

I want you to remember this lesson when I am dead and gone. Or when you are dead and gone. Such things do happen.

Lovingly,
    Jeremy

Taking the paper out, I folded it neatly in four and dropped it on the pitted concrete floor. It would reach its destination; I was in a universe where no action ever went astray.

Outside, the sun lay folded into the ragged squares of the old runway. Our usual building had come back. Rooks sat on the fake battlements. Some things had to be eternally re-enacted, like death. There were no truths unless they were eternally remembered. I said to the soldier who staggered dying at my feet, "All that really interests me is truth. Pretences and deceptions are my toys, my favourite toys."

He rolled over, groaning.

It was Uncle Gilroy.

I bent over him. It was impossible not to be moved by his look of agony, as he crushed the rusty sorrel under him.

"They're coming, Jeremy," he gasped. "The enemy. There's been a revolution. The earthquake destroyed the central world communication system. They'll be here in force soon . . . Never mind me, get into the house, as fast as you can."

Kneeling beside him, feeling his pulse, I whispered into his ear, "Don't worry uncle. It's only a game. You'll be back tomorrow."

I ran towards the house without looking round.

Slipping into one of the rear doors, I bolted it behind me. Silence filled the house. As I tiptoed along the corridor, I heard voices at the far end and proceeded even more carefully.

My sister was in the kitchen, talking to Mrs Gubernater and Grandfather. I paused by the door, listening. Of course they would be talking about me.

"His current obsession is that we are all manifestations of some interstellar entity which is engaged in single combat with him."

"What nonsense!" said Mrs Gubernater stoutly. "Now, mind out the way while I put these rock-buns in the oven. And why should they pick on him, of all people?"

"There could be something in his theory, though," Grandfather said in his creaky voice. "Single combat has an honourable tradition, and not only in boyhood games you know. There's plenty of precedent for it as a substitute for battle and war."

"Please, *not* a lecture, Grandfather," Bathsheba said, but he continued with scarcely a pause.

"Long, long ago, when the Vandals were at war with the

Alemans of Spain, the hostile parties decided to have their conflict settled by a single combat. They considered it as an appropriate substitute for war, a concise proof of the superiority of one party over the other, in which victory proved the support of gods and justice. Even very early on, there's the case of the Berovingian king Theoderich at Quierzt on the Oise, where his warriors said, 'Better for one to fall than the whole army.' And there's the more recent case of China settling its war against the Indo-Pak States with single combat, and retiring from much occupied territory when their man proved the loser. I'd imagine that single combat might well prove the only way of waging interstellar warfare, at least between two civilised planets.''

I could not help laughing. As I walked into the kitchen, expressions of astonishment registered on their faces, to be followed in Mrs Gubernater's case by one of anger.

"Little boys who eavesdrop never hear good of themselves. If you don't behave yourself better, Master Jeremy, you'll get no rock-buns for your tea."

"The rock-buns are just a minor part of the day's score in the silly old electronic game, Gooby." All the same, I liked Mrs Gubernater's rock-buns. "But I couldn't help hearing what Grandfather said. Will you tell me about the Vandals some time, Grandfather?"

"Of course, my boy. I'll tell you about them this evening, at bedtime."

When I slipped out of the kitchen, Bathsheba followed me, clutching at my hand.

"Promise you won't turn into a monster, Jeremy?"

"I am trying to but I can't because I've just swallowed one of the enemy's enchanted antimorphosis rock-buns."

"Ha ha. I'm still mad at you because you wouldn't tell me the answer to that riddle about the ping-pong ball."

As we raced up the main staircase, I said, "It's not a proper riddle – you could easily work it out for yourself if your powers of visualisation were as good as mine. That's all it needs – visualisation." I lowered my voice because we were passing the suit of armour standing on the first landing. It could hear everything. Grandfather used to collect armour, thousands of years ago. This suit stalked the house at midnight. "In any case, General, that's irrelevant now. The Sioux are surrounding the ranch and we've got to hold out until the sheriff and his men get here."

She gave me one of her sly looks. "I can't keep up this pace, by the way. This poisoned arrow wound in my leg is still agony."

"We'll probably have to cut the whole leg off."

"I expect so. In hand-to-hand combat, I can hit the Indians with it, like a club."

We climbed the narrow stair that led to the battlements. I pushed the door open. The prairie grass was high; herds of buffalo filled the distant horizon.

We crawled forward on hands and knees. I whispered, "Truth is so precious that it always comes attended by a bodyguard of lies."

"Mother may be coming to see us next month."

At the battlements, I raised my hand, squinting along the barrel of my shotgun.

"Smoke signals!" Bathsheba whispered beside me.

"Worse than that – the Vandals, and they're invading in force."

They were mustering on the hill, under the cedars. Hard little leather-clad men in helmets, with great swords glinting at their sides. They rode ponies, adorned with antlers to make them look more ferocious. A whole army was gathering for the attack on our castle, the last bastion of the Roman world.

"This will be a bloody day," I said grimly.

At least I knew that, despite the big heavy ball of time which we immortals rolled before us, I had thousands of golden centuries of childhood left to enjoy.

(1977)

Creatures of Apogee

From a distance, the one-storey palace appeared to float on the ocean like a wafer.

Three beings came springing out of the lighted rooms of the palace behind the long colonnade, he, She, and she. They ran over the flagstones, laughing. Night crackled overhead in tones of deep blue and sherbet. Joy flared like lightning across two opposed points.

From the chambers behind them, music overflowed. In that music moved nothing but harmony itself, complete in its own cadences, yet the key in which it was pitched carried an oblique reference to the particular loaded time changes of this world. Things grew, eyes sparkled, joints were as nimble; yet this was this fateful planet and no other in the universe.

Take that great terrace, paved with flagstones in which mica emicated beneath advancing feet: across its expanse, illumination played with as many variations as the music. The night itself was a great source of light and, like an upturned cauldron, the sky spilled its nourishments over the intricacies of the building. Into the vaulted ceiling behind the colonnades, the sea smuggled its own messages of light, for oceans have better memories for heat and day than does air. The glaciers, too, and seven tiny moons, all contributed their share of luminance.

And yet those three who ran laughing – they rejoiced in night, he, She, and she, rejoiced and lived for its qualities. Now they had reached the very end of the terrace, and rested against the last slender column, with its faded paintings of sorcerers and cephalopods. Their regard went first, instinctively, to the lapping waves, as if to penetrate beneath them and view the creatures who lay waiting in the depths, waiting for the appropriate season. They smiled wryly. They raised their heads. Together, they gazed across the auroral sea, watching great glaciers floating on pillows of their own cool breath. Dawn was coming. Dawn, without responding pallor in the sky.

Dawn, the magnet of life. Take their great eyes, set in faces pale, evanescent, baroque; inescapably, the gaze of those eyes was drawn to an iceberg that floated in the east. It lay on the deeps like a memorial to time itself. Its cliffs were of a remembered grey, sombre, stony . . . until the moment of dawn. Then the ice lit like a distant signal.

As a flower unfolds from its buds, revealing its voluptuous couchy pinks, the iceberg changed inward colour. The grey became dove-grey. The dove-grey turned chalk, turned to a tender pink wash, all promise.

Between day and night was no severance: their embrace was not to be prised apart by dawns such as this. As the sun rose further, as the iceberg, forgotten by its lamp-bearer, sank back into gloom, it was not radiance which changed but sound. The music ceased. Stale inside their satins, the musicians were stealing home.

The sun was just a point of pleading light, too far from anywhere to prevail. A pearl tossed into the sky would have cast more lustre.

The three turned away, he, She, and she. Very calm, they walked hand in hand upon the edge of the terrace, where the deep ammonias of the sea cast reflections like passing thought upon their countenances.

"Is it brighter?" she asked, referring to the Sun.

"Brighter than in our childhood," he replied.

"Brighter than yesterday, even," She said.

Now that the music of the night was hushed, the susurrus of ocean and air moved closer, speaking to them of the whole poignant fulcrum of existence. Overhead, a seabird sped between the high arches, coming from nothingness momentarily into the orbit of civilisation before it disappeared again into the void. At their feet, a concatenation of waves tossed spume on to the terrace, where it soon evaporated into space.

In the three of them moved an intense love for one another, so that they drew closer and walked like one. Not only was life short: far more touchingly, it was cyclic. The leaves that turned brown and died would spring up verdant again in many generations' time.

He said, "We are now so far from apogee."

She said, "The sun grows nearer, and nearer to the Time of Change."

And she said, "Our world has its set course – without a course there is no world."

Their silence was assent; but inside them, where things tangible met things intangible, was a great sense of awe, transcending joy or sorrow, as they considered the planetary motions within which their delicate part was cast. They were the life of their world; but on this world, all life was a mirror image. Two types of life – as different, as dependent, as yin and yang – existed . . . yet never met, yet never held converse, yet could not even breathe the other's atmosphere. Each type of life existed only in the death of the other. At the Time of Change, the centuries of being changed sentries.

So She said, "As a creature of apogee, I fear . . ."

To which she added, ". . . yet also perforce love, the creatures of perihelion."

Which he finished as, "For they and we together must form the sleeping and the waking of one Spirit."

They paused to look again across the rolling liquids, as if hoping for sight of that Spirit, before they made the decision to go inside their palace. In turning, they case their united gaze upon a broad flight of steps which led down from the terrace into the ocean. That was not their way to go. Other feet, of different shape and intent, would walk those steps, when the terrible Time of Change was past.

The steps were worn, their very grain obnubilated, as much by centuries as by tread. Many atmospheres, many oceans, had washed over them, as the world moved on its attenuated elliptical course. Small the world was, and a slave to its lethargic orbit; for in the course of one year, from the heats of perihelion to the cools of apogee and back again, not only lives but generations and whole civilisations underwent the cycle of birth and decay, birth and decay.

As the three looked at those broad steps leading down into the opaque fluids of the ocean, they held inside them the knowledge of what would happen in the spring of the year, when the sun showed a disc again and Change overthrew their kind.

Then the oceans would boil away in fury.

The tides would withdraw.

The steps would dry.

The palace – their palace – would be transformed, would stand revealed as merely the top floor of a mighty pyramid with many floors. The steps would lead down to the distant ground. That ground, no longer an ocean bed, lay over ten kilometres below.

All would be hushed after the storms of Change, except for the wail of atmosphere with its new winds.

Then the creatures of perihelion would muster themselves, and would begin to ascend the stairs. Under the blaze of the swollen sun, they would march up to this topmost place. In their own tongues, with their own gestures, they would obey their own deities.

Until the autumn came round again.

The three beings took firmer hold of each other and retired into the palace, to rest, to sleep, to dream.

(1977)

The Small Stones of Tu Fu

On the twentieth day of the Fifth Month of Year V of Ta-li (which would be May in AD 770, according to the old Christian calendar), I was taking a voyage down the Yangtze River with the aged poet Tu Fu.

Tu Fu was withered even then. Yet his words, and the spaces between his words, will never wither. As a person, Tu Fu was the most civilised and amusing man I ever met, which explains my long stay in that epoch. Ever since then, I have wondered whether the art of being amusing, with its implied detachment from self, is not one of the most undervalued requisites of human civilisation. In many epochs, being amusing is equated with triviality. The human race rarely understood what was important; but Tu Fu understood.

Although the sage was ill, and little more than a bag of bones, he desired to visit White King again before he died.

"Though I fear that the mere apparition of my skinny self at a place named White King," he said, "may be sufficient for that apparition, the White Knight, to make his last move on me."

It is true that white is the Chinese colour of mourning, but I wondered if a pun could prod the spirits into action; were they so sensitive to words?

"What can a spirit digest but words?" Tu Fu replied. "I don't entertain the idea that spirits can eat or drink – though one hears of them whining at keyholes. They are forced to lead a tediously spiritual life." He chuckled. This was even pronounced with spirit, for poor Tu Fu had recently been forced to give up drinking. When I mentioned that sort of spirit, he said, "Yes, I linger on life's balcony, ill and alone, and must not drink for fear I fall off."

Here again, I sensed that his remark was detached and not self-pitying, as some might construe it; his compassion was with all who aged and who faced death before they were ready – although, as Tu Fu himself remarked, "If we were not forced to go until we were ready, the world would be mountain-deep with the ill-prepared." I could but laugh at his turn of phrase.

When the Yangtze boat drew in to the jetty at White King, I helped the old man ashore. This was what we had come to see: the great white stones which progressed out of the swirling river and climbed its shores, the last of the contingent standing grandly in the soil of a tilled field.

I marvelled at the energy Tu Fu displayed. Most of the other passengers flocked round a refreshment-vendor who set up his pitch upon the shingle, or else climbed a belvedere to view the landscape at ease. The aged poet insisted on walking among the monoliths.

"When I first visited this district as a young scholar, many years ago," said Tu Fu, as we stood looking up at the great bulk towering over us, "I was naturally curious as to the origins of these stones. I sought out the clerk in the district office and enquired of him. He said, 'The god called the Great Archer shot the stones out of the sky. That is one explanation. They were set there by a great king to commemorate the fact that the waters of the Yangtze flow east. That is another explanation. They are purely accidental. That is a third explanation.' So I asked him which of these explanations he personally subscribed to, and he replied, 'Why, young fellow, I wisely subscribe to all three, and shall continue to do so until more plausible explanations are offered.' Can you imagine a situation in which caution and credulity, *coupled with extreme scepticism*, were more nicely combined?" We both laughed.

"I'm sure your clerk went far."

"No doubt. He had moved to the adjacent room even before I left his office. For a long while, I used to wonder about his statement that a great king had commemorated the fact that the Yangtze waters flowed east; I could only banish the idiocy from my mind by writing a poem about it."

I laughed. Remembrance dawned. I quoted it to him:

"I need no knot in my robe
To remember the Lady Li's kisses;
Small kings commemorate rivers
And are themselves forgotten."

"There is real pleasure in poetry," responded Tu Fu, "when spoken so beautifully and remembered so appositely. But you needed someone to prompt you."

"I was prompt to deliver, sir."

We walked about the monoliths, watching the waters swirl and curdle and fawn round the bases of a giant stone as they made their way through the gorges of the Yangtze down to the ocean. Tu Fu said that he believed the monoliths to be a memorial set there by Chu-ko Liang, demonstrating a famous tactical disposition by which he had won many battles during the wars of the Three Kingdoms.

"Are your reflections profound at moments like this?" Tu Fu asked, after a pause, and I reflected how rare it was to find a man, whether young or old, who was genuinely interested in the thoughts of others.

"What with the solidity of the stone and the ceaseless mobility of the water, I feel they should be profound. Instead, my mind is obstinately blank."

"Come, come," he said chidingly, "the river is moving too fast for you to expect any reflection. Now if it were still water . . ."

"It is still water even when it is moving fast, sir."

"There I must give you best, or give you up. But, pray, look at the gravels here and tell me what you observe. I am interested to know if we see the same things."

Something in his manner told me that more was expected of me than jokes. I looked along the shore, where stones of all kinds were distributed, from sands and grits to stones the size of a man's head, according to the disposition of current and tide.

"I confess I see nothing striking. The scene is a familiar one, although I have never been here before. You might come upon a little beach like this on any tidal river, or along the coasts by the Yellow sea."

Looking at him in puzzlement, I saw he was staring out across the flood, although he had confessed he saw little in the distance nowadays. Because I sensed the knowledge stirring in him, my role of innocent had to be played more determinedly than ever.

"Many thousands of people come to this spot every year," he said. "They come to marvel at Chu-Ko Liang's giant stones, which are popularly known as 'The Eight Formations', by the way. Of course, what is big is indeed marvellous, and the act of marvelling is very satisfying to the emotions, provided one is not called upon to do it every day of the year. But I marvel now, as I did when I first found myself on this spot, at a different thing. I marvel at the stones on the shore."

A light breeze was blowing, and for a moment I held in my nostrils the whiff of something appetising, a crab-and-ginger soup perhaps, warming at the food-vendor's fire further down the beach, where our boat was moored. Greed awoke a faint impatience in me, so that I thought, before humans are old, they should pamper their poor dear bodies, for the substance wastes away before the spirit, and was vexed to imagine that I had guessed what Tu Fu was going to say before he spoke. I was sorry to think that he might confess to being impressed by mere numbers. But his next remark surprised me.

"We marvel at the giant stones because they are unaccountable. We should rather marvel at the little ones because they are accountable. Let us walk over them." I fell in with him and we paced over them: first a troublesome bank of grits, which grew larger on the seaward side of the bank. Then a patch of almost bare sand. Then, abruptly, shoals of pebbles, the individual members of which grew larger until we were confronted with a pile of lumpy stones which Tu Fu did not attempt to negotiate. We went round it, to find ourselves on more sand, followed by well-rounded stones all the size of a man's clenched fist. And they in turn gave way to more grits. Our discomfort in walking – which Tu Fu overcame in part by resting an arm on my arm – was increased by the fact that these divisions of stones were made not only laterally along the beach but vertically up the beach, the demarcations in the latter division being frequently marked by lines of seaweed or of minute white shells of dead crustaceans.

"Enough, if not more than enough," said Tu Fu. "Now do you see what is unusual about the beach?"

"I confess I find it a tiresomely *usual* beach," I replied, masking my thoughts.

"You observe how all the stones are heaped according to their size."

"That too is usual, sir. You will ask me to marvel next that students in classrooms appear to be graded according to size."

"Ha!" He stood and peered up at me, grinning and stroking his long white beard. "But we agree that students are graded according to the wishes of the teacher. Now, according to whose wishes are all those millions upon millions of pebbles graded?"

"Wishes don't enter into it. The action of the water is sufficient, the action of the water, working ceaselessly and randomly. The playing, one may say, of the inorganic organ."

Tu Fu coughed and wiped the spittle from his thin lips.

"Although you claim to be born in the remote future, which I confess seems to me unnatural, you are familiar with the workings of this natural world. So, like most people, you see nothing marvellous in the stones hereabouts. Supposing you were born –" he paused and looked about him and upwards, as far as the infirmity of his years would allow " – supposing you were born upon the moon, which some sages claim is a dead world, bereft of life, women, and wine . . . If you then flew to this world and, in girdling it, observed everywhere stones, arranged in sizes as these are here. Wherever you travelled, by the coasts of any sea, you saw that the stones of the world had been arranged in sizes. What then would you think?"

I hesitated – Tu Fu was too near for comfort.

"I believe my thoughts would turn to crab-and-ginger soup, sir."

"No, they would not, not if you came from the moon, which is singularly devoid of crab-and-ginger soup, if reports speak true. You would be forced to the conclusion, the inevitable conclusion, that the stones of this world were being graded, like your scholars, by a superior Intelligence." He turned the collar of his padded coat up against the breeze, which was freshening. "You would come to believe that that Intelligence was obsessive, that its mind was terrible indeed, filled only with the idea – not of language, which is human – but of number, which is inhuman. You would understand of that Intelligence that it was under an interdict to wander the world measuring and weighing every one of a myriad single stones, sorting them all into heaps according to dimension. Meaningless heaps, heaps without even particular decorative merit. The further you travelled, the more heaps you saw – the myriad heaps, each containing myriads of stones – the more alarmed you would become. And what would you conclude in the end?"

Laughing, with some anger, I said, "That it was better to stay at home."

"Possibly. You would also conclude that it was *no use* staying at home. Because the Intelligence that haunted the earth was interested only in stones; that you would perceive. From which it would follow that the Intelligence would be hostile to anything else and, in particular, would be hostile to anything which disturbed its handiwork."

"Such as humankind?"

"Precisely." He pointed up the strand, where our fellow-voyagers were sitting on the shingle, or kicking it about, while their children were pushing stones into piles or flinging them into the Yangtze. "The Intelligence – diligent, obsessive, methodical to a degree – would come in no time to be especially weary of humankind, who were busy turning what is ordered into what is random."

Thinking that he was beginning to become alarmed by his own fancy, I said, "It is a good subject for a poem, perhaps, but nothing more. Let us return to the boat. I see the sailors are going aboard."

We walked along the beach, taking care not to disturb the stones. Tu Fu coughed as he walked.

"So you believe that what I say about the Intelligence that haunts the earth is nothing more than a fit subject for a poem?" he said. He stooped slowly to pick up a stone, fitting his other hand in the small of his back in order to regain an upright posture. We both stood and looked at it as it lay in Tu Fu's withered palm. No man had a name for its precise shape, or even for the fugitive tints of cream and white and black which marked it out as different from all its neighbours. Tu Fu stared down at it and improvised an epigram:

"The stone in my hand hides
A secret natural history:
Climates and times unknown,
A river unseen."

I held my hand out. "You don't know it, but you have released that stone from the bondage of space and time. May I keep it?"

As he passed it over, and we stepped towards the refreshment-vendor, Tu Fu said, more lightly, "We take foul medicines to improve our health; so we must entertain foul thoughts on occasion, to strengthen wisdom. Can you nourish no belief in my Intelligence – you, who claim to be born in some remote future – which loves stones but hates humankind? Do I claim too much to ask you to suppose for a moment that I might be correct in my supposition . . ." Evidently his thought wandered slightly, for he then said, after a pause, "Is it within the power of one man to divine the secret nature of the world, or is even the whisper of that wish a supreme egotism, punishable by a visitation from the White Knight?"

"Permit me to get you a bowl of soup, sir."

The vendor provided us with two mats to lay over the shingle. We unrolled them and sat to drink our crab-and-ginger soup. As he supped, with the drooling noises of an old man, the sage gazed far away down the restless river, where lantern sails moved distantly towards the sea, yellow on the yellow skyline. His previously cheerful, even playful mood had slipped from him; I could perceive that, at his advanced age, even the yellow distance might be a reminder to him – perhaps as much reassuring as painful – that he soon must himself journey to a great distance. I recited his epigram to myself. "Climates and times unknown, A river unseen."

Children played round us. Their parents, moving slowly up the gangplank on to the vessel, called to them. "Did you like the giant stones, venerable master?" one of the boys asked Tu Fu, cheekily.

"I liked them better than the battles they commemorate," replied Tu Fu. He stretched out a papery hand, and patted the boy's shoulder before the latter ran after his father. I had remarked before the way in which the aged long to touch the young.

We also climbed the gangplank. It was a manifest effort for Tu
Fu.

Dark clouds were moving from the interior, dappling the landscape with moving shadow. I took Tu Fu below, to rest in a little
cabin we had hired for the journey. He sat on the bare bench, in
stoical fashion, breathing flutteringly, while I thought of the battle
to which he referred, which I had paused to witness some centuries
earlier.

Just above our heads, the bare feet of the crew pattered on the
deck. There was a prolonged creaking as the gangplank was
hoisted, followed by the rattle of the sail unfolding. The wind
caught the boat, every plank of which responded to that exhala-
tion, and we started to glide forward with the Yangtze's great
stone-shaping course towards the sea. A harmony of motion
caused the whole ship to come alive, every separate part of it
rubbing against every other, as in the internal workings of a human
when it runs.

I turned to Tu Fu. His eyes went blank, his jaw fell open. One
hand moved to clutch his beard and then fell away. He toppled
forward – I managed to catch him before he struck the floor. In my
arms, he seemed to weigh nothing. A muttered word broke from
him, then a heavy shuddering sigh.

The White Knight had come, Tu Fu's spirit was gone. I laid him
upon the bench, looking down at his revered form with compassion. Then I climbed upon deck.

There, the crowd of travellers were standing at the starboard
side, watching the tawny coast roll by, and crying out with some
excitement. But they fell silent, facing me attentively when I called
to them.

"Friends," I shouted. "The great and beloved poet Tu Fu is
dead."

A first sprinkle of rain fell from the west, and the sun became
hidden by cloud.

Swimming strongly on my way back to what the sage called the
remote future, my form began to flow and change according to
time pressure. Sometimes my essence was like steam, sometimes
like a mountain. Always I clung to the stone I had taken from Tu
Fu's hand.

Back. Finally I was back. Back was an enormous expanse, yet but a corner. All humankind had long departed. All life had disappeared. Only the great organ of the inorganic still played. There I could sit on my world-embracing beach, eternally arranging and grading pebble after pebble. From fine grits to great boulders, they could all be sorted as I desired. In that occupation, I fulfilled the pleasures of infinity, for it was inexhaustible.

But the small stone of Tu Fu I kept apart. Of all beings ever to exist upon the bounteous face of this world, Tu Fu had been nearest to me – I say "had been", but he forever *is*, and I return to visit him when I will. For it was he who came nearest to understanding my existence by pure divination.

Even *his* comprehension failed. He needed to take his perceptions a stage further and see how those same natural forces which create stones also create human beings. The Intelligence that haunts the earth is not hostile to human beings. Far from it – I regard them with the same affection as I do the smallest pebble.

Why, take this little pebble at my side! I never saw a pebble like that before. The tint of this facet, here – isn't that unique?

I have a special bank on which to store it, somewhere over the other side of the world. Only the little stone of Tu Fu shall not be stored away; small kings commemorate rivers, and this stone shall commemorate the immortal river of Tu Fu's thought.

(1978)

Just Back from Java

The telephone was ringing in Morbey's study. In his dreams, the sound underwent a transformation. A brilliant bird was calling him, calling to his very spirit, through a tropical jungle. Then it invaded the building he was in, calling so stridently that he struck out at it – and woke up.

It might be his wife. More likely, it was his grandmother. Ludicrous fears filled him at these second thoughts, and he hastened down the corridor without stopping to throw a dressing-gown over his pyjamas. It was cold: he had a glimpse through the hall window of the night outside, with January's trees bare and crisp against a remorselessly starry sky.

He did not put on the light in his study, since a wedge of street lighting filtered obliquely through the north-facing window. Reaching for the phone, which stood on his desk, he knocked a pile of books onto the floor and heard something break.

"Hello, who is it?"

An old and quavering voice responded.

"Alan, I thought I ought to ring you. I thought you should know that water is rushing through the house. Isn't that a nuisance? I can't find where it is, although I've searched and searched. Perhaps it's in the roof somewhere. I wondered if you would get a ladder and go and see for me. I've been to fetch the ladder myself but it is a little too heavy for me. It's such a bother. I can hear it rushing at a terrible rate. It must have been pouring with rain all day, and I didn't notice. It's the fault of that gardener. He will leave the hose out."

Morbey switched on his desk light while his grandmother talked, by way of occupational therapy. His favourite china mug, which Maureen had bought him in Ludlow, lay smashed on the floor among scattered books. Dregs of coffee soaked into the carpet. He saw by his clock that it was seven minutes past two in the morning. Frost glittered on the garage roof outside.

"Granny dear," he said, shivering, clutching a cushion for warmth, "the night is perfectly fine and there has been no rain, I promise you. You should be in bed asleep. Didn't you take your sleeping pill?"

Muffled noises from the other end, as if she were trying to resite the telephone and its table in her bedroom.

"If you come round, Alan dear, you will hear the water for yourself. Perhaps a pipe has burst. It sounds like the Nile. We ought to stop it before it gets worse." She spoke tolerantly.

"The Nile's all in your head, Granny, all in your head. There really is no water. You cannot find anything wrong because nothing is wrong. Go back to bed, dear, and tuck in, or you'll be getting cold."

"If you say so, dear." She sounded doubtful, and he spent some minutes persuading her. When he put the phone down, he stood there thinking, prey to a familiar conflict of emotions.

She wanted him; whether the rushing water was real or not, her anxiety was real. She was ninety-three; perhaps at that age the passage of time took on a sound of beating wings. She needed him; that was what she was really saying. She was all alone in that bloody house of hers. Perhaps he had been too abrupt with her. In any case, there was no guarantee that she would comply with his wishes and return to bed.

Switching the light off, Morbey circumnavigated the disaster area and returned to his bedroom. He got into bed, still shivering, and switched on the bedside lamp. After a minute, he got out again and started dressing; he had to go and see that the old lady was safe. He feared more than she the Nile that threatened to bear her away.

The bedroom had been a breakfast room, in more spacious Edwardian days. Now the house was divided into two. Morbey rented the rear half, the Judges the front half. The fireplace had been filled in – no coal fires now – and an electric fire inserted in the grate. Morbey switched a bar on as he climbed into his trousers. On the mantelshelf stood half of a face, carved from grey volcanic stone and mounted on an oak plinth. It was the face of a Buddha, the left-hand side of the face. The ear was there, some of the stylised hair, the smooth and extraordinary cheek, part of a serene mouth, not quite smiling, and a clearly defined eye, oval and drawn out at the corner. The eye regarded Alan Morbey fixedly, without hostility but in a way that penetrated all his shams to the centre of his being.

The half-face had no nose. Morbey had acquired the smaller half of the face. Somewhere in the undergrowth of Central Java, the other, larger half of the face lay, awaiting a miracle that would render it whole again.

The Buddha, in his undivided days, had adorned the grandest holy place in all South East Asia, the great temple of Borobudur. For centuries, jungle had covered the ruins. Now the Indonesian government was restoring Borobudur, with UNESCO aid. This ancient eye, this element, had come West to watch over Alan Morbey.

Morbey underwent his familiar routine of self-scrutiny, liking it no more this time than before, feeling that the Buddha understood all his weaknesses. On the one hand, it was bloody good of him, a lecturer in geology now in his forties, a busy man with plenty to do in college, to turn out at two in the morning to go and comfort a senile old woman who lived ten miles away. On the other hand, it was weak of him to be so tied to her, and he was going to see her only because his conscience nagged him, telling him that he should make better arrangements for the old lady.

He dressed and went out to the garage which he shared with the Judges, while the self-catechism continued. The cold was bitter. As he dragged open the garage doors, grating them over the gravel of the narrow driveway, he saw that Candy Judge's bedroom light was still burning. Candy Judge, twenty-two or some similar absurd age, part-time punk, idler, whore, terrible girl. Vamp. That old-fashioned word – vamp. He had once felt her left breast. He thought of it now, comforting himself with the memory of its shape, so plump and nutritious. It was amazing how exactly he could recall its shape, although the occasion had been over a year ago, after Maureen left him.

His grandmother's house stood on the other side of the university town. At this silent hour of night, with no traffic in the streets, he drove easily through the centre, through the university area which, in its stone slumber, heaved shoulders and spires and minarets and domes like Candy's breast up towards the chilled stars. A poor English replica of the stone mountain of Borobudur, he thought.

When he turned on the car radio, some young fool was shouting, "I ain't gonna stand and moan no more." Morbey left him on for a minute, before telling himself that he did not have to listen to such noises if he did not wish. He drove the rest of the way in silence, dreaming of jungles and warm nights.

His grandmother's house was the last house in Convent Hill Road. She had lived there for forty years, being widowed for thirty-five of them. The house had stood alone in its grounds, with fields round it. In the fifties, semi-detacheds had climbed up the hill to Grandmother's gates. All the semis appeared deserted at present. Not a light showed anywhere. He saw that as he turned into his grandmother's drive lights burned in several windows of the old house.

The unintended welcome gladdened him. He nodded with approval. Belle Ravens had more life in her than anyone else in the street. Impending death made her defy the middle-class conventions of sleep.

The garage door was open and a naked electric lightbulb burned overhead. He saw the wooden ladder to which she had referred over the phone standing at the far end by the rusting lawnmower. Leaving the light to burn, he went to the front door, inserted his latchkey, and entered the house.

"Gran!" he called.

His grandmother slept downstairs nowadays, to avoid climbing the stairs. A bedroom had been improvised at the back of the house, in a room which, before the Morbey and Ravens families were scattered by death and travel, had served as the dining-room. Now there were commodes and wardrobes among the dressers and sideboards.

There was no answer to his call. The chill of the house got to him as he listened. Lights burned upstairs. He started to search the house.

His grandmother was in a room upstairs which had served as a bedroom for old Nurse Donnally, until old Nurse Donnally had died last October. She leaned against an overturned chair, most of her body sprawled over the floor. Her eyes were closed, her mouth open. She wore fluffy red bedroom slippers, an old blue night-dress, and nothing else. Her arms and face were extremely pallid and splotched with brown. Morbey ran to kneel by her, and put an arm round her. She felt very cold.

Belle Ravens, Alan Morbey's maternal grandmother, who had outlived not only her husband but her sisters, her brother, two sons and a daughter – Alan's mother – had travelled very lightly into her ninety-fourth year. Never of substantial build, she was in age little but flesh and bone. Her face and her torso and her legs were amazingly wrinkled; Morbey remained shocked at the extent and complexity, the over-elaboration, of the wrinkled skin, as he lifted his grandmother and carried her downstairs to her bed. She began panting uncomfortably.

"Don't try to speak. Just lie quiet and try to get warm. It's foolish of you to wander about the house – and outside – with no clothes on on such a cold night, isn't it?"

He tucked her into her large double bed and switched on the electric blanket. After standing looking pensively down at her, he went into the kitchen and switched on the kettle to make a cup of tea. Then he patrolled the house, turning off lights. As he did so, he conducted his self-interrogation.

This was the second time in a fortnight that he had been up at Convent Hill in the middle of the night, summoned like a doctor to the sick. Did he mind that? No, not as far as he knew. He felt he ought to mind it, that some people would mind it, but not he. Did he mean that *normal* people would mind it? Not necessarily.

Did he mind having to deal with this ancient lady, to associate so closely with deterioration? No, not as far as he knew. As far as he knew, he was glad to help her, although he was not able to offer much more than he was called upon to give: they had a truce there, old Belle and he, born of long acquaintanceship. Each knew the other better than anyone else on earth knew them. For instance, only once had she requested him to come and live in the house with her; that was when the old nurse-companion, Mary Donnally, had died. When refusing, he had given as a reason his reluctance to leave his own house in case Maureen returned.

Did he mind that his grandmother monopolised his life? Well, you couldn't call it monopolising. He liked seeing her. Besides, his life was so empty at present. She filled it, in a way. You had to care for someone. Wouldn't some people – the Judges, for instance – call the relationship rather a morbid one? Who cared what they thought? Also: who was there to give a fig, or any other fruit, for his relationship with his poor old grandmother? It was, after all, a relationship based on love and duty and compassion, all qualities in which he believed.

But did he mind, he asked himself, this whole situation, which some would surely regard as entrapping, by which it had fallen out that he alone was at hand to accompany this ageing woman through her last years?

As he went out to the garage to close it up, listening to his footsteps on the frosty ground, he pondered the question. Of course, he was able to pay his ageing relative so much attention only because his life was such a vacuum at present; but, given that fact, no, he could not say he minded.

Frankly, he minded very little these days, he was in a state of not-minding. He just did what had to be done, in college, or at Convent Hill. Since there was nothing to enjoy in life – he hated admitting that to himself – nothing but the odd left tit – there seemed also nothing to dislike. Indifference was all. And when his grandmother was well, he had to admit that there was a sort of sunset pleasure in discoursing with her and listening to her anecdotes of long ago. As Thomas Carlyle said, the past was safe.

When he took the cup of tea in to her, Belle Ravens' flesh was a more natural colour. "Have you been upstairs?" she asked.

"I've put all the lights off. What were you doing, wandering about? You know you have a tendency to hypothermia."

"Oh, I was warm enough, if that's what you're worrying about."

It was time to deliver his standard lecture on hypothermia. As he did so, he wondered if she was aware what the time was; after all, time of day mattered very little to her.

When his little lecture was finished, she said, "I suppose I shall have to phone someone to come and look at the roof. I can't think why the gardener hasn't been this week."

He sat on the side of the bed and held her seamed hand. "You sacked old Spinks three years ago, Gran. Remember?"

"So I did. You know, Alan, his wife said to me once, 'Mrs Ravens, I don't think I could bear marriage if it wasn't that we had a dog as well.' I've never forgotten it. She got very fat." Belle laughed.

"Are you going to be all right? Don't want the doctor?"

"What do I want the doctor for? He only gives me pills. You might ring a man to come and look at the roof. Ring straightaway." She grinned at him, mischievously.

"Granny, the roof's just fine. All that rushing water was in your head. Really. The house is as dry as a bone."

"If you say so, dear."

"You've got to get some sleep now."

"Bless you for looking after me the way you do. The roof can wait till the morning – it's all this heavy rain that does it. You will come and see me tomorrow if you can spare the time?"

The row of slender prunus trees Belle Ravens had planted during World War II had grown year by year. They spread along the side of the house, reaching out to other trees along the boundary fence, creating damp conditions. Their fallen leaves were left to moulder from one year to the next. Occasionally, Morbey would make an effort and rake them into a far corner of the lawn. He backed the car slowly along by the trees and headed out of the gate, down Convent Hill Road.

His grandmother lived in, as the phrase carelessly had it, a world of her own; she had suffered what Dr Dalton termed a minor ischaemic episode, and would probably recover – as she had recovered before – thanks to her amazing constitution and will-power. The rainstorms were fantasy, though strongly supported by the evidence of her senses; who could doubt that in the brain stem, where the hurricanes of thrombosis occurred, monsoons of blood took place?

Driving slowly downhill, scrutinising the blank windows of the semi-detached houses, he saw a light come on in a downstairs room. Who was it? What was going through their minds? His own fantasy, which he now brought out and held before his intellectual gaze, had had far less foundation in reality than his grandmother's. He had expected that, one night, when he was succouring Belle, a neighbour had arrived, coming to see what was wrong and if she could help. *She*, of course, you poor fool. Late thirties, rather smart, dark hair, energetic, willing to do anything for anyone.

Recently widowed. Husband left her. Unhappily married. Just back from Java. And after she and Morbey had put Belle to bed, she invited him back to her snug little house down the hill for a cup of instant coffee. She and Alan got along famously, laughing in the kitchen. She looked good without her coat, good figure, rather over-large breasts. Not an intellectual woman like Maureen; no degrees, no interest whatsoever in studying the Anglo-Saxon legal system or being chairman of the local neighbourhood committee or the sports centre, no ambitions to collect Victorian biscuit tins or to review for the *TLS*, no obsession with college dinner parties, no nonsense with speaking on behalf of the Conservatives or going out to Kampuchea to see for herself what was happening there. No prejudice against television or Morecambe and Wise. A rather ordinary woman, but warm-hearted, humorous, and pleasantly ready for what she jokingly called a bit of slap-and-tickle.

Etc. He pondered the paradox that even while his intellect inspected this bit of hokum with disfavour, he enjoyed it and adorned it with extra detail. They got on so well together that he chucked in his post, to the horror of the principal, who publicly admitted that Alan Morbey's work had been undervalued, and went off together on a long trip to see Java and, more especially, Borobudur. He sighed.

When he got back to his house, Candy's light was out. He entered silently by his door and went straight to his bedroom. Back in bed, he lay wide awake for a long time, unable to decide what he was thinking about or how he felt, if he felt anything. He also wondered if he was insane. As usual, he came to no conclusions.

Although, or perhaps because, Morbey disliked cats, they often came and sat on his knee. The Judges had a tabby cat called Sianouk, a sly emitter of concentrated bowel gas, one cubic inch of which was sufficient, if expanded, to poison a whole room. It climbed upon Morbey's knee as he accepted Laura Judge's invitation to sit down.

Edward Judge fiddled about in a cupboard of the large dresser which dominated the Judge's front room. He was, as they all knew, looking for drink and, as they also knew, the selection was limited to a popular brand of whisky and an unpopular brand of pale dry sherry. But E. H. Judge, Professor of Oriental Studies, made the quest look as if he was rifling through an ancient tomb for the birth certificate of the Buddha himself. At last he emerged with a bottle in his hand.

"Ah, whisky, Alan, would you care for some whisky?"

"That's sherry, darling," his wife said. Laura Judge, in her mid-fifties, was an elegant lady, her pale yellow and white hair piled in a bun at the back of her neck. She wore a violet velvet dress and stockings of an almost similar hue. As if in imitation, her husband wore baggy corduroy trousers which were nearly violet.

He removed his spectacles and peered closely at the label of the bottle.

"Yes, lucky dip, sherry, so it is, the luck of the draw. We're rumoured to possess whisky also, Bell's best, somewhere within this commode cribbed and confined, if you'd prefer."

"Sherry'd be fine," Morbey said, removing a set of cat claws from his thigh.

"Sure you wouldn't prefer whisky? It's no trouble. Well, not much." Judge made a stingy gesture of largesse, spreading his arms, then closing them too quickly, as if miming "scissors" in some donnish party game.

"Sherry, thanks, Edward."

Muttering to himself, Professor Judge poured three glasses of sherry.

Edward and Laura frequently invited Morbey in to their half of the house for an evening drink and a chat – both of their rather idiosyncratic vintage. It was kind of them. They were both busy university people, with little time to themselves. Even on this occasion, a very poor specimen of a student was present, awaiting attention, sitting uncomfortably in one of the large armchairs, clutching an untidy sheaf of papers and books and drumming on his knee with a spare hand.

As he handed the brimming sherry glasses round, Judge gave a small start to indicate that he had just noticed the student.

"Dear, Pristone, I'd forgotten you. You'll have a sherry, too, won't you?"

The student stopped drumming. "Whisky for me, please, Professor Judge."

"Sorry, we've run out of whisky, foolish of me. Have a sherry, go on. It's coming back into fashion, so you'll be OK. A swinging sherry, eh?"

As he was providing Pristone with a glass, he said to Morbey, "Do you know what I read in a Chinese encyclopaedia today? If you make your bed of bracken, the rats can't get at you. They can't gnaw through the bracken because it ruins their teeth. Do you think that's true?"

"An old wives' tale," Laura said, laughing.

"I thought you might know, as a geologist," Judge said, ignoring his wife and appealing to Morbey. "The Chinese are often right in these small matters. Very practical people, the Chinese. I noticed last year, when I was in Kunming, that the men who pedalled the trishaws for hire always carried umbrellas . . ."

He launched into a long anecdote which illustrated his own and the trishaw driver's perspicacity in roughly equal amounts. Quite amusing, thought Morbey, sipping his sherry. He liked Judge and his wife, and was able to like them and their mannerisms more now that Maureen was off-stage. With her, he had made fun of the Judges; she had found E.H. irritating, whereas Morbey enjoyed the man's intermittent sense of humour.

". . . it just shows the Chinese passion for secrecy. Their complex script announces that secrecy to the world. Even there, as you probably know, Alan, there are four sorts of script, the standard form, the small seal script, the bronze script, and grass script, together with a special form used for chops, their official seals."

"What would you say was the predominant English passion?" Laura enquired of the company. She had not gone with her husband on the China tour.

"Melancholy, without a doubt," Morbey said. "We've been famous for melancholy, hypochondriasis, the spleen, gloom, and general depression since Elizabethan and Jacobean times. What's our greatest tourist attraction? The deeply morose Tower of London."

"Shakespeare wasn't too gloomy," Laura said.

"I never found his jokes very amusing, I must say," Judge admitted.

"Webster, Burton, Milton – not a chuckle in the whole of *Paradise Lost*. Hardy, Margaret Drabble."

At that moment Candy Judge entered the room. News of her

arrival had preceded her, in the form of a general banging about, upstairs first, and then, accompanied by a sort of hopeful swearing, pitched to arouse compassion, or at least fury, in a mother's heart, along the hallway. Candy had dyed one half of her short-cropped hair blonde, the other half pink. The pink half stood up in spikes. A safety-pin was stuck through the lobe of one ear. She wore a type of shiny black jeans and a black satin blouse. There was a dog collar round her neck. A swastika was pinned over the breast Morbey had once fondled, a Snoopy badge over the breast he had still to tackle.

"I cannot find my poxing bloody boots," she said, discovering them, even as she spoke, on the top of the piano. They were black with sharp heels. Grabbing them, she disappeared again, leaving the door into the hall wide open.

Maintaining the flow of the conversation, such as it was, Laura, rising to close the door with a gracious wave of the hand which invited the company to assume it had never been opened, said, "I hope you are not suffering unduly from melancholy at present, Alan. It is tiresome of Maureen to stay away so long, but you may have to resign yourself to the fact that eventually there is a . . . well, a tide in the affairs of men which reaches the point of no return."

"What Laura is trying to say, with such ludicrous finesse," Judge said, "is that, as a student of human nature, she opines – and said as much to me at breakfast only this morning –"

"Yesterday, dear, at supper."

"– that Maureen, having flown the nest these many months, is probably fixed up now with another chap. She may not care to tell you as much, for reasons good or ill, compassionate or financial. I don't know your arrangements. Or of course the chap may be someone of whom she is vaguely ashamed. I read somewhere that absconding wives in retreat from a situation where they have been civilised and respectable, often opt for dreadful companions: criminals, black Africans, Welshmen, or the traditional army captain."

He peered over his glasses suspiciously at Laura, as if she were bound to admit that she had several army captains to her credit.

"The thought has crossed my mind, of course," Morbey said. "Would you mind not drumming, old boy, while we are holding this rather personal conversation? My wife has absented herself from felicity awhile, as the previous remarks may have given you to understand, and my nerves are in consequence somewhat unsettled."

The student, to whom this last remark had been addressed, rounded off the drumming and slipped his hand into his pocket, keeping it well out of Morbey's range. He said, "I didn't know I *was* drumming. I'm sorry if it disturbed you. I don't usually do it, as a matter of fact. It's just a habit I've got into recently – I mean, I've noticed it myself, ever since last term. It indicates strain."

"It indicates a desire to masturbate in public, if our psycho-therapeutic friends are to be believed," Judge said, with a snort of laughter. "Anyhow, Alan; Laura and I worry about you, don't we, Laura, and we –"

"We worry about you in the nicest possible way, Alan, you know, non-inquisitively, and simply as old friends and neigh-bours. You cut yourself off from others too much, you isolate yourself, when –"

"To hell with the amateur psychiatry," Judge said. "We think you ought to fuck some girls."

"What's that if not amateur psychiatry?" Laura asked him.

"That's the real professional stuff, my dear. Fucking, 'getting laid', in today's pathetic jargon, which when I was young denoted something which happened only to paving and a few foundation stones, is a great healer. It would probably solve your troubles too, Pristone, take my word for it. Supposing Maureen does come trooping back sooner or later, well, you'll need to keep in practice for that event, won't you?"

He looked over his spectacles at Morbey with some humour, to see how his advice was going down.

"Fornication's a bit like swimming, you know, Edward," Mor-bey said. "Once you have learnt how to do it, you never forget." He had observed in himself the feeble way he so easily fell into the Judge style of diction when he was in their company. Recalling other sports, he added, "It's as easy as falling off a bicycle."

"Not as painful, surely," Laura protested. "What would you say, Mr Pristone?"

"Trouble is, I've got a bike. I haven't got a girl at the mo'."

"Ah-ha, you should padlock them up, the way you do your bike," Judge said. "I suppose I shall have to offer you all another sherry. Courtesy demands no less."

"Thanks, but I'm off," said Morbey, rising slowly from his chair so that Sianouk fell off bit by bit, digging its claws into Morbey's kneecaps as it went. At least the repulsive creature had proved incapable, this evening, of bracketing the room with one of its high-impact farts. "I must go and visit my illustrious grand-parent."

Laura rose and laid a delicate finger on his sleeve. "We also, Edward and I, at the supper he just failed to mention, talked with some concern about your illustrious grandparent."

Smiling back at her, Morbey asked, "And what was the consensus of your opinion, over this semi-mythical meal?"

"To be candid, we thought either that the old lady was a defensive construct on your part, a smoke-screen behind which you were – to use another expression which Edward dislikes – *having it off* secretly, perhaps with a dear friend of ours. Or, that the old lady monopolised your time to the point where you had no time to have it off to any noticeable degree."

"Which particular dear friend of yours did you have in mind?" Morbey asked, thinking that any dear friend of theirs might become a dear friend of his.

"In other words," Judge said, pouring himself another sherry with some show of deliberately not doing it surreptitiously, "is this melancholy to which you lay claim induced by the company of that senile old hag of a grandmother, or just a cloak beneath which you operate amorously? We're fairly keen to find out, if you don't mind spilling the beans."

"I'd have thought that was another expression you'd dislike," Morbey said, heading for the door. "I presume it is also trans-atlantic. Meanwhile, I must ask you to leave my grandparent alone whilst I keep her company. And thanks for the sherry."

As he was closing the door, Laura said to her husband, "And not a bean was spilt."

His grandmother preferred men in ties, so he went to his bedroom to put one on before going to the car. Avoiding his face in the mirror, he looked at the half-face of the Buddha of Borobudur on the mantelshelf. The profile promised serenity and, by the curl of the corner of the mouth, fecundity.

"Fecundity," Morbey said to himself aloud, savouring the

word; the most barren life was fecund compared with what was to come.

The invisible side of the stone face, the side that still lay hidden in the muds of Central Java, was threatening by its mere absence. Ever since Morbey had bought the half-face from an Australian in Jogjakarta, he had worried as to whether it was a good idea to possess half a Buddha, whether the symbolism was not malign.

Uneasily, he pushed his thoughts to recall the pleasant Hotel Trio, run by efficient Chinese, in Jogjakarta. That was where the deal had taken place. He had been invited to Borobudur by UNESCO, to survey the ground before the major work of reconstruction took place on that ancient stone mountain.

It had been a pleasant hotel, he thought, getting his car keys out as he approached the garage. Those weeks in Java had been the best time in his life, in some ways. No worries. It ill repaid the Javanese to come away with half of a stolen Buddha's face in his baggage. Typical Western swinishness, he told himself. He had returned home to discover, slowly, his wife's involvement with – whoever it had been. Most probably old Judge was right: a crooked black Welsh army captain . . .

He had slept on the site some nights, under the brow of Borobudur. Cones of ancient volcanoes guarded the valley. Mist lay in strata across the ornate terraces, lit by a moon that sailed dangerously among the stupas. Marvellous, marvellous, he told himself, a cosmic Max Ernst. The energy that the modern world expended in restoring that ancient monument was also marvellous. He was powerfully moved by the project.

A different music came to him, disco music, with little twitchy bitch voices going "Bop, bop, bop," as if their teeth were made of tinsel and their throats of bubblegum. He had left the car radio on, it seemed. He climbed in, and switched the radio off. The Nolan Sisters might be in the mood for dancing, but he was not.

"Hello, Alan," Candy said, as he started the car.

With the headlights on, he looked back and saw her, illumined strangely by the reflections off the inside of the garage. Her face shone. It was thin and pallid, but young. Age had yet to damage it. Morbey checked momentarily to find out if he was in another fantasy.

"Sorry, are you into the Nolan Sisters?" He believed it was called "keeping your cool", not to exclaim in surprise.

She climbed over into the front of the car with him, sharp boots first, black-clad legs, smart little bottom, torso. The Snoopy badge slid by within an inch of his shoulder.

"Thought I'd give you a surprise. You're not stroppy, are you?"

"I'm pleased to see you." He moved slowly out of the drive and down the road. Whatever was going to happen – nothing would, knowing his luck – he saw immediately that it was more likely to happen where Professor and Mrs E. H. Judge could not interfere.

"Where you going?"

"Where are *you* going?"

"Oh, just out, you know. Mum worries if I hang about the house. We could go for a ride."

"I've got to visit my aged grandmother. I always do, every evening about this time."

"Fancy you having a grandmother! It sounds daft. Both my grandmas are dead and buried. Anyhow, you drove out in the middle of last night. I heard you, because my bedroom's on the garage side of the house. I bet you weren't off to see your granny then. Where were you going?"

The home-going traffic was thick, and they became caught in a slow-moving queue.

"You've been discussing my problems with your parents, I see."

"It's only friendly. Everyone needs some excitement, don't they? I never did like your wife, anyway, if you must know. You want to get someone else, cheer you up." She slipped an arm through his and cuddled against him. "Do you want to feel my breasts again?"

"What do you mean, 'again'? I've only ever felt one of them."

She grinned up at him from under magenta eyelids. "Go on then, have a go now, while we're stuck in this traffic jam."

Keeping his left hand on the steering wheel, he leant over and thrust his right hand into the satin blouse. Her right breast was every bit as pleasant as its predecessor, and perhaps a little sharper at the point. He moved to the other for comparison. Both were deliciously warm and firm. She did not wear a bra, or not on her punk days.

"Jolly good," he said. "I can't think when I liked the feel of anything so much."

"You haven't seen anything yet."

He kept his hand on the left breast, even as they moved slowly up London Road. It was still his favourite. The delicate nipple rested between his index and middle finger. Despite the tightness in his trousers, he could not stop himself wondering why she had suddenly decided to show an interest in him, after months of indifference.

"That feels just lovely, Candy. I'd like to get at it properly, and the rest of you. But I can't help worrying about your motives . . . You know, I enjoy a vivid fantasy life. When things like this happen in fantasy, there's no reason to worry about motivation – motivation is the enemy of fantasy. Because I've recently been having problems with motivation – my own, I mean, as well as other people's – I think I'd better stick to fantasy, thanks."

"Oh, we all have fantasies. But fantasy is only half a life."

He withdrew his hand, pressed it against his lips and nose, then applied it to the steering wheel, as the traffic speeded up.

"At present, mine *is* only half a life. Sorry."

After a silence, she said, "Go on, are you really on your way to your granny's?"

He nodded. "I'm just going to stop at a shop and get her some flowers. They've got tulips now, a sign of spring for the old lady. She may not live that long."

Depressed, he thought, it will be a relief when she dies and I don't have this responsibility; yet I'll miss her so much. How is it I've gone on this half-life trip, as Candy would say? The curse of the Buddha . . . Her death seems to be hanging over me . . . Here's Candy offering me life – somewhat ambivalently, I'm sure, but ambivalence is part of life. Only death monopolises certainty.

They drew off the road and stopped at the modest row of shops where a greengrocer-cum-florist remained open to catch the home-bound trade, hopeful suitors, grateful lovers, faithless husbands, dutiful grandsons . . . As Morbey jumped out of the car on one side, Candy jumped out on the other.

"I've got a friend round the corner, I'm going to see her. Thanks for the lift – see you. Tarr-ra!"

"Candy, it really is my gran!" He watched her spiky part-coloured head disappear among the pedestrians on the pavement. There had been no resentment in her tone. What did she think? Was she disgusted with him? Was it better or worse for him to prove to her that he was only going to see his gran?

Maybe he should have persuaded her to come along too; Belle would have enjoyed her company, if she was well enough today.

Of course, she could be lying dead in her front room when he got there.

"A dozen tulips," he said.

Alan Morbey drove slowly up Convent Hill, keeping a sharp eye open to left and right for the possible fantasy woman. Late thirties, rather smart, dark hair, energetic, willing to do anything for anyone. Recently widowed. Just back from Java. Nobody answering that description was in sight. Indeed, the only person visible at all was a youth in a green pullover looking under the bonnet of a Ford Capri painted four colours, and he was probably a Libyan. One of Colonel Gaddafi's men. "His green pullover gave him away," stated Mr Alan Morbey in court later.

He pulled into his grandmother's drive and climbed out of the car.

The house badly needed repairs. It was easy to distinguish houses occupied by old people. Their paint was flaking like skin, their tiles were coming off the roof, and all the downpipes were choked.

He inserted his latchkey and entered the house. Cold and silence greeted him in the hall.

"Gran!" he called.

No answer came, not her usual cheerful response.

"Gran!" This time more a statement than an interrogation. He went through to the back of the house, to her downstairs bedroom which had once been the dining-room.

She was lying in her bed with her pillows neat behind her grey head and her hands relaxed on the turned-down sheet. Her mouth was stretched open and her eyes were closed.

Dropping the tulips, he ran forward and grasped her hand, apprehension gripping his heart. It was cold as stone.

"Oh, Gran, don't be dead!" Immediately, the whole world

turned to stone. The light lost all its luminance, the room became infinitely gloomy and sinister in a way he would not have believed possible. Even more terribly, he saw that his future was lopped off, like a chunk of salami. He was now himself in the forward firing-line, and he crouched there awaiting a burst of celestial machine-gun fire.

He was scarcely surprised when the celebrated popular singer, Cliff Richard, appeared on the other side of the bed, strolling along perkily and regarding Morbey with a somewhat condescending grin.

"Your gran's dead, then, at last," Cliff Richard said, cheerfully.

"What do you mean, 'at last'? Her life seemed very short to her. One more day, just one more day would have been welcome to her. Decrepit as she was, she enjoyed every minute of life."

"Don't sound bitter. How about a song, if you like, to cheer you up?"

"Thanks, I don't feel like singing."

"No, I didn't mean *you* have to sing, stupid, I meant that I'd sing."

"Sorry I don't feel like listening to singing."

"Not even 'Congratulations'?"

"Especially not 'Congratulations'."

Morbey rose from the bedside rather distractedly, thinking that he now had a number of things he should set about, though none actually came to mind, chiefly because he was rather puzzled by the unannounced arrival of the popular singer.

"Is there something I can do?" Cliff Richard asked.

"I suppose you could phone the doctor."

Cliff laughed boyishly. "The doctor won't be able to do her any good, believe you me. Your gran's dead. I'm the only one who can do anything now. Go on, be imaginative, try me. What can I do?"

It felt to Morbey that he was totally enshrouded in a grey area, from which he stared helplessly at the youthful, lined face on the other side of the bed. The death of Belle Ravens had caused time to solidify, leaving him alone with her, stranded on a shoal from which it was impossible to wade ashore to the old world he had known before he dropped the tulips. He could feel the longing on his own face as he strove to reach out towards some kind of response. Nothing came. His skin was flaking like old paint, his hair was coming away like tiles, and all his downpipes were choked.

"Uhhh . . ."

"How's about the Nolan Sisters?" Cliff Richard asked. He did some neat little steps about the room, holding out his hands, snapping his fingers, singing "I'm in the Mood for Dancing". He was a natty little mover.

To Morbey came a vision of the bright tinsel world of pop that Cliff Richard was holding out for him, compounded of all those easy sub-musical resolutions, all those simple words and rhymes about parting and everlasting love and finding the one true love, all the fake philosophising over lust – what E. H. Judge had referred to once in Kantian terms as "the *Ding-a-ling-an-sich*" – all the trivialising of viscerally real phenomena. And that bright tinsel world revealed itself to him as a sort of bubble of death within life, swallowing young people, robbing them of felt feelings almost as effectively as death.

"Stop it!" he shouted. "If you're not here to torment me merely, then give me something real, anything, but not the Nolan Sisters."

Cliff Richard came neatly to a halt, gave a twirl, bowed to unheard applause, and manifested a breast.

The breast was of modest proportions, definitely female, pleasantly plump about its rotund base, with a delightful convex curve upward from the nipple. The aureole was slight, the nipple itself pink and cheeky. It was, as Morbey immediately recognised, Candy Judge's left breast. It floated just in front of him, hanging like a peach on a tree. When he reached out to it, it was warm. He kissed it reverently, pressing his nose against it.

The breast gave him courage, and brought his thoughts out of the grey jelly into which they had congealed. He worried about Candy. Was she somewhere with a friend, and suddenly utterly discomfited to find one of her breasts missing; or was this transcendent moment happening beyond the normal parameters of space, time, and brassieres? He hoped so.

Hearing his voice tremble, he said, "Am I alive or dead? If you're who I think you are, why use the persona of Cliff Richard? Why not reveal yourself as you really are?"

The room shuddered and grew dark. Cliff Richard gave an athletic prance, smiled a self-deprecating smile, raised his arms as if at the conclusion of an act, and darkled into nothingness. The nothingness spread at a remorseless rate. In the middle of it appeared a naked man. The man was small, olive-skinned, stocky, and quite as alert in his movements as Cliff Richard had been. He wore tight-fitting bracelets at ankles and wrists. He performed a dance, curious but menacing, with his feet raising high. There was only one side to his face. It spoilt his looks.

Shaking all over, Morbey reached for a chair and sank into it. He could hardly hold himself together. Now he understood the Cliff Richard manifestation; the familiar is always less frightening than the unknown.

"I sort of imagined you with a white beard and a flowing robe," he faltered, attempting to think how wittily Judge would have passed off this terrifying moment.

The god said, "Morbey, you poor anxious creature, how silly I'd look in that sort of garb in Borobudur. Pull yourself together and ask for whatever you want, if not the Nolan Sisters."

"I just want my grandmother back. For her sake."

"Don't be stupid. She's had her natural term and more. She died happy. Ask for something for yourself. How about your wife back? Or Candy, delivered naked and whole? Not just one lousy breast."

Sudden suspicion filled Morbey. "So often, when I've been researching, or occupied with a geological question, or something really important, I've suddenly found myself thinking about sex. Was that your influence? Can't you think about anything but sex?"

The god suddenly executed a few lascivious dance steps, light, predatory, clipped, erotic. "First things first and last."

"You don't help a bit. You are simply teasing me."

"I'm taking your mind off your bereavement. Don't you see that you suffer in hell every day, simply because you will not want anything for yourself, because if you allowed yourself to want it you'd reach out and grab it? And your silly restrictive culture forbids wanting and reaching out and grabbing because such things are reckoned impolite. So all the time you are settling for half of what you might have. Why, you even settled for half my face."

Behind the blackness, music was tinkling and booming, like an ocean driven mad by its own shoals of fish. The mutilated god was green now, the colour of ancient bronze, his flesh speckled as he darted this way and that among stylised vegetation. Morbey was completely disoriented, or reoriented, or cisoriented, or at any rate, as far as he could tell, was back in the Orient – *Zurück im Morgenland* was a phrase that occurred to him – because he distinctly saw, through a thicket of rattan and palm, the familiar terraces of Borobudur. A lot of people were dancing there, fleet, *svelte*, carnal.

"Half a god's face? Isn't that enough?" he was laughing rather stridently, triumphant at being able to answer the god back – though, truth to tell, the god was rapidly becoming less interested in him, as the music took hold and the smooth muscular figure threw itself into a provocative dance.

"Is it enough? You can choose . . ." The throwaway line was delivered as the god pranced off, moving rhythmically up and down the terraces with dark sunlight running like molten gold from his body. But that remark, more than any of the other casual remarks the god had made, sank through to Morbey. Perhaps he could choose.

The god's dance once more brought him close to Gran's bed. Music seemed to pour from his outstretched, vibrating hands, which moved so rapidly that his fingertips could not be seen.

As if she could no longer bear to lie still while such compelling music was playing, Belle Ravens suddenly flung back her bed-clothes and jumped out of bed. She wore her old blue nightdress. She ran up to the god and they began to dance together, not touching each other.

Nymphs with sloe Eastern eyes executed pliant steps behind the shimmering god. E. H. Judge and his wife arrived, together with other Oxford characters Morbey thought he recognised. One of the nymphs floated up to Judge, smiling, revealing perfect white teeth.

"*Noli me tango*," he said, but then impulsively he clasped her, and they went whistling away like Paolo and Francesca in Dante's wind.

Meanwhile, Morbey could still see, far away, the green-skinned god with his grandmother, dancing, capering, laughing. Minute by minute, Belle was growing younger. Vigour had returned to her limbs with the dance, her skin had become smooth again, her hair dense and black. Never had he known her so young in his lifetime. "She always lived for the moment," he said to himself, conscious that they had all been caught in some eternal moment.

The thought that time was no longer passing, that he had the power of choice, made him also lighthearted. He began to sing to the tune, jumped across the bed and the dying tulips, onto the lower terrace.

Someone caught his arm, laughing into his face. Laura Judge. In the wind, her pale yellow hair had blown free of its bun and unwound. It cascaded about her slender neck. She still wore her velvet dress, but was bare-legged and barefoot.

"Come on, Alan," she said, "don't waste time chasing my daughter. Choose someone who really understands what you want."

He laughed, not even bothering to respond in words. Instead, he whirled her up, godlike himself, prancing up along the terraces of the great ornate temple, which revealed itself steadily, bit by bit. Laura's face too was released from the everyday lines that had meshed it, floating before him on the sea of dance.

"We're free, free," she cried to him. Why was ecstasy accompanied by so much merry noise?

"Oh yes," he said, "Free – because I know what I want."

He felt her body hot against his as they whirled ever onwards through the great illuminated glooms of green and gold. She also knew.

Together, they ascended the elaborate terraces towards nirvana.

Alan Morbey's body was not discovered until twenty-four hours later. It lay sprawled in a room to the rear of the house, its cold cheek resting on a bunch of tulips, under a bed bearing Morbey's defunct elder relation.

The body was discovered by a neighbour from five doors away, on Convent Hill. She was a lady in her late thirties, rather smartly dressed, with dark hair, energetic, willing to do anything for anyone. Recently widowed. Just back from Java.

(1980)

A Romance of the Equator

Friends, very long ago in the old tropical green world, a boy lived whose name was Kahlin. Two strange things befell him in his life.

First of all, when he was a mere youth with limbs smooth as twigs, his home was demolished by a volcanic eruption. So great was that explosion that it could be heard by man and beast all round the world. Pieces of the earth were thrown into the air and landed across the seas two hundred miles and more away, where they still stand today as lines of hills.

The volcano destroyed Kahlin's home and killed both his parents and his little brothers.

Kahlin was so frightened that he ran and ran towards the north, away from the eruption. His legs carried him eventually to a narrow isthmus, fringed on either side by cliffs which fell sheer to the sea.

The boy heard a pathetic crying. He went to the edge of the nearest cliff and looked down. Two young gazelles had fallen over the side and were resting perilously on a ledge some feet below. Every effort they made to scramble up again endangered their foothold on the ledge. He could see that they were doomed to slip and fall.

Being a compassionate child, Kahlin removed his cloth headgear and used it as a rope to lower himself to the gazelles. He took one of the poor little things under each arm and climbed with them up to safety.

The animals were exhausted. He improvised shelter for them that night on the far side of the isthmus, and lay down between them, gazing piteously into their faces. One of the gazelles was white, the other brown. He put his arms about them and slept.

During the warmth of the night he heard a sound like the distant booming of the sea. He woke at dawn, and found that the two gazelles had turned into young women. They lay naked beside him, their eyes closed, one brown, one white. Still he held them, and his heart beat strongly and his breath came fast as he gazed at their beauty.

The two girls awoke and gazed at him, the white one with blue eyes, the brown one with eyes of amber.

Kahlin had heard of such things happening in fairy tales, so he covered his nudity and said to the girls, "How beautiful you are, both of you! My guess is that you were both princesses, turned into animals by some great enchanter. Is that so?"

The girls sat up and concealed some of their nudity. They denied that what Kahlin said was true. "We were animals, and were happy as animals. It is only the enchantments of your love that make you see us as girls. You are in a spell, not us."

"So how do you see me?" he asked.

"As a handsome male gazelle."

He snorted with disappointment, but the girls said sweetly, "We love you as we see you, and you must be content to be loved according to our interpretation. Truly, if we saw you as you see yourself, we could not love you."

Because he was a sensible boy, Kahlin saw some force in this argument and, because the world was young and its core still molten, he made love to the two girls, to the brown and the white, with equal passion.

Afterwards, the girls rose up and bathed themselves in the sea for a long while, standing below a waterfall, and washing each other's hair, the fair hair and the black. They wove themselves grass skirts before returning to Kahlin's side.

They regarded him with their large gazelle eyes and said, "Now the time is come when you must choose between us. It is not right that you should have us both. You must choose me or my sister to be yours, and to accompany you through the world until the last sunset, whilst the rejected sister goes on her way."

Kahlin grew angry and swore that he could not choose between them. They insisted. He threw himself down on the grass in a passion, beating the earth, swearing he loved them both, the one with hair like a raven's wing, and one with hair like honey.

"But we are going to live in different parts of the world," one sister said. "The pale to the north, the dark to the south."

Still he swore that he loved them both equally and would die if either left him. Dusk fell and they were still arguing.

A moon rose like a washed shell on the blue beaches of the sky, and eventually the girls came to an agreement. They said to Kahlin, "We see that you hold us both dear. Very well, since you saved us both from death on the cliff, then we will make a bargain with you. You shall enjoy us both, but a price must be paid, and that price must be your peace of mind. You will be forever trying to decide which of us you love the better, the brown or the white."

"I shall love you both the same."

Both girls shook their heads wisely, and wagged admonitory fingers, white and brown.

"But that is impossible. Since we are different, so we must be loved differently. Did you not know that that is one of the great secret truths of human companionship, and the cause of all its torment as well as its happiness? There is a configuration of love to fit the needs of every configuration of personality."

He threw his arms round them, crying, "There's no difference between you, except that one of you is brown and one white. How can I ever say which I love best, the limbs of ivory or the limbs of gold?"

And the two girls smiled first at him and then at each other, saying, "Just as you see us only as female, so your love makes you blind to our real differences, which are many. But you will grow to see. Your blindness will not long protect you."

"You women talk too much," Kahlin said, clapping his hands together. "I will accept the terms of your bargain and love you both." Whereupon, he coaxed them to lie down beside him, and the women did not take a lot of coaxing.

The moon set. It rose and set again many times, undergoing its small but magical span of changes, rather like a chime blown by the wind. And with every moon, Kahlin grew older in experience.

He saw that it was as the girls said. They differed greatly in their natures. He could scarcely believe it. In the first flush of his love, he had been blind to their personalities.

Then they had seemed merely like personages from some deep

dream. Now they slowly became human, with all their faults and contradictions.

One of the women was extremely passionate, and desired always to be close to Kahlin, never letting him from her sight. The other woman was cooler and more casual in her manner, teasing him in a way that alternately infuriated and delighted him.

One of the women was a good cook, and spent long hours over her stove, preparing with infinite patience dishes of great delicacy which could scarcely appease the appetite. The other woman cooked indifferently, yet bestirred herself occasionally to provide a great feast which they ate till their stomachs groaned.

One of the women was not greatly fond of washing, and was lazy, and spent much of her time lying about with her toes curled, prattling and laughing. The other woman was as neat and clean as a cat, and spent her days trying to keep everything impossibly tidy.

One of the women was highly intelligent, making clever or amusing remarks, and scolding Kahlin for his ignorance. The other woman was not intelligent, and repeated everything Kahlin said in honest admiration for his cleverness.

One of the women was most active by day, and leaped up with the dawn, calling Kahlin and her sister to join her. The other woman was a night creature, and came alive only after sunset, when she seemed to glow with a special light.

One woman was frank in all things, the other rather dishonest, full of amazing little secrets.

One woman painted and decorated herself, the other refused to do anything of the sort.

One woman had a gift for music and danced beautifully, the other could not sing a note but designed exquisite clothes for the three of them.

One woman smelt of musk, the other of honeysuckle.

One woman liked to talk about forbidden things, and cast a languishing eye on other men, while the other made a mystery of herself and disliked Kahlin's men friends.

One woman kept a pet monkey that pulled Kahlin's ears, while the other doted on three cats.

One woman seemed to be never quite content, while the other was completely uncritical.

One woman let her hair grow long, while the other cut hers short.

As the years went by, one woman became surprisingly plump, while the other became surprisingly thin.

By the same token, Kahlin also grew old, and his hair turned grey. No longer was his step as certain as it had been, or his gaze so keen.

Every day of his life he worked for the two women, and felt his love split between the brown woman and the white. Finally he rose and said to them, "Although I still have strength, yet I now know my days to be numbered. I have a desire to return to my origins, so I am going back to the mountains where I lived with my parents before the volcano erupted. You may come with me, or you may stay here, as you please."

This was in part his way of testing them, for he thought that perhaps only one woman – the white or the brown – would follow him on his journey.

So he travelled without looking back. He could hear that someone walked behind him, yet he refused to allow himself to turn to see who it was. He crossed over the isthmus where he had saved the two gazelles, the brown and the white, so many years ago that he went past the spot before recalling it.

Still he plodded on, and came at last to the mountains where he had been born. As he climbed the sides of the final hill, scenes from the distant past swam before his eyes. Recollecting his parents with love, he was granted insight, and perceived for the first time how his father and mother had differed in every way, almost as his two women differed. Only his childish love, with its quality of blindness, had allowed him to see his parents as two equal gods.

"So I glean a grain of knowledge," he said aloud to himself. "Was it worth travelling all these years for?" But he answered himself that a grain of insight was indeed better than nothing.

So Kahlin came to the top of the rise. There before him, greeting his eyes, was a magnificent sight such as he had never seen before. Spreading from horizon to horizon, steep slopes clad in jungle led down to a vast lake reflecting the sky. It seemed to him that this lake stretched to eternity, cradled at the bottom of the encompassing slopes. Not a single boat or sail crossed that silent surface. The lake was like the heavens themselves, without wave or ripple.

Only after he had gazed for a long while at the vista before him did Kahlin realise that this was the enormous crater of the volcano which had destroyed his parents, his brothers, and many other people besides. Now the place of death had become fertile through the ceaseless processes of nature.

Kahlin turned. Both his wives stood behind him, the white one and the brown. He embraced them warmly.

"You see there is an island in the middle of this new lake," he said. "We can make a boat and sail to the island, and there the three of us will live out the rest of our lives."

But the women said, "First we must speak. We made a bargain many years ago, the three of us. You agreed to love us both, at the expense of your peace of mind. We knew then, as we know now, that no man can love two women and be at peace in his mind. Every day of your life, our differences have tortured you. Well, now we release you from your bargain. You have often been unfair and cruel, it's true; once or twice you chased after other women, you even beat us, you sulked, and you did a lot of terrible things. You belch at your meals. All those things we now forgive, firstly, because we understand that such shortcomings are in man's nature, and, secondly, because despite those shortcomings, you did honestly try to love us both."

Kahlin looked from one to the other of them suspiciously.

"So, I'm free of the bargain, am I? Is this a new kind of trick? What follows next?"

The women, the white and the brown, smiled at each other, and then said, "We think you have learnt the lesson that as we have different natures, so it is necessary to love us differently. You have done well, considering your limitations as a man. Therefore we set you free and give you a further choice."

One woman kissed him on one cheek and one on the other, and they said, "You need take only one of us over to the island in the lake. Whichever one you choose will remain close to you for all the rest of your days. As for the other, you need never think of her again."

Then they walked about him and about, smiling mysteriously, and as they walked, they divested themselves of their clothes, for their bodies were still beautiful even in age, the brown and the white, and carried fewer lines of experience than their faces. And they watched him, the white one with blue eyes, the brown one with eyes of amber.

"Which of us do you choose, Kahlin?" they asked, at last.

He looked away from them, across the lake lying far below, across the uninhabited island, into the blue distance, and he said, "It really needs three people to build a boat, particularly if two of them are women. You had better both come with me. The three of us will live together on the island."

Without giving them more than a glance, he started down the steep slope towards the far gleaming water. The two women followed, waving their hands and protesting, "But you could be free, you could be free . . ."

At the water's edge, they built a small boat, making a sail of woven palm leaves. They slept on the beach that night and, next morning early, before the sun peered over the lip of the great crater to disperse its dews, they rose and launched their boat towards the island.

The two women stood by him with their arms entwined about his shoulders, and teased him, saying, "So, after all these years, despite all your lack of peace of mind, you still cannot decide which of us you love the better, the one with the hair like honey or the one with hair like a raven's wing. Really, Kahlin, you are a funny man! Now you're stuck with us both for the rest of your life."

The mysterious island was drifting nearer now. Kahlin could not help smiling, though he fixed his gaze upon the distant trees leaning out across the hazy waters, rather than on the two tormenting ladies by his side.

For he had his secret. Whereas once, as a youth, he had loved them because he thought they were almost identical, he had learnt through many long years to love them both more deeply because of their differences.

(1980)

Journey to the Goat Star

Fiction should imitate life only in being purgatorial
C. C. Shackleton

Further research revealed a copy of "The Journal of Psychiatry" for August 1995.

Evidence has come to light which indicates that there existed during the twentieth century a certain piece of writing which ran as follows:

William Frayser recovered – or believed he recovered – consciousness. The world about him was totally dark. Pain racked him as he confronted the idea that he was in hell. Only gradually did he realise that he was lying on a carpeted floor with his face against the front of a sofa.

With the realisation came layers of inter-connecting knowledge and memory. He had been working in his study, sitting on the sofa with a glass of martini on the table by his left hand. It was night. Snow fell slowly outside the windows, a blind being drawn down forever.

He had not heard the intruder. His record player was issuing Lutoslavsky's Fourth Symphony as he worked. No second sense had warned him of the approach of the intruder. Suddenly, he was struck on the skull, just where his hair was thinning, by a blow from behind.

Even as he toppled to the floor, he remembered he had once watched a play in which a similar attack had occurred, and had time to think to himself, "It would make quite a dramatic opening to a short story." Then all thought disappeared – except, he now reflected, on various sub-levels of the implicate order of the universe, where thought maintains independent existence.

He rolled over onto his back. The sofa smelt unpleasant.

There was light in the room. Over him stretched the freckled infinity of the ceiling. The sofa loomed above him like a mountain range. The low table stood there, with the glass of martini half full; it had not been knocked over in his fall. Everything was upside down: the liquid rested in the top of the glass.

The intruder sat at Frayser's desk. The table-light was on, his back was to Frayser. He appeared to be reading.

Frayser became very still, frightened that the man might turn, see his eyes open, and attack him again. He closed his eyes and only then became aware of a blinding headache which seemed to move cautiously about inside his skull as if looking for a secret place in which to hide.

With a twinge, Frayser re-opened his eyes, and found that the intruder had turned to look at him. He had swivelled round in the chair, and was holding a piece of paper. Seeing Frayser was conscious, the intruder extended the paper and asked, "Did you write this?"

"Ride? Ride what? A horse!"

"Write. Did you write this stuff?"

Because of his dizziness, Frayser found the question unanswerable.

After a pause, in which the intruder continued to regard him, Frayser asked, "What does it say?"

Holding the paper at the length of his arm, the intruder read, "I should begin with the undivided wholeness of the universe; the task of science is to derive the parts through abstraction from the whole, explaining them as approximately separable, stable and recurrent, but extremely related, elements making up relatively autonomous sub-totalities, which are to be described in terms of the explicate order." He paused and then repeated with some relish, "Sub-totalities . . ."

There was silence in the room. Outside, the snow was still falling past the window; either that, or it was suspended in the air and the building was slowly and grandly rising through it.

"Did you write this?" the intruder asked again, rustling the paper.

He was a big man in his middle forties, well built, with a solid and not displeasing face. His clothes were shabby, his shoes down-at-heel, and there was a general air of neglect about him. He bit a fingernail as he waited for Frayser's answer.

Frayser lay on his back and contemplated the ceiling.

"I can't remember," he said. "It's a sub-totality of what I'm working on now. Either I wrote it or it's a passage I quoted from David Bohm's *Wholeness and the Implicate Order*. I'm trying to formalise the nature of reality and the nature of our interpretation of reality as unitary relationship."

"You mean that matter and consciousness are one?"

"Well not quite . . . Anyhow, I can't explain my theories while I have this raging headache." He could hear his own voice, being reasonable, as he had always been.

The intruder looked disappointed. "What you've written I consider quite brilliant, quite brilliant. I mean, I only broke in here to steal your silver and whatever else I could get hold of, but this thought is worth far more than gold. It's a revelation." He shook his head over it in bemused admiration.

"It's not all that good," Frayser said, with some irritation. He wanted to ask the man to leave, but was not quite sure how the request would be received.

"Perhaps I might offer you a view of the matter," the intruder suggested, turning more squarely to face the recumbent Frayser.

"That wouldn't be of any interest to me," said Frayser.

"I suppose you're a bloody intellectual snob, like the rest of them." He made his voice thick and menacing.

"I work in a very specialised field, between science and philosophy. I hardly think that a common burglar would have anything to contribute to the debate."

"*A common burglar?*"

The intruder stood up and walked forward to loom over Frayser. Hands in pockets, he stared down at the horizontal man.

"Does it strike you that this is an archetypal situation, somewhat reminiscent of the relationship between psychoanalyst and analysand, you being the patient? Or, indeed, between parent and child in bed? Or between doctor and patient? I might, just might, have something to offer in the way of a valuable comment."

"It strikes me that this is an archetypal situation between defenceless, law-abiding man and merciless aggressor."

"I only hit you once." He squatted on his heels and casually felt Frayser's pulse. "You don't need an injection. While I have you here, Dr Frayser, I just want to tell you something that I've been longing to get off my chest for years."

"I suppose you murdered your parents."

"Now, no sarcasm or you'll get my goat! Something more interesting than murder. Some years ago, when I was in a different line of business, I had a revelation which is very apposite to the work you are at present engaged on."

Frayser rested his hand over his eyes. There were stars in his sky.

"Perhaps you'd be good enough to phone for the police, would you?"

"Try to be serious for a moment, please. You are one of the greatest theoretical scientists now living, and plainly if your theories are to have any relevance in daily life they must be acceptable to the common man – such as me. That is to say, I must be able to glimpse their essence, even if I cannot fathom the equations."

"There is something in what you say."

"There's everything in what I say. Are we dealing with the implicate order or aren't we? As I was saying, I was involved a few years ago in one of those relatively autonomous sub-totalities to which you refer, or, to put it another way, I visited an exhibition of the paintings of Braque."

"Don't be a fool, man, Bach was a composer, not a painter."

"I'm referring to Georges Braque, the French Cubist painter, born 1881, son of a house-decorator, just like me. To my mind, Braque is the greatest painter of our century." He squatted down on his haunches as he spoke, gesticulating grandly. "The greatest painter."

"Greater than Picasso?"

"An impostor, a mere con-man."

"Greater than Dali?"

"A poseur, a charlatan, a would-be monster."

"Greater than David Hockney?"

"Don't make me laugh, Frayser! Around 1910 or 1911, Braque

made one of those conceptual breakthroughs which happens once every generation, if as often. I'm talking about the hermetical cubism in which colour is dissociated from form, form from representation, and matter from energy. Either Braque had read Einstein, which seems unlikely, or he was somehow on the same wavelength, producing in paint the equivalent of the theory of relativity. Yet the result is pure painting. In his canvases, the implicate order was first made manifest for those who could see."

Frayser groaned.

"Of course, we have to treat these magnificent discoveries of Braque as paintings, and in that respect they are unrivalled, to my mind. Yet his Cubist vision managed to embrace not only the latest scientific thinking but also . . ."

The intruder paused, thinking deeply, eyes downcast towards the bird and animal patterns woven into the carpet. "On that point, modern Chinese scholars agree with me. Braque's Cubist vision also encompasses, in a prophetic way, all the social and economic problems which became more and more intractable as the twentieth century progressed.

"I mean, although he was the most self-absorbed of artists, a contemplator of his own artistic navel, one might say, yet he was of course affected by the social pressures of his day, and responded to them with staggering and almost unacknowledged perception . . ."

Frayser groaned again.

"Oh, you disagree, do you?" said the intruder. "Have you ever *looked* at Braque – I mean at his original canvases, not at reproductions, which tell nothing while pretending to tell everything?"

"Sorry, I was not really disagreeing with you. I know very little about art. I was just groaning. Do you think you could help me up off the floor?"

The intruder got his arms under Frayser's armpits and pulled. The older man being fairly light, he was soon dragged up into a sitting–reclining posture on the sofa.

"This is important to me, and you're hardly listening," the intruder grumbled.

"Oh, bugger Braque," said Frayser, clutching his head.

"You scientists are generally pretty philistine, aren't you? Never go to an art exhibition in your lives, do you? Yet you might have got your paper finished by now if you'd gone to see Braque years ago. You won't live for ever, you know."

"We're not on a spaceship, are we?" Frayser asked anxiously.

"What makes you think that?" The intruder went over to the window and peered out. "Blimey, it's still coming down. It's like Manchuria out there. I'd better go, or I'll be snowed in. Can't stand here talking like this. I'd like to tell you about the lovely bird symbol in Braque's later work, but I don't suppose you'd be interested. I must go."

"I might be interested some other time, if you'd like to come back."

Pausing with his hand on the door, the intruder said, "I'm not sure I trust you. But have a look at some Braques and see if they don't prefigure the whole dilemma of modern science, including Bohm's work. The whole *Weltanschauung*, really. I mean –" He turned earnestly back into the room, gesturing with his hands. "Braque's shadows have a substance, while the whole substance suddenly turns out to be a shadow of it. Forms are flattened, flatness has form. Planes merge, what is opaque becomes transparent and vice versa. Lines define nothing, yet everything is defined. If that isn't a vivid picturing of contemporary science – executed before the First World War – then I don't know what it is. I've been obsessed with the master's work ever since I saw it, and I suggest that he has a lot to say to you – and through you the world. Goodnight."

He went out into the darkness, disappearing as if he had never been, like a character out of fiction.

Frayser reached out gingerly for the glass of martini, and found a vase of flowers in his hand. He smelt them.

"Orange blossom," he said.

On the floor before him lay the piece of paper the intruder had dropped. He could see writing on it, but the writing would not resolve into words.

I should begin by saying that I have not been particularly satisfied with the performance of the crew since the start of the voyage. There was some answering back which I resented. To give a trivial example, being busy in my office one morning, wrestling with a problem, I asked a rating who wished to speak to me if he would mind waiting awhile in the passage, and he replied familiarly, "Ah, the passage of time."

The remark distracted me. As captain, I have complete control of the ship. But it is essential that the crew appreciate this if we are to survive happily for the entire forty-six years of the journey, otherwise we shall get nowhere.

There is also the knowledge that time is passing more slowly with us than back on Earth, relative to Earth, although naturally we are not conscious of differing temporal perceptions. I introduced the crew to jogging, a pleasantly rhythmic exercise, and each watch jogs regularly round the creative area. My idea is that everything should be as normal as possible, and to this end discipline has to be maintained.

Some of the conditions in deep space are not what were anticipated. It was hard not to mistake the stars for orange blossom, sinking across the universe.

In the control room, direct-vision panels stretched from floor to curved ceiling. The universe is out there. I could not take my eyes off the falling blossoms.

They fell slowly towards a great deep pool, and were mirrored there, so that their reflections came up to meet them. The blossoms vanished into each other, merging with flashes like silent summer lightning. Of course, there is no sound in space. The birds too – swallows or martins – are also illusions, but we have to take care in case they soften the hull. That would entail a return to dock.

However, to get to the incident you requested me to write about.

As I said in an earlier interview, the medics back on Earth secretly gave me injections to make me immortal. This was undemocratic, so none of the rest of the ship's complement have been told, even the officers. The injections make me tired and rather irritable.

Last evening, when everything was under control, I took the opportunity to retire early to my berth, I slept well. When I woke, it was light, and birds were singing in chorus. It's what musicians call *a capella*, and somehow it made me feel uncomfortable, reminding me of when my mother left me unaccompanied as a small child.

I shaved and dressed, feeling the deadness of the ship. I was getting nowhere. I addressed the crew over the intercom, but there was no response. It was fitting to make a complete inspection of the ship. I did so, despite the objections of the nurses, and found the place completely empty. When I spoke to one woman about it, she pretended to be doing something else.

Anguish gripped me. To have come all this way for nothing! Of course, I knew they were hiding from me, but in a way that made the matter worse. Now I proceed as best as I can alone. I have no intention of giving up now, and I will do all that is required of me.

Unfortunately, it will be rather a hollow victory.

The patient had signed his short statement with his name and rank, Gregory Grant, Captain, and underlined it.

As I read it, he sat rather brightly in the easy chair, watching me with his head slightly on one side. Like a child hoping his best efforts will be approved.

I said, "Well, Greg, the musical term for unaccompanied choral song is *a cappella*, with two 'p's. *Capella* with one 'p' is a she-goat."

"That was what I meant."

I gazed out of the clinic window, thinking how beautiful was the mind, how out of the darkest suffering came glimpses of poetry and light.

"You wrote this statement for me last night. Do you feel this morning that there is anything you wish to elaborate, any detail which could be expanded?"

"No." He was forty-six years old, a big man, well-built, and generally held himself well, only his clothes were shabby, and there was a decided air of neglect about him. His hair needed washing and cutting. He still bit his fingernails.

"Well. The woman who was doing something else when I spoke to her . . . The one I mention . . ."

"Yes?"

"I think she was nursing a small bird. Its wing was broken."

"A martin?"

"A baby one. Straight from the nest. You know how it's impossible for a bird to fly in space, owing to lack of air."

"She was looking after it?"

"She was pretending to look after it. I couldn't get any help. I feel I'm wasting your time, with these sessions, Dr Frazer. You don't believe a word, do you?"

"I didn't say that."

Silence fell between us. I never let silences extend themselves too long. I spoke at random, for almost any trail leads back to the centre. "You were a science-fiction writer at one time?"

"I sold a few stories in my late teens. To magazines. Not here – Peking. One was about a long voyage on a starship, so it came true, in a way."

"What do you think such a journey represents?"

He laughed. "You have me there. It's a wish to escape, I suppose, isn't it? To get away from this life, I suppose."

"You mean a death-wish? Where the time is out of joint."

"I see what you mean. The passage of time. I am immortal though, don't forget."

"The only effect of the immortality serum is to make you almost comatose – near to death. Let me remind you that we have come up against evidence of your death-wish before, and you always brush it aside."

He laughed, and sought as he usually did when the subject of death arose to dismiss it with a joke. "If you were aboard my ship, I'd discipline you for such remarks."

"Then you'd be the little martin, the martinet. Whose hands were you in? Who was the nurse not attending to your troubles, do you think?"

He sighed wearily, and looked down at his clasped hands. "You would say she was my wife. I mean my mother, of course." Silence. "The she-goat. Instead of unison singing – the she-goat, always butting her way in where not required. Re-choired. I used to sing about the house, but she could not bear that. She preferred silence. She said I sang flat."

"Do you?"

"Yes, Dr Frazer, I sing flat, and I'm also flat-footed . . . Just to oblige her." With a flash of insight. "So as to prove she wasn't a complete bloody liar, I suppose. There must have been some good in her, even if I got nowhere with her."

"That phrase, 'getting nowhere', also occurs in your report. How does it square with this forty-six-year journey you are

making? You mentioned you are travelling at the speed of light. Is
that 'getting nowhere'?"

"I believe that was why the oranges were bursting. They weren't
oranges as much as worlds, whole planets, dropping down into
oblivion and meeting themselves coming up. I was terribly excited
because for once I had seen through reality. At least, I had proof
that reality was not eternal, that facts had no form. No, I mean that
I always felt I understood reality better than other people. That
even the most solid objects, chairs, rooms, lives, were merely the
outward forms of something else, or lines defining nothing. That a
more real, more beautiful world lurked beneath them. That's what
faster-than-light means, incidentally; it has nothing to do with
Einstein, it's to do with people seeing through appearances. The
other planets are like Earth, but more real; only a few people can
see that. You need a captain with vision . . . Isn't that why you
enjoy oil paintings? It isn't really a portrait of father, oh no, it's a
veneer of colours, and the real thing is just a piece of stretched
canvas. Father himself, perhaps he's not real either, just a veneer
stretched over . . . No, that's too silly . . ."

"Why do you stop?" Often his ramblings continued for hours at
a time.

"Father – I'm talking nonsense. Besides, my mother said she
used to tease him about his warts and say 'He's no oil painting'."

"You were a father to your men aboard ship. But they wouldn't
accept your authority."

Grant chewed a fingernail and looked down at the floor.

"They answered me back, and now they have disappeared. But I
shall survive. Psychoanalysis will not prevent me from continuing
the journey. Much of what we say here is – well, it applies only to
one level of reality, doesn't it? In another half-hour, I'll be back on
watch and laughing all this off."

I rolled up a copy of *The Journal of Psychiatry* and hit him with it.

"It would be better for you to be off-watch, off your guard, and
to accept your feelings. Your mother rejected your feelings as a
child, so you tell me, but this is no reason why you have to reject
them. Your feelings of pain and isolation are real. I accept them as
real. Psychoanalysis can help you to accept and adjust to your past
pain. The pain will then become less."

"How can it be less?" he exclaimed, impatiently jumping up.

"Those things happened. My father died before I was born, mother rejected me in favour of my younger sister. They're facts. They distorted my whole life. You in your academic dream-world may not accept them, but they are facts, even if buried in the past. But for their pain, I would never have thought of going on such a long journey. And you expect me to be happy?"

"I fully expect that if you face the true nature of your pain, you will be – not happy exactly, but no more miserable than other people."

"You're ordering me to return to Earth, captain?" He grinned dangerously as he spoke. "Is the expedition to Capella cancelled? Are you relieving me of my command, is that it?"

"I'll see you again tomorrow," I said. "You can go back to the bridge now."

"No more cards, thanks. The other patients cheat."

I sat for a while, free-associating, having switched off the Lutoslavsky. Capella was a binary star, forty-six light years from Earth. However much he struggled, Grant in the middle years of his life was still moving towards a collision with the binary system of his parents, long dead though they were. No wonder he felt himself getting nowhere. That was one of the paradoxes about stellar journeys – one travelled impossibly fast, at the speed of light, and still arrived nowhere. The ship was a womb, protecting him from outside interference. The jogging, "a pleasantly rhythmic exercise", was the only movement experienced in the womb.

The beauty of mental illness, with its entanglements of words, and appearances which dissolved like figments of a dream, was indeed a place to go to, much like an alien planet. It was a journey into the Self, that jungle lit by an earlier sun. The spaceship with its metal hull represented the Ego. Perhaps it represented the future also. There was hope for Grant in the reported fact that the hull of his spaceship was not of entirely impervious metal: it could be softened by illusory birds; and birds – always messengers in such cases – had somehow managed to get through to the suffering psyche within it. Self and Ego were trying to communicate.

That was a sign of improvement in his condition. There had been a time when Grant discovered that his crew were all androids, when the "veneer of colours", of flesh, had been peeled away to reveal metal. When Ego conquered Self, then the human man was dead; androids had no Self. The rejection by the mother of her babe's hurt feelings was the first step towards that conquest; the grown babe found it too painful to confront the side of reality which the all-important mother had rejected.

I looked up at the painting of the bird on the wall. It seemed like the human race, always in flight from or to something.

At last I was ready to face my tormentors. Opening the desk, I pressed the red button.

At once, the accustomed outlines of the room, with its coffee machine, its lines of scholarly books, began to fade, and was replaced by the no less familiar plastic shell. The window, with its view of buildings, trees, and sky, also faded. Here was a veneer, I thought to myself, peeling indeed. Here was Grant's reality giving place to another layer of reality below. For all his delusions, he thought he was deluded; but it was not so.

The transformation was complete. I stood. A door opened in the shell, and I stepped out. Into the challenging environment beyond.

My heartbeat altered and my breathing quickened. The air was different. It sparked with a kind of dust that was not dust. Seeing was different, as if I were in the polar regions, in what explorers term a "white-out".

After a few steps, clumsily taken, I saw the Pillar appear before me. The hairs on my neck stood on end.

I knew that the Pillar, and the civilisation which controlled it, had heard everything which transpired during Grant's analysis.

"Are you making progress?" the Pillar enquired. Its voice spoke in my head, tickling the left hemisphere.

"If you have watched Grant's and my interviews with perception, then you will know that that question should be addressed to Grant rather than to me. However, if you were to reveal yourself to Grant and ask him, you would undoubtedly set back his progress. Instead of wasting time, let me ask you some questions. Mankind is an inquisitive species, and there is much I wish to know about you."

The Pillar glowed, and a – noise? – like a cello started in the recesses of my mind. I suspected that it tried periodically to communicate with me on a variety of telepathic bands, before reverting to less satisfactory speech.

"Ask," it said.

"The most important questions are always the most difficult ones to ask. Let me start by saying that I, Wilson Frazer, am not yet entirely certain of your objective reality. Either I am undergoing a schizophrenic illusion related to the dilemmas of the patient I am trying to help, or I am undergoing mankind's first encounter with extra-terrestrial beings."

"The latter, rest assured."

"So you tell me, but obviously I seek objective corroboration. Don't interrupt. You have yet to master human codes for when the end of one period of discourse has been reached. Supposing you have objective reality, then I take it that the most important question you could answer is a twofold one: how you have evolved – I mean from what kind of life-form – and whether you consider that the structure of your mind resembles that of human minds. My thought is that if our mental structures are totally dissimilar, then no real communication is going to be possible."

The response came unhesitatingly.

"We evolved from what you call amino acids."

"That's not the level of answer I required. So did mankind evolve ultimately from amino acids. I was thinking of more immediate ancestors. Mankind developed from a kind of intelligent primate only a few million years ago. And you?"

I stared at the Pillar, as if hoping to see there a fallible human countenance. It seemed to me the voice that spoke was tinged with loss.

"We evolved many millions of years ago – from amino acids. We are a fluid intelligence, totally unlike you. Our thoughts are our shapes. No, you would say, 'our shapes are our thoughts'. Forms are illusory, in other words."

I wanted to sit down. I wanted a drink. I did not want to converse with what might be my own delusion.

But perhaps one should take a new view of delusions, Frayser thought, gently peeling his clothes off and climbing under the shower. Blood ran down his shoulders from his skull, but he hoped that the blow was less serious than he had at first thought.

His headache had gone; indeed, he felt rather well, if lightheaded.

As he stood under the warm shower, listening to the water pattering into the china tray at his feet, he tried to recall exactly what the intruder had said about the paintings of Georges Braque. He admitted ruefully that he had scarcely heard of Braque. He had spent years incarcerated in one learned institution or another, and had not heard of a painter that at least one man – a ruffian admittedly – thought to be the greatest of the century. Why had none of his colleagues directed his attention to Braque's canvases? It could be that there he might find some of the formal illustrations he needed to buttress his theory, an illumination from an earlier generation hitherto overlooked. The prospect excited him.

Frayser remembered that there had been a builder near his home outside Nottingham called Brake. It was irrelevant, except for the fact that nothing was irrelevant in the implicate universe. One thing leads to another. Blake, Brake, Braque.

Had there been a Brake-in? Had, in other words, the intruder existed? He felt his skull tenderly as he turned off the water and climbed from the shower. Was the intruder merely an illusion brought on by an accidental bump on the head?

Wrapping himself in towels, he opened the bathroom window and peered out. Snow fell as orange blossom, deluging the world with its beauty. It was like the awesome and silent onset of schizophrenia, he thought.

Below his window, a small black car was trying to rev itself out of a snowdrift. But the great black ship ploughed on through the falling particles. Lutoslavsky played.

"You are using force in keeping me and Grant captive. Therefore I am justified in believing you hostile. I have committed no hostile act against you. Why do you do this to Grant and me?" I said to the alien when it appeared.

A cello sounded in my mind again, causing a vibration in the left hemisphere. The Pillar spoke once more.

"We are not hostile. We are simply curious. We cannot understand much you say when you speak to us direct. On the other hand, we think we understand more when you talk with Grant, even if what we understand is a mystery. For instance, the idea of parentage, which takes up a great deal of Grant's thinking, is new to us. Fatherhood, motherhood – brilliantly original! We now ask you: are you hostile to us?"

My efforts to interpret what was being said to me by this possibly imaginary being were dual and conflicting. I pretended, on one hand, that I was conversing with aliens in reality, and, on the other, that I was merely dealing with a sick patient – aware that the patient might be myself. When dealing with sick patients, I was never less than honest, but at this juncture I saw that caution was necessary.

"Hostility is like love. It really needs a response to awaken fully. Studying our own prehistory, experts once assumed that we came from killer apes, and that killing and hatred were in-built in our genes. The theory was unscientific, pessimistic. Our species became human not through killing but through co-operation. We were not hunters but scavengers. We carried back food to weaker members of the tribe. It was not hostility but love which coaxed us into real communities. Unfortunately, our communities became too big. Big communities kill those inside and outside. We are seeking a way out of that dilemma now. If your history parallels ours, we would be glad of helpful suggestions."

"What sort of suggestions?"

"Don't be stupid! You ask me to define what I would not need to ask if I could define it. I stand before you naked. Stop hiding behind words and lights and show yourselves to me. Then perhaps we might get somewhere. Scrap this pillar-thing. Otherwise, I want to go home."

"Apologies. You say your communities became too big. Is that why you are at present destroying each other?"

"I will say yes, although behind that simple syllable lies much complexity. Is it the same with you?"

"We like big communities. We only prosper when many millions of us are together."

"Show yourselves to me."

"What are these complexities of which you speak?"

My senses whirled. Perhaps I was talking to myriad micro-organisms with some kind of corporate mind. In which case, I would have anticipated no understanding between us. Yet it seemed as if some kind of understanding was growing, as with Grant.

"Create me a chair and let me sit down. Then I will speak further."

My first command to them, which they obeyed. A beautiful crimson chair materialised. It looked the size of a house. I could not tell how close or far it was. It shrank and became solid. I went over and lowered myself cautiously into it. Again the note of a cello in my brain, deep melancholy. There was something they unappeasably wanted from me.

"I'm only a psychoanalyst, and a rather unorthodox one at that, with as many broken marriages behind me as most of my patients. Why you picked on me, I don't know. My chief interest is in the structure of the human mind, and let me tell you that there is not just a single level of consciousness. You observe as much with my patient, Grant. He perpetually glimpses other levels of being. You may regard this as a drawback for us; indeed, I believe that it is so, on an evolutionary scale. We are multivalent. Perhaps we are like the flightless archaeopteryx, using our wings as yet merely to hop more easily from branch to branch, with flight still an accident in the future. But much of our creativity comes from conflict between these different levels of mind. Do you have similar problems?"

The Pillar appeared to come a little nearer, and again I was gripped by a sensation of unreality.

"Our shapes are our explicated thoughts."

I waited, but there was no more. Possibly they were telling me something profound about their psyches. If so, I failed to comprehend. Possibly – there was the gulf of comprehension I feared, across which no human words could be thrown, as Grant and I hoped to bridge the gulf dividing him from his feelings. Once more, I had the impression of trying to speak to a sick patient, this one monstrously sick, in a way rivalled by no sort of human illness. The white-out began to close in on me.

I said, "You'll have to try to explain."

The Pillar said, "You must sleep now."

No matter how hard the intruder struggled, his little black car sank more deeply into the snow. In the end, he left the engine running and lay back in the driver's seat.

"This is the second consecutive year that it's snowed on mid-summer's day," he said. "The implicate order –"

His crippled wife, sitting patiently beside him, said, "The Greenhouse effect. Did you get what you wanted, that's the main thing?"

"I told him about Braque, if that's what you mean, Nan, but –"

"No, but really –"

"It wasn't exactly a personal –" They rarely finished sentences when talking to each other.

"No, I didn't mean that, but since we've been living in Manchuria –"

"That was your choice."

"I'm not disputing that so much. It's just – well, if Braque had been alive . . . Have you talked to the Premier again? You know you said –"

"About Braque? The Chinese don't seem interested. Tanguy now, that's –"

"Don't fret, doll, we'll sort it out. That's you all over. I –"

He put his hand consolingly on her knee, and fell asleep.

The car engine purred, the Manchurian night was thick as owl's feathers. They might have been the only two people left alive. Over in the barracks, defectors were being shot. A dissident was beheaded. It was a one-off operation.

Next day, Greg Grant arrived as usual at the time appointed. He wore his old creased suit. I suspected that he had slept in it. Someone had.

He gave me one of his cautious grins and settled down in my battered easy chair, where so many patient sufferers had sat. His fingers drummed on its arms.

"I can spare you an hour off duty. The ship is more or less running itself. With the aid of the computers, of course. It gives me greater freedom that way, and I'm getting reconciled to being alone in space. We're moving through an area of dense foliage now. The airlocks are filling up with leaves and we can hardly keep pace with them."

He looked puzzled by his own remark.

"Greg, I don't exactly know how to put this, but maybe I am no help to you. It is just possible that I am suffering from sudden hysteric outbursts. Did you come in a car? I imagine things when you're not here. I think we had better skip this session."

"Or all of them? I feel I'm wasting your time. Have you discovered anything wrong with me?"

I hesitated. "Your cerebral hemispheres are possibly out of synch. Too much vigorous fornication will do it."

Grant smiled. "I see. 'And consummation comes, and jars both hemispheres.' You're imagining things, doctor."

"I do imagine things."

He laughed, a pleasant human sound.

"We all imagine things. Don't worry. When I'm up on the bridge, I often imagine that I imagine you. Yet here you are, real as anything, warts and all."

"But you don't think anything is real – evidence the hemisphere's are out of synch."

"What do you mean? I know the spaceship's real. I know the foliage is real. I brought you along a leaf."

He pulled a green leaf out of his pocket. It was fresh and cool. I stared down at the structure of its veins as if looking into the mind of a god, or the retina of a goat.

Grant said, "We need this session, both of us, you old goat. I had a wonderful dream in the night. You remember our joke about the martin and the martinet yesterday? Well, I saw the little bird again in my dream."

He dreamed that the bird came at dawn and took him to a little deserted place in a wood. He crawled in on hands and knees, feeling excited. It was like a rabbit burrow, and warm. Inside was a big box with four locks on it. He felt sure there would be treasure in the box but, when he opened it up, he found it was empty.

At this point, there seemed to be a break in the dream. When it began again, he, or someone rather like him with a fat stomach, was giving him a doll. The doll had a little dress on. He accepted it with delight and found that it was a precious doll with a china head. Its eyes opened and shut.

He took it over to show to his wife, Judy, who lay near the box, but she was dead. He dropped the doll and it broke. The bird flew away with a worm in its mouth.

Grant laughed. "That was all. Pretty silly dream." He rubbed his hands on his knees.

"Belittling your feelings again." I hit him with a rolled-up copy of *The Journal of Psychoanalysis*. I can't bear being reminded of knees.

"You should know what my laughter means by now."

"We have met the doll before," I said. He did not evade that issue. "Doll, dollar, dolour . . ."

"Of course. It's Eggy again. Greggy's boring little Eggy."

It often happens in psychoanalysis that the most intractable problems, those most deeply buried, camouflage themselves against discovery under protective layers. They may appear to have been resolved, but are not. Appearances, as Grant knew, are not everything, though everything is appearances. That this dream was important I understood when he insisted on telling it me against my will. I was excited. We might be near a resolution of his central problem of relationships. How he related to this doll, a recipient of infantile feelings, was important. The china head meant nothing; for some reason, everyone on spaceships dreams about china.

Early in the course of analysis, Grant had told me how he had been born to a mother still mourning the death of her husband in a motorway accident near Ovum, NC. She took him to live in Siberia. He thought that this accounted for her coolness to him as a baby. When he was four years old, his sister was born. The mother became cheerful. This had served to make him jealous of the new baby, and also guilty, because he felt he had betrayed his mother in failing to be a satisfactory love-object for her.

He had then stolen a doll from a toyshop – another crime – and fussed over the object, which he called Eggy. The toyshop closed shortly afterwards.

He had laughed greatly when first relating this episode. He revealed that at a later date, in despairing adolescence, he had interpreted this brief period – the doll had soon been abandoned in disgust – as a sign that he was willing to become a baby girl himself, if it would please his mother. In other words, he felt he was a homosexual, and for a while toured Siberia on a 1000cc motorbike.

Although he had had no homosexual encounters, nor was he the Don Juan type whose rather frantic pursuit of women reveals to an educated eye a crypto-homosexual, I had accepted this perception of his at face value, and we had proceeded from there. He showed me the motorbike.

I say we proceeded, but in fact we made little progress. We had been getting nowhere.

In the light of the new dream, I saw that I had swallowed the earlier explanation – a tritely standard one in psychoanalytical terms – too easily. Beneath that first interpretation lay deeper ones. We had not yet arrived at the bottom layer of paint. The forms were merging into a new pattern. I excused myself and gave myself a shot behind the screen.

"Why have we come up with Eggy again?" I asked.

"Eggy was only one aspect of the dream. What was the treasure I expected, do you think?"

"Don't you know – not even when the four apparently function-less locks represent your four years?"

"I know the treasure wasn't there . . . There was just the empty box . . . Oh, Christ, I suppose the box is a womb symbol. We're back to mother again. That's what I hate about psychoanalysis – the same old subjects return over and over again. It's always sex, isn't it? This was a dream about my mother . . . Her empty box . . . The love she never gave me . . ."

"Only your mother?" I was smiling now. I felt great. I knew the Pillar was just an illusion.

"Well . . ." He paused, sighed. "My wife was dead, remember. She just lay around near the box."

(I had a box at the opera that night. *Turandot*.)

Then I understood. The box was as empty as the spaceship. The crew, those missing father figures, were subordinate to Captain Grant because he felt that his father, by dying, proved himself inferior. The box in the dream represented his mother and the hard case he thought her to be. Grant had always complained that his marriage failed because his wife was unresponsive. The dream showed his understanding of that situation – she had been too close to his mother. Hence the way she lay next to the box. In other words, Judy had accepted his mother's interpretation of him as a difficult boy. In "giving no response", she might as well have been dead as far as his emotional needs were concerned. He had got nowhere with her either.

(Was *Turandot* seven-thirty or eight-thirty?)

As we teased this out, he became more lively, and drummed his fingers on the arm of the chair like a maddened Paderewsky.

"There's a bit of the dream I'd forgotten. It comes back to me now, but it's not important."

Vital keys often pretend to be forgotten, to arrive before the footlights exactly when wanted, like Turandot herself. Their timing is faultless. The mind is its own stage-manager, and waits on its own wings.

"It's a contradiction, but it's what happened. The box was empty, yet the doll came out of it. That's me when I – or whoever had the fat stomach – handed Eggy to me."

He began to rub his knees, then thought better of it.

"Your pregnant mother had a fat stomach. Events in dreams have synchronicity."

"Of course. Of course. Listen, the doll was my sister. Eggy was my *sister*. Not *me*."

Grant sat silent, luxuriating in his sense of revelation before he continued. "The family used to pretend I loved the doll. I've always accepted that, accepted their blindness, quite wrongly. Memories get lost: the truth is, I see now, I *hated* the doll. I could not identify with it. It degraded me – down-graded me." The admission exhilarated him. "It was my *sister* I hated so much I had to conceal the knowledge from myself by using a surrogate doll, as the target for all my wounded feelings. I couldn't bear so much hatred; that was why I wished I was dead.

"The doll was a dead thing. It could be controlled, unlike my mother's little treasure wallowing at her breast and shrieking for more.

"In my dream, by dropping the doll, I killed my sister when mother wasn't looking, didn't I?"

"No one was looking."

He shook his head, smiling. "Only the bird – myself. You have to watch yourself."

"Why do you think you were pleased to receive the doll if you hated it so much?"

"My mother gave it me, that's why. Her 'little treasure' – that was her term of endearment. That damned effigy! The hatred of that thing . . . The hatred of everything . . . It paralysed me. I feared – I feared everything, myself especially. All because my father got himself killed in a car crash. Near Ovum NC, of all places. It was no one's fault. Mother mourned him because she loved him. I was so greedy that I couldn't bear to think she loved him . . . It's the old, old situation – Oedipus again. You still envy your father even if you don't have a father."

He broke into laughter. This time I joined him. We triumphed together. It was a good day.

He jumped up and grasped my hand. There were tears in his eyes.

"I need to think all this through. Get it clear. My head's straight at last. Then I'll come back. Then I'll be cured. The hatred will fall away like ashes. I know it, I feel it. A little bird tells me . . . And that little bird . . . The martinet. With a phallic worm."

"What do you make of that?"

"It's obvious now, I have turned myself into a martinet. Martinets have no love life. They are themselves one big stiff erection. *Vigor mortis*. With nowhere to put it."

Grant laughed with a pinch of hysteria. "God, you should see me, so damn stiff and spruce in my space uniform . . ."

"All dolled up, eh?"

"I'm free now. I'll be free. You wait till I get to Capella."

"There may not be any girls on Capella."

"Then I'll speak to the computers. We'll return to Earth. My wife will be waiting for me to come back."

With a muttered word of excuse, he crossed the room and headed briskly through the door.

Outside, the little black car awaited him. The driver opened the rear door and Grant climbed in.

"Still snowing, I see."

The crippled woman in the passenger seat gave a laugh. "Harbin's a cold city and, besides, it is the Year of the Goat. You know what Shakespeare said, 'All things in their declensions interfuse, Save where a bloody separation comes 'Twixt logic and the thing direct perceived . . .' That's the implicate order for you . . ."

"*Romeo and Juliet*," said the driver.

"*Hamlet*," said the passenger.

"*Titus Andronicus*," said the wife, firmly. "Where else?"

"I suppose we have to wait for Frayser to connect."

"What I really meant was –" said the woman.

"We can't sit here for ever," said the driver. "At least, only in a sense . . ."

"And meanwhile just hope that the universe becomes explicate without any assistance from –"

"We could get a cup of tea. At least, when I say 'cup of tea' –"

"I'd better get back to the hardship as soon as possible," Grant said. "I think I have now resolved various contradictions in my inner life. Free from self-hatred! Maybe I've the fortitude to let truth shine in and obliterate evil memories. I've willed myself . . ."

"What?"

"Cured."

"You've punished yourself long enough," said the woman with a laugh. "At least as long as I've –"

"Sure."

"OK," said the driver. "No traffic tonight."

They set off along the dull suburban Manchurian motorway. The wipers clicked to an old tune of Lutoslavsky's.

Long after he had gone, I stood looking out of the window, at the lawns, at the great trees, at the other buildings, and at the birds sailing in the summer air above the trees. I contemplated the complexity of the human mind. Yet I contemplated its simplicity too. As Freud has said, beside every bridal bed stand four mute witnesses – the parents on either side. Grant had chosen an unresponsive wife because there is a demon of repetition in human affairs; hating his mother's supposed unresponsiveness, he had nevertheless selected a wife with her attributes. Well, if he sought her out after his years in the cold interstellar spaces, a magical transformation would have taken place. The transformation would be in him.

He would be able to stop acting the goat, to come down to Earth. And I?

I would be able to ascend.

As I thought the thought, the outlines of the room where I had been imprisoned for so long began to dissolve. There was no longer need to press any red button. Away went the windows with their splendid view, and my comfortable study. All had been borrowed from my mind. The amino-volk – as I thought of them – were interstellar refugees, but they had their powers. To them, my memories were as real as Grant's long-vanished (and in many respects illusory) past was to him.

My breathing quickened, my heartbeat altered. My left hemisphere tickled.

Through the white-out, the Pillar appeared. Perhaps it was a needed symbol of stability for their shifting minds.

"Are you making progress?" Its invariable question.

"Grant has made progress. He has resolved various contradictions in his inner life. I think he has the fortitude to let truth shine in and obliterate evil memories. He has willed himself cured. He has punished himself for long enough, and will now forgive himself."

"You have cured him within the time-limit we set. Congratulations. We selected Grant because we believed he was in many respects a hopeless case."

I laughed. I had to keep the laughter under control. "And is that why you picked me?"

"You were like a father to him. That could be something we also need and will pay for."

But Grant's father was long dead . . .

"Sorry, I want to go home now, just like Grant. I am interested in you, and don't wish to be insulting, but I can't believe your species will be half as absorbing as our suffering, hopeful species, struggling along as best we can, failing yet often scoring considerable successes."

"Please don't start denying us. We need to speak to you much more about parentage."

I scratched my neck. The remark was so stupidly human that it threw me.

"Look, you have just witnessed some of the problems that parentage brings to people on Earth. You say you don't reproduce by that method. So what point is there in discussing it?"

"We sympathise greatly with Grant. We also have no father. We become born through fission. That is why we now migrate through interstellar space, seeking, seeking . . . we know not what . . . We will tell you all you wish to know, open the secrets of the universe, if you will help us . . ."

Suddenly my patience was at an end, my pride roused.

"Look, my job is analysing humans, and that is exhausting enough. Humans *are* the secret of the universe. Whatever you are, you're irrelevant, an orphan species wandering the spaceways. I can do nothing for you. Now – beat it!"

The Pillar turned a shocking mauve. Cello notes turned into a trumpet call inside my brain. I was rejecting their hurt feelings. Then silence. The first silence I had heard for a long while. Reality returned. Like Grant, I was free to be myself. A bit of a problem, that. I knew only how to be my professional self.

The silence continued.

They had gone. Why? A species that could take no for an answer? No wonder they were permanently lost.

I felt a rush of love for my patient. Grant had never taken no for an answer – not even from himself. He had won through.

Somewhere, every moment of the day, some human was making another human miserable, knowingly or unknowingly. Everywhere, humans were struggling to be happy. How could another species help that process? I felt proudly, yes, we have problems, but we can solve them – and we have the right to privacy before we do so. *The Journal of Psychoanalysis* is a testament to human will-to-live.

"Isn't that a fact?" I said to Frayser as he entered the room.

William Frayser was still wrapped in his shower towels, two blue ones and one green. The warts on his face shone in the artificial daylight.

"I think that in the coming thought-revolution the word 'fact' will have to be interpreted in a different light. In the implicate world, there are only planes and interfaces." He spoke off-handedly while regarding his fingernails.

Stung by his superior tone, I said, "You scientists think yourselves so clever, but anyone who has studied the human mind knew that long ago."

Frayser drew himself up grandly. Perhaps he thought the towels made him look like a Roman in a toga. "What do you do as a psychiatrist but contemplate your own navel all day?" he sneered.

"Have you ever tried contemplating *someone else's navel*?"

My question took Frayser aback. I pressed home my advantage by reminding him that he was an intruder.

The word "intruder" seemed to agitate him, and he muttered something I did not understand about human beings not being interchangeable.

"Everything's interchangeable," I told him. "You as a physicist should know that." My confident mood allowed me to speak out. "Why, you yourself are made of the matter of dead stars – as both myth and science confirm."

I thought of the world's broken dolls and hopes; but, after all, in them lay renewal and life everlasting.

Frayser shook his battered head.

Perhaps he was about to deliver a lecture on the implicate order – in which, admittedly, we are all implicated – but thought better of it. Perhaps he saw the gleam of triumph in my eye. He cleared his throat and pretended to admire the Georges Braque painting of the bird on my wall.

"Why, that's magnificent, a magnificent painting," he said. "Who is the artist, may I ask? Did you paint it yourself?"

But I took the opportunity to slip past him. I had better things to do than chop logic with that man. After all, I had won through in a battle that perhaps decided the future of the universe.

Grant and I had both won through. There was every cause for rejoicing.

Things would be better on the ship from now on, and I could take credit for that, too.

I made my way to the nearest elevator, and thumbed the button for Bridge.

Bright light greeted me, noise and bustle, people busy but smiling. Floor reflective, crew unreflecting.

Grant was in uniform again. The crew had reappeared. Life's journey was back on course. Full speed ahead.

A sweeper was sweeping the leaves up. Birds chirped among the air-conditioning units, changing the recycled spring.

Beyond the ports, great bouquets of blossom were falling grandly through space, falling light and lissom as snowflakes.

Grant was singing in tune.

★

The evidence recently amassed suggests that this piece of writing was entitled "Journey to the Goat Star". No such title is registered in the bibliographies of the period. Nor has the piece itself been discovered. Researches continue.

from *Recent Bibliographical Rarities*
(Twentieth Century Cubist Studies)
by Wym Flah-Zee

(1982)

The Girl Who Sang

Mochtar Ivring peered over the flowers on his balcony and saw in the street below a beautiful girl, singing. It was the sound of her voice which had brought him to the balcony.

Most of the street lay in shadow, but the girl's head and torso were in sun. Her dark glossy hair shone, her cheeks shone. When she glanced up at him, green eyes dazzled for a moment in the early light. On her arm she carried a basket. She disappeared into a house, taking with her all the magic from the scene.

Craning to catch the last glimpse of her heel, Mochtar heard his landlady from the room behind say, "Mind my jissikla plants now!" He returned into his room where Mrs Bornzam was clearing his modest breakfast and making his bed.

"Beautiful singing," he said, explaining away his supposed threat to her windowboxes.

"That's the girl who sings," Mrs Bornzam said, with her customary air of setting in its place all that was known about the world.

The singing and the sight of the girl had momentarily lifted Mochtar's spirits, though they sank again when he contemplated the grey-clad bulk of Mrs Bornzam. The city of Matrassyl was stocked with people like Mrs Bornzam, all fat and corsetted and dull and ungenerous of spirit. He had been here far too long, but was too poor to afford to leave. So he lodged with the Bornzams in the back street, and advertised in their front parlour window for pupils. At present, the number of his pupils was precisely one. The war. Everything could be blamed on the war.

Although he had all day to kill as usual, Mochtar left the house in some haste, pulling on his yellow coat as he went, buttoning up its fur collar, as he hurried into the street. Not only did he wish to avoid Mrs Bornzam's conversation which had for its leitmotif the contemptible inability of teachers to earn good money, but he wanted to catch another glimpse, if possible, of the girl who sang.

The street was full of Matrassylans trudging to work. They were a dumpy race with a preference for grey cloth. Mochtar raised his eyes to the distant hills, but no one else looked. When he came into a grander thoroughfare, men on horseback mingled with the crowd of pedestrians, and a cabriolet laboured slowly up to the castle, the driver lashing his horses. On the corner of this thoroughfare and the street where the Bornzams lived stood a tavern. As he paused there, the girl who sang left by one of its side doors.

The way she swung her basket told him that it was now empty, and he guessed she had been delivering bread. As she paused in the sunlight, a few notes escaped her lips. Then she saw Mochtar staring and stopped, smiling, her lips apart, to give him an enquiring look.

She was more lovely than he had imagined. Her face was rather long, though this was counterbalanced by a round little nose. Her mouth looked generous, her eyebrows were arched and a trifle severe. Heavy lashes offset her light green eyes. If these features sounded miscellaneous when catalogued, when glimpsed together their effect was delightful – even breathtaking. Mochtar thought, and before he could allow shyness to overwhelm him, he had stepped forward, raised his hat, and addressed this beautiful creature.

The beautiful creature regarded him from under her lashes. With a disarming smile, she sang a few bars of a melody and then passed by, tripping daintily up the side street. Thus a chance was presented to gaze at her slender figure, in which the dumpiness of Matrassyl was nowhere apparent.

He had certainly never heard a more delectable sound than her singing. Cloddish bodies pushed by him as he stood, striving to capture her elusive tune in his head. At one moment he thought it familiar, at the next not. The harsh sounds of Metrassyl, thrown against stone walls and cliffs and echoing back, drove it from mind.

He moved on when a squad of infantry marched noisily by, and made his way to the Question Mark. The usual one-armed beggar stood outside, but Mochtar brushed past him. He favoured this coffee house because one of the waiters was friendly, hailing from the same distant country, born within sight of the same sea, as Mochtar. After greeting his friend, he retired to his usual table and abstractedly unfurled a newspaper to see how the war was going.

War had been raging for nineteen years, prowling back and forth across the continent of Campanlat like plague, springing up again when seeming exhausted. It showed no sign of reaching any conclusion, despite the oratory of statesmen.

It was the war, and the prankish accidental nature of war, which had stranded Mochtar, at the age of twenty, in Matrassyl. Innocent of all knowledge of any such city, he was studying in a university in the Qzints when the university town had been invaded by a Pannavalan army. The invading army took over the university buildings as its headquarters. Mochtar and other students had been made prisoner and forced to work in gangs, towing barges south-eastwards for several hundred miles along the towpaths of the Ubingual Canal, which cut through the heart of the strife-locked continent. One stormy night, Mochtar had dodged the guard, crossed the canal, and escaped, to find himself, after months of wandering, in Matrassyl. He was too ill to go further. Although his strength had by now returned, return to his home by the Climent Sea was impossible; for that he needed money, and a cessation to the fighting in the western sector.

Sipping his free coffee, he scoured the blurred newsprint before him.

According to the latest report, the enemy in the west was at last in retreat, following the bitter winter campaign. The double-headed eagle had gained distinct ascendancy over the sun-and-sickle – although, in the east, in Mordriat, prospects were less bright. Somehow, the news brought Mochtar little joy, certainly not enough to dislodge the girl's tune from his head. The words . . . The words of the tune . . . Suddenly, he resolved a part of the puzzle. He slapped his hand on the table, rattling his cup. The girl – he should have realised as much earlier – was not singing in Olonets, the local language. She sang in Slachs, an eastern language with which Mochtar was only slightly familiar.

The friendly waiter ceased his favourite occupation of staring over the green curtain into the street, and said, mistaking Mochtar's gesture, "The news is gratifying, yes?"

"Very gratifying. We'll be home some time, and away from this prison of a town."

"This is the day you go to teach your lame boy?"

"Yes. He's now my only pupil, and he's a fool. Hence my failing finances."

The waiter nodded and bent closer. "Listen, I have a titbit for you. A fellow told me yesterday that the duke's language teacher has gone for a soldier, silly ass, to try and find his brother lost in the eastern war against the Kzaan of Mordriat.

"The duke's enlightened about foreigners, they say. Why don't you go up to the castle and try your luck?"

"I'd never dare."

"It couldn't do any harm. Try your luck, I say, or you may be forced to take up a waiting job too. Better to teach the surly Matrassylans than serve them, I say . . . Have another cup of coffee before you leave."

The next morning was positively springlike. When the sun Freyr rose high enough above the shoulders of the Cosgatt Mountains to shine upon the domes of the city's churches, Mochtar was already dressed and breakfasted.

Mrs Bornzam disapproved of this departure from routine as gravely as she disapproved of lateness, and expressed her displeasure by hissing through her false teeth, but her lodger escaped without delay into the street. He walked slowly up it, up to the top. It was a direction in which he rarely ventured, for the alleys became narrow and steep, and the people increasingly xenophobic. Deformed phagors lurked in slavery here. He observed that a water pump was being repaired. Cobbles had been taken up, a spring gushed down an adjacent way from a broken pipe, bubbling across the street.

Blessed water, he thought, which has diverted the girl who sang from her customary path towards my irresistible clutches.

As he stood where the ways met, his initiative was rewarded. Echoing among the shadowy alleys came a haunting song, and in a moment the dark girl was in sight, her basket over her arm. Her step was firm. She was as trim a vision as he had ever set eyes on.

Immediately, his hatred of the city left him. According to legend, Matrassyl had once been the capital of an empire; now it was a dull provincial town. But the beauty of the girl who sang transformed it into a miraculous place.

He raised his hat as she approached.

"May I walk with you on your way?"

She smiled with a reserve which Mochtar felt he already knew by heart. A fragment of song drifted from her red lips. Prepared for the foreign language, he thought he grasped its simple meaning: "I care for nobody, for nobody cares for me."

She gave no other answer. He had the benefit of her profile along most of the street. At the door of the tavern, she turned her eyes towards him and sang a few pure notes. Then she went inside.

He waited with a light heart until she emerged with a light basket. It was puzzling: the girl who sang attempted neither to evade nor to address him. Pretty and pleasant though she was, there was something withdrawn in her manner, something which made him feel it would be impertinent to return up the street with her.

"May I see you tomorrow?" he asked. He thought, if I don't see her, the sun will not shine.

When she sang, he recognised the Slachs word for "tomorrow", but could not understand the rest of it. That vexed him, but he went on his way rejoicing in the memory of her parting smile. What a strange, what a marvellous girl . . . And not from these parts, praise be . . . Perhaps unhuman blood ran in her veins – the blood of the Madis, let's say . . . Before he knew it, he had climbed the hill and was at the Anganal Gate of the castle.

The dukes of Matrassyl had seen grand times, but misfortunes of war had reduced their pomp. Mochtar was shown into a room with an unlit stove where the curtains, funereal at long windows, had moth holes in them. He sat on a side-chair, contemplating a portrait of the Emperor, above which hung a tattered flag bearing the double-headed eagle, the bird of Oldorando-Borlien. Clutching his hat, he thought how the world was loaded against the young; even the expression about the Emperor's whiskers proclaimed as much. You had to fight back as best you could.

When a withered clerk entered the room, Mochtar stood up. The clerk asked him a few questions. After another wait, he was shown into the presence of the duke.

The duke sat at a polished table. He wore a green velvet jacket with lace cuffs. And a wig. Apart from a large ruby ring on one finger, and a melancholy expression, he appeared much like any ordinary human being in middle life. Unsmilingly, he motioned Mochtar to sit on the opposite side of the table, so that they could both study the other's reflection in the polished table-top.

"I have three children. I wish them to be taught Ponpt, which I understand is your native language, to a standard where they can speak it fluently and read its works of religious literature with ease."

"Yes, your grace."

"The times are ill, M. Ivring, and will remain so until the forces of the sun-and-sickle are defeated. Because of the confounded war, I wish also to have my children coached in the barbarous eastern tongue of Slachdom. You have no command of Slachs, I assume?"

Caught between a wish to be honest and a wish to secure the job, Mochtar paused. Then, rather to his own surprise, he sang in his light tenor voice, in Slachs, "I care for nobody, for nobody cares for me."

The duke was impressed. He screwed a monocle into his left eye and surveyed Mochtar carefully.

"You are engaged, sir. My clerk will furnish you with details of salary and so forth. Before you go, outline for me your philosophy of life."

In the midst of the paralysis which this question induced, Mochtar thought that, very likely, dukes were trained to freeze the air about them; it went with their exalted station in life. He recalled his pleasant home-city by the western sea, where the gulls cried: he thought of the desolate plains and mountains within which Matrassyl was ensconced; he thought of the yet more desolate lands to the east, the lands which led ultimately to the High Nktryhk, from whence, mysteriously, a girl who sang had come, emerging from clouds of war. And he thought of saying to the duke, There is no philosophy, only geography; Helliconia is a function, and humanity a part of that function. But that might not meet the case at all.

"I believe in rationality, your grace. That people should conduct their lives without superstition . . ."

"It sounds commendable enough. How do you define superstition?"

"Well, your grace, we should trust to the evidence of the

intellect. I can believe in this table because I can see it; yesterday, if challenged on the point, I would have been within my rights not to have believed in it, because my senses had not informed me of its existence. Hearsay evidence would not have been sufficient."

The duke's hand went to an elaborate inkstand and played with it, seemingly without permission from the duke, who sat stiffly upright.

"You chose a trivial example upon which to suppose yourself questioned. Let us say the interrogation concerned not a piece of furniture but Almighty Akhanaba, who elects not to show himself to us. What then?"

"From this day on, I shall believe in your table, your grace, because I have witnessed its existence, and could if necessary give some account of it."

The duke rose and pulled the bell-cord. "Be sure you teach your charges your language and literature, not your philosophy. I also am a rationalist – but one evidently of larger capacity than you. I believe in this table as evidence of God Almighty as well as mere evidence of itself. As I see my reflection in it, so I see His."

"Yes, your grace."

As the dry clerk returned to escort Mochtar out, the duke said, "Undiluted rationality leads to death of the spirit. You sing. Remember that songs are frequently to be trusted above prose, and metaphor above so-called reality."

From that day on, Mochtar's affairs prospered. He saw more of the girl who sang – and not only in the mornings but in the evenings and on her free afternoons. He put one or two rivals to flight. Discovering more about her became one with the advance of spring, which grew greener everyday although Helliconia was entering the autumn of another Great Year. They walked in the daisy-starred meadows above the grey town, and she sang, "Love is all lies and deception, And my lover hides in the dark wild wood."

They sat on a fallen tree trunk, looking down at the city below, where little dumpy people moved in miniature streets. Beyond the town flowed the river, the chill Takissa. Above them, steep meadows gave way to the harsher slopes of the Cosgatt. Somewhere up there, so rumour had it, an army flying the banners of the sun-and-sickle was approaching Matrassyl. The girl hugged her

knees and sang about a house untended, where women's hearts
were empty because their men were off to fight at a place called
Kalitka.

Beyond the city walls, the life of the country reasserted itself.
Fish flashed in the river, and a heron waited immobile for them on
the bank. Butterflies and bees were at work in the scantiom
nearby. Beetles glinted in the tall grass.

Both suns shone. Everywhere lay double shadows, double
highlights.

He gestured contemptuously at the city which distance had
diminished. "Look at it – you could put it in your pocket, castle
and all."

But she had no answer for him, only her touching lament.

"Never mind Kalitka," he said. "What about Matrassyl and you
and I? What about those highly important topics, eh?"

He grasped her impatiently, but she shook free and jumped to
her feet. She looked blank, and the song died on her lips. Standing
with her mouth slightly open, she presented a picture of maimed
beauty.

One evening in her doorway, he kissed her lips. She put an arm
about his neck and softly sang, "Don't drive the horses too hard,
coachman. There's still a long long way to go."

Together with the spring and their developing relationship went
Mochtar's increasing involvement with the two sons and the
daughter of the duke. Their ages were five, six, and eight. Though
they were haughty with their language tutor, they attended to his
lessons, and made steady progress in Ponpt.

Sometimes, the duchess, a thin lady in velvets, arrived at the
door of the schoolroom, and listened without speaking. Sometimes
the duke would appear, cramming his bulk into a small desk to
attend, frowning, to what Mochtar had to say. This embarrassed
his employee, all too aware of his scanty knowledge of Slachs.

Sombre though the duke's demeanour was, Mochtar detected
an errant spirit under the surface; whereas her grace appeared to
possess no character at all, beyond a stifled way of breathing.

"M. Ivring," said the duke, drawing him aside on one occasion,
"you may apply to the librarian, with my permission, to refer to
my books. You will find there a section of volumes on Slachdom,
including – if memory serves – a grammar of the Slachs tongue."

Not since he had been forced to leave his university studies had Mochtar seen as many volumes as the library contained. The section printed in Slachs was particularly precious. It drew him nearer to the girl who sang. Here he could study her language, and make out something of the history of her race.

One afternoon, when he was sunk deep in a leather chair, reading, the duke appeared and screwed his monocle into his eye.

"You are deriving benefit from the library, my rationalist friend?"

"Yes, your grace." Mochtar realised that this stiff-backed man, the Duke of Matrassyl – not ancient, perhaps no more ancient than twenty-eight years old, though that was ancient enough – was attempting to be friendly. Beyond closing his volume with a finger in it, Mochtar made no move to respond.

"You probably wonder how I come to have such a collection of volumes relating to Slachs."

Having wondered nothing of the sort, Mochtar kept silent.

The duke walked about before saying, "I led a campaign to the east, very successful. We put the forces of the Kzaan of Mordriat to flight. A great victory, a great victory. That was ten years ago. Unfortunately, it did not end the war, and now the enemy has gathered strength again, and isn't too far from here . . ." He sighed heavily.

"Anyhow, we plundered one of the strongholds of the Kzaan, and these books were part of the booty. They're decently bound, I'll give the barbarian that."

He swung about on his heel in a military way, leaving as abruptly as he had come. Dismissing him from mind, Mochtar returned to his history of the Slachi.

The Slachi were a nation within a nation. They lived chiefly in the mountain ranges of the vast country of Mordriat, often as shepherds or brigands. They were persecuted from time to time. Many of the men were forced through poverty to join the Mordriat Kzaan's armies, where they served the sun-and-sickle loyally. Indeed, their prowess in war had enabled some exceptional Slachi to become Kzaans. Despite such occasional glories, the history of their race was one of misfortune. There had once been an independent Slachi nation, but it was overwhelmed at the Battle of Kalitka ("still a subject for epic poetry", said the chronicle) six centuries previously.

As Mochtar's friendship with the girl who sang grew, so grew his knowledge of her ethnic background, and of her language.

So also did her mystery grow. She never spoke. She could not speak. She could only sing her songs. Though people in the back streets of Matrassyl knew her because of her singing, no one was her friend. None could say her name. She was the eternal foreigner.

The girl who sang worked in a bakery and lived in a garret. She had no parents, no relations, no one near her who spoke Slachs. She had no possessions, as far as Mochtar could discover – except for a long-necked binnaduria inlaid with mother-of-pearl, with which she sometimes accompanied her songs.

So beautiful was her singing that the birds of garden and meadow ceased their own warbling to listen. They would gather about her high window as they never did about the casements of those who threw them grain.

"I'm a foreigner in this town, as you are, my darling. Where were you born? Do you remember?"

"The walls of Lestanávera stand high above the stream. But life in Lestanávera is nothing but a dream," she sang in her own tongue.

"Is that your home, Lestanávera?"

"Alas, the traitorous Vuk at night who opened up the gate, Betrayed old Lestanávera and Slachi fate."

"Were you there then, my poor love?"

She could not reply, unless her lingering regard was a reply.

In the duke's library after lessons the next day, Mochtar found a reference to Lestanávera. It had been a great fortress on the Madavera, the main river of the vanquished kingdom of Slachi. A traitor named Vuk Sudar had opened the gate to the Mordriat enemy and the impregnable fortress fell. Two years later came the fateful battle of Kalitka, when the Slachi nation was finally defeated, its leaders and soldiers slain.

In so many of her songs, Mochtar reflected as he walked back to his room, she made reference to events long gone. The realisation came to him slowly that not only was song her sole means of communication: her songs were traditional, referring to events long past. The shadowy power of Lestanávera, a place he had had to look up in a book, might be either the power natural to her birthplace, or to a legend born long before her grandparents' time.

"Late again, and me standing over the pot for you," Mrs Bornzam said, when he entered his lodgings. Mochtar took his evening meal with the senior Bornzams and their two loutish sons – a doubtful privilege. Since he was late, and politely brought up, he apologised.

"I should think so," the lady said, in a tone implying that she found his apologies as irritating as his unpunctuality. "Just because you work for the duke, you needn't ape the manners of the duke."

He let his anger simmer throughout the meal, eating little despite the blandishments of old Bornzam, who was a civil enough fellow, considering that he worked in the town abattoir. He waited until after the meal, when Mrs Bornzam stacked all the dirty plates and cutlery into her sink, added her pair of china false teeth to the pile, and began the washing-up. Her teeth were always done with the dishes, and dried afterwards on the same towel, before being reinserted in her mouth.

Mochtar worked himself up to deliver something cruel, but managed only to say, "Mrs Bornzam, I shall be leaving this house tomorrow. I will pay you till the end of the month. I refuse to eat at your table again."

She looked round at him in horror, her cheeks turning a dull red. Fishing in the washing-up water with one hand, she brought her teeth up dripping, and pushed them into her mouth to say, "And what's so wrong with my table, then, you little scholarly prig? You won't get better meat at any other table, that's sure."

"It's not at all sure. It's a very debatable statement. Mrs Bornzam, your temper might be better if you sang everything you had to say. You might then be less intolerable."

"You cheeky little pipsqueak!"

"Though doubtless if you attempted to sing, your teeth would fall out. Goodnight, madam."

Feeling less triumphant next morning, Mochtar told his troubles to the girl who sang.

"Hide away your tear, Only the binnaduria sounds sweet year-long."

He kissed her passionately. "Why can you not speak, you beauty? Yet how I love your voice. What has happened to you that the ordinary power of words has deserted you?"

What with the practice that she and his pupils gave him, he now spoke easily to her in her native tongue.

"Only the binnaduria sounds sweet year-long."

"It's not true. You also sound sweet – always."

That word "Always" lingered in his mind as he climbed the road to the castle. To have her for always . . . To take her away from grey Matrassyl, away to the sea . . . But his daydreams shattered as ever on the rational rock of his having too little money. He had received a letter from his father – it had been on its way for months – but it enclosed no money for him. Damn his father, the old rogue.

Fortune, however, still smiled on him. At the close of the morning's lesson, the duke entered the schoolroom. He had a widowed cousin who also wished to learn Slachs. Would M. Irving be her tutor for a salary she and he could agree between themselves? They expected the lady at the castle on the following day.

Mochtar had had to give up his lame pupil, the son of a burgher, in order to teach at the castle. With four pupils, his salary should be sufficient to get married on, if he could find a good room locally.

The dream changed. He would live for ever in Matrassyl with the girl who sang, and she would slowly come to speak prose like everyone else.

That evening at Freyrset he asked her to marry him. He thought she accepted him. She sang that all the girls of the village admired the handsome young shepherd, but he had eyes for only one of the girls. She sang of a handkerchief that gleamed in the moonlight by a ruin where two young lovers had met. She sang that the River Madavera flowed by a cottage, where all who passed in boats heard a young girl singing to express her happiness. She sang, she played her guitar, she danced for him, she wept. It seemed like an acceptance.

There was no difficulty in finding a pleasant but rather expensive room in which to set up house. They consoled themselves for their extravagance by admiring the beautiful view of the river. The girl who sang knew many songs about rivers. Rivers, with ruins, broken wine-glasses, soldiers, deserted lovers, lost letters, and old mothers, formed a large part of her repertoire.

The wedding ceremony presented difficulties, but Mochtar, aided by his waiter friend, found an understanding priest who agreed to join them in matrimony.

"I knew a nun with the same affliction," the man of God observed. "She had been raped by an enemy soldier, or perhaps it was a friendly one, and never after uttered another word. Except for her devotional singing, which was much valued in the nunnery."

So Mochtar and the girl who sang were married, and returned in happiness to their room with a view. The bride clutched her groom, kissed him, and sang sweetly, but evaded all the usual pleasant intimacies of the bed.

It was therefore a rather gloomy Mochtar who returned to the castle to meet his new pupil. The Lady Ljubima was not the gaunt old figure in black his imagination had painted. She was a fair-haired woman of his own age, brightly dressed and flirtatious of manner. Even the duke looked more cheerful in her presence. She informed Mochtar immediately that she liked him and had no intention of mourning an old husband who had been foolish enough to get himself killed on a silly battlefield.

Standing like a statue to integrity, Mochtar informed her that while he was prepared to teach her a foreign language, he felt bound to tell her that he was newly married. She laughed, not at all put out, and named a generous sum she was prepared to pay as long as the lessons were not too dull.

Despite himself, he found himself growing to like Ljubima. She had wit, and she detested Matrassyl as cordially as he. She treated him as a slightly dim equal, and told him amusing stories of life in what she termed her "tinpot palace", now overrun by the hated sun-and-sickle. Their friendship progressed faster than their lessons.

When Mochtar returned to his room, there was his lovely wife, to sing to him and kiss him and cook him gorgeous meals – but not to grant him the intimacies he craved. Every day he discovered how expensive meat was, and how dusty repressed desire.

"What ails you, my love?" he asked her tenderly – he was tender to her at this time. "What has befallen you?"

She took up her long-necked binnaduria and sang him a heart-breaking song of a lass who walked late in her garden one night, and none thereafter knew why she pined away, pined away.

He took to writing down the words of her songs that summer. She gladly helped him, singing each phrase over, her hand resting on his shoulder. At first, he did it for love, without mercenary intention. Growing more ambitious, he took music lessons in the evening with an old crone in the lower town, in order to be able to transcribe the notes of her songs into his book.

As he was walking home one evening late, Mochtar was hailed from a hansom cab. It was his fair pupil, the Lady Ljubima. She offered to drive him home, and he climbed up beside her. But she called to her driver, and they clip-clopped to her house at a great rate.

"For a glass of wine, no more!" she cried, laughing at his concern. "Don't think I'm offering you anything else, little scholar."

"I don't doubt that!" he said, suddenly bitter. "Women like to lead men on – only to deny them the one thing they want."

"Oh, la! And will you name that one thing?"

"You know what I mean – the rational end of desire."

More sympathetically, she said, "You speak with experience."

"With *in*experience, more like."

When they reached the mansion, Ljubima said she was tired, she dismissed the servants and took him into her boudoir, where she poured him a glass of spiced wine. They sat companionably on a *chaise-longue*, and Mochtar found himself pouring out the story of his strange wife. At first, he felt ashamed of his loose tongue, but a passion for declaration soon overcame him.

Silence fell when he finished.

A tear stole down Ljubima's cheek. "Mochtar, dear Mochtar, thank you for confiding in me. Your wife sounds such a rare person. No doubt she underwent some terrible experience as a young girl – that's a tragedy. But it is obvious how much she loves and trusts you. No doubt in a year or two she will feel confident enough to grant you all you desire and more."

"A year! A year or two! You think I can wait so long?"

She tried to calm him. He seized more wine and drank it down, flinging the glass on to the rug, where it lay without shattering.

"You must wait. Oh, yours is such a rare love! I will never do anything to sully it. Forgive me! I admit that, on a whim, because you're amusing, I did play with the idea of a seduction scene, this being a night I am free, but now –"

He turned furiously on her.

"Played with the idea – played with me, you mean! Just as she does. A rare love! Rare indeed! Take your clothes off, you bitch, or I swear I'll kill you."

"I'll call the servants and have you shot. One scream is all it needs."

He stood back. "Ljubima, forgive me, I'm not rational. Let me stay with you tonight, I beg. I will offer no violence, only love. I'm not a violent man. Please, if you find I'm acceptable. Amuse yourself, as you intended. For myself, you know how I have grown fond of you."

She sat. Then she raised her hands and began to unpin her hair.

"Are you sure this is what you most want?"

"Oh, yes, yes, darling Ljubima!" He fell on his knees, seizing one of her hands and kissing it. "How can you be so sweet to me, a commoner?"

"Ask nothing – just accept," she said. "And don't flatter yourself by thinking of me as nobility. I'm just a woman overtaken by war."

He did not pause to puzzle out her remark.

The girl who sang did not reproach her husband when he appeared late next day. Instead, she gave voice to a slow song of intricate rhythm, to which the refrain was, "Oh, Marick, Marick, are you dead, as in my dreams you were?" Smiling, she executed a gentle dance before him. He covered his eyes.

During the next afternoon lesson, Mochtar and Ljubima were formal. At the end of it, as they rose from the schoolroom table, she said in a low voice, "I accepted you last night because of the touching story of your marriage, nothing more."

"That is not what you said then. When may I come and see you again?"

She looked down at the worn carpet. "The war from the east

draws nearer Matrassyl, day by day. Who knows what will become of us all?"

He thought that her words could have been set to music.

As she left the room, she said casually, "You could come tomorrow night. I'll be free then. My cab will pick you up in the Old Square."

Because she seemed so wealthy and he so poor, he thought, I'm really lucky, but everything would be better if only I had more money.

The next time the Duke of Matrassyl entered the classroom to observe the progress his children were making, Mochtar ventured to address him.

"Your grace, your children are both brilliant and diligent at their studies. However, they lack mastery of the correct Slachs accent, that all-important matter, which I, not being of Slachi origin, am unable to impart in all its nuances. May I make so bold as to suggest that I hire for you a lady I have encountered, a Slachi, who could come to the castle and enunciate for your children and your Lady cousin, to their decided advantage?"

The duke regarded him from under his iron eyebrows.

"When you were first engaged, young man, my impression was that you had little Slachs, though I grant you progressed rapidly. Supposing this lady you have encountered . . . proves herself a better teacher than you. Will you not then have engineered yourself out of a job?"

"This lady, your grace, speaks only her own language. She will be a perfect example but an imperfect teacher, you'll find."

"You are still a rationalist, I perceive. Very well, bring her along."

"She is much in demand, your grace, and not only comes somewhat expensive, but requests strongly that your grace pay her through me before she appears."

The duke took a long look out of the window towards the mountains.

"Well, the enemy may be at the Takissa before autumn. Before that fate befalls us, we must all enjoy life as much as we can."

He sighed heavily. "I have reason to believe that our old enemy, the Kzaan, will raze Matrassyl to the ground if he gets here . . ."
And he paid Mochtar the amount he demanded.

When Mochtar arrived home, he explained to his wife that she would have to sing at the castle the next day. "Sing and dance, that will be best. We must earn some money. When the enemy gets near the gates, we are going to escape, and that requires resources. My friend in the Question Mark will come with us. Three will travel safer than two."

Her breasts heaved beneath her blouse, and she began to sing quietly of Lestanávera, now only a ruin, where once many a handsome man and maid were seen.

"Never mind Lestanávera, my dear, let's eat supper fast, because I have to go out this evening."

Over the pot on the stove, she hummed quietly to herself. It was the song, he recognised, about a girl who looked after her father's swine; she called to them and the swine heard her voice; but the one whom she longed to hear was dead beneath the winter's snow. He checked to make sure it was in his collection.

By now, he had over two hundred Slachs folk-songs, many of them several centuries old. In the civilised capitals of the West, the collection would be worth a great deal, and his name would be made when they were published.

There was great activity as Mochtar made his way to the castle with his wife. Soldiers were marching through the streets, and a band was playing. As the band stopped, Mochtar understood the reason for the excitement. Distant cannonfire boomed in the hills. The forces of the sun-and-sickle were nearing the Takissa. He said nothing to his wife.

She sang a repertoire of songs to her audience of four, just as Mochtar demanded. To his disappointment, the duke and duchess did not appear. As they were about to leave the castle, however, the duke was standing in the hall talking to two army officers. He also was in uniform, with sword and pistol at his belt, looking formidable. A line of armed phagor guards waited motionless behind him. When he saw Mochtar, he called him over. The duke's manner was curt, his expression grim.

"I may be absent for some while. You are dismissed, Ivring. Draw what salary is owed you – my clerk will see to it – and don't come here again, ever."

Mochtar was dumbfounded.

"But why, your grace?"

"You're dismissed, I said. Go."

"But I must say goodbye to Lady –"

The duke, in turning a uniformed shoulder on him, noticed the girl who sang for the first time, and beckoned her to him. He said something to the generals, who immediately became interested.

She approached, and eyed the duke with an open curiosity in which her usual innocence protected her from fear.

"What's your name, my dark-haired beauty?"

She sang a few pure notes, "My name is sorrow, I'm from Distack." It was number 82 in Mochtar's book.

One of two officers immediately took the girl by her arm, while the other officer drove Mochtar away.

"I never argue with an armed man," he said, and fled, ignoring his wife's cries.

When he had collected his fee from the duke's clerk, who would tell him nothing, he hurried from the castle. Pushing through the crowded streets, he went to cheer himself up at the Question Mark, where he gave an account of the duke's behaviour to his friend, the waiter.

"I can't understand it," he said. "I was the perfect teacher."

"The war's coming this way," said the waiter. "Faster than expected. You're a foreigner, aren't you? Well, that's the way they treat foreigners in this rotten town. I should know."

"Yes, you must be right. Then why did they seize my wife?"

The waiter spread his hands. It was all so obvious to him. "Why, she's a foreigner, too, isn't she? What else can you expect in a place like Matrassyl?"

"I suppose you're right. Get me a bottle of wine, will you? What a mean way to behave to an honest chap . . ."

He spent several hours drinking in the coffee house and studying the newspaper, which was full of bad news from East and West. The only item to offer encouragement was an obscure paragraph on a back page, which announced the death of a composer in his home country. Someone would have to take his place. Composers were always needed, in war as in peace. He would have to see about arranging the songs, to make them more palatable to a cultured public.

Going heavily home, he was surprised to find his room empty.

His wife had not yet returned. Who would prepare his supper? Why, their bed was not even made, curse her.

Suddenly, he was angry. What pleasure had he ever enjoyed on that bed? She gave him nothing, never would. But there were others . . .

His mind dwelt luxuriously on Lady Ljubima, on her beauty and ardour. Also on her way with words, always so precise, always saying exactly what she intended. A rational person, like him. Really – one had to admit it – being married to someone who could not talk or make love was misery.

He took a drink from a brandy bottle, tramping round the room, and came suddenly to a decision.

Pulling his old pack from under the bed, he stuffed some essentials into it. The bottle went in. So did the priceless folksong collection. At the door, he paused and looked round. Her long-necked binnaduria lay on the dresser. Yes, it would serve her right if he took it. At least he'd get something from her. He grabbed it.

As he walked through the streets of Matrassyl for the last time, he saw his future clear. He would be doing Ljubima a favour. He was rescuing her from certain death. Rape. Torture. All the rest of it. This was one of the evenings she had forbidden him to see her – but what of that? Her cab was what he needed. They would escape in the cab. She would have valuables. They'd drive westward, never stopping. Never stopping till they reached the western sea. There they would live happily and prosperously, and he would be famous.

It was a long way on foot to her mansion. Double darkness had fallen by the time he arrived. As he passed under the light by the gate, he saw her holding a candle at an upper window. Ljubima saw Mochtar and waved frantically.

"She's crazy for me," he told himself, smiling.

Her footman opened the door. He stepped into the hall. The Duke of Matrassyl emerged from Ljubima's parlour. His monocle was in his left eye. He levelled a double-barrelled pistol at Mochtar. He trembled with suppressed fury.

This apparition so astonished Mochtar that his legs began immediately to quake. He could hardly stand up, never mind speak.

"I'm glad to see you so dismayed," said the duke, speaking in a thick voice. "You have earned yourself a reputation as rather a cool customer. I discover you have had the infernal temerity to visit my mistress here, in the very house in which I have installed her. She has told me everything, so don't deny it."

"But, but she –"

"You are going to be shot. I am going to shoot you. Say nothing. Pray to Akhanaba."

Mochtar's knees collapsed. He fell sobbing to the marble tiles.

"But my poor wife . . ."

"A little late to think of her." The duke had a grim smile on his face, as if he was enjoying these moments considerably more than Mochtar. "Ten years ago, when fighting in the eastern campaign, one of my generals took an enemy position, and we found we had captured the family of the Great Kzaan of Mordriat – the Kzaan having fled in true Slachi fashion. My men put all the family to the bayonet, except for the Kzaan's wife and daughter, the latter scarcely seven years old. They were seized for ransom. That was a lucky day for us."

Mochtar looked up supplicatingly, but the duke kicked him back into a crouching position.

"Both the mother and the daughter were raped on their way back here, and unfortunately the Kzaanina died. The daughter escaped from us one night. We assumed she had either died or found her way back to Mordriat. But no. You, my resourceful little trickster, found her in the back streets of this very city. Her mind's gone, but she's still of great value. The Kzaan will spare Matrassyl in order to get his daughter back alive."

Through his snivels, Mochtar had been listening hard. He rose to his knees now, to say, "Your grace, please believe me, I was about to hand her over. That was why I brought her to the castle, don't you see? You can't shoot the saviour of Matrassyl."

A pleasant laugh sounded behind the duke.

"You can't shoot him, Advard. Let him go. He means no real harm – unlike the Kzaan, with whom you are prepared to deal. I wish more of your soldiers had Mochtar's nerve."

The duke turned scowling to where Ljubima stood, tall and fair, holding before her a candle in a golden candlestick.

"You love this crawling commoner," he said, raising the pistol.

"Oh no, no, Advard. On the contrary. He almost raped me. I'd be glad to see him go. But I hate seeing people being killed."

Mollified by this response, the duke turned back to Mochtar. This time, something sheepish had entered into his manner.

"Listen, I shall count to ten, boy, and then I shall shoot you if you are still here. One."

Mochtar was through the door by Three.

By Five he was back.

He smiled nervously at the duke and Ljubima.

"Sorry. I forgot my pack and my binnaduria."

He grabbed them and ran for the door.

"Nine. Ten."

Both barrels of the pistol fired. But Mochtar had fled into the night.

(1982)

Consolations of Age

The hill was broken and, on the face of it, forbidding. Two tribes lived on the hill, the Antall on the east slopes, and the Zambill on the west.

Perched in their watchtowers, the tribes could see welcoming savannah and jungle. From the shelter of those distant trees they had come, and to it they would have returned, had not fiercer tribes driven them to their present refuge and taken over their ancestral groves. Their defeat, their flight, was not forgotten. They hunted with circumspection.

A stranger knowing something of the history of the two tribes might suppose that they would ally themselves against common, powerful enemies. It was not so. The Antall and Zambill were perpetually at war with each other.

That they survived at all was due to an accident of geology. The broken hill was all that was left of what had once been a great mountain, drained by a grand river. All that remained of the river was a cleft in the rock, deep but fairly narrow, which divided the hill into two unequal parts – the land of the Antall and the land of the Zambill. This cleft was known as King's Leap.

To the Zambill fell the larger part of the mountain, stocked with small game and watered by brooks. The Antall, in the east, had their sacred pools in the rocks, and lived off the great variety of birds which nested among the crags of the broken hill.

In accord with these marginal variations in territory, the two tribes observed different customs. Their customs governed every event in life, from birth to death, including such matters as food, and how to cook and eat it.

Both tribes were patriarchal, and ruled by savage chiefs. When the young men reached puberty, they were forced to undergo initiation rites. These rites also differed between the tribes. The youths of the Antall were required to disappear into the wastes of the hill, there to slay a mountain cat barehanded. Before the youths of the Zambill could become fully-fledged warriors, they had to vanish into the rocks of the higher hill, there to mate with a female baboon.

The local game, needless to say, did not observe human customs. When chased, goat, cat, and mountain sheep often fled to the heights, jumping across the gulf of King's Leap to safety from their pursuers. This frontier meant nothing to them. But one day, two old men met at King's Leap, and confronted each other across its rocky lips.

Of recent years, drought had stricken this part of the world, and game was scarce. The result was an intensification of the hostility between the Antall and the Zambill. Any member of the other tribe who was captured was put to death after cruel torture. Raids were undertaken, crops and huts burned, women raped, children taken into slavery.

The instigator of warlike activity on the Zambill side was Chief Whiili-An. On the western slopes of the broken hill stood a gate of clumsy design, its two round towers linked by a wooden gallery stretching across the top of the doors. Behind this gate was the citadel of Zambill, a crowded, uncomfortable place which gave shelter to animals and insects as well as humans. The towers were of stone, the inhabitants were stony-faced, and behind the market square stood the stone palace of Chief Whiili-An. Here he lived with his five wives, plotting destruction on the enemies of his tribe. The skulls of past enemies, grinning from his walls, were constant reminders of his prowess.

Just as relentless was Chief Maani-Mjmu of the Antall. He lived with his six wives in a decorated mud fortress behind the mud walls of his citadel on the eastern slopes. His life was dedicated to inspiring his warriors to fresh atrocities against their neighbours on the other side of the hill. His fortress bore on its battlements gruesome testimony to his past successes.

Many a night, under the great moons that sailed over the hill, blood was drunk in the citadels of Antall or Zambill, and yet another victory of one or other chief was celebrated with drum-beat, sweat, and liquor.

Within their own territories, the word of Chief Whiili-An and of Chief Maani-Mjmu was law, and unchallenged. Only one thing prevailed above their word. That was the custom of the tribe.

It so happened that in both tribes the chiefs were worshipped as gods. But when divinity fell from the brow of the god, a younger chief was appointed, who immediately dispatched the old god without mercy or reference to his previously unblemished record. The tests for failing divinity differed between the tribes, although both were equally stringent.

One afternoon late in the year, when the sky was full of flocks of mourner-birds passing overhead for days at a time, Chief Maani-Mjmu of the Antall climbed to the top of the eastern side of the hill and stood leaning on his spear, breathing hard, and looking down into the abyss of King's Leap. While he rested there, an old man appeared on the western side of the Leap and slowly drew nearer.

Although Maani-Mjmu's eyesight was not what it had been, he knew this must be an enemy. He prepared to fight. Then he recognised Chief Whiili-An of the Zambill.

Chief Whiili-An saw the stationary figure at the same time and recognised his enemy. Hefting their spears, they confronted each other.

Both were boney and pot-bellied. Their eyes were sunken. Their skin was finely wrinkled, as if time had cast a specially tailored net over them.

For thirty years, they had been at war. To each, the other ranked as little less than a demon. So engrossed had they been in the organisation of hunting and fighting, that neither had noticed the years go by. But great suns had plunged into the savannah, great moons had sailed above the jungles; sons had grown up and wives had grown old. Somewhere beneath the skin, below the bone, a magic spell of decay had been cast – a spell which finally even gods had been forced to recognise.

"You thief, you fecundator of monkeys!" shouted Maani-Mjmu. "I piss in your food-bowl."

"You murderer, you strangler of feline young!" called back Whiili-An. "My dung shall daub your cheeks."

Both men began to jump up and down, waving their spears and bawling ritual insults across the frontier.

Finally, Maani-Mjmu stopped and said, "Phew, that's enough. I'll have to sit down." He stooped and seated himself carefully on the edge of King's Leap.

Whiili-An hesitated, scratching his greying hair. Then he said, "That's not a bad idea. My legs aren't what they were."

They sat facing each other across the divide, listening to the stridulations of the cicadas.

Finally, Whiili-An said, "Well, you old villain, I suppose they've decided you're no longer a god."

Maani-Mjmu said nothing for a long while. His silence was adequate answer. "How about you, you old brute?" he asked.

Whiili-An sighed. "I may as well tell you, since it's plain you're now no better than a clapped-out old cormorant. I'm up here for my divinity test. I've got to jump across this stupid King's Leap. I know I'll never do it. It's too wide for anyone to jump. Only a fool would try."

"I hear you tried and managed it last year," said Maani-Mjmu maliciously.

"My left leg's been playing me up lately, to tell the truth," Whiili-An said. "Anyhow, smartass, what are you up here for?"

Maani-Mjmu let another of his long silences elapse.

"Never mind having to jump over this ridiculous abyss," he said. "I've got to jump *into* it. I've just failed my divinity test."

His enemy eyed him craftily. "Which was?"

"You know."

"How should I know the customs of a gang of poachers?"

"Well, I failed to satisfy all my six wives when we performed before the warriors last night." Maani-Mjmu hung his head.

Whiili-An laughed again, slapping his knees.

Growing angry, Maani-Mjmu got to his feet and brandished his spear.

"You gibbering gorilla, I satisfied five of them before daybreak."

"You couldn't satisfy a female dog turd."

"I'll satisfy you, you python fart!" So saying, Maani-Mjmu flung his spear. It missed his enemy by a hand's breadth, as once it would never have done, and skittered harmlessly across bare rock.

Scared, Whiili-An hurled his weapon, only to miss the other old chief by a few inches.

"They don't make spears the way they used to," he said, scratching his thigh.

"Well, the damned women don't cook like they used to,"

Maani-Mjmu explained. "You see, if the women won't cook properly, the men won't make spears properly. I've told them dozens of times. Do you think they listen?"

"You've nothing to complain about. You should see the trouble we have in Zambill. The warriors are lazy. They sit on their bums all day. No wonder the women won't cook for them."

"With us, it's the other way round. The women won't cook properly so the men won't work properly."

"So you just said, you old nut. Are you going cracked in your old age?"

"Cracked or not, I could jump this leap, which is more than you can do."

"You could never jump that," Whiili-An said, spitting into the gulf to show his contempt.

"I could have done last year."

"Do it now."

"Tomorrow. My back's troubling me a bit today."

The sun prepared to plunge into the savannahs, wreathing itself with band after band of purple heat.

"It's a silly test, anyhow," Whiili-An said, turning away. "I always said it's a silly test. Doesn't prove a thing about a man's ability. This last year or so I tried to get the custom changed, but your warrior of today is a bone-headed fellow. Won't listen. Refuses to listen."

"Don't talk to me about the younger generation. When I think of all the things I've done for them . . ." His voice trailed off into bitterness.

"Maybe we could join forces, you and I, and start a new tribe," Whiili-An said, as the sun disappeared.

"What was it *like*," Maani-Mjmu asked, as the moon appeared. "You know, mating with that female baboon?"

Whiili-An laughed. He settled himself more comfortably on his side of the abyss. "Funny you should ask that. I was thinking about it only the other night. You see, the trick is to drop on the animal from above . . ." He laughed again. "Well, I might as well tell you the whole story. We've got plenty of time . . ."

(1983)

The Blue Background

To the north stretched the line of the Carpathians, unvisitable. Although the mountains could be seen from almost every hut in Drevena, they played little part in the lives of the inhabitants; this contemporary generation did not even believe that demons lived in the mountains, as their forebears had done throughout countless generations.

The little river Vychodne flowed through the village, and perhaps formed the main reason for the hamlet's being where it was. A crude waterway system had been set up – no one remembered by whom – to help irrigate the stony land cultivated by the peasants of Drevena; for the land flooded in winter and became dry in the hot summer months. The sea lay a long way distant: no man of Drevena had ever set eyes on the sea and returned to tell of it; so that its moderating influence could not alleviate the harsh climate of the region.

On the outskirts of the village stood a ruin, still referred to as the House. It had been considerably grander than the rest of the poor buildings, and its stones were still mined to patch walls. Since its destruction, which even the oldest inhabitant, spitting into his fire of a night, failed at some length to recall, nobody grand, or with any claims to grandeur, lived in Drevena. Only the poor remained, stranded in the middle of the stony land, compelled to earn their living by tending the reluctant soil.

Beyond the ruin of the House was a hut where the Lomnja family lived. Poverty in Drevena was fairly shared, but the Lomnja family was poorer than any of their relations. Old man Lomnja had been partially blind since youth; his wife, Katja, was frail, good-hearted but improvident. Of the six children she had borne to Lomnja, three survived, a boy, girl, and a younger lad, Lajah. All of the work on their sparse acreage was shared, though the brunt of it fell on the males, Lomnja and his two sons, Hlebit and Lajah.

Just as the home of the Lomnja family was furthest from the centre of the village, so their holding was furthest from the River Vychodne.

The exact characteristics of their land were familiar to all the family; they worked it over ceaselessly throughout the seasons.

The family had a cow named Marja. Marja spent the night in a small lean-to stall tacked on the back of the Lomnja dwelling. Every morning, weather permitting, she was driven down a narrow track to the family holding.

The holding began after a creaking wooden bridge, which was no more than a few planks laid across a shallow ditch. The land consisted of three ridges sloping towards the west, where they became one. This western end was most fertile; stones had been extracted from it over the ages and a wall built with them, to keep Marja out. A few vegetables; lettuces, radishes, spring onions, tarhuna, and green peppers, grew there.

On the rest of their land, the Lomnjas grew potatoes, mainly on the lower ridge, and barely on the two upper ridges. Beyond the ridges was wild land where little grew but patches of grass and occasionally wild sages. There, Marja was left to forage while the others worked the soil.

The landscape in which they bent their backs was austere. The mountains lay distant in one direction, often lost in cloud. In the other direction lay flatness, bisected by the dusty road which led from nowhere to nowhere and passed through Drevena as it did so.

There was another landmark nearby.

On the middle strip of land tilled by the Lomnja family stood an ancient ruined church.

Most of the church roof had fallen in; the dome had collapsed, perhaps in the time of the Turk, over two centuries ago. But the walls still stood, and against the south wall old Lomnja grew his vines. Katja and her husband made a few barrels of wine every year, wine acknowledged to be the best in the village. The small income they gained from the wine kept the family together.

All that the ruined church meant to the family was a windbreak; it provided a sheltered place in which their precious vines could grow. Only to little Lajah did the church mean something more.

Lajah was a dark, undersized, skinny lad with black questioning eyes – just like all the other boys in Drevena. He wore an old jacket of his brother's and a pair of trousers, and he went barefoot most of the year, even when snow lay on the ground. He worked no better than any other boy. He was no more intelligent. He was not especially handsome. Since he never spoke much, he was not regarded as particularly bright, and in consequence he was not much spoken to, even by his contemporaries. His old grandmother, who had died the previous winter, when the wind from the east was at its height, had talked to him, telling him old dark legends, and had taught him ancient songs. Yet he could not even sing particularly well.

Lajah loved the decrepit church. He did not care about poverty; poverty was a natural condition. He was proud to be a Lomnja, because the Lomnjas had the old church on their land.

Every day, when the family rested at noon, sitting with their backs against the ruinous southern wall to eat their blinis (and a bit of cold fish if they were lucky), little Lajah would enter the church by the broken door and stand among the weeds and rubble.

The space inside the church seemed large to him. Nothing of the landscape outside could be seen. The clouds formed the roof. He climbed over the rubble and stood at the far end, where once an altar had stood.

Here, a portion of roof still overhung. It sheltered an old wooden figure secured with arms outstretched to the wall. The boy would look up at it open-mouthed, until his father called him back to work.

"Who put the figure there?" Lajah asked his father.

"It's Kristus."

"But how long has it been there?"

"I don't know, do I?" responded his father. "Centuries. Before the Turk. Stay away. The building is dangerous."

In the centre of the village was a hut, almost as humble as all the rest, which served as a meeting place. There the men smoked their pipes together and sipped a little tea or wine or pear water. Sometimes, they spoke of Christ. Sometimes they spoke of Muhammad. But the names came out with a deep peasant contempt, exhaled among blue smoke, as if they had no substance. Christ and Muhammad had come and gone. The land had re-

mained. And the people had remained to farm it. Whoever the
gods were, whoever the lord was, what was important was the state
of the crops.

"Neither Christ nor Muhammad could put up with life in
Drevena," one old man said, and the rest of the group chuckled.

Lajah was listening with his elder brother, Hlebit.

"But Christ's still here in the Lomnja church," he said.

More chuckling. One of Lajah's uncles said, with kindly
contempt, "That's just an old stick of wood with the worm in it,
lad."

Lajah's brother punched him in the ribs.

Next day, Lajah went back to the church and looked at the
figure hanging on the wall. It moved him deeply. Christ had his
arms outstretched, and the arms were too long and did not fit
properly to the body. His body was thin, like an old peasant's. He
wore only a brief garment over his lower body, the folds of the
cloth crudely indicated by the carver. His legs hung down like two
sticks.

The head of Christ was turned to one side with a simple gesture
of pain. His crown of thorns was carved almost carelessly, so that it
looked as if his head was bound about by rope. His mouth hung
open in a human despair. He looked rather stupid, as if the
wood-carver, for all his piety, was unable to imagine intelligence.

"Christ must have been a peasant too," Lajah said to himself.

What also moved him was the ancient and faded colouring of the
figure. The body was yellow and cancerous with age, as if Christ
were already far gone in leprosy when crucified. His garb was
carmine, the colour still clinging in the deeper folds, his hair
brown, his face a mottled red and brown.

These simple earth pigments stood in contrast to the blue
background against which Christ's figure was set.

The crucified Christ had no cross. Wood was scarce in these
parts. The distorted capital T of his figure was nailed against the
plaster wall of the church with rusty iron spikes.

The wall was knotted and lumpy. However long ago it had been
plastered, it still retained the impression of carelessly applied
downward brushstrokes. The pigmentation had once been deep
blue. Now the richness of that colour lingered only where the
timber body afforded it some protection from sun and rain;

elsewhere, it had faded to a delicate sky tint, a blue that spoke of seas and distant eternities.

It was to this background as much as to the figure that Lajah directed his gaze. It seemed to him that Christ was stepping forward from the blue of heaven. When the sun shone in, the shadows of the stiff arms endowed Christ with spectral wings, blue on blue.

Nothing of what he felt could the boy declare, so he said nothing, even to his sister. He worked beside his elder brother and his father in silence.

A day came when summer was advanced, and grape harvest nearing. The distant line of the Carpathians had lost their caps of snow. Katja was picking the first fruits from their apricot tree when she espied a man on horseback, distant, tremulous in heat.

In wild excitement, she ran out to the smallholding to tell the family. They straightened their backs and peered when she pointed. Even old Lomnja shaded his eyes and looked, though he could see no further than the end of his beard.

There on the road which bisected the olive green landscape was a man riding a horse, even as Katja claimed. He must be coming to the village – no avoiding that, as the road unrolled – and maybe he would stop. Surely he would stop. Perhaps Drevena was his destination.

They all laughed at that idea, even old Lomnja, because it was difficult to see why anyone should want to come to Drevena.

"Perhaps he's heard tell of our wine, father, and wants to sample it," Katja said to her husband.

All round them, sparsely dotted about, the rest of the population of Drevena stood upright in their fields, flexed their backs, and stared towards the dusty road. As if by common consent, all began to trudge towards the village. The crops would not die for want of an afternoon's attention. Strangers were worth investigating.

When the stranger arrived in Drevena's one street, the whole village – every man, woman, child, and dog – was waiting for him. The sun was low by then, and he cast a long shadow as he dismounted from his mare.

The men of Drevena were not certain how to greet strangers. They remembered a time some years before when "the army" – as they called the platoon which had appeared one winter – marched through Drevena on Franz Josef's business. Then they had wisely taken to their heels and hidden in the fields. To this solitary man, they merely doffed their hats and waited for him to speak.

"Greetings, my friends. I am a traveller. Miltin Svobodova by name. I have come a long way and still have far to go – to Ostrava, in fact. Your village does not look very hospitable, but heaven knows how far it is to the next one, so I have decided to stay here for the night. The Lord God will guard me."

The man's accent was so astonishing, as was what he had to say, that no one could answer him. The men huddled together and discussed with each other. Eventually, one of them said, "What makes you think you can stay in our poor village? Suppose we decide to beat you up and rob you, God or no God? You've a strange fancy to come to a place like this on your own, haven't you?"

"I take you for simple Christian folk, as I am myself, and expect no harm from you, since I offer you no harm."

The man was quite slender, pale of face, dressed in black, with a silk hat on his head. He confronted them in a confident way, though without swagger.

"There's nowhere fit to sleep in Drevena. Nor do we have anything to do with religion. Ride on down the road. It's only two hours to Goriza Bistrica. That's a better place. Everyone says so."

"My mare's too tired to go further. I shall pay for my lodging – more than the miserable billet is worth, no doubt."

At this, they conferred again.

The cottage in the middle of the village which served as a meeting place was an inn of a kind. There lived old lame Varadzia, who had Turkish blood; he was prevailed upon to make such accommodation as he could for the traveller.

The villagers peered in through the one curtainless window of the cottage. There they watched Svobodova unload his two packs, from one of which he brought a mysterious rosewood box with a handle and a pipe of some kind protruding from the front of it.

"No doubt he keeps his jewels in there," said one of the more imaginative peasants. "Perhaps we should cut his throat and share them out between us – then we'd all be better off and I could buy a cart. No one would ever hear of the crime."

"Franz Josef would hear of it," another answered.

After Varadzia had served Svobodova with sturgeon and the local delicacy, a hatchapuri – a sort of paratha stuffed with cheese – washed down with a glass of the Lomnja red wine, he sat down and took a pipe with the stranger. After a while, he let in a few cronies, all eager to hear what the traveller had to say about himself.

Svobodova talked grandly of life in Bratislava, of the beauty of its thoroughfares and churches, of the loveliness of the Danube with its bridge, and of the singing in the cathedral.

"What about the loveliness of the women?" Varadzia asked, boldly.

"That's not for Christian men to dwell on," said the traveller, severely.

"I'll bet they're a sight more attractive to look on than our lot, though," one of the peasants remarked.

Changing the subject, Svobodova spoke of the rest of Europe beyond the Dual Monarchy, of how powerful Germany and Great Britain were, the latter with vast possessions overseas. And of how brilliant was the organ in Notre Dame cathedral in Paris, though the city was notorious for its sinfulness – almost as bad as Prague in that respect.

"So I suppose you have come to these arid parts to escape from the sinfulness, sir," said Lajah's father. "Almost no trees grow near Drevena, so sin is sparse also."

"I am a photographer," said the stranger. "That is God's will. Happily, I have private means, and I travel about recording a vanishing way of life with the new photographic equipment. I am convinced that Europe is becoming too steeped in the flesh, and that the Lord in his wrath will soon punish her with a war more terrible than any before, waged with all the modern weapons at our command. So I travel throughout our country, compiling a record of what is and may not remain for long."

"Nothing's going to change here, you have our word, sir. Life goes on here as ever. We can't even afford a new bridge. We'd never have a war here."

"That's as may be," said Svobodova. "Now I wish to sleep. In the morning, I shall photograph anything here you consider of significance."

The men looked at each other uneasily over their pipes.

"We've nothing here of any significance, depend on that," they said, as they took themselves off to their flea-ridden homes.

Next day, the sun rose in majesty from its mists, and the inhabitants of Drevena went out before the heat arrived to tend their acres. They ignored Svobodova, having decided that he was a harmless madman. Anyone who considered that there was anything in Drevena worth photographing was mad.

Svobodova stood in the middle of the road in the middle of the village and photographed the road. He photographed the ruins of the House. He photographed Varadzia standing self-consciously before his doorway.

"You'll do better in Goriza Bistrica, down the road," Varadzia said. "It stands on the edge of a gorge and its houses were built in the Turkish time. Besides, there are priests and things there which would appeal to you."

"I'll be on my way, then," said the photographer. Settling his account with Varadzia, he loaded up his mare, carefully stowing the precious camera in a pack, and set off down the dusty road.

As he went his way, figures straightened up one by one in the fields and stood like statues to watch him. It was as if they speculated on the sights he would see beyond the horizon. Then they shrugged and turned their heads down towards the earth again, almost with the gesture of cattle grazing.

Svobodova was aware that a small boy was running towards him over the broken terrain to the right of the track. The boy grew nearer and for a while ran parallel with the track, on the far side of the babbling Vychodne. When a bridge came, the boy crossed it and ran in front of the man on his slow-moving mount.

The photographer halted his mare and looked down at the boy without speaking.

The boy was about thirteen years old, as far as Svobodova could judge. He wore an old tunic-jacket, a pair of baggy trousers, and very little else. He looked up at the man with an open and trusting expression, and asked, "Did you photograph anything important in Drevena?"

Svobodova rubbed his chin.

"Everyone told me there was nothing worth photographing in Drevena. You people are not very proud of your village, are you?"

"There's one important thing you must photograph."

The boy turned and pointed back across the fields to where the church stood, vines growing up its southern wall.

"Well, my lad, unfortunately ruined churches are two-a-penny in Slovakia. What's important about that one?"

"Inside, sir, come and see. The important thing is inside."

Miltin Svobodova was kind-hearted as well as principled. He imagined that the Lord might have sent this boy as a messenger. Without arguing, he climbed from his saddle; he followed Lajah across the fields and his mare followed him.

Lajah led him to the old broken door of the church, where Svobodova tied up his horse. Boy and man entered the ruin together, while the rest of the Lomnja family straightened their backs and watched this strange event open-mouthed.

At the far end of the shell stood the ancient wooden Christ against its blue background. Lajah led the man forward without a word.

When they were near enough, he simply stood and gazed upwards. The stiff mediaeval figure remained, recording the agony of spiritual man; the shadow of the broken roof was high at this hour, cutting across the coarse texture of the blue wall and shading the roughly carved head of the sufferer.

The photographer crossed himself, bowing his head before the ancient symbol.

"Here is the true spirit of this harsh, godless land," he said. "God may be despised, ignored, but he is never absent. This poor representation, quite untouched by Renaissance values, was doubtless carved and painted by some dumb serf such as that fellow outside, to express an inner light struggling for expression. That inner light, my boy, is the one hope for our sinful world."

"But it's beautiful, isn't it, sir?"

Svobodova looked down at Lajah, head on one side, and then permitted himself to smile.

"It's certainly worth a photograph."

Lajah watched as the magic box came out and the photographer prepared his plates. On the top of the box, which was of rosewood, an oval plate was affixed; on it were embossed the words, "London Bioscope Co., 1911". He scarcely listened while Svobodova worked at setting up his tripod, explaining as he did so that a firm of publishers in Vienna and Bratislava had commissioned him to produce a volume of photographs of rural Slovakia. If the photograph of the Christ figure was successful, it would appear in the book.

A deal of fussy preparation followed. The boy became bored. Christ remained as he had been through the centuries, hanging cankered from the old wall. Finally, the shutter of the rosewood box clicked and the picture was taken.

"I'm grateful to you, my lad," Svobodova said, as he stowed away his things. "You are the one spiritual person in a heathen village. You represent the hope and the future of Drevena. Now, let me write down your name and address in my notebook and I will see that you receive a copy of my book when – the Lord willing – it is published."

It was done. He remounted his mare, gave a farewell wave, and headed for the delights of Goriza Bistrica. He was never seen in the area again. For a while his visit was talked of – since there was very little else to talk of – and then he was forgotten.

Lajah grew to manhood and married a girl called Magdalena, who was known to cook a delicious stew. For a few weeks, life for them was paradise; but the demands of toil eroded the edge of their happiness. There was no freedom from the fields. They became just another couple. Soon, there was little to mark them out from the rest of the villagers, except that Lajah still made infrequent excursions to the ancient church to look at the timber in its anguished gesture against the blue wall.

Winter came. Magdalena carried Lajah's child. The winds blew from the east, loaded with the destructive fury of winter. The distant pass was blocked by snow. Drevena was cut off completely from the outside world. The villagers stayed in their poor huts, shivering and starving.

Spring brought heavy rain. One morning, when the peasants waded out into the fields to plant their crops, or salvage what was already planted, they found the church had collapsed. The old wooden figure of Christ was buried under the rubble.

"It had been there a good long time, mind."

"Long before the time of the Turk, they say."

A few days later came the post wagon, carrying letters and passengers for Goriza Bistrica. The pass was clear again. On its rare appearance, the wagon stopped always at Varadzia's, where the driver paid well for a bottle of Lomnja's red wine. On this occasion, the driver handed over not only a silver coin for the wine but a parcel heavily wrapped in cloth and addressed in large letters to Lajah Lomnja.

"What do you think it could be?" Magdalena asked, excitedly, and Lajah turned it over and over, admiring the stamps. "It has come all the way from Bratislava just for you, Lajah. I didn't know you knew anyone there. You are a one for secrets, and no mistake."

At last they opened the parcel. They knelt on the stone floor over its contents. Inside was a large impressive book with padded covers. The mauve cloth was emblazoned with gold lettering which read, "Scenes of Rural Slovakia – Our Vanishing Heritage, by Miltin Svobodova." The edges of the pages were gilt.

Lajah turned the pages with clumsy hands. There were many pictures. They meant nothing to him. Nor could he struggle to decipher the text underneath.

Towards the end of the book, he came upon a photograph of something he recognised.

It showed the Drevena Christ, the Christ now vanished, the spindly Christ nailed to the old wall, arms outstretched, head to one side in a toothless grimace of pain.

Lajah put his finger on the photograph and said to his wife, "I was there when the man came to Drevena and made that picture. See, it's part of the old ruined church that collapsed in the last rainstorms. I used to go and look at it when I was a kid."

She looked at the picture and at him. He said nothing more. Leaving the book lying open on the floor, he went outside. His hoe leaned against the mud walls of the building. Taking it up, he went back into the fields, sparing never a glance towards the pile of rubble which marked the site of the church.

As he bent his shoulders towards the soil, he thought with contempt of the foolishness of that photographer who had come long ago. A city man. He had photographed the old timber figure, certainly. But his photograph was in sepia. It failed to capture the blue background, the glimpse of infinity, that Lajah had once loved, before life closed in.

(1983)

The Plain, the Endless Plain

The forest, which had been growing slowly more impenetrable, ended without warning.

Relieved to escape from the trees, the Tribe emerged one by one and grouped together to stand gazing at the territory which confronted them. Ahead stretched an almost featureless plain.

In their weariness, they did not communicate. No statement was needed to convey the starkness of their situation.

The plain which stretched before them was so immense and nondescript that it existed almost as an abstraction. Its indeterminate area presented itself as little more than a texture under the drab sky. Nothing moved on it. Such contours as the plain possessed were lost in its colossal scale. Such colours as it possessed were also lost, submerged in a prevailing tawniness. Over all of its expanse, no hill or tree or monument broke its supine geography; so that despite its magnitude it did not transcend the petty, as if it were there only to be sucked at and finally devoured by the hazes of distance.

In all the expanse there was no sign of welcome for the Tribe, no refuge. They stood there in a group, appalled, bludgeoned by the dimensions stretching before them.

Behind them, however, the Enemy still advanced through the green intestines of the jungle, moving confidently, without caution, as the noise as from a steel foundry testified. To survive, it was necessary for the Tribe to venture out into the wilderness, hoping that the Enemy would not follow but instead turn back into the fastnesses from which it had emerged.

A consultation was held, in which all members of the Tribe joined. They could not agree to press forward on to the plain. They had not determination enough. Some argued that they should skirt the jungle and hope to discover a river or safer place where they could take refuge.

Only when, among the thickets to their rear, the heavy metallic noise of enemy pursuit, coupled with the macabre wail of an electronic bugle, persuaded them that haste was required of them, did they understand that they must retreat into the plain or perish. The enemy advanced on too broad a front for any other manoeuvre to be feasible.

At this time, the Tribe numbered only twenty-one. Some of them still remembered the time when their peaceful existence in the hills had been shattered. The arrival of the Enemy had been sudden and remorseless.

Goaded into haste, despite their weariness, they moved forward. The Tribe had no banners as did the Enemy. Their progress was humble, their movements dogged. They walked close and in single file, keeping always to a strict order.

They soon became engulfed within the great volume of the plain.

The first time they stopped to rest, they could look back and see the forest, an irresolute strip of blue-green behind them. At the time of their second rest, distance had dissolved the sight. They were absolutely alone in the annihilating marches which the plain represented.

Courage – or a kind of dumb continuance – was a distinct feature of the Tribe's group characteristics. Each supported the other. Nobody spoke of turning back. Their sense of direction was good. They proceeded forward without hesitation, travelling westward. Day followed day.

These were the twenty-one referred to later as Generation One.

As they became more familiar with the plain, they found that its monotony was broken by features not apparent to anyone viewing it from a distance. There were lines of low hills, rather like the ripples in a quilt, which formed obstacles to their progress. Colour, though muted, was abundant: the plain was no desert, and supported mysterious lines of low vegetation of various hues, purple, green, brown. The general colour of the land was sepia, or oatmeal.

No rain fell, yet there were winds which were no more than whispers, bringing a spray of moisture. More frequently, clouds of dust blew in their faces. The prevailing weather was tepid, without force.

The Enemy followed them. The dull glint of its armour could be seen when its extended lines crossed the low hills. Its clangour could be heard. The Tribe remained constantly alert, never resting for long, never sleeping for long, pressing ever forward into the heart of the plain.

Only at one period did they halt, for any considerable period, when it was the time to reproduce. Many progeny were born to them. As soon as the young were strong enough, the march forward was resumed. The pace increased, watch after watch, in order to draw further ahead of the pursuit.

The field of their vision was circumscribed. The light was constant but dim. All that could be determined in the sky overhead was a whitish haze. When the Tribe came to a line of hills, they would stand there on each other's shoulders and stare ahead. Never were they rewarded with the sight of anything that promised change. All that existed was the plain, the endless plain – and the senseless pursuit.

Generation One became old and died one by one, but within a short space of each other. Their deserted husks were left behind as quickly fading landmarks. Generation Two continued as their parents had done, and begat a further generation. Generation Three numbered three hundred and two thousand, four hundred individuals, the number divided equally among the seven *septs*.

Like the previous generation, Generation Three progressed ever forward across the plain, walking in parallel single files. The Enemy continued to pursue, its menacing blades sometimes lost in the prevailing haze, sometimes appearing dramatically near, its cruel noise intensified. Food was always available. The terrain underfoot was of a curious texture, stiff yet yielding. The Tribe walked, in fact, over the tops of a stiff, dense, shrublike vegetation. The vegetation turned dry small leaves to the air and conserved moisture at its roots, where darkness prevailed. Down there in the darkness lived lumbering cretaceans the Tribe called Arntrods.

The Arntrods were numerous and easy to hunt. The hunters of the Tribe pushed their way down through the stiff foliage to where, among the stems, there was room to crawl. Here herds of pallid Arntrods browsed. They could not elude the hunters. In no time, they were speared and their twitching bodies passed up to the surface.

At feeding time, the grey Arntrod carapaces could be cracked as easily as the shells of eggs. The flesh inside was of a lumpy texture, like scrambled egg, and almost tasteless.

Harmless though the Arntrods were, they sheltered a small parasitic creature called a Toid, which the Tribe feared. The Toids, tiny, ginger, nimble, ran everywhere, their feet stinging all they touched. They worked their way into the joints of the Tribe, causing intense pain and sometimes death. The progress of the Tribe across the plain was often halted when they were forced to disinfest each other of the hated Toids.

Despite casualties, the generation managed to reproduce itself. The *septs* gathered in traditional fashion, six bodies interlocking, matching sides, with the mother locked inside the sexagonal, penetrated from all angles simultaneously. Out from her ruined body spurted the ova, some of the young hatching while still in the air. Generation Four numbered over thirty-six million, two hundred and eighty thousand. As undaunted as their predecessors, they continued across the expanses of the plain, moving ever westwards.

Generation Four, progressing in long parallel files through the wilderness, were beset with rumours and speculations. In particular they discussed the nature of Generation One, what had been its objectives, its characteristics. Had the twenty-one members of Generation One known where the plain would end? Had they an intuition of how many generations were needed to cross it? Did they know what lay on the other side of the plain? Rumours abounded of a beautiful land, where rain fell and sun shone and there were no Toids.

More pessimistic stories described how much knowledge had been lost, generation by generation. Some claimed that Generation One were giants who had conceived a great Plan, now unfolding, unbeknown to the present generation. One day soon, it was whispered, the Twenty-One would reappear, reincarnated, and lead the present generation to a better land, where they would not have to travel and food would be plentiful.

But it was not until Generation Five, which numbered over four billion, that such speculations gave way to action. Generation Five became sure of its strength, and resolved that a stand must be made against the Enemy. It refused to retreat further as its predecessors had done.

A range of hills, slightly higher than others which had been traversed, came into view. Generation Five climbed to the long crest and arrayed itself along the crest in battle order. It turned to await the approach of the Enemy.

So poor was the general visibility that it was hard to determine the strength of the Enemy. As it approached with its horrible machine-noise, with that thudding clangour as characteristic as a scent, its metallic banners could be seen to spread across the horizon from one side to the other. Yet the Tribe kept their formation.

The Enemy's rate of advance slowed. Now the Tribe could discern both the huge units and the small which comprised the force. Some of its battle-towers were the size of large mobile pyramids.

Fear struck the Tribe. But all individuals held their ground without panic. Saboteurs were sent out, who progressed along the true ground, close to the roots of the vegetation where the Arntrods grazed. These saboteurs were able to move unseen as far as the enemy engines, destroying their tracks and feelers.

Slower and slower went the Enemy's foremost wave. It ground to a halt. The two forces confronted each other. Nobody moved. Food became scarce as day succeeded day.

The Tribe grew anxious. They dared not attack, so formidable did the Enemy appear. On the other hand, they were loath to resume a progress which would now seem more than ever like a retreat. A further dilemma was that the time for reproduction approached; at that period they would be most vulnerable to an aggressive move, and could easily be overwhelmed by a remorseless foe.

In the end, it was starvation which drove them back into the level plain. The Tribe had no idea whether the Enemy needed to eat or whether it drew its nourishment from radiations in the air. They knew only that they were beginning themselves to die, to wither inside their carapaces. Leaving a line of dead husks still to face the Enemy, the surviving members of Generation Five crept

down the far side of the hill and resumed their progress towards
the west.

The generations passed. Each generation travelled across the
endless wastes, multiplied itself, and perished. Generation Six was
the lost generation, striving to repair the damage done to morale by
the previous generation. Generation Seven suffered immoder-
ately, since they came upon a region which was increasingly desert.
The stiff vegetation was eroded, the Arntrods disappeared. There
was nothing for it but to progress relentlessly, leaving the dead and
dying behind.

But the desert dwindled, giving way to a territory marked by
brighter colours which dyed the landscape with complex patterns.
Some of the patterns were traversed only when many days had
passed, but there were those who suggested that they represented
diagrams of living things, drawn on the surface of the plain on a
gigantic scale. It was Generation Eight which was christened the
Parrot Generation.

Generation Eight, in traversing the plain, made the discoveries.
In the first place, they discovered that they were no longer being
pursued by the Enemy. The Enemy had gone. There was no
Enemy any longer.

Perhaps the Enemy had been deterred by the barrier of dead
bodies of Generation Five. Whatever the reason, it became apparent that pursuit was no more. Generation Eight, now numbering
itself in trillions, was shocked into immobility. One of the chief
motivations of the Tribe had suddenly been removed. Nobody
knew how long it was since the Enemy had withdrawn; all they
could say was that the conditions of life were suddenly altered.

The Tribe was unable to advance further. They spread over the
plain in all directions, aimlessly looking for sustenance, but
not progressing. So they happened on the Parrot, as it became
known.

The elders among the Tribe had been studying the strange
patterns of the landscape, hoping to discover there some hint as to
which way they could best advance. Permanent watch was kept on
the sky, in case the gigantic and presumably supernatural beings
who had inscribed the landscape on such a gigantic scale should
return. Word spread among them that the Tribe was now covering

an area on which had been emblazoned the likeness of one of the parrots which, folk-memory insisted, once haunted the forests from which the Twenty-One had emerged.

At last a sign had been given to the marching generations. Amid great excitement, the Tribe assembled itself along the outlines of the supposed Parrot. Hunger was forgotten in a great surge of optimism that they were at last to be released from their travails.

When the outlines of the Parrot were covered by individuals, one wing of the Tribe could not see the other. Those who stood on the supposed beak could see no further than those who stood on the supposed feathers of the stomach. Nevertheless, the speedy scouts who were despatched to circumnavigate the figure returned to report excitedly that the configuration definitely conformed to the popular conception of the designated bird.

The elders now proclaimed that the gift of flight was about to be bestowed upon the Tribe. The next generation, Generation Nine, would be able to fly, and would then lead the rest from the accursed plain. Everyone sat back to await the time of reproduction with positive determination to believe this desired result.

That time came. Once more, the *septs* assembled, the mothers linked into the middle of the rings. Penetrations took place. Followed by the usual long, locked expectation.

Then ova issued.

How few! How disappointingly few ova!

Why were the mothers barren?

But the ova issuing, the progeny hatching in the air as before, were this time taking wing, hovering uncertainly over the multitude.

Conflicting cries of dismay and wonder filled the air. The noise alarmed the flying young. They set off towards the west on their new wings.

Despite the shouts of those below – their parents – to come back, to come down, the fliers flew on, slowly flapping their unprecedented wings, and disappeared from the sight of the Parrot Generation.

After an hour or two, the fliers of Generation Nine became tired and settled on the plain. They huddled close, rested unaccustomed muscles. There were no more than four hundred of them; they were oppressed by the solitude, the mute desolation of the place.

All round them lay the plain, covered in its mysterious patterns, leading nowhere. Deep silence prevailed.

At length, a venturesome *sept* struggled into the air and spiralled higher and higher, in an attempt to see what lay beyond the plain. Up and up they climbed, until the ground was lost in haze. The air became sultry. Still they flew. Far, far above them, they glimpsed a pale globe, thrilling in its implications. Then their strength failed them, and they had to glide back to earth. They landed convinced that they had seen the sun at last. But of the plain there had been no visible end.

After more practice, the flying Generation Nine found itself able to stay aloft without fatigue. It continued in the direction the Tribe had maintained over the generations, making for the west, winging along close to the ground, stopping only to sleep or eat. So its days were passed, eternally on the wing.

Generation Ten numbered only thirty-two thousand, but at least numbers were increasing. Some of them were born without wings. These unfortunates were left behind without compunction. Generation Ten was sure of itself, and sure of reaching its destination, flying great distances without rest. Still the dull brownish landscape unrolled below, without feature or monument.

It was this generation, in its overconfidence, which almost came to grief. No longer did they bother to post sentries while they rested. The Enemy was nothing more than a fairy story, told to scare or amuse before they closed their eyes for sleep. The Twenty-One had passed beyond legend, becoming mistier than the horizon itself. Even their dreams were dreams of disbelief.

And then the Forager came.

The Forager was gigantic beyond imagining. Those waking to look upwards in incredulous horror could see only its fangs, lubricated and clicking in anticipation, with a body suspended high in the air. Great stalks of legs, angled this way and that, supported the body.

Unlike the steady monotonous movements of the Tribe, the Forager's movements were rapid but intermittent, a veritable stutter of muscles. A blur of action, death of an individual, stillness – then fast swallowing as the warm food went down. Then stillness again, followed by another swift pounce.

Terrified, Generation Ten took to flight. It had no weapons of offence, no defence but retreat; but its anger and surprise were such that all its members swooped on new wings down into the eyes of the monstrous invader.

Those eyes, various and fur-rimmed, seemed to burn darkly for a moment – until spiked feet quenched them. Then Forager reared like a startled horse, combing the air with its leading limbs. Then it ran blinded from its attackers.

Its high jointed legs carried it rapidly over the plain. It plunged away on an erratic course. Long after the thin limbs were lost in the haze, the bulbous body could still be seen, bobbing above the undulating ground.

Ten of the Tribe had been killed. The remainder, much disturbed by what had transpired, flew to a nearby strip of purple, there to rest and discuss what they should do.

A stale, sluggish wind blew across the face of the endless plain, carrying dust with it. The survivors of Generation Ten huddled close together. They had lost the initiative even to forage for Arntrods.

It was then, in this hour of despair, that one of the individuals chanced to look towards the north-west.

In excitement, he called to the others. Soon all were staring where he pointed. It seemed they could see something, they knew not what.

Together, they mounted into the air, climbing high, ever watching as they circled.

There was no doubt. A formation of some kind lay low to the north-west. The general opinion was that it was a range of mountains, half-concealed by the haze. There was to be an end to the plain at last.

Somewhere there must lie a land promised by the ancestors, where food was abundant, where there was shelter and variety of forms and a more pleasing way of life.

The Tribe landed again, abuzz with excitement.

And at that moment enormous lights lit the sky overhead, such as none had ever known. And there were huge roaring noises. The ground shook. And a dazzling brilliance such as they had never known shone down from above and extinguished them utterly.

(1984)

You Never Asked My Name

In the days beyond the future, a town existed on a rocky peninsula some two days' journey south from where Athens had once stood.

The peninsula began with a swollen knuckle of rock and tapered off like a pointing finger into the blue sea. Along its spine grew fragrant pines the shape of opened umbrellas, cacti, cypresses, vines, and olive trees flecked with fungus like mildewed lace. Where the peninsula ended, at the very nail of the finger, stood the small city-state called Tolan. Its inhabitants called it The Perfect Place.

The human beings who lived in Tolan, in their ordered society, counted themselves fortunate. They considered themselves safe from the post-bellum wars which raged elsewhere over the face of the ruined world. They had escaped the worst physical effects of The Deterrence. Nevertheless, their minds were less unscathed than their bodies by all that had happened.

From a distance, Tolan looked like a toy. Everything about it seemed artificial, from its miniature palaces to its tiny walled vineyards. The people themselves, aware of their brittle survival, walked like dolls.

No two houses in Tolan stood on the same level. The steepness of the hillsides precluded it. The roof of one house came level with the herb-strip of the next. Their white walls marched down to the sea amid broom and boulder, and stood at angles to each other like a family whose members have quarrelled. A stranger arriving by mule over the mountains from the ruined world would come first to the house of Nefriki; Nefriki's house stood highest up the slopes and furthest from the centre of the town.

There Nefriki lived with his sister, Antarida. Nefriki and Antarida lived apart from the town and apart from each other.

Nefriki was a strong young man, magnificently muscled, with a ferocious head of golden hair like a lion's. His face counted as handsome, being finely moulded, with blue eyes and a strong jaw, to which latter clung a sparse golden beard. He smiled most of the time, even when he was angry. Nefriki was generally angry. His duty was to kill people.

His sister, Antarida, was a different type of person. Her movements were as languid as Nefriki's were charged with tension. Her skin was pale. Her dark eyelashes and brows sheltered pupils of an intense grey, of a shade otherwise seen only in the eyes of cats. She was slender, her breasts and hips were small. She shaved her skull so that, in her twenty-first year, she reminded strangers at once of foetus and aged crone. Her duty was to tend the dead.

In order to defend themselves from the technological barbarism which had descended upon the rest of the planet, the people of Tolan had formed themselves into the most rigid of societies. Every family held an unalterable position in the caste system, from the lowest trawler for kelp to the highest official, from the foot-washers to those so refined they were forbidden sight of their own excrement. The codes of Tolan were many, and known by all; memories were sharpened by the fact that death immediately followed any transgression. Survival lay in obedience to the law.

The utopians of Tolan had established what they called The Perfect Place: and in doing so they had killed joy.

Puritanism and sensuality were intertwined like two vines which will destroy each other. Although the men had absolute autocracy over the women, yet, by starlight, they desired only to be defiled by them in every way possible. Lies were revered, castration was frequent, sadism was beauty. Chastity was praised and all perversions practised. To the sadness which prevails over human life, Tolan had added its own superstructure of misery, which it called utopia. Thus the ways of pre-Deterrence societies were preserved.

Sometimes refugees from the ruined world came climbing along the tumbled spine of the peninsula. Sometimes small boats sailed up the Gulf of Spetsai, attempting to moor at the harbour of Tolan.

Nefriki was always waiting for the invaders. He had his own area of the frontier to defend. Nefriki's arm was strong, his spear sure, his arrows unerring. He was the outcast hero. Because of his prowess, only the dead entered Tolan.

Antarida's trade was with the dead. To her the town scavengers brought the corpses her brother had killed. Lovingly, Antarida laved her bare skull with perfumes and assumed a gown of pure white. Then, with delicate hands and mincing fingers, she set about cleansing the dead enemy. Those hands and fingers went everywhere, into the most obscure corners, prying, preening. The hairs of the dead were washed and numbered, their orifices filled with wax from the wild bees of the peninsula. Then the corpses were buried beneath the excreta of the women of Tolan.

For those born in The Perfect Place, the last rites were different. They too, when life had left them, were taken into the care of Antarida for her minutest attentions. It was Antarida's fingers which were the last to invade their privacy. Burial for the native Tolanese was by water. Their bodies, laved and perfumed by the arts of Antarida, were taken to a stretch of shore preserved for such purposes.

A few feet below the clear waters of the Gulf, a shelf had been built. On this shelf were iron rings, to which the deceased were secured. Mourners could stand on the shore gazing down on them. The naked corpses lay with arms spread and legs apart, as if beckoning voluptuously to the living. There were no tides in the Gulf, nor had been since the Moon, the huntress of Earth's skies, had been destroyed in The Deterrence. The dead seemed to move only by virtue of the small lapping waves, which entered them as delicately as Antarida's fingers.

Shoals of tiny fish soon destroyed the virginity of the dead. The fish glinted like needles, they rippled like fabric. A haze filled the water. Soon those who had lived were no longer recognisable.

While the latest sea-burial was taking place in Tolan, another post-bellum engagement was taking place across the territory where the ancient city of Athens had once stood. Here the remnants of the human race were fighting against their own inventions. A group of refugees from the battle fled southwards. Day by day, eluding pursuit, they neared the peninsula over which Nefriki watched.

On the subject of love, or what passed for love in The Perfect Place. In no other aspect of life was the difference between brother and sister more marked. All men desired Antarida. They desired her youth and pallor; they desired the fragile beauty of her skull;

above all, they desired her for the obscenity of what her hands and fingers did. From the highest to the lowest, all men and some women yearned – even more than for death – to be encircled by the embrace of Antarida.

Nor did Antarida deny her suitors. It could not be said that Antarida had passion. But it suited her to be rendered entirely naked, to be slobbered and pawed over, to be clutched by older men in the rictus of orgasm. She herself did not move during these encounters, but lay as still, as well-mannered, as one of her corpses.

Her brother, from the small watchtower above their house, looked down through the skylight in the roof. He could see her spreadeagled in the posture of sea-buried corpses, while men had their way with her. In this sight, Nefriki took a melancholy pleasure; for he knew – such were the mores of Tolan – that these couplings added greatly to the prestige of his sister.

Occasionally Antarida was visited by the man Nefriki feared most, Reeve Ikanu. This dark-visaged man was the reeve of the city to whom Nefriki was answerable. Ikanu ruled the frontier. Ikanu could dismiss Nefriki from his post or sentence him to death for the smallest infringement of the law.

Ikanu's face was heavy and pale with compressed cruelty, although his body was thin and dark as if stained. The skin of his hairless cranium was multitudinously veined, so that it seemed as if his brain were visible. When Ikanu lowered his stained body on to Nefriki's sister, his savage watchdog sat outside the house, close by the door, guarding his master. When the dog caught a glimpse of Nefriki on the watchtower, it would growl, "Guard yourself," in a voice as deep and threatening as its master's. The dog ate meat; its master subsisted on a diet of wine and gnats.

Sometimes, Nefriki allowed his thoughts to turn to the past, and to Etsimita, the love of his early adolescence. Etsimita had been of a higher caste than he. Their love had been forbidden. Had it been known, both Nefriki and Etsimita would have suffered death. Perhaps this peril made their brief passion all the sweeter.

In those days, Nefriki had been able to love. His soul had been like a country in a fairy tale, conquered by love, and he had wished only to be possessed by Etsimita and to possess her, soul to soul.

They could meet only at night. One night of unclouded stars, they had met by the seashore and walked along it barefoot, holding hands. They had been talking low and seriously of subjects lovers talk of – those conversations so intense that they can never be recaptured afterwards, no matter how hard the bemused lover tries.

Etsimita had been overcome by happiness and by the beauty of the occasion. She hauled up her long skirt to the top of her delectable haunches and plunged into the breakers, which were made silver by the Milky Way which shone aslant them. As she went, she cried to Nefriki to join her.

He wished for nothing better. But hardly had he entered the foam when a black shape rose from the water before Etsimita and dragged her down below the waves. Uttering a cry, he dived to her rescue.

She came floating up in a pool of blood, and he dragged her ashore. Both her legs had been severed almost to the knees. The cuts were clean. It was no shark which had seized her but an anti-personnel war-machine, drifting far off-course, an accursed product of the ruined world.

Etsimita died before Nefriki could carry her home. His sister sealed up the wounded leg-stumps and went about her mortuary business with her deft hands, her diligent fingers, her probing thumb. Then, since she had transgressed inviolable rules of her society, the remains of Etsimita were consigned to the excreta beds. Something in Nefriki had passed from him at that time.

These memories returned to Nefriki as he sat on the watch-tower, regarding the prostrate body of his sister below. They fled at the sound of a stone bouncing down the mountainside some distance away – a sound only his ear was acute enough to catch.

Immediately, Nefriki was alert, again the guardian of the community. He slid to the ground, took his long bow and the quiver of arrows which leaned by the door, and moved into the concealment of the broom bushes. Climbing among boulders, he quickly reached the spine of the peninsula, where rock piled on rock like mating geckos.

Wedging himself between two boulders, Nefriki could see blue sea far below on either side, gleaming in the sunshine. Ahead of him was movement. Among the umbrella pines, a party of men was approaching. High overhead, Ikanu's trained birds of omen soared, screaming to the foe in their artificial voices, "Distance yourself, distance yourself!"

There were other guards Nefriki could summon. Attached to his quiver was a shrill reed which would call them. Such was Nefriki's confidence that no such thought entered his head. He was filled with excitement at the anticipation of killing.

Of recent years, mountain lions and wolves had been returning to the mountains of Greece. They moved no more silently than Nefriki amid his allotted territory.

As he worked his way forward, he saw that five men were approaching. Ahead went a scout, moving with caution – and more difficult to keep an eye on than the four who followed him. Of these, one was plainly the chief; he rode on a kind of legged machine which squeaked softly as it progressed. The other three men followed with the dogged and enduring manner of subordinates. It made good sense to kill the leader first.

The leader was a proud man. He looked about arrogantly, his bare chin jutting. He had already sighted the toylike Perfect Place. He wore a helmet with visor, perhaps to protect himself from harmful radiation which still invaded the air. Over one shoulder a carbine was slung.

Above the leader, above the pines, wheeled Ikanu's birds of omen, still calling, "Distance yourself, distance yourself . . ."

Nefriki slid one of his powerful hands across a rock, flexed his muscles, dragged himself against the rock, waited motionless until the scout had passed within a few yards of him, and then fitted an arrow to his bow. He raised himself slightly and drew back the bow with all his strength.

The five men were passing behind a thicket of cactus. As they emerged, Nefriki let the arrow fly. It sped to its mark with a powerful angry sound. It penetrated the thin metal-plating the leader wore across his chest and buried itself in his ribcage.

The leader made no comment upon his dying. He was evidently a man of decision; on receiving the arrow, he fell without hesitation backwards from the machine. As his head struck the ground, blood pumped from his mouth and ran into his helmet.

Nefriki released a second arrow and ran forward without waiting to see it strike its target. As he dodged behind boulders, he swung the bow over his shoulder and drew his short sword. He rushed out to confront two demoralised men; their companion lay on the ground beside the leader, an arrow through his chest; one of his legs was still kicking, scattering small stones.

"Distance yourself," screamed the birds of omen.

One of the two survivors was too frightened to shoot. The other brought up a self-focus heat weapon and fired wildly. A pine tree burst into flame above Nefriki's head. Nefriki sliced off the man's right arm. The other man turned and fled.

Breathing deeply, Nefriki picked up a heavy round stone, took aim, and flung it at the head and shoulders bobbing down the hillside. He heard the brutal sound of stone connecting with skull before dropping to the ground as bullets sang through the air in his direction. The scout was returning.

Since the scout kept up intermittent fire, he betrayed his position while Nefriki worked behind him. It was no great matter to attack silently from the rear, to bring the short sword into play, to thrust its already bloodied blade upwards right under the scout's ribs. While the scout shuddered in the dust and died, Nefriki went back to finish the man whose hand he had severed. He smiled all the while.

Among the dead stood the legged machine, bearing a burden slung on its back. It spoke in a gentle voice as Nefriki approached.

"Master, I will serve you. I am made to serve. Do not destroy me as you have destroyed those humans. I can work for you all the days of your life."

Without replying, Nefriki went cautiously nearer to inspect it. The machine's parts were painted a dull green. Its four legs were multi-jointed and ended above its body; it could adjust to function as a taller or a smaller animal. Set in its square head beside its eyes were the muzzles of two guns. They pointed at Nefriki, awaiting his reply.

He took an enormous, sudden kick, catching the machine under its chin. For a moment, he thought he had broken his leg or at least his toes, but his strength and his sandals saved him. As the pain left his limbs, he saw that he had jammed the machine's head back at an angle which rendered its guns useless.

He turned his attention to the burden on the machine's back. Strapped there, wrapped in film, unmoving, was what he thought was a beautiful dead girl. He took a step nearer. As Nefriki looked down at her, the girl opened her eyes and gazed up at him. He ceased smiling and tugged his golden beard instead.

Breaking the straps that bound her, he lifted the fragile burden from the machine, to set it rustling on its feet. He balanced her in an upright position, one arm encircling her waist. Then with another kick he sent the machine trotting downhill towards the distant sea.

The imprisoned girl's lips moved. "Spare me," she said. No mist from her breath obscured the wrappings over her face.

Shouts sounded near at hand. Other Tolanese guards were coming, called Nefriki by name. Nefriki did not reply. Half-carrying, half-dragging the film-wrapped girl, he made his way to a shallow cave he knew of, its entrance concealed by bushes. He climbed in and pulled her after him. They lay together until the hue and cry faded, and sunset melted in patches among the rocks outside their hiding place. All that while, he gazed at her silvery face.

When everything was quiet, Nefriki began to unwrap the girl – gently at first and then furiously, as the film resisted his tugging. When she was free, she gave a sigh and stretched her arms above her head, so that her flimsy tunic rumpled up over her body. Her hair was dark and hung to her shoulders without a curl.

She was thin, even spindly. The joints of her arms clicked slightly as she raised them. Nefriki could feel in her the gentlest of vibrations, and knew that her heart was of plastic, not flesh. He lay against her, terrified. This was the enemy, forbidden in The Perfect Place. The inhuman. The inhuman and female incarnate.

His body was touching hers. The workings of the engines inside her gave her synthetic flesh warmth. He could easily kill her.

She said, "Thank you for saving me. You do not have to be frightened. I should not be able to resist you if you wished to demolish me. All men are my conquerors, that I know." Her voice was lightly accented with regret.

"The men I killed were your friends."

"The men you killed . . ." She let the phrase dangle, perhaps in contempt, then said after a pause, "I was only their *thing*. I told you, you do not have to be frightened."

"Frightened of you? How could I be frightened of you? You saw what I did to the men you were with."

When she said nothing he declared, "I'm frightened of nothing." He raised himself on one elbow to look down at her face. She did not reply.

Angrily, he said, "What are you, anyway? You're an artificial creation. You don't even understand what I say."

"Yes, I'm artificial. I'm an atrinal android, designed to appease man's need to touch. A plaything." Her tone made him feel naïve.

It was his turn to say nothing. She said, "Relationships between men and women are so bad that men have had to invent something like me, to avoid their pain in true human relationships."

"Is it possible to have a – true relationship with you?"

With a hint of coquetry, the android said, "That is for you to say. It depends on your character."

"Come out into the open. I want to look at you. Don't try to run away." He made his voice rough, masculine.

She climbed out of the cave after him and stood relaxedly, her eyes turned to the sea murmuring far below, so that her perfectly formed, anonymous face took on a pensive expression.

Nefriki caught her wrist. "Take off your dress."

"You wish to see me naked? I am formed like a living woman. Of course I will do that for you, but first you must answer a few questions about yourself."

"What's that to you?"

"So that we can be close. Or do you fear that? What is your name?"

"I'm Nefriki, the guard of this place. You have seen what a good guard I am. I kill anyone who comes near Tolan. I keep Tolan safe. I am stronger and more deadly than anyone in Tolan. I can have any woman I want. Every woman desires to lie with me."

The atrinal android said in a soft voice, "I also wish to lie with you, Nefriki . . . But first tell me who you are."

"I told you. I'm the guard, the strongest man here. This is The Perfect Place. Everyone fears and respects me. Last year, I killed a mountain lion with my bare hands."

She sat down, so that her face was hardly to be seen in the velvet of early night.

"Anecdotes, boasts, Nefriki . . . But what lies under them? Tell me who the real man is, and then we can make love."

He squatted beside her and gave a short angry laugh. "Is it such a privilege, to make love to a machine? Pah, any woman in Tolan would throw themselves at me and beg for my love. They never ask who I really am."

"Perhaps they dare not ask. Perhaps they dread to know . . . Do you know that there are a few wise humans who believe that The Deterrence came about because the world's leaders suffered from man's common fear of women, and of themselves being women? They had to prove they were men even to the extreme of ruining the planet. And they rose to power over populations who felt as they did. Women know these things."

"What can women know that men don't?"

"They know that men desire their bodies but fear their minds."

"Rubbish. You're a demented machine."

She beckoned him nearer. "Before you discover how human I can be, Nefriki, tell me your deepest secrets, your deepest truths, tell me who your real self is . . . I don't ask it to achieve power over you but to free you, to make you free."

He moved closer, took her in his arms, kissed her roughly on her lips.

"You see. I have no fear of you." He laughed. "Suppose you tell me your secrets, if you have any."

She put a finger to her lips. "I will tell you my deepest secret. It is so profound that you will think it trivial. I am only a mirror. I can only mirror the men in my life. So was I designed, as a machine; but I can tell you this – I have found that many human women are also mirrors. They have turned themselves into mirrors. Simply through fear."

The conversation was not to his taste. He did not understand her. Besides, he felt hungry.

He jumped to his feet, called to the android woman to follow him, and headed down almost invisible trails to his house.

Antarida was not in. She had left the house empty, the door open. No doubt at this time of night she would be lying on a bed in one of the small palaces of Tolan, prostrate beneath some gallant necrophile.

He lit a lantern and brought forth bread, cheese, and the cloudy wine of Tolan. He offered them to the creature who stood just inside the door, watching him with her narrow eyes.

"I do not eat," she said, regarding him steadily.

"Sit down while I eat. You worry me."

She came to the table with a wanton step. She was designed to please, for all her riddles; he saw that. He wondered how best to kill her.

"What sort of secrets did you expect me to tell you? I've no secrets."

She said, softly, "You are so vulnerable, Nefriki. I hear the way your voice dies at the end of a sentence. I love the sound of it."

"You'll never capture my heart by such talk." He spoke through a mouthful of bread.

"It's not your heart I want but your soul. You brought me to your house to show me one of your secrets."

"I brought you here because I wanted to eat. It's my home, you silly hen, that's all. I could break your plastic neck."

She shook her head sadly.

She rested her hands together on the table and said, "No, you brought me here to show me that you live with a woman. Her scent is about the room. But you never make love to her. Why do you live with a woman to whom you never make love?"

He struck the table with his fist.

"Because she is my sister. You expect me to make love to my sister? Whatever happens in the ruined world, here we have the death penalty for such obscenity."

"Otherwise . . ." she said, and let the word hang in the air, like the dark trail that rose upwards from the wick of the lamp.

He lowered his head and ate without looking at her, pressing the food into his mouth, scowling.

At last he rose, still chewing the last crust of bread.

"The night is fine. We will go and swim. Then we'll see what happens. Can you swim or do you sink?"

"I swim, Nefriki, thank you. I can do most of the things men wish me to do, like other women."

He led the way down the hillside. Occasionally, he looked back over his shoulder to see that the android woman still followed him. She appeared all obedience, but he could not trust her.

It was his duty to kill her. If Reeve Ikanu discovered that he had spared an invader from the ruined world, Nefriki's life would be forfeit. Inside him, he felt a reluctance to do the deed himself; this creature was a powerful witch, with an understanding of men

Nefriki regarded as almost uncanny. There was another way to dispose of her.

As they climbed down to the shore, they had to pass by the slope-shouldered villa which was the residence of Ikanu. The villa was composed of small towers, featureless except for small square windows here and there, designed to keep out sunlight. The building resembled a tropical ants' nest. As man and android woman passed by its slanting sides, they saw a light in one of the small windows. As they passed by the front door, soft-footed, the watchdog sitting at the step called in its deep growl, "Guard yourself".

But for once Nefriki was too intent on his purpose to feel fear for the reeve. He ran down on to the sand, and the girl followed.

The night was lighter on the beach. The star-blaze overhead reflected on the waves, and there was a dazzle of luminescence in the warm water just off shore. Fireflies darted along the beach like miniature ball lightning.

He kicked off his sandals and then, after only a moment's hesitation, pulled off his clothes. Meekly, the android woman also undressed. She stood before him without defences, her firm breasts close to his chest. He caught the thickness in his own voice as he said, "You go in the water first. I'll follow."

It was a long time ago that his love Etsimita had ventured into this same water to her death. Nefriki had never dared to plunge into the tempting waves since. He stood on the shore, fists on hips, watching as the android girl obeyed and waded deeper.

"Stop!" He could bear it no longer. The water splashed against her meek shoulderblades. She turned back to look at him when he shouted. Nefriki plunged out to her, calling incoherently.

He grasped her arm and ran back with her to the shore, dragging her against the undertow. "It's dangerous," he said. "Dangerous. Machines in the water . . ."

They flung themselves on to the sand. He took hold of her and began to kiss her passionately.

"You must forgive me, you must forgive me."

She said, "Was it courage which made you run in after me?"

"No, no," He was burying his face in her damp synthetic hair. "It was fear. I couldn't lose you. You offered me something . . ."

She was breathing more deeply, stirring in his embrace. "No, leave me alone. You wanted to kill me. To dispose of me."

She tried feebly to break from his grasp, but was unable to.

Nefriki thrust his face into hers until his lips were almost touching her lips. His face was distorted. She felt his damp beard against her throat.

"Listen woman, you gave me the chance to speak the truth about myself. I couldn't take it – so covered is my life in lies. You're right, all men are liars. Well, now I've caught you again. I've got you and I will tell you the truth, and you will listen."

She turned her face away. "Death excites you so much, doesn't it? You're preparing to lie again."

"I will tell you the truth only if you will believe it, if you will keep still, if you will accept what I say."

"There can be no such contract," she said. "You may tell me what you claim is your truth – then I will tell you if it is credible. The more insane you think it, the more likely it is to agree with horrible human normality. Do you understand that, Nefriki, you weakling, you fool? Laid open, humanity can only squeal out madness and terror – the madness of being born, the terror of dying, of confronting death.

"And for men there is something more: the dread of the female . . . Every man is infiltrated by that dread, although he never escapes sharing all his chromosomes but one in common with womankind. Western man I'm talking about – the sort of man who unleashed The Deterrence on the whole world. Now – speak, Nefriki, if you must, knowing that I will believe you only if you reveal yourself as unutterably vile."

She had pulled herself free during this speech and knelt above him, as he had earlier knelt above her. He clutched her, his arms about her waist, and spoke in a low choking voice.

"Very well, then. Vileness, yes, vileness. I am utterly destroyed by Tolan, by its mores, its society . . . There's no one I love. Even my sister I hate . . .

"And I suppose that I dream of defiling her when she is dead . . .

"Yet I am a man. Towards every approach I must be tough. If the waves devour my sweetheart, I must not weep. I must be tough – to myself as well as to women. I poison myself thereby.

Women. Yes. I hate them, their weakness . . . Their strength even more . . ."

The android woman made to speak but he silenced her, sinking lower, his lips against her thighs.

"There's no escape for me. Besides, to escape would be a womanly act. I'm a guard, a man among men, all male. Of course I hate women – yes, fear them . . ."

"Why fear them?" she asked.

"Years have gone by . . . I touch nobody . . . Love means weakness, surrender. A true man like me must be all hard. Sword in hand, no feeling. If you want me to say it so much, then I'll say it to you because you're only an android. I hate and envy women. There!"

As she looked down at him, her face was calm as usual. She opened her mouth, hesitated, and then said, "It's on that hatred, that ingrained sexual hatred, the world wrecked itself. The madness of the male, deterring real feeling, leads to The Deterrence. And the fears of women make them turn themselves into mirrors."

Nefriki was not listening. He said, "How can I escape my prison? I hate myself, I long – I long to be a woman. Yes, there, woman, there's my damned soul you asked for! Have it, take it for the little it's worth."

Nefriki burst into furious tears, burying his face in his muscular forearms and his elbows in the sand.

She rose and stood above him, like a statue in her nakedness. It was darker now. The luminescence had disappeared from the sea, the fireflies had gone.

"All this is more of your posturing, Nefriki. It's not your soul you're offering, it's a posture, nothing more. You're diseased, you can't speak truth – you wouldn't know truth if you saw it. I recognise what you say as a kind of truth, but mainly it is just your posture. No one confesses except to gain pity or admiration."

"You're being cruel," he said into his arms.

"I told you I am only a mirror. A mirror is all you require for your narcissism, not a living woman. That's why men invented my kind. You give me nothing. You never even asked my name."

She began to walk away down the beach, away from Nefriki, away from Tolan, The Perfect Place.

He shouted after her. "You demanded my soul, you damned bitch, and I gave it you. Give me something in return."

Light swept across the sand, bright enough for Nefriki to see that the android woman had paused. He turned to see where the light came from.

The cruel reeve, Ikanu, had thrown open the front door of his house and was marching forward, sword in hand. Beside him was his faithful dog, shouting, "Guard yourself", in its hoarse voice. A woman stood in Ikanu's doorway, holding a torch above her head. Nefriki saw that it was his sister, Antarida. So she wished to be witness at his death.

For a moment, Nefriki stood undecided, attention caught between sister, reeve, and android woman.

The dog advanced croaking its cry in its artificial voice, "Guard yourself". After it came Ikanu, now raising his sword threateningly. He wore a robe which trailed to the sand and a flowing wig to cover the baldness of his head, which flapped as he trudged towards Nefriki.

An unanticipated noise broke from Nefriki's mouth. He was laughing involuntarily. The figure of Ikanu, half-man, half-woman, suddenly embodied all the theatrical insanity of Tolan: Ikanu's melodrama, Antarida's necrophilia, the destructive lifestyle into which isolation had forced the beleaguered city.

In the middle of his laughter, Nefriki saw how he himself was living out a sham. He could give no coherent account of himself even to the android woman – there was no valid context from which to deliver it. His emotional life had frozen. He laughed to think he could have acted out a role without knowing it.

The laughter began high and fell to a low grating sound, much like the artificial voice of the dog.

On Reeve Ikanu the laughter had an extraordinary effect. The reeve dropped his sword, to stand in puzzlement, thin arms outstretched. Slowly, his sandalled feet lost their purchase on the shifting sand. Slowly, he lost his balance and fell backwards. His dog rushed to him and began licking his face. "Guard yourself, guard yourself . . ."

Nefriki turned. The dim light from Ikanu's doorway, where Antarida still stood transfixed, lit the retreating back of the android woman. It looked as if the darkness would swallow her at any moment.

He called to her and started running along the beach. "I want to know your name! I want to give you something real . . ."

Without turning back, without ceasing to stride along the beach, she said, "What have you got that's real?" Her voice was almost drowned by the sound of the surf.

As he ran, Nefriki shouted, "My soul! Isn't that what you wanted? You haven't got one. Help me find mine and we might manage things better between us. Where are you going?"

She made no answer. In desperation, he called again. "Why should I want to come with you?"

This time she stopped and half-turned to deliver her response.

"The ruined world may resemble hell, but perhaps hell is where mankind belongs, not in perfect places. At least hell does not dissemble. You have vomited up some of your lies, Nefriki. If you dare to come with me, you may some day find your system cleansed entirely."

"I hate you," he said.

And then he took hold of her hand.

(1985)

Lies!

Never will I forget how she spoke to me that night. So calm, so white was her face, so dark and stormy were her words, so tense and compressed her meaning. Beautiful? Oh, she was beautiful all right – but what you should first ask is, was she truthful?

Of that I cannot say. Certainly she meant to torment me, to wound, perhaps even to kill. But in such objectives, truth is often the sharpest weapon.

This is what she said, as far as I can recall her actual words. No one can reproduce the manner in which they were said, or the curl of her lip, the glint of her teeth, when she said them, when she forced them from her.

"In me are three women. The woman I present to men, the woman I present to other women, and the woman I present to myself when I am alone, secret, a million miles from others. You alone, Rupert, have seen that third woman, and how should you expect to survive the encounter?"

She came near then, so I felt her hot breath and spittle on my cheek. I could not move. I understood that Little Sinnenlugen would kill me. In truth, I half wished for it.

It was the year of 1986. Business had taken me to Bavaria and business had failed. The enterprise I had undertaken for my company had not met with success; on my return home, I would be dismissed for a certainty. So I took some days off to walk alone in those mountains and forests which divide Germany from Austria.

The weather was miserable. There were no tourists about. Even the small farming villages seemed deserted. Soon I was walking high above those villages, in venerable forest land. The trees carried an additional burden of misery, for the rain that fell on them contained precipitations from distant manufacturing centres, making them sick.

For some while, as I wandered among the brakes and tracks under dripping foliage, I pretended to myself – such was my mood – that I was lost. Only as evening descended, and a curtain of lead, rimmed on its underside with gold, began to close on the horizon, did I realise that I was in truth lost.

My first alarm was almost pleasurable to me. But the horizontal light, infiltrating the tall trunks of the trees, shone on a myriad beads of moisture, dazzling me, disconcerting me. It was as if I advanced upon the bayonets of an elfin army. An evil enchantment was all about. When I heard the thud of my boots on the pine needles underfoot, it was as though I listened to the advance of an invisible enemy. Shielding my eyes from the glare, I hurried forward. Once I called. There was no response. The answering silence was too terrible for me to dare repeating my cry. Who would hear that I would wish to hear?

The confusion of the light died suddenly. I was alone in twilight. Emerging on to a ride through the gloomy ranks of the conifers, I began to trot, hoping to outpace the dark. The ride went on for miles, occasionally dipping down or rising. The silent presence of the trees became ever more gloomy. At last, out of breath, I stopped by a fire-fighting station, where wooden beaters stood on a rack.

After I had recovered my breath, I set off again. Darkness surrounded me, a darkness of quite a different quality to the dark of towns. This darkness was personal to the forest, and waited there in hiding during the day. Engulfed by it, I somehow strayed from the broad path, and found myself staggering among brambles and bracken I could no longer see.

Humans are strange creatures. We are not our own best company on such occasions. For we find, rational beings though we are, that there is another being within us, who emerges in feral mood and scares us with stories – perhaps they are memories – of long ago, when most of the world was covered with forest. This ancient and unreasonable being will not be talked down. It does not understand our tongue.

After banging myself a dozen times on unyielding timber, I realised that the night must somehow be passed in the forest.

Nor was I entirely displeased. A masochistic side of me even rejoiced at the prospect. But on the whole I was dismayed at the thought of a grim and spooky night in the wet, with no warmth and nothing to eat.

I settled down as best I could, with my back to a tree in a comfortingly traditional way. There is only one attitude at such a time: knees up, arms folded, head resting on knees. I fell asleep.

Fear woke me. Some great creature was crashing through the trees in my direction. In a moment, I had scrambled to my feet and was peering into the pine-choked dark.

Perhaps whatever approached rapidly would have appalled me. Perhaps even a simple woodman, axe on shoulder, would have frightened me. What alarm was mine when I saw a coach and horses coming my way!

Fond though I am of horses – I began to ride as soon as my father would teach me – they somehow alarm me when they are seen head-on at full gallop, manes flying, eyes staring, lather at their mouths. Who could reason with a runaway horse? More alarming still, these beasts pulled an ancient coach. It rattled furiously behind them – the sort of vehicle that became obsolete I know not how many years ago.

The horses – a pair – were grey, and of heavy build. The coach was black. It bore two carriage-lamps. Up on the seat, lashing on the animals, was a figure more alarming than they. It wore a black leather outfit. A cloak fluttered from its shoulders. It plied a whip over the backs of the horses. Its hair streamed in the wind. It was female.

The young woman's feet were bare. I glimpsed that incongruous detail – among the general incongruity – and yet it did not register on my perceptions until later. For I was taken by her face and its ghastly expression. The arched eyebrows, the pinched nostrils, the mouth tensed open, displaying white teeth, the eyes glaring forward over the necks of the careering animals – all these were tokens of a woman seized by . . . but I knew not what. Terror? Certainly they struck terror in me, terror both of her and of whatever might be pursuing her, real or imaginary.

Paralysed as I was, I yet realised that I had only to stay still and she would be past in no time. Whether real or apparition, she would be lost in the dark almost at once.

At that instant – I can hardly describe it – there was an immense explosion. Or rather a noise, a concussion, and perhaps a flash too. I was temporarily blinded. When I saw again, the coach was gone, the horses were gone. Not along the track they were following with such uncanny haste. Simply gone, disappeared into nowhere. The young woman stood there, a few paces from me, her cloak about her shoulders.

She did not see me. She began to curse, furiously, hotly, with the most awesome obscenities and blasphemies. Nobody cares greatly for blasphemy these days; the religious fervour which once gave blasphemy power has faded; but this ferocious woman swore against the holy powers with all the vehemence of faith.

So she continued for a while. She walked about in a circle, kicking at sticks and mud as she went. Then she saw me. The disgusting words died on her lips.

She approached, neck arched forward like a swan's.

"Are you from my sisters?"

I stammered something in reply.

"Whoever you are, get me out of this accursed forest. I must be home before daybreak." She spoke in a formal, precise way, coldly but quite calmly, in a manner totally unlike the one she had used before realising she was observed.

I felt less fear of her now, and was recovering enough from my state of shock to ask her where she thought her coach had gone.

She laughed. "If you witnessed its disappearance, then I imagine you have sense enough to guess its destination. I only wonder I was not carried there with it!"

Looking down, I saw her bare feet already covered with mud. The riding outfit she wore was tattered and torn. Beginning to feel some compassion, or at least a fellow-feeling in distress, I offered to walk with her through the forest if she wished.

Later, I wondered how she was so visible, after midnight in the thick of the woebegone forest. At the time, all that seemed natural enough, and I watched her smile with no surprise.

"We can go together. I imagine that my father's house is not far."

"I do not believe there is any habitation within miles."

"We shall see."

So we began to walk together. She was a tall person. Her dark hair drifted beside me at the level of my eye. Neither of us spoke, though I was full of curiosity.

As if in reaction to my recent dismay, my mood became one of complacency. To an idiotic degree, I felt cheerful and trusting. By quick sideways glances, I perceived that her face, no longer distorted, was remarkably fine, the skin clear, the structure good, the features trim and positive, as only the features of those who are dark of hair and pale of skin can be. Her eyes were a deep blue, or possibly a velvet, or possibly some other colour that had no name. She was beautiful: so beautiful that I felt her nature to be beautiful as well. And this assumption I could persist in even while reminding myself of her recent sacrilegious fury.

After a while, she took my arm. Neither of us made any comment. For me, it was enough to feel her warmth against me.

"We shall be at my father's house soon," she said, at one point.

"Is he awaiting you?"

"Oh, father will be asleep in the arms of my stepmother, no doubt."

Something in her tone prevented my questioning her further.

It was to my relief, and also regret, that I saw a light among the trees.

We emerged at last from the repressive confines of the conifers and walked along a road leading uphill. Dogs were barking somewhere not far distant.

The house loomed black against the sky. We went through an iron gate and up a drive. A great grey dog came whisking up to us, sniffed at the woman, and disappeared again into the undergrowth. The woman said nothing. She was still clutching my arm.

"Can you put me up for the night –"

"Of course. I expect that you will stay." She held my arm even more tightly, although there had been no invitation in her tone.

The light we had seen through the trees shone from a window high up in the serrated line of roof now towering about us. Evidently it was a grand house – and rather unwelcoming in aspect, I thought.

We walked round the building until we reached a side door, at which my companion halted and produced a key from her pocket.

"Look here," I said, responding to some inner prompting,

"perhaps I should not come in and trouble your family. I don't even know your name."

She paused with the key in the lock.

"I mean, I can walk along the road to the nearest village and knock up someone at the inn."

In a hard tone, she said, "People round here won't open up at this time of night."

We entered the house. She switched on a light.

"My name is Sindy, short for Sinnenlugen – although my sisters call me something else."

As she made this casual introduction, as I told her my name, she looked straight at me. Her beauty was startling; but, as I stared, her aspect changed as if by magic. Her shoulders softened, her whole stance changed, her head was lowered. No longer was she commanding; she almost cringed.

When she snatched a smock from behind a door and wrapped it about her, hiding the riding outfit, she was scarcely recognisable as the prideful woman who had walked beside me in the night woods. She was now more like a little drudge, paid to clean this great house. Her demeanour, as she led me forward, was mouse-like and obsequious. She put a finger to her lips to motion me to silence.

We passed through a large, old-fashioned kitchen, with a great stove on one side, over which washing was hung on suspended poles to dry. The great grey dog had slipped into the house with us. It went over to the fire and curled down beside it with a heavy sigh.

The mysteriously named Sindy led me up through the house without putting on any more lights. A light was already burning in the hall. We ascended a staircase of some grandeur.

"This is where my sisters sleep," she whispered, as we reached the first landing, passing by portraits in gilt frames.

We went down a side landing, through a door, to a part of the house that seemed both unfurnished and undecorated. The air struck chill. Up a bare stair we went, along another passage, with closed doors leading off it, up a winding stair, and so to Sindy's attic rooms, where the light burned which we had seen from the forest. A fire of logs flickered in a little black grate.

All was stark here. The furniture, what there was, was of the poorest. The one mat on the floor was worn.

She looked searchingly at me. Now her pupils appeared dark.

"It's my place," she said, as if by way of explanation.

She turned and went into a further room. Uncertainly, I followed. In this room stood an old four-poster bed, much the worse for wear, with its canopy in tatters, but well furnished with pillows and linen. A black cat sat in the middle of the bed, gazing at an indeterminate point in space.

"Well." Sindy gave me one of her searching looks. "Now you are here. What more do you expect of me, master?"

Startled, I said, "Nothing."

"Oh, yes, you do. You expect to get into bed with me, to climb on to me and penetrate me, don't you?"

I did not reply.

"Don't you, Rupert?"

I laughed. "It would be agreeable if you found it agreeable. Not otherwise."

"Why should I find it agreeable?"

"Women do, by and large." I laughed again.

"Why do you laugh at what is not funny? Are you embarrassed? Are you *afraid*?"

"Come, now." I crossed the room and took her arm as gently as she had taken mine. "It is you who is afraid. I will not harm you. I am no rapist. Perhaps it would be pleasant for us both to be in this bed together. At least it would warm us up."

Again her manner changed. Suddenly, the challenging manner was gone. She wrapped her arms about me, snuggling against me like a large animal.

"You wouldn't hurt poor Sindy, would you? You'd be kind and nice? I'm so scared of men, really, really scared, though I never admit it."

By such coaxings, and with coaxings from me of a parallel kind, we threw off our damp clothes and climbed – by degrees and endearments which were enough to intoxicate me – on to the great bed. The warmth and aroma of her body was like a drug to my senses.

"You're going to take advantage of me, I know. I fear it, Rupert. Oh, Rupert, I am so scared of you, really. The way you appeared in the forest . . . Swear you will not suddenly turn savage . . . Well, then, let me have a guarantee. Just to please me, to make me feel less frightened so that I can enjoy your caresses . . . Let me tie your hands for a little while, just in case you should be urged to strangle me in your embrace. Your darling hands . . . Mmm, yes, oh, Rupert, dearest, give me your hands for safety, fast . . . Then all the rest of your body can be free with all of mine. My poor tender body . . . Yes, here . . ."

Before I fully understood what was happening, my wrists were imprisoned above my head. Under her blandishments, her naughty wriggling, I had allowed my hands to be locked into iron gyves secured to the mighty wooden beams at the head of the bed.

As they snapped together, I knew I had been trapped. Immediately, my sensuous mood was broken. I fought and kicked to get free. The cat, hitherto impassive as a Buddha, went flying and disappeared out of the door. Sindy jumped from the bed, to stand naked where I could not touch her. Though I twisted about, writhed, shook the bed, I was caught. At last I lay still, gasping, and glared at her. But she was lovely – I thought so even in that moment of fury.

"What are you, you hateful creature?"

"You may find that out," she said.

Then she put on a gown and went from the room, leaving me alone, sprawled on the bed.

For a while, I struggled in the dark. By stretching myself, I could get my bare feet on the floor. There was nothing within reach of my exploring toes which could be used as a weapon. She had caught me so easily. Now there was nothing for it but to await her pleasure and see what could be done to reverse the situation.

Angry – and with my masochism fuelling a certain elation in the absurd situation – I crawled under the bedclothes, pulling up the blankets with my teeth. I had been chilled to the bone. Gradually warmth returned to me and I slept.

It was still dark. Sindy was sitting by me on the bed, poised – I could tell it even as I returned to my senses – poised for flight.

"I am so scared of you, Rupert. You understand, don't you? So scared. I really desire you, but first we must understand each other. I want to tell you something, something extremely private, something nobody else knows. Do you like the sight of blood?"

"For the love of God, woman, stop torturing us both and let me go. I will leave here at once and not lay a finger on you, that I swear."

Her whisper came through the dark to me. "That's not what I want, Rupert."

I refused to speak. In the dark, I could only sense her exact position. My thought was that, with a spring, I might get my legs about her throat and drag her down. There would be only one chance of success. After that, doubtless she would bind me tighter. As I moved, she moved. She was off the bed as if she read my thoughts.

I lurched uselessly to one side, tearing the flesh of my wrists against their iron bonds.

Sindy went to the door, opened it ajar, and softly called a name. Next moment, I felt a heavy body bound on to the bed. Low growls came to me. Somehow, that great grey dog – or maybe it was another dog – was there with her.

"Now, Rupert, now . . . Now you must lie still or you will find yourself attacked. I would not attack you because I don't want to hurt you, but my friend here feels differently. If he makes a good guard, and I don't doubt he will, then I shall reward him at daybreak in a special way – and you may watch."

She laughed. By now, she was back at the bedside and looking down at me.

Afraid to move, I lay and allowed her hand to move over my body. Despite the threatening presence of the hound, I became intensely excited.

"Now you know the reason why I am scared, Rupert. In spite of your violent nature, I will be gentle with you. Women are gentle, you know. I want to tell you a very private story, and I hope you will listen.

And she began.

When I was born, it rained blood (whispered Sindy to me). To be exact, three basins of blood. My mother could not stop bleeding. I was the first of three babies to emerge from her womb. Although I escaped unscathed, my two sisters were less lucky. They were breech births, and both midwife and doctor were distraught, fearing never to draw them into this world. The doctor drank a bottle of brandy during the crisis. Yes, and the midwife another bottle. My father said so.

While I lay swaddled safe by my mother, the tussle went on. It lasted all night. One of my sisters was almost torn in half, I was told. Both died during the following day, without uttering a cry.

As for me – it was a year and a day before I gave so much as a whimper.

My mother was never to recover completely from her ordeal. She became a permanent invalid, shunning men, lest she was forced to undergo such torture again. Do you wonder, Rupert, I grew up with a fear of your sex?

My mother was everything to me. I worshipped her. Anything she wished I would do. I used to take her for long rides in the forest in my little trap.

We used to visit the midwife, who lived deep in the forest. The forest was more extensive in those days. Her husband was a woodman and made furniture. The midwife was gifted with magical powers, said my mother, though I never believed her. If she had such powers, why did she let my poor sisters die? But mother insisted that she was my fairy godmother.

My thoughts were always with my dead sisters. I communed with them, Rupert, I imagined them close to me.

Just over a year ago, my mother died. I will not dwell on that, or I shall weep. She was so beautiful. Exquisite – yes, exquisite, and told the most beautiful fairy stories. Dead, Rupert – but still close to me in every way . . .

I begged my father to let me have her preserved, so that I could keep her in my room and talk to her. At that time, I had a suite of rooms on the first floor. Father would not hear of such a thing.

Did I tell you about my father? He's so respectable, so rich. Richer than grandfather, even, who started our pharmaceutical company in Hitler's days. Also he's on all sorts of committees – oh, I don't know, to do with the law. And he's a hermit, really – he collects stamps, yes, that's it, stamps . . . Can you believe it?

I made such a scene on the day of mother's funeral that father had to lock me in the cellar. Oh, I went mad, I can't tell you. I seized a chopper and tried to cut my way out. I was possessed. You know how gentle I am, you've seen how gentle I am. Yet I have kept that chopper with me ever since, to protect myself, just in case I have to kill myself or my father or anyone else who threatens me.

My two sisters were there with me in the dark cellar. Being dead, they have no personality, so they share mine. That's fair and reasonable. One of them – I don't know if you can understand this, my dear, but one of them loves men, while the other hates them.

Sometimes, they nearly drive me mad. Sometimes I really think I am mad. Now, lie still when I laugh. Remember that faithful Karl is here, with his sharp teeth, yes, to stop you doing anything you shouldn't.

What a horrible shock when my father married again, almost immediately after the funeral. Who should he marry but his housekeeper, that terrible woman, Ingeborg, Ingeborg whom I hated, who tried to keep me from my mother. Fat Ingeborg. He married her, would you believe it?

Then I understood! Between my tears I understood. I understood the whisperings, the lights fluttering in dark rooms, the rustles, the sudden closing of doors, all those sly dishevelments. Oh, yes, I understood why my father sometimes looked like a dog with the whites of its eyes showing, what she did when she sat by him with the rug over his lap in the orchard in the heat of a summer afternoon. Why she was there and not there, here and there. That Ingeborg!

They married in town, curse them. Half the population of Bavaria was there. I was locked in the cellar.

When they returned, all in their stiff dead clothes as if there was nothing under the clothes but more clothes – why, she brought with her two daughters from her first marriage. Yes, she was a widow, Ingeborg, she knew all the tricks of marriage, all the syrups – oh, yes . . .

And those two girls . . . My age, but so simple, so foolish, so trusting. How they capered that first day, in their little frocks. How they ran about the house, shrieking and calling. How they simpered before me and cried that they longed to be friends and love me.

They put their fat arms about me, hugged me. Ingeborg too. Said she would care for me like my mother, as she breathed on me.

Oh, when she said that, did not I feel the chopper twitch under my pillow upstairs!

So I smiled and told those two little pets, my new sisters, that I had two other sisters already, who lived in the cellar. I went into a great fantasy about them, so that those little pets had their tongues hanging out. I told them they lived down in the cellar for ever, because they were afraid of daylight.

Down went the little pets to see them, nothing suspecting. As soon as they were safe in the cellar, bang, I slammed the door on them and locked it. Yes! How the little brats screamed, but no one could hear because my father had gone for an afternoon's drive with his beautiful new wife.

Out to the stable I ran, got the hose, turned on the tap, ran with it, spewing out water like blood, down the hall, thrust the end under the cellar door. You remember, don't you, Karl?

In the water rushed, flushing those little pets to the bottom of the stairs. There I stood laughing. I could imagine the water flowing higher and higher. I thought perhaps it would take an hour to drown them. How they screamed! How they screamed!

Through the house I ran, glorying, destroying all their pretty clothes and dolls and toys. What excitement! Oh, I was so brave that afternoon, Rupert, and the great sun swung through the windows, all gold and tawny, as if it would hang where it was for ever.

Then father came home with Ingeborg. Well, they could not see the joke. I can't tell you what they did to me. Well, I'll whisper to you and see if you can believe it. My father stripped me naked, whipped me with a whip and then raped me, all in the sight of Ingeborg, who became so excited that she tore her own clothes off and fell on me too. There! That's what they did, I swear to god. And those two little pets, all wet and bedraggled, peeped round the door to watch, clutching at each other in a disgusting frenzy. What a scene, Rupert! Imagine! Don't you wish you had been there? You could have joined in too . . .

Ah, you don't like to be caressed like that? You get so excited. Stop wrenching at the bedhead. Stop it! You will injure yourself. Look, you have made your wrists bleed, you wretch. You men are so violent. Well, then I shall teach you a lesson. No more story. I will bathe those wrists for you – with some boiling water.

During this recitation, which sounded to me much more like a dreadful fairy story than the truth, Sindy's attitude had changed yet again. She had become nothing so much as an innocent waif, sitting for the most part with her hands folded in her lap, like a

child reciting a rhyme. Her eyes became curiously light, her
eyelids heavy and dewy. Her head came forward on her slender
neck, her gaze sank down to her hands, all with a kind of feigned
innocence at variance with the obscenities she uttered.

She switched on a dim light in one of two ante-rooms which led
off the bedroom and busied herself with water. Although I could
not see what she was doing, I heard a metal basin fill. All the while,
her great grey hound sat on the bed, watching me, its black jaw
slightly open, its tongue trembling, as if its ungainly body was
filled with a barely controlled passion to devour me.

My wrists were giving me pain, yet I scarcely dared move in case
the brute leaped on me.

After some while, the demonic woman emerged from her
ante-room, carrying a huge bowl of steaming water. Also gripped
in one of her hands was – I recognised it immediately as the sort of
chopper which featured in her depraved mythology.

Her face shone yellow through the mounting steam.

"This will cure you," she said, with a horrid smile.

The faithful hound looked round to see what his mistress was
doing. It was my chance. With my right foot, I gave the brute an
enormous kick in the entrails. The force of the kick sent it flying
off the bed, right into the scalding water.

Water splashed everywhere amid howls and screams. The bowl
rattled across the floor. Sindy fell over. Sliding the lower part of my
body off the bed, I reached out with my feet for the chopper.
Securing it with my toes, I dragged it nearer, until I could pick it
up between my feet, drop it on the bed, and grasp it with one hand.

Desperately, frantically, I chopped at the bedhead, striving to
release myself. The wood splintered under my blows, but the
chains held me too close for those blows to have real strength
behind them.

While the hound dashed scalded from the room, Sindy got to her
feet again.

"Please let me have that chopper, Rupert, dear. You will spoil
the bed. I will climb in with you if you are good – I know you want
me to."

I hacked away. Given time, I could cut myself free. She kept
begging for the chopper, promising more and more explicit
pleasures while I rained blow after blow on the wood.

She had had enough. She ran from the room, but was back in no more than a minute. In her hand she carried a flaming brand, advancing with it to the bedside, holding the flame above her head. I watched the smoke go up and scrawl its signature over the ceiling.

"Give me the chopper or I shall immediately set fire to the bed."

Did she mean it? What was this demonic creature not capable of? I passed over the chopper, handle first.

She threw it into a corner without removing her gaze from mine.

"You look so beautiful and harmless there, Rupert, that I can scarcely bear to kill you. How awful your screams would be! Don't you want to hear the rest of my secrets? There are many terrible things yet to be told, and dawn is a long way off."

"I don't want to hear a word more from you."

"Let me tie your feet to the bottom of the bed. Then I can trust you and come and lie beside you."

She went and laid the brand in an empty grate in the corner of the room, where the flame died and a sullen trail of smoke rolled out across the floor. She returned to the bed and stood by its head, looking down at me, smiling. Truly she was beautiful. Again she was the imperious beauty I had encountered in the forest.

With another change of mood, she snatched up a sheet, draping it about her shoulders with a fold over her hair, and immediately became nunlike and wistful, as befitted the opening of the second part of her story.

Poor little me, how I suffered. Even you, hard of heart though you are, would have pitied me in my suffering. How dearly I paid for my prank. How I wept, wept for weeks, became a shadow.

Feeling my disgrace, I left my luxurious compartment downstairs. Would you like to feel my disgrace, yes? I brought myself to live up here, in these desolate attics. My two new sisters were full of forgiveness, and would scratch and whine at the other side of my door, for all the world like animals, begging my blessing. They swore they would exhibit themselves. They swore they would lick me all over to show their penitence. Yes, Rupert, that is what they most longed to do. Would you also like to do that, Rupert, if I let you?

At night, I used to escape into the forest. I found I could jump from these windows and wish myself safe to the ground. Yes, it's true. Truly good people can do most marvellous things like that.

To shame my father and my new mother, that Ingeborg, I would put on ragged clothes and go to work in the kitchen. The dirtiest jobs I did – the dirtier the better. Ingeborg would stand by and weep. I knew all that sort of thing hurt them more than it did me. What a martyr I was! How I abased myself! Shovelling up ashes, scrubbing floors, cleaning toilets, talking to the builder's man, working in the stable – anything degrading, I did it. Oh, what savage delight it was, yes. And Ingeborg wept, and my father wept and even those wretched little sisters wept, sharing a handkerchief between them.

Those sisters had lovers who called on them. One sister, the one who was mad about men, had a fellow who owned a factory in town. He came here. And the other – she had gone the other way, she hated men and had a girl her own age who called here, all elegant in a green corduroy suit. Well, I'd go on my hands and knees and scrub round their feet, or vacuum-clean wherever they sat down. I took care always to appear filthy and sluttish. And I would fawn to them, saying, "Yes, miss, thank you, miss, what next, miss?" and so forth. You could see how they hated it.

One day, the postman brought an envelope addressed to me. It was an invitation to Herr Ottetrant's annual ball. Herr Ottetrant is the great landowner hereabouts and his parties are very splendid. This party was to celebrate his fortieth birthday. Since he had just done a great business deal with the Americans, celebrations were to be on a grand scale, and there was to be dancing on three successive nights.

Let me just whisper to you that Herr Ottetrant and I are very well acquainted. He is a very prim and proper man, but at the same time lecherous. I like him, to tell the truth, and I never minded a bit what he did to me when I was only a young girl. In fact, I believe that in a number of cases molestation by a man as handsome as Ottetrant, with a splendid physique and so forth, has a steadying effect on a girl.

His invitation arrived three weeks ago. In my mood of abnegation, I decided I would not go to the parties. My father begged me. He said that Ottetrant had a romantic interest in me, that he might wish to marry me, and such nonsense. The more he said, the more adamant I was. I fell fainting at my father's feet, and had to be carried to the sofa. What a fuss! I even wetted myself for verisimilitude, Rupert, darling.

Papa was distraught. He swore that he would make my new sisters go in my place.

Very well, I said. Since he loved them more than me, it was right and proper that he should send them in preference to me. My only suggestion would be that he should send Ottetrant a note beforehand, warning him not to waste his time on the lesbian sister.

Last night was the night of the first of the three balls. I had made myself especially drab, and sat by the old grate downstairs in the kitchen, looking woebegone, with my hair straggling down about my neck. The new sisters were all painted and made up, the very portraits of middle-class success.

"Oh, how lovely you look!" I cried. "All the men and one or two women I could name will admire you." Then I burst into floods of tears. It was very well done, and they went off in their taxi looking more shamed than I had dared hope.

I was alone with Karl. My father and stepmother had gone out. So I proceeded to go as insane as I dared. I began by breaking all the crockery in the scullery.

The noise, the sheer noise! I was just going into some sort of a – it was a trance, I suppose, a sort of possession – oh, you should see me at such times! When suddenly – I can't tell how it happened, but suddenly, it seemed to me that my fairy godmother stood in the kitchen. The place was full of smoke where I had flung the cinders over the floor, but there she stood and she was talking to me. At first I could not understand a word. The truth is, I hate words – they're like snakes, yes, like snakes.

"Poor creature," she kept saying. "Poor, poor creature! What would your mother say if she could see you in this state?"

Then it seemed to me that I was ordered to go into the garden and fetch a pumpkin. I hardly knew how to move. Everything was a complete blur.

Why a pumpkin? I kept asking myself. Maybe it was just a wrong word.

Somehow I managed to drag a huge pumpkin into the kitchen and set it on the floor. Why I did it I can't tell, because I hate pumpkins. I hate the look of them, as well as their name. They're very obscene in appearance, the very opposite of me, dressed as a nun, which I suppose I should become. Taking holy vows . . . Goodbye, naughtiness, hello, Jesus!

As I stood there, breathing heavily from the exertion, the pumpkin began to change. I was terrified. It went black and then began to swell, as if it was pregnant. You will never believe this, Rupert, but it grew and grew, that pumpkin – I had to jump out of the way – and it turned into a *coach*. Don't laugh. For once I'm telling the truth.

There stood this great coach, shafts and all, in the middle of our kitchen.

There was no way in which anyone could get it out of the kitchen.

I thought I was mad. I thought I was haunted. My godmother was nowhere to be seen.

I rushed from the house, screaming my head off, and jumped straight into the old lady.

"Calm yourself, Sindy," she said. "I wish you to go to the Ottetrant party. You are too much alone. It will do you good to mix with other people. Here's your chance."

"I shall scream again in a minute, I warn you."

"What you need is the formative influence of good conversation."

Although it sounds ridiculous, there stood the coach, outside now, complete with two greys chomping at the bit, large as life.

"Couldn't I have a taxi? Please?"

"A *taxi*? Out of a *pumpkin*?" she asked incredulously. "Now, don't be tedious, Sindy, do as I say. Go and get into some decent clothes and drive to the party like a sensible girl."

I started to scream. I can't bear to be called sensible. She soon made me be quiet. She clouted me with a wand she was carrying.

"You are far too highly-strung. You always were. No wonder your poor mother died."

"She's not dead."

"Don't be cheeky, girl! Go to the party and don't stay too long. Don't drink, be sure you dance with Ottetrant, don't let him slip a hand down your corsage, or anything else, and – remember this – leave there before midnight. Promise? Before midnight."

I promised. Of course I promised. When she had gone, I rushed inside and put on some decent clothes. I kissed my dear mother goodbye. Then I lashed up the horses and drove to the party in style.

Rupert, you can tell I am not a boastful girl, I hope, but I was such a grand success at that party. How I pranced and flounced and gave myself airs, yes! Oh, I danced with Ottetrant, I insisted. I wore a cat mask and looked immensely sexy. Men are always positively salacious about cats, aren't they? My sisters, my new sisters, were there, but they didn't guess it could possibly be me. I rushed about flirting and drinking, and having a simply terrific time. Ottetrant put a hand down my corsage and felt my breasts. Both of them. Do you know, one young man got me out on the balcony and started being romantic in such a silly old-fashioned way that with one swipe I – wham! unzipped his fly! He practically fell into a flower bed.

While I was laughing, my digital watch buzzed midnight. Then I remembered my boring godmother's boring instructions. Without waiting to say goodbye, or even to grab my wrap, I raced across the lawns to where one of Ottetrant's men was holding my horses.

In a flash, I was up on the box and driving hell-for-leather home. In the excitement, I lost my shoes. I decided to try and take a short-cut through the forest, which was fatal. My godmother must have put a curse on me or something, because suddenly – pow! – well, you saw it, didn't you, the coach and horses just disappeared . . .

You see how my life is? Nothing has ever gone right, ever since the hour I was born. I deserve nothing but the empty life of a nun. And pumpkins every day for breakfast.

During her narrative, Sindy had been all energy and gesture. I almost saw her coach and the two greys conjured up before me. Now, she again brought the sheet lugubriously over her head, to give a sweet impersonation of a nun, her delicate lips bowed as if about to utter a Hail Mary.

Reaching out to the full extent of my chains, I grabbed the ends of the sheet and wrenched her towards me. Taken by surprise, she lost her balance and fell across me. I had a leg locked round hers in a moment, holding her in place before she could run for the chopper, gripping her slender body against mine.

"Now, you crazy little fiend –"

"Oh, you do love me," she cried. "Yes, yes, be masterful, Rupert, ignore my fears, kiss me, please kiss me . . . All over the place . . . Uhh . . ."

And she pretended to swoon, falling limp in my arms.

As I looked down at her, full of mistrust, I heard noises outside. A vehicle was approaching the house. Glancing up, I saw a pallor at the window. The hour of dawn approached, bringing the inevitable regrets and promises of a new day.

Sindy stirred and murmured as if in her sleep, eyes closed, "Oh, feel my breasts, please, darling, please. That's what all women need, that and no more, and that is what they dare say only to themselves, their real selves; not to men, not to other women. Only to themselves, feel my breasts, feel my . . ."

"There's someone outside. Release me at once. Unlock my fetters."

At that, she sat up, to listen for a moment to the noise of wheels outside.

"My sisters are returning from the party. I wonder what luck they had, the little beasts. I hope they were both brutally de-flowered. I hope the blood runs down between their legs. I shall creep down and spy on them. You can come with me, Rupert, as a reward for not strangling me just then."

She saw my eyes light, and laughed. "No, you can't come! I'm making a fool of you in my evil way, yes. You just stay there and I will be back." At the door, she paused to blow me a kiss. "There's lots more to tell of my secret life, Rupert." Then she was gone.

I waited until she had been gone for the count of fifty. Then I lifted the key clutched in my right hand – I had stolen it from her pocket when she lay in my arms in her swoon – and unlocked my gyves. Running to where my clothes lay discarded, I threw them on and went to the door.

The scalded dog, Karl, had disappeared. Trying to subdue the loud pulse of my blood, I began the descent through the old house.

By a faint dawn light seeping in through a stained-glass window, I saw that the floor below, on which Sindy said her sisters slept, was not as sumptuously furnished as I had imagined. Indeed, it was scarcely furnished at all. There were no portraits. Wallpaper hung from the walls in long curled strips, as if damp had got to it, and a section of the plaster ceiling had collapsed. The place looked as if it had been deserted for years.

Trying to avoid creaking stairs, I found my way down to the ground floor and so to the kitchen into which Sindy had first led me, which announced itself by its warm, sad smell.

With extreme caution, I eased myself into an alcove by an immense dresser. Something told me that she was near at hand. It was impossible to guess what sort of mood she might be in, so unpredictable was she.

A pallid luminosity filtered into the stale room. Nothing is more antagonistic to the human spirit than that particular straminious light, when the night has stood too long and curdled. Once, labouring men trudged to work in it. Now, by common consent, people have abandoned the ill hour; it is witnessed only by those whom sickness, love, or a secret anguish have kept wakeful. Only their pallid faces greet that pallid hiatus in Earth's round which the Romans called *prima lux*. And the eyes in my pallid face turned until they saw the female figure at the table, seated there, motionless.

Motion is most hard to detect at that wan hour. I thought, Ah, another game. Suddenly, something changed in my mind. I filled with grateful feelings. She played rough, perhaps, our demonic Sindy, but at least I had her full attention. When did that happen in my life before? I also could play . . .

I dashed forward from my concealment, seized the figure, kissed it full on the lips –

Except it had no lips.

It had no lips. It had no flesh, only a dusty fibrous matter clinging to the bone, which choked me as it reached my mouth.

"You kissed my mother, yes! Yes!" screamed Sindy, pouncing from her hiding place behind a curtain and rushing, rushing towards me, arms extended.

Sick with disgust at this last humiliation, I ran from the ancient corpse, made for the door, flung it open, and burst into the waning night.

A builder's truck stood there. Two men were unloading bricks from it with the aid of a small derrick attached to the side of the vehicle. So there were no sisters at all, perhaps no ball, perhaps no father, no anything. All a lie, a part of a poor girl's delusion . . .

I began to run. She was coming after me, calling my name.

Down the drive, along the road, through the thick treacherous light. The promise of another day stained the horizon.

The conifers were sombre and unstirring. I plunged in among them, glad now to return to their diseased concealment. And almost at once I tripped over an unnoticed branch and fell full length.

With a kind of despair, realising that fate was against me, I lay there panting. Made no stir as Sindy came up to me, did not move as she cried with triumph and ripped off her clothes. Did not turn away as she kneeled by my face.

"You can't leave me, Rupert! Kiss me where I need it most – then we shall always be together."

So I put an arm about her waist. I moved nearer to her flesh. To press my face into her hair was like burying it in damp moss. It had a fresh field scent.

Only I was burying my face in real moss. Gradually, as gradually as the dawn succoured the world, I came back to my senses, to find myself with an arm about the bole of a pine and my face pressed into the mossy carpet below the tree.

Slowly I sat up, groaning. The forest stood tall about me and I was lost again. All had been a dream, the demon woman no more than a vanished figment. I scarcely knew whether to be glad or sorry. All I knew was that I was now free to return home and face whatever problems awaited me.

Who could resist adding a postscript to such a tale? Not I! Yes, I found my dear little Rupert's fantasy, hidden in a drawer like a dirty thing, tucked away behind a roll of fabric, and all a fabrication.

"Feel my breasts, please, darling . . ." Stupid erotic fantasy! Why should a man think I want his clumsy paws on my breasts? All the little liar gets is an occasional lick of a nipple when I am feeling generous. Quite often I'm generous, really.

Males are so ill-equipped to face the crises of life. They do not possess the same three dimensions women have, so they have nowhere to retreat to except their fantasies. Yes, it's no wonder he can never sum me up, but must simply enmesh me with his lies. Wanton lies.

Why must he pretend our first meeting was all a dream? Because life to him is a dream. He has never woken to its terrors, its magnificences, my Rupert. Since he sleeps, I can be my true, secret self . . . I live, while he sleeps his way through life, pretending my needs do not touch him.

Lies!

Yet I love them. For those lies protect us from our fears of each other, yes! For if our life so close together is not happiness, what is? We can lie *to* as well as *with* each other, here safe in our immense house, he, I, my mother, my sisters . . .

(1986)

North Scarning

Norah said, "I don't really want to go this way." She pouted more heavily than before.

"Nearly there," Tom said.

They had turned off the main road and were driving slowly down a lane signposted "By-road". A second sign, older, more weathered, said "North Scarning Broad. Private". To their left curved a high brick wall, without gate or feature. To their right were hedges with starved winter fields beyond. No cattle moved in the fields. A speckled frost covered everything, and mist lay over the land. Temperatures had not risen above zero all day.

"The place is dead," Norah said, not without relish. She retreated a little into her coat and wrapped her arms about her body, although it was perfectly warm inside the car. "Can't we go back to Norwich?"

"It won't hurt just to have a look. Don't be silly."

Norah made no reply, which was her way of showing contempt for any man who thought her silly. Norah Utting was a lightly built woman in her thirties with dark hair and an air of wishing to be amused – which, in general, it was not difficult to do. Tom Bridges kept his gaze on the road ahead. Frosted panes of ice covered the ruts scored by a recent tractor. He slowed and dropped into second gear.

"I was eleven when I last came down this road," he remarked.

"Have you changed much?" Norah asked. He ignored the remark.

She switched on the radio and filled the BMW with drumming and shouting.

Where the lane took a turn to the right, an iron gate stood

straight ahead of them. The gate had been fortified with boards and barbed wire. Tom stopped the car.

"Looks as if we can't get through to the Broad."

"Good, let's go back. Wasn't the funeral enough for you?"

"I must see the old Broad while we're here. It's only just beyond the gate. Are you coming?"

She shook her head. She was a pretty woman who liked to have her own way.

"I'll park the car under those trees, just in case of traffic."

She laughed. "Traffic? This place is like the realm of the dead."

The car rolled on to the crisp grass. Tom reversed it under a group of pines so that it faced back the way they had come.

"Don't be long, Tom. I don't fancy being stuck here on my own. It'll be getting dark in another hour."

"You'll be OK. You can see the old house from here; look with reverence on my birthplace. I won't be long."

She turned up the radio as she watched him walk back to the gate, a tall figure in his black suit and coat. Beyond where the wall ended she could see the solid bulk of the house Tom had indicated, featureless against the heavy pallor of the sky. There was too much sky in Norfolk for her liking. As Tom disappeared, an upper window lit in the house, like a small square eye observing her.

Tom Bridges' mood was resentful. He did not greatly enjoy this expedition, but Norah's opposition had kept him up to it. Like her, he wanted to get back to the comfortable hotel in Norwich, where they could meet up with some of the rest of the family, assembled for his grandmother's funeral, and have a drink and a little fun. Tomorrow, it was back to work in London. Also, he did not greatly relish these trips to the past, which had contained more humiliation for him than he could admit to.

A plane roared low overhead, startling him. He shook a fist at it as it disappeared in the direction of the North Sea. In his boyhood, the planes had been a source of pride and excitement; he had spent hours watching them take off and land on the local aerodrome; now, they signified only complex international politics which he did not understand.

It was easy to climb through the hedge by the old gate. Little weals of frost clung to his coat. His grandfather's house appeared quite close. His memory from childhood suggested that it was a long trudge away. Old outhouses which had stood here had collapsed and were now buried under a tumble of ivy and dead vegetation. The oaks he remembered were still standing. He walked under them, treading quietly, aware of the hush that possessed the world since the aircraft went over. It was remarkably still.

Everything had shrunk since childhood days. It proved to be no distance at all to the Broad. The cart track leading to the little quay had dwindled. No vehicle had come this way in many years. He was confronted by a sign which told him that the Broad was now the property of the local council, that it was dangerous, and that trespass was forbidden. Desolation prevailed. The notice had been defaced, the fence broken down. Fires had been started. Broken bottles and beer cans lay about, painted a temporary white by frost.

Scarning Broad still retained a private face. *His* Broad it had once been. Beautiful even in the depths of winter: still, calm, one of the last havens of that tranquillity of mind which is the monopoly of childhood. Open to the sky. Accessible, yet not exactly welcoming. Far out on the ice, where a slow current kept a stretch of water unfrozen, ducks were busy, secure from interference.

Almost despite himself, Tom felt contentment steal over him. He reminded himself to be happy. This was the scene which had contained eternal moments of delight. This was the place where he and his friend Ed used to swim with Daisy for hours at a stretch. This was the spot where he had fought Will Court all one summery afternoon – and won. So he told himself, kicking a can on to the ice, watching it slither and clatter.

He stood hunched in his black mourning coat, remembering, editing memories. He turned to look back at the old house, his grandfather's house – owned by the council now, of course – but it was hidden by a rise in the ground behind tall untidy hedges whiskered in white. For a long while, he stared at the hedges, fighting off the idea that evil could have an independent life, or rule in a hedgerow.

As the shadows lengthened during those bygone summer evenings, when elms still dominated the ripening Norfolk landscape, and the moon, rising early, fragmented itself among their branches, Tom's mother would come from the house, walk through the vegetable garden and raspberry canes, and call to him as she strolled down the lane. He would answer or not, as the fancy took him. Sometimes he would hide from her.

She would enter into the game, walking to the water's edge as if she were about to fall in, softly calling his name, letting her voice sink till it was no more than the distant coo of a dove. Then he'd run out and capture her and lead her back to the house, past the great buddleia bushes which grew by the stables, aflutter with butterflies almost till the moment the sun went down.

It was his grandfather's house. Grandfather was still active in those days. He helped Tom's father run the agricultural equipment business which he had started as a youth, the first man in all Broadland to sell tractors. He lived with grandmother on the first floor of the big house, over Tom's parents, who occupied the ground floor.

Grandfather Bridges was an independent-minded man who preserved some of the old ways of the countryside, despite the innovations introduced by his company. He still walked ten miles each Sunday, rain or shine, to see his widowed sister over in Coltishall. He kept his old shire horses in good pasturage long after his machines had rendered them unprofitable. And he resolutely refused to believe in the ghost, Old Court, which haunted his rambling house.

The other occupants of the house had every reason to believe in Old Court. Old Court's presence moved about the upper floors most nights, bringing with it a terrible sense of dread. Only Grandfather was immune from the dread. Small Tom slept with a night-light by his bed, but the flickering shadows the flame created were almost as intolerable as the darkness it was designed to fight. His lifelong insomnia sprang from the time when he sat hunched up between the sheets, staring about him, dreading Old Court's visitation.

Once dawn came, matters were better. Yet he could look out of his window at the garden and the meadow where the wild poppies bloomed red and imagine a kind of curse, as if the ghost ruled there too, spreading its disease over nature.

"Mummy, do we have to live here?" Tom asked his mother, one breakfast, heavy-eyed.

"We're quite safe, dear. Old Court keeps to the upper floors. Besides, why should he harm us? His wife was my friend, and I was good to her when they fell on hard times."

She understood her son's anxieties. The tale she told of Old Court was amplified as his understanding grew. The Court family had been wealthy landowners at the turn of the century. Both the house and North Scarning Broad were mere entries in their property ledger. Then the first World War had come – "The Great War", as men called it then. Old Gregory Court's two sons were both killed on the Western Front, one leaving behind a young family. Old Court never recovered from the loss of his sons. His fields fell derelict, he refused to adopt modern farming methods. Parcel by parcel, he sold off his land to meet his debts. One night, he took his best shot-gun up to the attic of the house, and blew his brains out. Grandfather Bridges, who had been his chief rival in business, bought up the house and the Broad for a song. There the Bridges children had been born, and their children after them.

North Scarning House had been a perfect if isolated place in which to grow up, apart from that frightening presence. Even into the 1960s, something of a Victorian peace had prevailed over this corner of the country. It had never been easily accessible. Many of the local people had never ventured even as far as Norwich. Little traffic rumbled down its leafy lanes, and the grocery van still called once a week. Yet all the time, there had been that awful manifestation, parading its distress in the upper floors of the house, wearing them down with its malignancy.

Finally, it had driven them away. The family had broken up. The old days were finished and done. His mother could not take Old Court any more. Old Court had descended into her very kitchen one autumn afternoon, and she had run screaming into the lane.

Tom Bridges listened to her cries now. A sense of horror froze him. He hunched himself in his dark coat without turning round and listened to his name being called. His teeth ground together. His arms wrapped him round until his fingers dug into his ribs. He could feel the pens clipped to his breast pocket.

Some mute thing inside him said, "Have I never escaped from my childhood? Were all those adult years just a dream?"

"Tom!"

He turned. She appeared blurred by mist, by the blueness of the late afternoon, by the sombre uprights of the bare December trees behind her. It took a second to perceive that it was Norah Utting who ran towards him, not his mother.

Norah almost collided with him. "Oh, Tom, Tom, there was someone there . . . Oh, I'm so relieved."

He was almost as relieved as she was. Holding her tightly, he drew out of her her explanation. As she was sitting in the car, she became aware of someone approaching through the pines by the roadside. The figure came close to the car, waiting behind the nearest tree. It was impossible to see him clearly. But she had become frightened and finally, she said, "Ran for her life".

"No, there was no one, Norah. Calm yourself. It was all just imagination. Who'd be about in the woods at this time of year, near North Scarning?"

"Murderers? Rapists? I didn't stay to find out. There are people in the old house. A light came on."

"Just council clerks. Come and walk here and calm down, then we'll go back to the car."

"I can't go back to the car."

He thought of how his mother had said almost the same thing, all those years ago: "I can't go back into the house."

When he first heard her calling, he was riding round the field on Daisy. He slipped from her back and went to the lane reluctantly, mistrusting the note of panic in her voice. Pigeons were calling serenely in Scarning Woods.

His mother stood by the lower garden gate, holding her hands together, her head slightly on one side in what was a typical attitude. Her hair was tied up in an old-fashioned bun and she was paler than usual.

Tom stopped, hating to have to confront whatever was troubling her. She came quickly towards him and put her arms round him, crushing him to her flowered brown dress.

"I'm never going back in there, never again," she kept saying. He tried to escape, but she held him tight, saying, "Oh, no, this time you don't slip out of your obligations. You stay here and comfort your mother, as a son should. I've had a nasty shock, a really nasty shock . . ."

They sat on the trunk of an old beech which had been felled in the spring. Although it was mid-October, the days were still warm and the leaves on the trees had not yet turned.

"I heard someone walking about upstairs, and there was no idea in my mind of Old Court. I thought by the heavy tread that your grandfather must have come in without saying a word to me. As far as I knew, I was alone in the house. So I went to the back stairs and called up 'Who's there?' You know how it's rather dark on those stairs. And the footsteps came on to the upper landing and then started to descend . . ." In her terror at the retelling, Tom's mother clutched him close.

"Tom, I couldn't move. I couldn't move. The footsteps came down towards me, till they were on a level with my eyes. I could see nothing, but – oh, how I felt – frozen! Frozen all over. I made a run for it at last, into the kitchen. The cat went flying. I slammed the door, and just stood there against the table, quaking – I'd been making a sponge cake. And what do you think? *The door swung open.* Oh – then I knew a terrible thing was after me, to get me, to have me, and out I ran, into the open."

He was terrified by the look on her face, and screamed to her to tell him no more.

Taking better control of herself, his mother said, "Now listen, for I may never be able to say this to you again. We're not a communicative family. There's evil in every one of us, which we have to fight. Evil and fear. They're related, though I don't know how. The most innocent-seeming thing can turn to fear and evil. Why the universe is made that way is beyond me, but so it is.

"This old house of ours is as peaceful as could be, you'd imagine, yet there's a spell over it. When it was built over a hundred years ago, the owner never set foot in it. I forget his name. He was murdered and his body never found. The stories said he was murdered, for he disappeared one night, never to be seen again. We've never told you, lest you'd be scared. So the house passed to the Courts. But I wonder if that original bad reputation hasn't encouraged the ghost of Old Court to get up to his tricks.

"However that may be, I cannot live in fear. It will breed evil in me, I'm sure of it. Fear breeds evil. I don't want you to be afraid, either, to grow up afraid. It is important for you to have courage burning like a fire inside you. Then you can be good, d'you understand?"

She shook him, gazing into his eyes very seriously.

"Do you understand? Look at me. I want you to be good, because people are happier if they are good. Do you understand?"

Sulkily, Tom said, "I am good. Can we go in now?"

It was growing dusk and a wind was rising. He was afraid.

"I can't go back into the house. We won't move till your father gets home. That's another half-hour or more. I won't be in there on my own, or with you. I won't sleep there another night. We can go and stay with your father's folk over in Coltishall."

"Did you see him, Mum? You know, Old . . . ?"

"No, I didn't *see* anything." Inconsequentially, she added, "I sometimes wonder if there really are such things as ghosts . . ."

There was silence. He saw her face working. She turned quickly away from him. Then she wept. The boy tried clumsily to comfort her.

"Oh, Tommy keep away from me, keep away. I want everyone to keep away from me. I'm bad, bad – miserable and bad."

He took her at her word. He ran away from her, ran down the twilight lane, away to the watermeadows. He had hated himself ever since for leaving her when she wept.

"I can't go back to the car," Norah said, looking weakly into his face.

Without contradicting her, Tom walked with her to the crumbling edge of the quay. The willow was still there, bereft of leaf at this season. Just below the quay, where Ed and he once moored their canoe, tall frosted sedges stood, brown, mottled, crisp and dead. The Broad was drying up, year by year, as it ever had done.

"This is where Ed and I used to swim, together with old Daisy. This was our place Norah. We'd spend all day in the water. We never caught cold. Sometimes we'd swim out to the middle of the Broad, to what we called Boot Island."

He pointed out across the ice to where the ducks were. "Somewhere out there. You can't see it now. We were happy then. Kids.

And we're standing on the very spot where I fought Will Court, all one summery afternoon."

"All afternoon?"

He told her his story. After Ed had finished work, he and Tom would fetch Daisy from the field where she stood deep in buttercup and clover, and ride her down to the quay. One day, they found a bicycle propped against the sheds, and a large brown boy swimming in the broad. The boy climbed out, saying that he owned this place. His grandfather had been Gregory Court, who owned all the land hereabouts.

"He don't oon no land hereabouts now, that's a fact, bor," said Ed. He and Tom had driven off the intruder with sticks. Will Court had pedalled away, dripping and naked, his clothes over the handlebars of his bike, shouting defiantly that he would be back to kill them.

He had come back, silent, unobserved. It was one midsummer day, when the long lanterns of the laburnum avenue were beginning to fall, and one side of the lane was flecked with red and white briar roses. The heat was so great that Tom ran down to the water on his own, without waiting for Ed to finish his labours in the workshop. He had stripped off his shorts and dived in, plunging through the clear brown water where shoals of minnows wheeled and turned like living galaxies. When he surfaced, Will Court was there waiting, and began throwing stones at him.

Tom scrambled out of the water through a bed of sedges, scattering the young frogs. Hidden by the sheds, he had crept up on Will Court from behind and attacked him with his bare hands.

"He was bigger than me. He stamped on my bare feet. I ran into the shed, but he followed, blocking the door. He swore he'd bash me up."

"Poor Tom," Norah said. "You should have run for the house, not the shed."

"A yard broom was standing in one corner. I charged him with it and banged him out of the way. We had a fist fight, right here on this quay. He knocked me down. My mouth was bleeding. I couldn't escape and I was afraid he was going to drown me. He kept saying that he owned the whole place. I broke away and climbed up a sloping willow that used to grow over the lane.

"Will Court followed, so I was trapped. He threatened to kill me. I pulled back a young branch and let go of it when he got near enough. It knocked him clean off the trunk and he crashed down to the ground. I went and jumped on him and hit him in the face. Then he'd had enough. He got up and ran – and never came back again."

"Oh, you were brave!" Norah exclaimed, hugging him.

"Well, I had no alternative." The story had cheered them both. Turning away from the frozen expanses of water, they walked, closely linked, back the way they had come, until the old house loomed into view, until they were safe on the by-road.

The BMW stood where Norah had left it, passenger door open, radio playing. As they got in, they looked round at the wood. Nothing presented itself except silence and stillness, nature withholding itself.

"I was imagining things," Norah said, with a small laugh. "I do find this a spooky part of the country. You're kind of weird, Tom, too, this afternoon."

Indeed a special melancholy had the land in its grip. The light waned perceptibly, although the featureless cloud-cover overhead seemed no darker than before. Dead bracken, sombre trees, and the long expanse of wall, were the only features to present themselves. None held any particular interest or comfort.

Starting the car, Tom said, "Just before we head for Norwich, I want a closer look at the house. For sentiment's sake, or whatever . . ."

He had chosen a good moment. She was unable to make any objection.

When they reached the main gate, he turned in and parked in the asphalt park in front of the building. Enclosed by the wall, under the shade of a line of conifers, they felt that night was nearer. He saw anxiety in Norah's restless eyes.

"Don't be long," she said, and lit a cigarette with her plastic lighter. "You're a bastard, you know."

As he approached the house, people were leaving it, buttoning up their coats, moving hastily, calling to each other with voices sharpened by the cold. Most of them were women, who hurried over to old cars, one to each vehicle, shouting farewells as they went. The staff was going home – rather early, he thought with disapproval.

A notice at the door said: NORTH SCARNING COUNTY COUNCIL. Head Offices. On the door was a brass knocker, dull brown from years of negligence, in the shape of old London Bridge. His grandmother had affixed it to the door when they took the house over in the twenties. Sixty years ago, he thought. Heavy stuff. He was pleased by the secret signal.

Without knocking, he went in, to find himself in a much-altered entrance hall. One half of the hall was taken up by a cheaply built wooden cabin, to which the unwelcoming word "Enquiries" had been tacked. The cabin was lit. A typewriter and a small phone-exchange sat bathed in fluorescent light, but he saw no one of whom to Enquire. Automatically, his gaze went to the staircase curving upwards at the back of the hall; he thought for a moment that someone stood on an upper step watching him. There was nobody in sight.

Taking advantage of the absence of a receptionist, he walked rapidly down the corridor to his left. In the old days, there had been only two rooms in the front of the house on this side, the breakfast room – so-called, although it was used as his father's snug little study – and the dining-room, in which his mother's old rocking-horse stood. Effortlessly, he found himself remembering every detail of every room – cosy, atmospheric, eternal, threatened. Now, there were five doors instead of two, each painted grey, with frosted glass windows; the original rooms had been partitioned to make smaller offices.

No one stopped him. A young woman passed without giving him a second glance, a Walkman clamped over her ears. It buzzed at Tom as she went by.

At the far end of the passage was another cubicle, labelled Pensioners' Queries. It came equipped with a glass sliding panel, a bell, and a pencil on a length of string. Once, the servants' back stairs had occupied the space, the very staircase Old Court had finally descended, to terrify his mother into leaving the house. Tom looked up to see the scars of removal, but a false low plastic ceiling had been installed from which hung fluorescent lighting, concealing evidence of the past.

He sat down on a bench provided for pensioners awaiting a response to their queries, realising how ill at ease he felt. More than that, ill. Why had he felt compelled to tell Norah the complete lie about the fight with Will Court?

The frosted glass panel slid open. A young lady stuck her tousled head half through and said, "Sorry, dear, closed. Come back tomorrow. Bye."

"Wait," said Tom, before she could disappear. "I want to speak to someone in charge."

He could hear his voice hollow and unnatural. Perhaps it accounted for the startled look she gave him. As she backed away into the room, he noticed she wore a green leather jacket. Evidently she was about to go home. Behind her, in the narrow room choked with desks, and a grey filing cabinet standing where the rocking-horse had once stood, two older women were examining Christmas streamers, probably with a view to decorating the office for that coming event. They too ceased what they were doing, and looked at Tom in consternation.

"I used to live here," Tom said.

One of the women dropped the box of streamers. The other ran into a further room, crying, "Mrs Dunwoody, Mrs Dunwoody, Old Court's come downstairs."

He caught sight of himself in a mirror behind the young woman's desk, pale face peering through the hatch, dressed in black, black tie, black suit, black coat, white shirt. All proper for his grandmother's funeral in Norwich. But to the women in the council offices, a visitation of a different kind.

It was immediately understandable. The Bridges family had believed that Old Court haunted them because they were in part responsible for the decline that led to his suicide. He had been *the family ghost*, dreaded but domesticated. After Old Court had come downstairs and confronted Tom's mother in her kitchen, the Bridges had moved to another part of the country, and prospered, never giving Old Court another thought, except to admit him to conversations at Christmas, in order to evoke an agreeable shudder. Thirty years later, people here still lived in dread of the same apparition; staff left before dark, women screamed at the sight of a pale face.

The young woman in the leather jacket showed resourcefulness. She dashed forward and slid the glass panel to in front of his face, as smartly as if it were a guillotine blade.

He stood in the chilly passage indecisively. Shortly after his parents had left North Scarning, his grandfather had died. His grandmother had then tried to sell the old house and move into Norwich. She could find no buyers. The evil reputation of a haunted house made it unsaleable. For weeks, then months, the place stood empty. As the weeds grew, so the price dropped. Some potential purchasers, inspecting the house, swore they had come face to face with Old Court on the stairs. As months turned into a year, it became clear that no one was ever going to wish to live in North Scarning House again. Eventually the council took it over and converted it into offices.

The women were talking behind the door with the frosted glass. Tom could see their blurred outlines as they conferred in the space where he had once played at being a great huntsman. He turned on his heel and hurried from the building. He could no more face Mrs Dunwoody than she, presumably, could face him.

Outside, the carpark was now dark. His BMW stood alone by the gate, apparently without an occupant. He could see no sign of Norah.

He ran across the tarmac with its white-painted rectangles and flung open the passenger door. Norah lay there with her head back, slumped half across the front seats. It was light enough for Tom to see a red weal across her throat.

Fear overcame him. He almost ran away, as he had so often run from any kind of difficulty before. This time, he fought the impulse. Reaching in, he touched her body tenderly.

"Norah."

She opened her eyes and began to giggle. Sitting up, she put one arm about his neck and kissed him.

"Sorry to scare you, you bastard. Couldn't resist it. You did just walk off and leave me, didn't you? I could have been raped and murdered fifty times."

He was almost mute with fury as she took out a tiny handkerchief, licked it, and began rubbing the lipstick from her neck. "Let's get out of here," she said. "Enough of this rotten nostalgia kick of yours."

He got into the driving seat, and backed the car round. In the squat old house, one light burned upstairs. That room had once been his bedroom. There he had sat up in bed in the corner of the room, afraid to close his eyes till morning came. His lifelong habit of cowardice must have been reinforced by those insomniac occasions.

To be behind the driving wheel gave him confidence. He began to laugh. "You're a real minx, Norah. I'll never trust you again."

"Just get me to Norwich. At least we buried your Gran – I want to drink to her staying good and buried."

As they drove down the winding road, he said, of a sudden, "Norah, I lied to you. I didn't fight Will Court, I wish I had. I hadn't courage enough. He came and caught me by the quay and flung me in the Broad. He was younger than me, too. I didn't dare get out of the water in case he hit me. I swam over to Boot Island and stayed there all day."

"Didn't you knock him out of the tree?"

"Sorry. I made that up, too."

After a moment's silence, she put a hand on his leg. "I'm sorry you felt you needed to lie to me."

"I was lying to myself."

And down below the quayside, where the water was deepest, he and Ed had found a disintegrated body, a skeleton with a half-millstone secured by a chain round its waist. They had been too frightened to tell anyone. Only now, as the car headed for the Coltishall bypass and Norwich, did it occur to him that his family had been too ready to expiate their guilt by giving Court's name to that haunting presence in the house. It was probably much older than Court, was engendered not by Court's suicide but by an older crime – the murder of the man who rotted under the piers of the quay. Evil had been more ancient than they imagined, and more durable, and still continued, under an assumed name.

"God, I need that drink," he said.

Norah was cheerful, now that Norwich and the comfortable hotel were somewhere ahead of them. As night closed in round the speeding car, she said, "Don't worry, Tom. You never have to go back there again, do you? Think of something nice."

"You're right," he said, smiling affectionately. He knew that he went back to North Scarning in memory every week of his life, that he was tied to it and could never escape. All the same, anything was better than actually living there. He did as Norah suggested, and thought of something pleasing.

Daisy came plodding over the field towards him as he unlatched the gate, whistling a boy's shrill whistle. She was a big old Suffolk Punch, the last of Tom's father's shire horses. Tom had a dim recollection from his earliest years of seeing Daisy pulling the plough over Barton Leaze Field, the blade turning up brown earth glistening like Christmas cake, a flock of gulls behind the plough-man screaming as they followed the furrow, and great Daisy leading the way, setting her tasselled feet down steadily, never hurrying, never tiring – and never as efficient as a tractor.

She ambled out of the field and waited for Tom under an elder tree while he secured the gate, taking her chance to nibble the special grasses that grew in the bank. From the bank, he climbed on to her back. Off they went, Ed walking beside her sucking a straw, slapping her neck occasionally, to drive off flies. Down the lane they went, Tom having to sit crouched to avoid willow branches overhead, and the waters of the Broad glittered through the trees. Never a sail on this private, secret water.

Often enough, Daisy would pause at the water's edge to slurp in the shallows as if testing the temperature. Sometimes Tom would slide off her back at this point. At other times he stayed on. The mare would then trudge into the water, moving slowly and quietly, from shallower to deeper water, from tree-shadow to open sun-light. Soon she would be swimming, only her head and craning neck above water, and Tom and Ed would swim beside her, calling and laughing with pleasure.

Daisy liked best to swim where the water was deep, away from clinging sedges and reeds, along by the quayside and the old dam wall. There she could raise her head and crop the lush grasses from the banks as she swam. She never tired. Nor did the boys. They could stay for hours in the soft water, until the sun made a golden path across the Broad and midges rose in tremulous clouds. They used to dive in from the side, sometimes plunging right under Daisy's broad belly. The embrace of the Broads was silken on their bodies. Time was suspended. Everything was safe and beautiful. Life was a dream. The water was the world.

One day, Tom dropped his watch in the water. That was the day they dived deep and found the skeleton, smiling as if it had been waiting for them all summer.

(1986)

The Big Question

If we look back a century to the 2080s, can't we see clearly why the period since has become known as the Age of Interrogation?

Isn't it obvious to us now that the twentieth century and the great part of the century which followed were bristling with certainties – ideological and scientific certainties above all? What but reaction could have followed from such a blind epoch?

How could anyone from that benighted period have visualised that ahead of all their stoutly held beliefs lay a tranquil age when everything would be brought into question? Including the very rules of grammar, which permitted sentences to end without the appetiser, the tasty carrot, of a question mark?

Who would wish to go back to those awful old days of the full stop? Even the most trite conversational transaction nowadays – doesn't it have an element of interesting ambiguity lacking in the past? May we conjure up a contrast from the two ages?

Shall we imagine an English country crossroads towards evening, where a motorised young woman speaks to an immobilised man on a stile?

"Am I on the right road for Bideford?" shall she say?

"Where else might you think this road would lead?"

"Oh, Sticklepath, Stadhampton, Strathclyde, Stockholm?"

"Be you trying to be funny, young lady?"

"Am I headed in the right direction?"

"Be there another road that leads into Bideford Town as surely as this one?"

"Bideford, then, definitely?"

"Where else, my dear?"

How might a similar twentieth century exchange go?

"Is this the Bideford Road?"

"No."

Wasn't all that decisiveness, that extraordinary ability to "make up the mind", an important factor in the general decline? Could it have been that the military mania, the love of grotesque destructive weapons, which gripped the Twentieth Century, depended upon a readiness to make a statement? A ridiculous firmness of purpose we have now fortunately lost? An unwarranted certainty of being right? In politics and everything else?

We may ask ourselves, mayn't we, where all that firmness of purpose came from? Was it not the more peculiar when we consider that the start of the twentieth century had seen the publication of Einstein's Theory of Relativity? How is it that his findings took so long to sink in, even among intellectuals? Today, when we perceive everything as relative, don't we inherit an amazing belated gift from Einstein's thought?

Of what use is it to look back at that questionable age without question marks? Of what use, indeed, is it to look forward, when we recognise even solutions as questionable? And what should we say of a time when the term "questionable solution" seemed like a paradox? Isn't paradox the very stuff of our civilisation? Where else should we look for uncertainties if not in the very bases of our laws? Haven't those laws been framed by a century of wise practice in order to protect us from what our deluded forebears regarded as the Eternal Verities? Eternal whats? When we are here today and gone tomorrow?

Are not our law courts and churches bastions of half-truths? What is truth? said jesting Pilate; and is he not the founder-member of the Age of Interrogation? As the improved version of the poet Keats has it:

> Uncertainty is truth, if truth at all;
> That's all – or more or less – ye need to know.

Is it not a fact that our primitive ancestors in the twentieth century tried to establish any number of wishy-washy fads as disciplines? Were there not attempts to elevate sociology, for instance, into a science? Why should we not rejoice that we now view human nature as elusive, and not susceptible to quantification? Was it not one of today's patron saints, Werner Heisenberg, who formulated the Uncertainty Principle – demonstrating that if you knew the momentum of a body you could not tell its speed? And vice versa?

Who these days does not realise that the New Uncertainty Principle builds on Heisenberg, formulating the semi-truth that if you happen to know where anybody is, you have no idea what they are doing? Eh?

Is this not also the philosophical impulse behind the Nine Commandments? From the First Commandment, "Shalt thou have no other gods but me?" through "Try to honour thy father and mother," to "Thou shalt not commit adultery much," do we not experience a wisdom which culminates in the edict: "Candidates are advised not to attempt more than one Commandment at a time?" These marsh-firm principles – are they not the solid sand on which our culture is founded?

So, is it surprising that our modern novelists have risen up to embrace the principles of the Age of Interrogation? Isn't the great Cadillac Bohm's masterpiece, *Looking at a Lighter Deed?* a rival to Tolstoy's *War or Peace?* Do we not see in this novel many of the Higher Uncertainties of our time? May we quote from Chapter 6, where Jake visits Lockerby in the prison hospital?

Why was it that he always looked at his watch at 5.40 every evening? Had he regularly had to catch a bus at that time when he was working in Milan? Was 5.40, perhaps, the time he had first made love to a woman? Had someone he knew died at that time? What prevented him remembering?

Did he shiver slightly as he passed through the grey doors into the ward where Lockerby was waiting to die? And the ward – what hidden meaning lay behind its name, Bodenland Ward?

Should Jake have felt surprised when Lockerby rose to meet him with something like his old exuberance? Was that sprightliness real or feigned? Wasn't his handshake friendly enough? (And yet, in his eyes – real or imagined reproach because his friend had not visited him before this?)

The grapes – why lay them down so tenderly, shrouded in their tissue paper, as if they were human?

"How are you?" If the familiar phrase escaped him unawares, was that not convention conquering a real concern?

"How do you like this dump I'm in, Jake? Isn't it elegant? Want to hear about Nurse Evita? Isn't she cute? Have a glass of wine?"

Wasn't this the old Lockerby still, despite the grey hair and ashen pallor of lip? Could anyone resist that infectious, if quavering, chuckle?

"Have they put you on drugs, then?"

"Let's talk about something else, shall we?" Wasn't that typical, in spite of an underlying nervousness? "How are things outside? I mean – on that planet you still inhabit and I have vacated, probably for good?"

Well, why not amuse him with tales of latest encounters with women, if that did not make him too jealous, and all the trials and tribulations at work?

How was it that Lockerby listened so restlessly? What was it that made those dark eyes of his seem to glow, and his fist pound on the edge of the bed?

"Jake, Jake, are you crazy? All the pain and pleasure of the world – don't you see it's here, locked up in Bodenland Ward? A world in miniature? The pain of suffering, the pleasure of a successful bowel movement, the tension of awaiting the next lousy meal, the highest ambition to get one kind word out of Nurse Evita?"

What gaudy melancholy then inspired him to draw an extended and amusing parallel between the various anguishes of his cancer-ridden body and the maladies of the universe outside? Could it have been something in his eyes, his body language, which almost had Jake convinced?

"May I have another glass of wine?" Why steal his friend's cheap plonk? "Isn't it true that the whole world is at death's door? Violence, cruelty, lust, religion, won't they be the ruin of us all?"

In the laugh with which Lockerby interrupted Jake, was there not something more than mockery? "Isn't it true," he echoed, "that that just ain't so if Nurse Evita has anything to do with it? . . . Oh, aren't I dying to get my hands on her . . ."

On the bus back to town, why did Jake find himself longing for a lighter deed? Wasn't everything that happened terribly heavy? How was it that everything had to depend on everything else?

Would it have hurt Lockerby to have preserved a little decorum, to have behaved more like a potential corpse, to have been less *fun*?

Stopping off near the shopping centre, he asked himself, Why not visit Lockerby's wife, Ludmilla? Who could say how much she might be longing for company?

Could she have been hoping he would call? Why else that look of delight and mischief on her attractive pale face?

How long did it take them to get into bed? How could they possibly stop laughing, laughing with delight? And who would guess, on this damp November night, what the pair of them were up to?

Wasn't this the way to get back beyond the bounds of civilisations and hospitals? Beyond mankind and the beginnings of the world? Beyond the limits of individual life?

"Jake?"

"Yes?"

"Do you care for me at all? You do, don't you?"

Should he answer? Or should he just go on staring down at the creases in the pillow?

(1986)

The Ascent of Humbelstein

It is said that no statue was ever raised to a critic. This may be because critics are such humble men, because they lead lives of blameless respectability, or because ordinary people have never heard of their names.

Harold Humbelstein was humble, blamelessly respectable, but far from ordinary. He had written no less than two critical volumes on the life of the great English poet and novelist, Thomas Grissing, and had besides, from the shelter of the English department of his university, written several popular novels. These novels satirised intellectual life. The most successful, *A Golden Slash*, had brought Thomas Grissing back to life in order to make fun of his sombre view of human society.

Humbelstein's reputation had been built on his demolition of Grissing's.

By his forty-fourth birthday, Humbelstein was a power in the land. Which is to say that he was feared by almost anyone who had to do with literature and disliked by many others, including his wife, Fiona, the great-niece of Thomas Grissing. Humbelstein was enjoying the fruits of his success: his publisher loved him more than his wife did.

That forty-fourth birthday found Humbelstein alone in Barnstaple, North Devon. It was November and raining. Humbelstein stood in the doorway of the Taw View Tea Rooms (closed), sheltering from the rain and gazing across at the statue of Thomas Grissing erected on the river embankment.

Though not handsome, Humbelstein photographed well, as he would be the first to admit. He was a tall man, cultivating a stoop to assert humility, dark, hairy, and with an air of having been, or being about to be, athletic. He dressed in jeans or tweeds as occasion demanded. But perhaps the most interesting thing about him, warm in an inside pocket, nestling against the red shirt with the white collar, was the letter from his media agent.

The letter set out the terms for a six-part TV dramatisation to be made of *A Golden Slash*. What most pleased the recipient of the letter was less the payment he would receive, for it was a principle with Humbelstein always to regard payments for his work as too low, than the news that Jenny Miles Adam, a beautiful actress and a hot property, would be playing the main female role of Liz Ratatouille. For all his raffish airs, Humbelstein was as guarded with the living as he was unbridled with the dead; but in this case, he felt he might venture. He had met Jenny Miles Adam once at a party, and fancied that she fancied him. If so, What ho! as Thomas Grissing would have failed to say.

The rain fell down on Barnstaple, thunder rumbled. Humbelstein waited. He was surveying the town for possible locations for the TV drama – alone. It would have been too much to have brought Fiona with him. Her Aunt Hermione lived on the outskirts of Barnstaple, and they would have become involved in a boring visit to the old lady.

Rain poured over the statue of Thomas Grissing and his pedestal, on which an elaborate plaque was carved, bearing an inscription to The Great West Country Novelist and Poet, THOMAS GRISSING, Son of Barnstaple and Father of The Barum Novels. His Prose was Exquisite, His Life Irreproachable.

"Well, I made mincemeat of that claim," said Humbelstein to himself, scratching an armpit. "Poor old Grissing. At least his plaque is worse than his plight." It was a bit too draughty in the doorway to bother writing the witticism down.

Grissing, as befitted a man who had followed a sedentary career, was portrayed in green lead, seated on a chair, legs folded, clutching those two indispensables of a Georgian literary existence, a pipe, and one of his own books. When the spear of lightning struck him, he uncrossed his legs and rose slowly to his feet.

His leaden gaze took in the river and then searched the deserted road and pavements. It lighted on Humbelstein in his doorway.

Grissing beckoned. "I say, old man, you, help me down off this confounded pedestal, will you?"

"Me?" Humbelstein asked.

"As soon as you can, old chap, thanks," said Grissing, somewhat tartly. "It's raining, you know."

Humbelstein looked round for a hiding place. A woman of some dimension moved slowly about inside the Taw View Tea Rooms, but gave no indication that she intended to unlock her door. He turned up his collar before walking slowly across the road to where the statue was waiting.

"Let's hope to god he doesn't know who I am," Humbelstein muttered to himself.

There was not simply the question of how furious Grissing would be to find that he had been made merciless fun of in two Humbelstein tomes; he might also demand a share in the proceeds of *A Golden Slash*.

It had always been the pleasant custom of Harold Humbelstein, six foot two, to mock Grissing's more meagre stature. But the grey hand which grasped his outstretched one was startlingly strong, the small figure he swung down from the pedestal remarkably heavy. The ancient tale of the Golem of Prague came momentarily to Humbelstein's cultivated mind.

"Where – where do you want to go?" Humbelstein asked.

"Out of this bloody rain, of course," said Thomas Grissing, stomping across the road towards the tea rooms.

Humbelstein was shocked. Not in the poems, not in the touching – and therefore infinitely mockable – memoir, not in the twenty-two lengthy volumes of the Barum novels, had the word *bloody* appeared. It had never entered Humbelstein's head that Grissing might use it in real life – if, indeed, this was real life. He had his doubts about that. The doubts were magnified by the miraculous way the blind snapped up in the Taw View Tea Rooms, the door opening just in time to admit the dripping figure of the local author. Humbelstein followed.

"Toasted teacake for two and a big pot of tea," Grissing said to the buxom lady when they had seated themselves at a corner table.

She smiled broadly at him. Not an unpleasant-looking woman, despite all the lipstick. "Very nice to see you in here, Mr Grissing. I'm a great fan of your books. So's my husband."

"It's fair brevish of you to say so," answered Grissing, with a Devon burr in his voice. "You don't have a drop of something strong to go with the tea, do you, my dearie?"

The waitress laughed. "I'll see what we have out back. Would whisky do?"

"It does most things."

She hurried out to the back of the shop in fits of laughter.

This homely little tableau, with Grissing playing up genially to the woman's admiration, claimed most of Humbelstein's attention. He did not fail to observe his surroundings, however. A few buns and cakes were on offer for sale, together with a himalaya of canned Vimto and other fizzy drinks. There were also tiny china animals, funny objects of coloured glass, neckties woven from matting, and a series of pallid greetings cards for occasions which had never occurred in Humbelstein's career. Posters on the wall advertised unlikely sounding events being performed in unlikely sounding halls: "Obeying the Great White Spirit" in the John Gay Theatre, "Embargoes: An All-Woman Revue" in Sticklepath Masonic Hall, "African Capitalists" in the Howard Cornish Rooms, and so forth. It was just the sort of environment he mocked mercilessly in his trendy class-conscious novels. At present, he felt too uncomfortable for mockery: he was confronting a man of whom he had said that he had concocted fake greatness from trivia, trivia from greatness, and fakery from all that grated.

"Sorry, you look a bit downcast," Grissing said, turning his scrutiny on Humbelstein. "Would you rather have sausage and chips?"

"No, no thanks."

"You look like a sausage-and-chips man. No offence intended."

Even in his shattered mood, Humbelstein wasn't taking that from the author of *The Hands of Ethel Bethesda*.

"I'm a vegetarian, thanks." The lie gave him consolation.

"All fish and fury, eh?"

"I'm an ovo-lacto-vegetarian, as it happens."

That should have silenced him, but all Grissing said was, "Food is there for us to enjoy, like sex." Sex was another thing that Grissing never mentioned in his novels. His life had been discreet. He had married at the age of twenty-two and had stayed married to the same woman until his death at the age of eighty-nine. Humbelstein's critical volumes had had sly fun with those grim facts.

The food came. The friendly lady brought Grissing a half-tumbler of whisky, which he offered to share with Humbelstein. Humbelstein refused.

"Teetotal too, eh?" said Grissing. "You've a lot to learn, old chap. I can honestly say that the best years of my life were spent utterly pissed."

"Oh? It's only the peasants of Exmoor who get drunk in your novels."

"I am a bloody peasant. A peasant who can write. You buggers in universities would not understand that."

The pleasures of the buttery teacake restored Humbelstein's equilibrium. Regarding the leaden and rather featureless face across the table busily swigging off the last of the whisky, he began to form a theory. He was, after all, good at theories. He preferred them to life, just as he preferred Grissing as a statue.

He was the victim of a hoax. Somehow, the Grissing statue had been exchanged for a real person. His colleagues at his redbrick university were getting their own back. Just because they did not have six-part plays on television.

"Better get back to the old pedestal now," Grissing said, standing up. "Would you mind paying?"

The rain had ceased. The river flowed sullen and undimpled towards obscurity, like deconstructionist prose.

They crossed the road to the deserted pedestal. Grissing put out a hand for assistance.

"I can't let them get away with this. Show some spirit, Humbelstein," Humbelstein told himself. "Remember what you tell students at the start of each university year about putting the heart before the course."

Aloud he said, "By the way, Grissing, I can't stand those stupid, staid novels of yours. They should have stayed unwritten."

"Then where would *you* be?" asked Grissing. He grasped Humbelstein's hands, and the latter found himself suddenly swung upwards, to land on the top of the pedestal, along with the chair, the book, and the pipe.

It is said that no statue was ever raised to a critic. But Harold Humbelstein sits on his pedestal still, looking rather forlornly over rainy Barnstaple and the world of the Barum novels.

(1987)

How an Inner Door Opened
to My Heart

"But only gods can make a tree" – old song

I found A walking in the sanctuary of the museum grounds. Just pleasantly walking. Strolling as if she did it every day. Naked, absolutely confident, friendly, anonymous.

Where she walked, flowers sprang up under the imprint of her bare feet.

We keep the grounds well guarded. Nobody can get to The Six. Nobody has ever managed to break in from the tormented outside. Not one of our trees has ever been stolen. How then did the beautiful anonymous A get in?

It was a question she never answered. She appeared to know nothing, not even her name. How did she speak? It was always hard to recall, after that musical voice had ceased. I only know that she spoke my language.

Encountering her suddenly, I prepared to challenge her, but the words died on my lips. To meet a young naked woman who greets you unsmilingly, without self-consciousness, without any attempt to cover herself, is confusing. The conventions fall away before that frank nudity. You feel humble. Whatever might be said would seem irrelevant.

So there it was. Suddenly the well-ordered world is mysterious. I had been dreaming of creating a banyan. Standing before her, I was the one at a loss.

She came with me complacently to my apartment, to my office, and allowed me to question her. There she sat, relaxed on my mauve sofa, one slender arm upon the sofa arm and her legs crossed. She regarded me through her violet eyes, courteously telling me that she had no idea who she was or where she had come from.

She waited upon my questions. She had no questions to ask me.

She showed no particular interest in her surroundings, as the daylight fell across her calm breasts and shoulders.

How could I help staring at her, at those shoulders, those breasts, that lovely face? Through my mind ran questions I could not ask. Was she in some way deranged? Could this be part of a criminal plan, involving others? Even more fantastic notions passed amid my thoughts. And – what would The Six say?

Did not the arrival of A signal a crisis in our relationships?

Requesting A to remain where she was, I walked over to my desk and rang Security. They had nothing untoward to report. The barrier on the wall had not been breached. As I talked to the captain, I studied a reflection of A in a wall mirror. Although it was difficult to see her clearly, I could appreciate how composedly she sat on the sofa, gazing ahead of her without tension. Her dark hair seemed to surround her head like a nimbus. Undoubtedly she was lovely – almost too lovely, too perfect, to be human. Her misty reflection seemed to fade and flicker at my thought. It was a relief that Stephanie was away on business that day, or no doubt I would be in trouble. Stephanie had no time for rivals.

Since this was a Thursday, we directors who formed The Six had an early meeting timetabled as usual in the museum. This presented a problem. I could not take A along with me, even if I dressed her in Stephanie's clothes; relationships between The Six were too delicate for that. Nor did I wish to leave her alone in the apartment, in case she did something unpredictable, or in case she disappeared in the same mysterious way she had arrived. I wanted her for myself. An intense yet oddly unfocused desire had seized me.

A must have sensed my uncertainty. As I went over to the music stack and let Scandinavian chords flood into the room, she moved to the window and stood gazing out. It was how I afterwards remembered her, looking towards something unseen. I found myself drawn to where she had been sitting. On the pink cushion of the sofa she had left the imprint of her naked bottom. I sank down and pressed my face to that perfect imprint.

Ashamed of the impulsive act – suddenly furious with myself – I jumped up and left the room. She would have to do whatever she had to do. I hated to feel a woman's power over me, however much I sought it.

In our museum – known simply as The Six – we housed reproductions of fifty-two kinds of tree. All were created in our workshops. Our rule was to work from photographs and paintings, and every tree was perfect in every detail, at whatever stage in its life cycle we chose to represent it.

The six of us – the six, that is, after Betty Jule died – had been interested purely in the artistic aspect when we were making our first three or four trees, shortly after graduation. A tree was just an art project to us, a series of moderately complex problems to be solved by the application of flair and logic, and perhaps with the correct plastic material. We might as well have tried to reconstruct a megatherium, but a larch had seemed at the time to present a more interesting challenge.

Our first exhibition was a greater success than even we had anticipated. The public which arrived to view our six trees was impelled less by aesthetic considerations than by nostalgia. They wanted to see, to walk round, to stand under objects which had actually still existed on Earth only a century earlier.

From then on, we never looked back. The very rich almost immediately wanted a The Six tree in their homes. We sculpted trees in all stages of their growth. We improved the quality of our material by shopping abroad. We automated our methods. Soon we were supplying stands of trees, copses, even woods, all over the world. All six of us became famous. Stephanie sang. I conducted symphonies. The great Aristo directed movies.

Always we made trees. Some were designed to recreate various times of year. We never did generalised trees; they were left to our competitors. Ours were always individual, sometimes with blemishes on them, fungi and so on. Once we created a dozen date palms in pure silver for the crown prince of Saudi Arabia. Within three years of our first sapling, all six of us in the partnership were millionaires. That was really before the contamination laws were tightened. Since then, we stayed within the ample grounds of the museum. It was our castle, its doors closed to the outside world. The public was allowed to view daily, but only by android extensions. The privileged alone had audience with us in person.

We were three women and three men after Betty died. The sexual tensions between us were considerable. Lust and jealousy were like tidal forces which threatened to tear us apart. But the sense of a prospering and worthwhile project kept us together. Besides, who would wish to be at large in the illness-crippled world?

Betty Jule and Aristide "Aristo" Smith had been the one married couple among the seven of us. She was artistic; he could handle money. We all worked together in a big warehouse studio and were pretty poor in those days. When we had a chance to buy the ground floor of the building, we took it. We all moved in. I should add we all got ourselves screened, to prove to each other and maybe ourselves that we were carrying none of the killer sexual diseases circulating in the city.

After three years of their marriage, Aristo found out that, for most of that time, Betty had been having a secret love affair with Winston Watson Bulawayo. Winston was really the guy who started us off on trees, back in college. A terrible showdown took place. Winston and Aristo traded blows, though neither were violent men. Aristo swore and emoted and threatened suicide, but it was Betty who actually overdosed in a friend's weekend compartment. She left a message saying she loved both men and could not give either up.

A bad time, that. I fell in love with Stephanie Hao, who had been living in a mildly lesbian relationship with our public-relations lady, Claudia Cadwallader. Stephanie was small, blonde, slender, not really my type, but she had something to offer I could hardly define. Gradually our relationship became warm, gradually she could accept me. She was a laughing lady, Stephanie. Claudia, by contrast, was solemn and cool.

After some while, Aristo, who was really the head of our outfit, took up close relations with Su Mindanao, the member of our team I have not mentioned so far. Su was a chemist, tall, slim, dark, inventive, sparkling, often moody. She and I had lived together our last year in college, and a stormy time that had been. Not that we regretted it, and I guess the fondness we felt for each other was still alive, because just now and then we managed to sneak a few private, lustful hours together without Stephanie or Aristo finding out. They were all so jealous. Well, we all suffered for love.

This Thursday morning, I was thinking of none of them as I crossed the path over to the main block. I thought of the meeting,

which promised to be a tough one. Aristo had summoned our chief
bankers because we had to decide whether to open a tree park in
the centre of Rigel City, on the other side of the continent. I also
thought of the strange woman, whom I have so far called simply A.
Soon, I took to calling her Mary – not because that was her name
but because such a womanly woman deserved better than an
initial.

Claudia Cadwallader came out of the building to meet me,
linking her arm in mine. Like the rest of us, she was in her
mid-to-late thirties, but there was something endearingly childish
in her appearance – a misleading impression, since Claudia was
nothing if not high-powered. Not only was she our most sensitive
sculptor, she also ran the actual museum itself, with all its adminis-
trative problems, as well as handling its delicate relationship with
the fevered and near-anarchic city beyond its walls.

"Aristo isn't here," she said. "He's had to jet to Venezuela to see
about that missing shipment of soya beans."

"I thought we had that all in hand?" I looked at her sharply.

"It is the third shipment to go missing this year." She spoke
in her normal reserved way which some found soothing, some
irritating.

"But why did he have to go today?"

I said nothing else as we went up the steps, and then, "We can
make no decisions without Aristo and Stephanie being present."

She squeezed my arm, "Dean, Aristo knows that. Don't you
think that's why he went off today? It buys us time with the bank."

We went together to the meeting. Winston Bulawayo and Su
Mindanao joined us on the mezzanine and we entered the board
room together. That's the way we always work, showing a united
front whatever our personal differences. There had been a time
when Su was fit to kill Winston. They had been living together, but
Winston was making it with Claudia. What a fight! We had all
become involved and no one was speaking to anyone else for a
whole week. Nevertheless, the six of us had walked together into
a meeting and together had staved off an attempt by Global
Glutamate to take us over.

So after the meeting, when we had managed to hold everyone off
on the Rigel City enterprise (Rigel was a fine commercial proposi-
tion but unfortunately its disease statistics were horrific – and

rising), we took a drink in Directors' Bar and I told the other three about Mary, my naked lady.

A lot of jokes went by. We all laughed, except Claudia, who smiled, but beneath it was a lot of angst. They were unwilling to believe me. Winston was jealous, the ladies suspicious, thinking maybe I was trying to smuggle in a pet without a health clearance.

"And what is Stephanie going to say?" Su asked.

It was all fun enough, no worse than I had expected, and it ended with a challenge to me. They should come over to my place and meet Mary. On the whole, we had tended to keep away from each other's places of late.

"Let's go," I said. The staff was taking care of public viewing. We could afford to have a little fun.

But Stephanie's and my apartment was empty. I called. We all looked. It developed into a game. There was no sign of Mary. Only the indent on the cushion. She had gone as mysteriously as she had come.

Of course I phoned Security, but again they had no report of anyone unlawful in the grounds. The others started on a heavy bout of teasing. I had to let them get on with it, while protesting that I had certainly not imagined the lady.

When they left, I sat down with a shot glass of whisky and asked myself, Had I really imagined Mary?

Only a moment of weakness allowed the question to slip into my mind. I was a rational person, leading a well-regulated life. My artistic ability was never in doubt, and I enjoyed the respect of my peers. My career was a success; I skiied once a year in American Antarctic; above all, my liaison with Stephanie was a fulfilling one. Mary had been real enough for there to be a prosaic explanation for her appearance. Mary? No, that was the wrong name, too tranquil. Madonna? Salome?

Unusually for me, I allowed myself to sit drinking, getting no benefit from the alcohol but enjoying the drama of the situation. I told myself I was waiting for Stephanie to ring. Stephanie didn't ring. I took another drink. I played my own music.

Then I went to bed.

On the wall of our bedroom hung a painting by Dante Gabriel Rossetti, the nineteenth-century English artist. It was called *How They Met Themselves*, and depicted a couple, richly caparisoned, meeting another identical couple in a forest. In these stiff figures I had always found a disturbing quality, which reminded me now, as I gazed at them, of Stephanie's pained exclamation when we had been having a quarrel, "Oh, living! Isn't it like being lost in some damned forest?" Just as if there were still forests, as I reasonably pointed out.

"More like being locked behind a door," I had replied.

Now I lay down, and the doors of sleep opened to me. I seemed to be moving over a stretch of water made dark by tall surrounding trees, approaching a mountainous island, where a grand gate opened into the rock. It was in doubt whether I entered there.

Before dawn I woke, roused by sounds in the room. As if a dream continued, I felt no surprise on finding that Mary was back with me. She stood by the tall curtains, pulling them aside just enough to peer out. Something in her attitude suggested anticipation. She was, as ever, naked. The pallor of the pre-dawn sketched in the outlines of her figure.

Kneeling on the bed, I began to recite to her, to utter an incantation. Perhaps I was drunk, not knowing where the words came from.

"Your womanly figure with its full hips, your virginal body with its pale flesh, your slender waist and swelling bosom, that mouth with greedy lips, that generous flowing hair – all make me repent how I hungered for so many lewd conquests. Come to me, Mary, come to bed with me and make me whole . . ."

It was like someone else's voice speaking. She turned, came towards me on naked feet. With an extended hand, she touched my cheek. I clutched her wrist. Yes, she was real enough.

"You don't desire me, and you must not have me. I am not yours to possess. What you wish for is my innocence, but I cannot restore innocence to you."

These words, spoken gently, had a profound effect on me. In contradictory fashion, they filled me with both joy and melancholy, just as the situation, though totally unprecedented, had for me a haunting familiarity I was at a loss to explain.

"I want you, I desire you, like no other woman I have ever known. Come into bed with me – we'll talk, only talk."

"You know what you have lost. You must understand that I cannot restore that loss; only you could do that. Look at the world about you and see its greed. See the misery that greed causes the greedy. You must not want so much. You must not want me."

Her voice sank to a whisper. Terrified, I said, "Don't leave me. I want to understand what you are saying. I don't understand a word of it."

Yet even as I spoke, I did understand. She had opened an inner door.

"You must not seek to dominate me. I have a gift to give." As she whispered these words, so bemusing to my senses, she sank down so that her breath was on my lips. Then she kissed my lips.

I sank back without attempting to capture her. Although it felt as if she was still talking, my curious state of mind prevented me from being sure. Never had I experienced such pure rapture. My mind filled with the idea that she had arrived from a distant saffron planet, yet, by a ridiculous contradiction, the planet was somewhere near at hand, concealed.

The phone rang, and by automatic reflex I switched on even before I was awake. The clear voice of Stephanie in my ear announced that she was at the skyport and would be back at the museum – she did not say home – in an hour's time.

It was a bright morning. The long drapes at the window had been parted slightly. So *she* had been there, and possessed corporeal being. A kind of lust and homesickness drove me out of bed and into a search of the whole apartment. She had gone again. Would she return? Had there been a finality about our conversation? And what on earth was it she had said?

In a rather lost way, I heated a cup of coffee, showered, had my daily injection, and made my way over to the museum. The earlier sunlight had been swallowed in the city's self-made overcast.

Winston Bulawayo greeted me cheerfully and took me to one side. "Hey, Dean, what do you think? I made it with Su last night! Just like old times, except – wuh, that lady's so much more experienced now . . ."

I did not immediately respond. He added, "Well, old Aristo was away, so I grabbed my chance . . ."

For some reason, I felt depressed. I clapped him on the back, but could not help saying, "There'll be hell to pay if Aristo finds out. He and Su were so happy."

"Not as happy as you might think," he said, looking rather angry at the implied criticism. "Nothing's permanent. In fact, Su is thinking of breaking it up and moving in with me."

"How's Claudia going to feel about that?"

He stopped and put his solid form in my path. "What's the problem with you this morning, Dean? You were always a kind of moody guy anyway. I've seen the way you look at Claudia. Lay off her, will you? I can look after Claudia *and* Su."

"And Aristo? Isn't he due back this morning?"

The two ladies, Su and Claudia, appeared on the scene, both looking rather upset. Winston's and my conversation ended abruptly, which was just as well, perhaps. He gave me a black look before turning to greet Su.

Inside, I felt deeply disturbed without knowing why.

"Did you have a good night with your naked lady-friend?" Claudia asked me, looking solemn as usual, so that it was hard to judge how seriously to take her. Before I could answer, she said, "Su says that Aristo rang her to say he will be back here midday. When does Stephanie get back?"

"Soon." It was all I could manage to say. A chill suspicion had entered my mind.

Excusing myself, I took the elevator to my office on the fourth floor. In a short while, I was through to our suppliers in Venezuela. They dealt with the growers who had cleared the last of the Venezuelan forests to grow the soya beans which formed a vital constituent of the plastic from which we made our artificial trees. Of recent months, they had been having trouble with hijackers who had stolen their products. They sounded calm enough over the air: No, they had not had the pleasure of a visit from Mr Aristide Smith.

I cut the link. Compelled by an inner pain, I ran down the emergency stairs and out across the park to the main gate, where the guard, recognising me, allowed me to escape into the street. There I walked, pacing furiously, not caring if I looked distraught.

There was no doubt in my mind that Aristo and Stephanie had met somewhere in a private rendezvous. They had spent the day in each other's arms. Laughing, lustful, extravagant Stephanie. Covetous, grasping, lascivious Aristo. The treachery of them both . . .

At the corner of the wall that surrounded the museum grounds was a big video advert for our exhibition. It showed the six of us, all immaculate and aloof, being beautiful people. Healthy, wealthy, glittering with success. Our clothes proclaimed our excellence. But under the clothes, I thought . . . I turned and pressed into the streets and arcades of the city.

People everywhere. Staring or not staring. Many talking to themselves. A man on a corner in a black outfit, cursing aloud. Many of the women veiled, toting guns. This was the place we had nicknamed the Big Addle. Despite the warmth of the day, men and women were wearing gloves, all naked skin being covered as a guard against disease. Everywhere, forms slouching, running crookedly, or moving hesitantly, anxious to avoid human contact. The rundown puritan world from which we, The Six, had escaped via our success.

And Stephanie had betrayed me. So upset was I that I paid no heed to the danger I was in. I simply had to walk, and be away from all the calculating glances of those I knew so well. What had Stephanie said after her last abortion? "Dean, our lives take precedence over anyone or anything else . . ." Our lives? We had no common life any more. This was going to be another of Aristo's triumphs, demonstrating his ascendancy. Bitterly, I thought how little he had cared about Betty Jule's death – and she so tender. Well, no, really a calculating woman, who had certainly been cruel enough to me when she had caught me with Stephanie, years earlier . . .

The crowds grew more dense towards city centre. There were queues at the clinics, the windows of which were protected by metal bars. Ambulances, flashing and blaring, made their way only slowly along the roads. CHASTITY SPELLS LIFE, said the hoardings. MASTURBATION SAVES, they said. CONNECTION BREEDS INFECTION, they said.

Mary was standing naked among the crowds. She was looking here and there in an abstracted way. The crowds jostled her yet curiously did not give her a second look. Possibly they were shocked. More likely they regarded this as yet another government attempt to enforce the puritanical way of life: anyone touching her would have been immediately arrested.

As I tried to make my way towards her, waving and calling, she turned and went down a side alley. Pushing people away to either side, ignoring their horrified looks, I ran after her.

The alley was empty. There was a church of some kind down there, advertising itself with a holosign: The Church of the Deep Minders. Not a trace of Mary. I ran down the alley, looked into the church. She had gone.

An acid sprinkle of rain drifted down. I sheltered in the porch of the church. Exhaustion and disgust overcame me.

There was no place for me here. I belonged in the museum. I was one of The Six. I must go back and face the latest crisis. Perhaps we were all on Earth to be tortured by our sexuality, that gift we had turned to such bad use.

As I started back, a copcar snarled to a halt. Two police jumped out and grabbed me. Despite my struggles and protests, I was thrown into the compartment at the back of the car. In short order, I found myself in a shabby precinct office, answering charges of indecent dress. I was wearing my usual gold lamé suit with my brown slippers and silver wig – my everyday dress in fact. But hands, face, and upper chest were exposed. It was a violation of the laws.

They were slightly impressed when I said that I was one of The Six. Had I proof that I was Dean Morsberg? No, I had no documentary evidence on me, but they had merely to ring the museum and confirmation would be forthcoming.

So they put me in a cooler. My clothes were taken from me, I was made to shower, blood samples were taken by a nurse in an air suit. It was afternoon before the police put a call through to The Six. No, Dean Morsberg was right there with them, and they did not know who the impostor was that the police were holding.

My rage knew no bounds. So that was what Aristo and Stephanie were up to! The forests of their lust had sprung up and lost me. This was their plan to keep me out of the way while they enjoyed the fruits of each other's bodies . . .

Charges of contamination and impersonation began to look menacing. My anger faded before outraged feelings of anxiety. How was I to get back into the stronghold where I belonged? I put a call through to our lawyers as soon as I could, but from their stonewalling responses I knew that Aristo had got to them first.

A year in the slammer would be what I would get. Then they

would have me back. After all, I was still a part of The Six. Twelve months was how long they calculated their passionate and eternal feelings for each other would last. Then they would let me back. If I remained free of disease that long . . .

That night, in the silences of the noisy station, my cell door swung open and in walked Mary again, naked, innocent, gentle of eye. She would not give herself to me. She uttered but one word.
   "Forgive!"

(1988)

Bill Carter Takes Over

That winter, dawn broke over Inkerman Terrace at about seven a.m., which was the time Bill Carter, obedient to his alarm clock, got out of bed.

Already there was a friendly rumble of traffic outside. As Bill peered from his bathroom window, he could see the traffic piling up on the raised Westway into London.

His wife Laura did not get up until seven-thirty. The arrangement suited Bill. He liked the peace in the house, liked to breakfast alone with the newspaper, liked a quiet half-hour before he drove in to work at Jackson's Alloys.

He filled the kettle, switched it on, and went into the living-room to have a look at God. A rainy light filled the room. God's tank was in shadow.

"Not much of a day, O Lord."

God was used to criticism. He said nothing. He curled a flipper and made a lazy circuit of his tank. God's tank was a standard size. God-tanks were mass-produced and measured the same the world over, being just under two metres square and one point four metres high. The tank was open to the air. It contained nothing but air and God.

Carter went nearer.

"I don't think Judy's flu is any better this morning. I'm just going to take her up a cup of tea. I can hear the poor kid sneezing in her room. Can't You do something about that, O Lord? You know her exams are coming up."

Privately, Bill Carter thought his daughter was backward. Privately, he blamed his wife. Not so privately, Carter was morose and often bellicose. On the recommendation of his doctor, he went to see a marriage counsellor every Wednesday.

"Well?" – challengingly to God.

God spake. "I do keep your daughter's interests in mind."

Sigh. "You know I don't like to complain, O Lord, but . . . please let today be something special. Just for a change."

God's single eye was rather like a peony. Its petals opened. Among dense stamens, something glittered. When God manifested Himself to a troubled world in the closing year of the twentieth century, He chose to appear universally in non-anthropomorphic form. People who were against racism applauded this; people who were for it thought God was being silly.

"All is well, Carter, and all is eternally well. Time does not really pass, you know. You live with me in an eternal day."

"Christ, You always fob me off with words. How about some action, Lord? I'm only worried about Judy's flu. And my wife's behaviour . . ."

"I am here on Earth only as witness to my presence throughout the universe. I really prefer not to work little local miracles, having found from experience that they are counter-productive."

Carter clenched his fists.

"But You're omnipotent, omnipotent! You made the damned galaxies! Don't give me that counter-productive nonsense."

"Carter, you must accept that even omnipotence has its limits."

"Oh, come on, will You, God? Just between You and me. You know the mess my life's in. Judy, Laura . . . I've got another session with Mrs Batacharya this evening. Help me, will You? I ask You every bloody day –"

"And every day I do help you, Bill, in many mysterious ways . . ."

"Oh, You mealy-mouthed –"

In sudden rage, Carter heaved himself into the big glass tank. God writhed away to the far side, but Carter grasped one of His trailing flippers and got in a swift kick at one of the three segments of His body.

"Ow, that hurts, Carter! You know we can't stand pain."

"That's ridiculous!"

"How else could we comprehend mankind's problems unless we suffered with you and felt pain? Owww!"

Throwing himself forward, Carter locked both hands round the

smooth neck-like stalk connecting God's first and second segments. He had God pinned down on one side of the tank in a fairly
undignified position.

"Now look here, Almighty, I want a miracle out of You. Then
I'll let go, understand? Quick!"

"Owww. What do you want me to do?"

"You can do anything, anything, and You ask me what I want!
How about a bigger house for a start. Far away from Inkerman
Terrace. On a hill somewhere, beautiful views, with a stream – yes,
a trout stream. And a pretty wife. Plus a lake and a power-boat on
it. Two wives. Sisters, who get on well together. Good dress sense.
And a full-size ivory statue of Ella Fitzgerald in the hall. And a
good job, forget Jackson's Alloys. No – no job, no work, just my
estate to look after. I want to be a crack shot, really crack. A private
armoury, the lot. Wild elephants in the grounds, really dangerous.
Servants. Drink. Women. Fame. A fax machine. You know what I
want. Make them materialise and I'll let You go."

"Yes, I do know what you want, Carter, and believe me I
sympathise, deeply. Owww-wow! All those things – those gross
material things – would really be only a substitute, a poor substitute, for a state of spiritual – Owww-owww! Mercy, Carter!"

"Cut that pious talk. One small miracle, come on, one small
miracle, or I'm keeping You pinned down here all day, O Lord.
Anything! How about – a palm tree in the back garden?"

"You know the neighbours would complain. Think not only for
thyself. Ohhhhh, Jesus Christ, Carter, you have a nasty streak in
you."

"Who put it there? Come on, a palm tree, or I'll tear this
flipper-thing right off."

Over the garden, a flash of light. By Laura's rockery, just where
she had buried the family cat, a palm tree appeared, its topknot of
leaves blotting out the chimneys of the houses opposite.

Carter climbed out of the tank, victorious but unsatisfied. God
relapsed sulkily into a corner. He was sick of doing palm trees.

Carter made time before work commenced to go and see his elderly
mother, Joyce Carter, in the old folks' home nearby.

Joyce Carter was eighty-one, her skin blotched by liver-marks
as if by a poisonous fungus.

She shared a room with Mrs Vera Walker. Their two manifestations of God circulated in their tanks, which had been pushed awkwardly together behind the commode, by the oxygen cylinders.

A nurse was taking Joyce Carter's breakfast tray away as the old lady began a litany of complaint before Carter had seated himself beside her bed.

"Oh, I can't tell you how sick and fed up I am of that Mrs Walker, I was just telling the nurse here, fed up. You should have heard her at two this morning. Stone deaf, of course. What a mess! No consideration, poor old thing. I keep trying to get them to move her. Might as well talk to a brick wall. God, God, why You don't help me I can't think. Nobody cares for a poor old woman like me any more."

"I care," said God. "Of course I care, Mrs Carter. That's why I'm here, suffering with you. Be patient, my dear. All is well and all is eternally well."

"That's a lot of help, I'm sure."

Knowing that his mother, who treated God much as she had her dead husband, could go on arguing for ever, Carter indicated that he had to be getting to work.

"You never stay long these days, do you?"

"You've always got God to communicate with. Bear that in mind."

"Oh, He's no company. He keeps going on about the Hereafter – not a very cheerful subject."

"That's untrue, Mrs Carter," said God reprovingly. "Didn't I read you a whole Barbara Cartland romance yesterday? But, as I told you then, the Hereafter represents a happier state."

"There He goes again. You see what I'm up against. Nag nag nag."

Carter stood up, glancing at his watch.

"At least He loves us all. 'Bye, mother."

The day's work at Jackson's Alloys passed smoothly enough. Carter left his desk promptly and, that evening, the traffic jams were not too bad. He was home by five-thirty.

Laura came down the stairs smiling, to greet him in the hall. He looked at her suspiciously, but she put her arms round him and kissed his cheek.

"Let's have some tea. Come into the kitchen and talk to me. Judy's a bit better."

Mollified by this, he followed. She turned the radio on automatically before she filled the kettle. They perched on stools as the kettle started to sing. Her God's tank was wedged in the space between the oven and the fridge.

As they sipped tea from their horoscope mugs, Carter said, "They were playing 'Eso Beso' on the car radio on the way home." He hummed a few bars. "Do you remember that one, darling, when we were kids?"

"Who was it used to sing 'Eso Beso'?"

"I've forgotten – it's so long ago."

God spake. "It was Paul Anka."

Laura took a biscuit out of the tin. "Those sixties songs had more zip than the stuff they pour out now. The nineties are a bit of a flop, aren't they? Perhaps next century will be better. But that's up to You, isn't it, O Lord Almighty?"

She threw Him a scornful glance and He coiled over to face her.

"No my dear, it's up to you and your husband, and everyone else on Earth. I can only work through you, as you strive for a better world."

"Crikey, me strive for a better world? I've got my hands full as it is. I took Judy up some Marmite. She wouldn't drink it. It's all I can do to hold my marriage together. I'm just not appreciated, that's the trouble. Work, morning, noon, and night . . . Debts, debts, debts . . . Without wanting to be unpleasant, God, I think You created a lot of unfairness between the sexes."

Carter said, "I wonder whatever happened to Paul Anka."

God spake. "Bill, it's six-ten, time you went to your marriage guidance counsellor."

"Oh, you've got to tittle-tattle to that woman again."

"Why don't you come with me, dear?"

"I've got other things to do. You ought to have a jog round the park, like Paul Gutteridge does. Much better for you than going to that awful Batacharya woman every Wednesday."

As he went into the hall, Carter called, "And you – please behave yourself while I'm out."

"And what's that meant to mean?"

"Just remember God is watching you."

He slammed the front door as he went out, and then regretted it.

He was early at the marriage guidance clinic in Profumo Place. The old habit of punctuality was hard to shake, even though Mrs Batacharya had once uttered a deadly insult and called him "anally-oriented". He read vintage copies of *Asia Review* until the bell tinkled and he went into Mrs Batacharya's room.

Mrs Batacharya sat in a creaking wicker chair. She wore a tweed skirt with jumper to match, a blue cardigan and green suede shoes. She had found room for her God and his tank between the old leatherette couch and the door.

He sat down, facing her, looking depressed.

"Well, how have you been, Bill, dear?"

"Bunty, I believe that my wife is continuing her affair with that bastard Gutteridge. Of course I'm not sure, but she mentioned him again this afternoon. I don't know whether I'm imagining things or not. What's imagination, what's reality? God's presence hasn't made the distinction between them any easier to grasp, I must say."

God spake. "Both are aspects of my eternal Being."

"Please ignore Him," Mrs Batacharya said. "He has no qualifications for counselling. Also, He has been very loquacious today. Just concentrate on me. How has your week been, Bill?"

Carter groaned. "I beat up God this morning until He produced a palm tree in the back garden. I suppose that's on my conscience."

"One measly palm tree?"

God spake. "It was a *cocos nucifera*, to remind Carter of how such trees dump thousands of tons of free fruit daily into the ungrateful laps of mankind."

Mrs Batacharya said, "You're always preaching, O Lord. Take it from me, it's counter-productive. That I can tell You from experience."

"Outside, in the real world," Carter said, "chaps must know for sure whether their wives love them or not."

"And, in that real world, does Laura know if her Bill loves her?"

"I tell her often enough," Carter said. "Don't I, God?"

"Love lives in deeds as well as words," God said, turning authoritatively in the tank. "When I created the world, that was a deed of love, and you are all children of it. You would save yourselves endless sorrow if you could remember that cardinal fact."

"Bill's trouble," Mrs Batacharya said crushingly, "is that, as well as Laura and himself, you also created Gutteridge."

Carter downed a couple of beers at the local before driving home. He went upstairs to see his daughter, but she was asleep, breathing laboriously, wearing her Walkman. Laura was nowhere about and there were no signs of supper.

After some hesitation, Carter went into the living-room to see his own incarnation of God. He switched the light on. Closing the door and leaning against it, he looked at the Being who moved languidly in His tank.

"Well, Wednesday's almost over, O Lord, and it didn't have much to offer. I'm sorry I hurt You this morning by the way. That was a really disgusting performance."

"I'm touched by your penitence, Carter, but you should learn to control yourself."

Sighing heavily, Carter went over to the window and drew the curtain.

"Isn't that part of Your job? You made us, after all."

"You see, that's what makes me so absolutely fed up. You humans whine and winge for autonomy. You get it. I give it to you. Then when anything goes wrong you blame me. Every time. How do you think I feel? Grow up, will you?"

"So what about Judy, then? Is she going to be fit enough to go back to school tomorrow, or isn't she?"

"I'm the Creator, Carter, not your family doctor."

"Surely You must be bored out of your wits in that tank –"

"– In these multitudinous tanks, Carter –"

"– not getting through to humanity, preaching, just performing a minor conjuring trick now and again. Why don't You try a really major miracle for once? It might improve Your morale as well as everyone else's."

"What precisely do you suggest?"

"You see, You've got no imagination . . ."

"So what do you suggest?"

"I wish I had Your job!"

Next moment, Carter found Himself dispersed among a myriad tanks, staring out at the whole of humanity. In the background, joy, illumination, trumpets, and the thrilling tintinnabulations of galaxies.

Countless representatives of humanity stared back at Him, aware that something inexplicable had happened. For once, everyone's attention was centred on God.

Carter spake. "All is well. And all is eternally well."

What else could He have told them?

He was to find that even omnipotence had its limits.

(1989)